# MY MOTHER'S LIE

BOOKS BY ANNA E. COLLINS

*Her Secret Life*

*His Other Life*

*Love at First Spite*

*These Numbered Days*

*A Life in Bloom*

*Worst in Show*

*Finding Mr. July*

# MY MOTHER'S LIE

Anna E. Collins

bookouture

Published by Bookouture in 2026

An imprint of Storyfire Ltd.
Carmelite House
50 Victoria Embankment
London EC4Y 0DZ
Uniter Kingdom

www.bookouture.com

The authorised representative in the EEA is Hachette Ireland
8 Castlecourt Centre
Dublin 15 D15 XTP3
Ireland
(email: info@hbgi.ie)



ISBN: 978-1-80550-409-2
eBook ISBN: 978-1-80550-408-5

*Parents make enduring impressions on their children, and with such great power comes great responsibility. This book is for all parents who treat this most important job with care and purpose, but most of all for mine—Marita and Per—for their always unwavering love and support.*

# ONE

## FRANKIE

Now

*Everything is fine.* Frankie Lavigne sucked in a breath, and it seemed to her as if the sound of it echoed through the quiet before she looked down to where her fingers were perched against the black and white keys of the piano.

Her entire field of vision was black and white. Black like the massive iron candelabra to her right, white like the candles lit within it. Black like the suit jacket on the man in the first row, white like the handkerchief his wife was clutching in her hand. Black like the casket at the front of the vast space, white like the roses cascading over it.

*Yes, everything is fine,* the little voice in her head said again. She just had to concentrate on the task at hand and get on with it. The piano was her safe place. Her escape. Her joy.

Somewhere in the church, a man cleared his throat, the noise quickly followed by a few more as if a secret go-ahead had been issued from the pulpit. They were waiting for her, and in wait, silence could be agonizing. She got that, and yet she couldn't make her hands move. For the first time in her life, they didn't want to play. How embarrassing.

She studied the ring on her left index finger—a silver treble clef with a white pearl in the middle that had been a gift for her high school graduation. She'd lost the matching necklace at some point over the years, but she always wore the ring, even though it tended to snag on things.

"Because music will always be a constant in your life, even though we've decided it's wiser to pursue a different degree," Estelle had said as Frankie ripped open the wrapping paper.

And her mom had been right. She was always right.

Well, except when she'd predicted she'd live to a hundred. She'd been wrong about that. Thirty-three years wrong to be exact, which made no sense at all.

Frankie's vision blurred, and she briefly withdrew her hands to her lap before steeling herself against the aching pit in her gut and trying again. Fingers set for the starting A minor chord. She knew this song. It was part of the very fabric of her life. All she had to do was press her fingers down and start. She could hear Estelle's voice and her guitar in her head.

A baby in the back let out a loud wail, pulling Frankie's gaze across the congregation before she could stop herself. She had deliberately avoided picking out faces in the crowd, but now there they were, red-eyed and sympathetic. The mayor was in the front row, having given a lovely eulogy for the local news cameras that were set up in the middle aisle, and even he was dabbing at his ruddy cheeks. Every seat was taken, and according to the priest, the overflow space in the high school gymnasium next door was full—several hundred more people who at this very moment were watching Frankie choke on live stream.

*What would Mom do?* Frankie thought. She closed her eyes and attempted to summon Estelle's voice. It was there with more ease than she'd expected. *The show must go on. Mind over matter.* A tremor rushed down Frankie's spine. Estelle had been so much stronger than Frankie. Her anchor and her guide.

Oh God, what would she do without her mom?

Frankie's fingers came off the keys again, her thumb slipping and sending a bright C into the rafters, which made the congregation stir as if a wind had blown through the room. She had time to think that she must have been keeping them waiting a long time if a single note could do that, then a low "psst" reached her from the end of the first pew.

Frankie turned her head, spotting her friend and colleague, Kayla, there with her hand on the shoulder of one of Frankie's more advanced piano students.

"Hey," Kayla whispered, her eyes soft. "You okay?"

Frankie wanted to say yes. She should have been able to say yes. Lavignes didn't crumble. But maybe a day like today it would be acceptable to admit this small slip? Especially when the alternative was dragging this silence out longer. She shook her head just enough for Kayla to see.

"Do you want Mira to do it?" Kayla mimed.

Frankie looked to the teen, at her blue, knee-length dress and yellow hairband, and her shoulders relaxed at the sight of color. Any color. She found the Kopps, Mira's parents, in the crowd, her dad nodding to Frankie in encouragement, as if to say they were fine with this turn of events. Which, of course they were—any parent who sent their kid to Starview Conservatory would see this as an *opportunity* as much as a way to be helpful. Not that Frankie begrudged them that stance—Estelle had made it part of the school's original mission statement after all. Whether a student of piano, voice, guitar, violin or ballet, there would be plenty of chances to perform. It was one of the reasons their school had reached such renown.

No, not their school anymore. Now it was Frankie's. Alone.

Frankie beckoned Mira forward and got up, the chair scraping mournfully against the wooden floor.

"I'm sorry, Ms. Frankie," the girl said in a low voice as they switched places. "We all miss her."

Frankie swallowed against the lump in her throat. "Thanks, Mira." Then she let Kayla tuck her close in a way she hadn't done since they were teens and steer her into a seat.

With a new player at the keys, the congregation straightened in anticipation, and before Frankie could conjure even a shred of protective armor, the first chord rang out, an arrow to the heart. How many times had she heard Estelle play this song? In small bars, on big stages, in their living room, on the radio, at festivals. It had been the pinnacle of Estelle's career and the foundation for Starview, but more than that, it was a love letter to Frankie, the miracle child who'd almost been lost. Stolen but returned.

Even though Mira's version was strictly instrumental, the words still floated on the air, as if every person in the room could imagine Estelle's voice brought to life, and Frankie closed her eyes as tears streamed down her cheeks.

*She wasn't in her room; not hiding in our van,*
*Her teddy bear left upon the floor; that's how it all began.*
*One hour was enough; she slipped into thin air,*
*A misguided moment of trust; a heavy burden to bear,*

*I searched through every nook; her name a precious song,*
*Lifted in prayer to the sky; please help me right this wrong,*
*Each second steeped in fear; I'll never let her go*
*I will not rest until she's back; this alone I know*

*Quiet places where laughter should be,*
*My only child is gone*
*Gone is she.*
*Empty arms and a desperate plea*
*My only child is gone*

*Gone from me.*

The reception was held at city hall, a large turn-of-the-century building with a wooden clock tower and immaculate gardens just off the town square. With less than five thousand in residence, Aspen Creek wasn't a big town, but much thanks to Starview, it had become the kind of place where once you settled, you stayed, and as a result, everyone knew everyone, and everyone especially knew Estelle. If Aspen Creek had any claim to fame it was the music conservatory and its colorful owner, and consequently, two hours after the service had ended, Frankie was still shaking hands and nodding at shared memories of her mother.

"Such a loss for the town."

"Only reason my daughter got into Juilliard."

"So grateful to have known her."

"I know you'll make her proud."

Just when Frankie's feet were going numb and her knees threatened to buckle, her sort-of cousin, Matt, sidled up next to her with a glass of white wine, a hand pie, and an apologetic expression that he leveled on the next mourner in line. "I'm so sorry, but Mayor Halloran needs her." Then he steered Frankie to a quiet corner of the room and set her down in a chair.

Frankie looked around. "Where's the mayor?"

"Somewhere over there." Matt tipped his head into the crowd. "But no one will be the wiser. Now eat or I'll shove that pie in your pie hole myself, Frankenstein." He sat down next to Frankie and crossed his arms.

"You don't have to be so mean about it," Frankie muttered before taking a bite and allowing the fruity filling to awaken her numbed senses. She sighed in relief as the sugar hit her bloodstream and rinsed the bite down with a gulp of wine. Not that she condoned the lying, but it would have looked even worse had she fainted.

Kayla, who was married to Matt, stepped up behind him and placed her hands on his shoulders. "How are you holding up, Frankie?"

"Better now," Frankie said, licking pie filling off her fingers. "All these people—it's just a bit overwhelming. But I'm okay. Everything's okay."

"Everyone loved Aunt Estelle," Matt said simply, standing and letting Kayla take his seat.

They weren't actually related, but Estelle and Matt's dad, Raymond, had known each other forever, so when Frankie and Matt were little, that's how they'd always thought of each other's parents. Aunt Estelle. Uncle Ray and Aunt Darla. Though Aunt Darla had not been with them for a good while, having upgraded her husband for a younger version and moved to Portugal when Matt was in college, only to pass away unexpectedly from diabetes complications a few years later. Uncle Ray was here somewhere though.

"I saw someone from work I need a word with over by the coffee, but I'll leave you in my wife's competent hands." Matt gave Frankie a smile, kissed the top of his wife's head, then stalked away.

"Is he ever not working?" Frankie asked Kayla as she finished her wine. A warm and fortifying buzz had settled in her legs, but she wasn't quite ready to head into the fray again.

"Working, yes. Networking, no." Kayla watched Matt disappear in the crowd, affection written all over her face. "And he's doing really well. Did he tell you he sold that historic Victorian on Monroe?"

"Good thing Estelle thought to introduce the two of you then." Frankie smiled at the memory of her mother's excitement at the match of Cousin Matt and Frankie's once-best friend.

"I'll forever be grateful."

"As am I for your support in this." Frankie gestured to the room, a wave of nostalgia sweeping over her at this rare one-on-

one time with Kayla. Nowadays, it seemed they only ever saw each other at work or with Matt also present. The school kept her so busy. "I know our lives have sort of diverged, but it means a lot to me that—" Her voice broke without warning as the brief respite came to an end. She dug her nails into her palms in frustration and turned her face away. *Get a grip.* The people of Aspen Creek would expect better of her.

But this was how it had been since that night a week ago when Charlie, the custodian at the school, had shown up at the house after hours to let Frankie know an ambulance had taken Estelle to the ER. Riptides of emotion without warning. Quicksand where she least expected. Because she didn't even get to say goodbye. By the time she reached the hospital, Estelle was gone. A massive heart attack, just like that.

"Of course," Kayla said, leaning forward in her chair. "You know I'm here for you. But if anyone can handle this, it's you. You guys basically ran the school together—you know exactly what to do."

Did she? Frankie wiped her tears as discreetly as she could.

*Of course you do,* Estelle whispered in her mind. *We're in this together.*

Except they weren't in it together anymore—that was the problem.

They both fell quiet for a moment, then Frankie sniffed, screwed up her posture, and rose to her feet. "I should get back to it."

Kayla reached out to touch Frankie's arm. "Let me know if you need anything."

Frankie nodded, then she ventured back into the throngs of guests who had come to pay their respects.

There was the florist Mom bought her seeds and bulbs from every year, Frankie's fifth grade teacher from the year they moved in, and several of her high school ones, the butcher on Main Street, Mom's hairstylist, the whole chamber of commerce board, and so many current and former students and their families. The room was lined with flowers, many of them with cards attached, sent by folks who'd been unable to attend, and in a corner, Starview's students took turns playing short tunes on their instruments. That wasn't something Frankie had arranged —they'd just shown up because that's what this town did.

New tears threatened at that thought, but before they could spill over, a shrill voice said her name right behind her.

"I've been looking all over for you." The woman was all rosy cheeks and solemn eyes, which struck Frankie as a contradiction. "I couldn't believe it when I heard. How are you holding up?" She pulled Frankie into an embrace that smelled of jasmine and money while Frankie scrambled to place her. "I came home as soon as Daddy told me of course. I mean, you know—I owe everything to darling Estelle. Chicago is still ah-mazing."

The penny dropped. She and Maddie had come up together at Starview, often playing piano duets that brought down thunderous applause, but after high school, Maddie had done what Frankie didn't and pursued her craft, which later led to her permanent appointment with the Chicago Symphony. Frankie had been happy for her when she'd heard. Happy with a sprinkle of "what ifs" for herself, but she would never say so out loud.

"Maddie, I almost didn't recognize you," Frankie said, fighting the urge to check her outfit for imperfections in the presence of Maddie's sheen. "It's been so long."

"You know. Just here and back. One night only. But you look good." Maddie paused, raising her eyebrows. "I'd hoped to hear you play earlier."

Frankie's fingers curled into her palms as if prompted to hide by the statement. *You and me both.*

There had been a certain level of competitiveness between them back then—who mastered "Fantaisie-Impromptu" first, who got the finale solos at the concerts, that sort of thing, but Frankie had long since accepted that when the dust settled, she was the one left behind. And she'd come to terms with that. Really. She and Estelle had carved out a nice life for themselves. They liked teaching.

"Who's your friend, Frankie dear?" Uncle Ray stepped up between them, saving her from having to respond. "I thought I knew every single soul in here."

"Oh, but you do, Mr. Clark," Maddie said. "It's Madeline Forrester. You were on the zoning board with my father."

"She's a pianist for the Chicago Symphony now," Frankie added magnanimously.

"No." Uncle Ray huffed in disbelief, a wolfy grin stretching his thin lips. "Not Peter's girl? I don't believe it." He took her hand in both of his as she preened. "What a clever young woman you've grown up to be."

He was such a salesman, Uncle Ray—could make anyone believe whatever he wanted them to. Right now, Maddie likely felt both younger than her thirty-six years and indeterminately brilliant. It was no wonder he'd built such a successful property development company for himself. Being able to make anyone feel special was a superpower.

Frankie had loved it as a child, but as she grew older, she'd occasionally spied the intent behind it, seen how the schmoozing preceded handshakes at a Christmas party or town picnic, and more than once, it had made her wonder what Estelle saw in him to have kept him a lifelong friend. Estelle was never bothered by it though. "He's good at his job," she'd simply said, which had ended the conversation if Frankie ever asked.

But while Frankie took his suave ways with a grain of salt, even joking about them with Matt on occasion, Uncle Ray was still the closest thing to family she had, and you didn't choose your family. Besides, he'd given her Matt, and Matt always took after his mom more and couldn't stand what he called Ray's "business face." Although the first time Frankie saw one of Matt's realtor commercials on TV, she'd called him howling with laughter over *his* business face. She wasn't sure he'd forgiven her for that yet.

The afternoon was drawing to a close and the crowd finally thinning, so Frankie left Maddie and Uncle Ray to their conversation, meandering from group to group to thank people for coming. There was a gorgeous floral arrangement on the entry table, and as the pressure of the day released its stranglehold, she stopped to smell the pink gardenias and read the card.

> *Loved and missed. Estelle, you had the patience of a saint. Neither one of my boys practiced their guitar, but you never scolded them, and they're still playing. Be with God. / The Henleys*

Frankie remembered them. They'd moved away a few years ago, but the news must have traveled. Soothed by the scent of the flowers and kind words she didn't have to interact with, she roamed the perimeter of the room from bouquet to bouquet.

> Tulips and peonies:
> *Deepest condolences, Frankie. I once suggested we'd name a room at the library after Estelle, but she wouldn't have it. Well, I'm telling you—I'm going to petition for it again. / Maria*

> A swathe of lilies:
> *Estelle—Aspen Creek's very own star. How very missed you'll be, but how fortunate we are to have had you in our midst these many years. Much love as you move on. / Herbert K.*

> Roses and carnations:

*I met my husband in college when we bonded over our time at Starview. We're expecting our first child in a few weeks, and if it's a girl, her middle name will be Estelle. Thank you for everything. / Candace and Leo White*

Frankie's fingertips caressed the expensive cardstock, the strumming beat of "Go Your Own Way" by Fleetwood Mac at a low volume cushioning another wave of disbelief that her mom was gone. There was so much love here—more than she'd known or understood while Estelle was alive. Estelle hadn't been just her mother; she'd been a mother figure for countless others over the years. A matron of Aspen Creek. And maybe that should have made Frankie feel less alone, but it didn't; it only amplified the loss.

Frankie forced herself onward, her eyes landing on one of the many framed photographs of Estelle scattered around the room. In this one, she was posing outside Starview with her guitar. The picture must have been twenty years old—her hair was longer, her eyes bigger but still lined with her signature kohl pen. There was confidence in her posture and pride in her smile, but she'd looked away from the camera at the moment of capture.

"She was looking at you, wasn't she?" a woman asked next to Frankie, startling her. "I can tell. I remember that wonder in her eyes when you were around."

Frankie studied the woman's profile. She was about Estelle's age, bottle-blonde hair in an updo, tasteful make-up, tailored but feminine pantsuit. "I'm sorry. Have we met?"

"Oh." The woman extended her hand. "Silly me. Of course you wouldn't remember. I'm Orla Monroe. I interviewed your mother for *Country Weekly* right after her song went gold, but you were still a little tyke then."

Frankie stiffened at the woman's name. She hadn't heard it in a very long time, but for a while, it had been synonymous with everything that was wrong with media's involvement in the music industry. *Give them a finger and they'll take the whole hand,* Estelle had griped.

"Right. Ms. Monroe." Frankie kept her expression neutral while wracking her brain for exactly what it was that had turned her mother off the reporter. She picked up another card.

"Just Orla. Please." She mirrored Frankie, grabbing a different one. "My deepest condolences. I stayed in touch with Estelle for some years after that interview, so I understand you were very close."

There had been a second interview, hadn't there? One Estelle had shut down. Something about getting unduly personal when all Estelle wanted to talk about was her music. They'd moved to Aspen Creek shortly afterward. How interesting that Orla had mentioned only the *Country Weekly* feature. It begged the question why she was here—to pay her respects or because nosiness was a lifelong affliction...?

"I appreciate it," Frankie said, though she wished the woman would go away both out of loyalty to her mom and so that she wouldn't have to repeat the same pitying conversation for the umpteenth time. "And thank you for coming." Frankie looked for an out and spotted Matt behind the reporter. She lifted her chin to signal she needed him.

The understanding that comes with growing up together delivered, and he meandered over. "Hey," he said. "All good?"

"Yep." Frankie glanced from him to Orla, hoping he'd continue to read her mind and save her.

"Day's almost done," Matt said. "Want to come to our place later?"

Frankie hedged. While she appreciated that he was sticking around, the invite put her on the spot. If she couldn't keep her emotions in check, it would be better to be alone. "Maybe. I still have a lot of these to read." She held up the card. "Am I supposed to respond, do you know?"

"I wouldn't," Orla said, inserting herself in the conversation. "Orla Monroe. Pleasure." She shook Matt's hand.

"Nice to meet you." He sounded perplexed, and if Frankie knew him right, he'd have a snappy comment or two later about the reporter. Turning his attention back to Frankie, he deliberately angled his shoulder to cut Orla out. "If anything, you could put a note of thanks in the paper," he said.

"If that's enough," she replied. She'd look it up later. Matt meant well, but he didn't have all eyes on him like Frankie now did. Estelle's shoes would be hard to fill.

"Oh, people do that all the time," Orla said from behind Matt. "You'll be fine. People can't expect handwritten notes with a turnout like this. Beautiful flowers. Gorgeous. Fitting. I hear she loved gardening."

"Did you know her well?" Matt asked, his manners taking over.

"Only in a professional capacity, and it has been years. We... lost touch."

"There are a lot of flowers," Frankie agreed, too tired to call out the euphemism for whatever disagreement Orla and Estelle had had. She held up the card in her hand. "And I really should try to get through these."

"Want help?" Matt asked, nudging it. "Who's that from?"

"The Peltiers. Their son was a student. He's at Berklee now."

"Impressive," Orla said, clearly believing she was still part of their conversation. She flipped open the card she was holding.

Matt took the Peltier one and read it for himself. "Aw, that's sweet. 'Will always remember her.' And Kayla told me Maria at the library wants to get a room renamed. I bet she'll make it happen. No one would vote no. Like I said—everyone loved Aunt Estelle."

"Um..." Orla looked up from her card. "Maybe not everyone."

Frankie and Matt turned to her.

"What do you mean?" Frankie asked, her irritation with the woman growing.

Orla handed her the card. "Look for yourself."

Frankie read the note, anticipating more laudations, so it took a moment for the sentiment to compute. Her brow furrowed as she stared at the words.

"What is it?" Matt asked.

Frankie showed him the card, and they read it together in silence, the message a stray thread in an otherwise perfectly embroidered tapestry of solicitude and praise.

"What the hell?" Matt said, which was exactly Frankie's thought as the words danced before her eyes.

*Now that you're gone, I have no choice but to forgive you.*
*Not that you deserve it.*

# TWO

## FRANKIE

Now

Frankie unbuckled in Estelle's driveway and pulled the wad of cards out of her bag, sifting through it until she found the one with purple fields illuminated by a sunset. She put the others away, then opened it and read the message again.

"Forgive for what?" she mumbled. And since when was Mom undeserving of forgiveness? It was such a ludicrous thought that somewhere out there, someone had harbored ill will toward her mom. Estelle didn't have beef with anyone as far as Frankie knew. It was a gift.

She got out of the car and rounded Estelle's Tudor style home, eyes glued to the neatly written letters as she followed the stone-set path past the left gable where the roof sloped dramatically into a trellis overgrown with wisteria. On the other side of the gate in the fence, she paused and repeated the words out loud to herself. Then she crossed the lawn, pulling her key out of her pocket.

Her tiny house in the back of the garden had been a compromise. After Frankie finished her degree in elementary education and was ready to start looking for jobs, Starview had just celebrated its tenth anniversary, and Estelle was looking to expand its part-time music program by adding a full-time academic curriculum for grades one through six. She'd needed Frankie's help, and the adorable cottage-style little house had been her graduation surprise for Frankie. "I know you need your privacy now that you're grown," she'd said. "Ta-da. Your first house, my darling."

There was a job in Charlotte that Frankie had been interested in at the time, but Mom had made it so easy to stay. She'd already drummed up excitement in the community that Frankie might be joining Starview as a piano teacher and head of academics, the pay was good, the tiny house had everything she could ask for, and if she needed more space, she could head up to the "big" house whenever she wanted. Plus, two months later, Mom had made them co-owners of Starview. Frankie had earned it, she'd said.

Frankie let herself into her home, flipping on the lights above the small kitchen counter before setting her bag down on the rolling cart that served as an entry table. With white interior, wood floors and trim, an abundance of windows, and multiple hanging plants, the house normally had the ambiance of a much bigger space. Today, the walls crowded her, and as soon as she'd washed up and had a glass of water, she fled back outside and inhaled deeply.

The setting sun reflected in the windows off Mom's patio making it seem like someone was moving behind the panes. Frankie hadn't set foot inside the big house since Estelle's death, but now, with that stupid card burned into her retinas, the building called to her as if Estelle herself would be there with an answer.

She hurried back across the lawn the way she'd come and let herself in through the side entry to the kitchen where the air hung thick with herbs and memories. She counted to three before forcing her gaze to the remains of a life cut too short. Grief stirred inside her, but she kept it at bay by focusing on action. The next step. *Lavignes don't idle.*

The garbage probably needed emptying and the fridge sorting out. Estelle had died on a Thursday, which was one of the days they both fasted until noon, so only an empty coffee mug sat in the sink from that morning—a clunky red thing that Frankie had supposedly made in some art program she didn't remember.

"Does this go in the dishwasher?" she called out before she could stop herself.

Her cheeks heated, that incessant burn starting up behind her eyelids again. No. She had cried enough. "Don't worry, I'll handwash it," she said in a lower voice, and then she did just that, drying it carefully and placing it back in its spot on one of the open shelves above the counter.

She glanced through the doorway to the living room beyond, wondering if today was the day she'd conquer that as well. "Mom could be at work," she whispered. Estelle was always at the school late. Frankie could allow herself to pretend, for a brief moment, that it was a day like any other. That she'd gotten home before Estelle and needed something from the house. From her old room even. Maybe she could make it all the way up the stairs with a little make-believe. At some point, she'd have to, and because of that card, sooner would be better.

"It's only a card—it doesn't have to mean anything," Matt had said before they parted ways after the reception, but Frankie felt it in her bones. It meant *something*, and judging by the way Orla had scrutinized the card, the reporter had known it too. The question was what—a misunderstanding, a prank, or something more sinister?

Frankie strode into the living room with determined steps, purpose momentarily replacing her grief. The more she thought about the card, the more it grated on her. It was offensive really, sending a note like that to a funeral. Estelle's standing in Aspen Creek was beyond reproach, and that extended to Frankie. They had earned their respect. Had worked hard to lift the town up. They were the Lavignes, dammit.

No, not "they" anymore. Now it was just Frankie.

The brief burst of resolve drained out of her as quickly as it had appeared, and she sank onto the couch as the emptiness around her pressed closer once more. Smudged fingerprints on the corner of the glass coffee table where Estelle usually put her coffee stood out in stark relief in the low light from the window. Frankie imagined Mom's tutted disapproval and went to rub them off with her sleeve, but she stopped a few inches short, a surge of protectiveness rising in her chest instead—an impulse to preserve them.

"Get it together," she said out loud, forcing her gaze to the corner of the couch instead where Mom would have sat, reading glasses on her nose and legs folded up underneath her if this had been any other Sunday. Frankie ran her hand across the cushion as a tremor coiled up her spine.

*Oh, Mom.*

She glanced over her shoulder as if to ensure no one was watching, and then she pulled a blanket from the back of the couch over herself and curled up underneath it, inhaling the faint whiff of Estelle's perfume that still lingered on the knitted fibers. Only a few minutes, she told herself. No one would have to know. This wasn't caving, it was... recuperating. It had been a long day, and Mom would want her to be fit for fighting again tomorrow. Frankie had every intention to make her proud, but if she could just press pause for a little, maybe things would start making sense again.

How many times had she rested her head on Estelle's lap here as a little girl while they escaped into fictional worlds? How many times had they played together on the piano over there? Watched the butterflies arrive in their garden outside? It was unfathomable that none of these things would ever take place again.

Estelle wasn't supposed to be gone.

*But now that she was, she was forgiven...*

Frankie's eyes drifted closed at the disconcerting thought as the ghost of Estelle's fingers caressed her temples in that lulling place just beyond consciousness. She was a grown woman and had long since outgrown this kind of comforting, but surely an exception could be made on a day like today. One elongated moment of indulgence, of being little Frankie, of belonging to someone, then tomorrow she'd go back to being Ms. Frankie, now sole proprietor of Starview. She would right the ship that had been knocked off course with Estelle's passing, and soon the community wouldn't know the difference.

Frankie usually dismissed her wake-up alarm immediately, but the next morning, the jaunty tune seeped slowly into her consciousness, a backdrop to kaleidoscopic dreams of packing for flights that were already departed. It wasn't until its gradually rising volume made the water glass on her nightstand tremble that she finally opened her eyes and realized where she was. She'd managed to drag herself back to the tiny house and her own bed last night after falling asleep on Mom's couch, but she was still wearing her funeral outfit, and her mouth tasted like vinegar.

The loft spun as she sat up and rubbed her hands across her face. Her dark hair hung lank down her shoulders, so she pushed it behind her ears before gulping down what water was left in the glass. Then she clambered over to the stairs, careful not to hit her head on the low ceiling, and hurried down the steps. She was ten minutes behind schedule if she wanted to be the first one at the school, and anything else was not an option.

Not when today was the first day back to business as usual at Starview.

Last week, they'd cancelled all after-school classes and forgone regular daytime scheduling, letting their three classroom teachers plan their days based on their students' needs. In Kayla's first/second grade room, they'd read a lot of books and drawn pictures of Estelle and the school. In Beth's third/fourth grade room, half the students had been out with a spring cold, so the remaining ones had picked a group project on famous musicians as their focus, and in Grant's fifth/sixth grade room, the students had opted to continue their academic studies because "that's what Ms. Estelle would have wanted."

Frankie had been in and out, dealing with the hospital and making arrangements for the funeral, everything made more difficult by the fact that there was no will. She hadn't thought it would be so time-consuming, but the days had passed in a strangely warped way where she never knew what time it was or where she was supposed to be. One day, she'd found herself in one of the practice rooms staring out the window until it was dark outside. After that, she'd stayed away from the school. The last thing she wanted was for a student or parent to spot her acting unprofessionally and spreading concern she wasn't up to this task.

But today, the break was over. She'd called a staff meeting at eight like Estelle always did on Mondays, and after that, their full-time academic students would be expecting normalcy, so that's what she intended to bring.

*It's a regular day*, she thought in the shower.

*It's a regular day*, she repeated, pulling a yogurt out of the fridge.

"It *is* a regular day," she said out loud upon parking behind the old rectory that now housed the academic program.

She checked her hair in the mirror, wondering if she should

have taken the time to blow-dry it, but before she could come to a decision Kayla knocked on her window.

"You're here," she said when Frankie got out.

"Of course I'm here," Frankie said. "It's Monday."

"I wasn't sure," Kayla said. "Yesterday was a lot."

Frankie hoisted her bag over her shoulder. "I'm fine."

"If you say so." Kayla started walking next to Frankie toward the music building.

This part of the school was housed in an old wooden structure that had once served as the community church, but the only thing that gave away its former use nowadays was the circular stained-glass window above the peaked entry and a narrow bell tower. Inside, the building had undergone a full renovation when Estelle bought it that added six small soundproof practice rooms, two offices, two bathrooms, a janitor's closet, a staff area on the balcony that used to house an organ, and a ballet studio with eighteen-foot ceilings in the back where the chancel had once been.

It was Frankie's second home, but when she stuck her key in the door to Estelle's office, she had to use both hands to stop her fingers from trembling. This door shouldn't be closed.

"I brought in the mail last week," Kayla said, trailing behind her. "There's a stack of cards from the kids too." She pointed to a bundle tied together with a yellow string that matched the school's exterior.

Frankie nodded but didn't look at the cards. Sure, supposedly these were from their students, but the memory of the anonymous one was still too fresh. She didn't need more surprises. Instead, she directed her attention to the bookshelves, the framed photos and interviews, the gold record of "My Only Child" in its honorary spot on the wall behind Mom's chair, before she inhaled deeply and rounded the desk.

As soon as she sat down, the phone rang. She and Kayla looked at each other, and her friend must have seen something in Frankie's expression because she reached for the phone after the third ring. Frankie stopped her at the very last second. The phone on this desk was Frankie's now, and she wouldn't let Estelle down.

She picked up the receiver and cleared her throat. "Starview Conservatory. This is Frankie speaking."

"Finally," a woman said on the other end. "This is Lauren's mom, Alicia Nolan. I left a couple messages last week. Did you get them?"

Frankie glanced at the receiver in her hand, noting with a drop in her stomach that the voicemail icon had the number seventeen next to it. "Hi. Yes, it's been... a busy few days."

"Yes." Alicia was quiet for a beat. "I understand that, and I hope you don't think me insensitive—I'm simply confirming that after-school classes will commence today? Lauren has a solo at her cousin's baptism coming up, and between you and me, she needs work. Where are you at with hiring a replacement?"

"Replacement?" Frankie frowned.

"You know..." Alicia let out a tense titter. "To take over Estelle's students."

A wave of nausea rolled through Frankie. Was this what people meant when they said the world kept turning? She'd heard it in countless song lyrics over the years, seen it on motivational posters, and even in memes, but the true cruelty of the notion had been hidden until now. "You're asking me if I've found a replacement for my mother?"

"Okay... I've got this." Kayla gently pried the receiver from Frankie's hand. "Alicia? Hi, this is Kayla Clark. Sorry—Frankie had to get on another call. I want to assure you we are addressing any changes that need to happen as fast as we can after our tragic loss and strive to have more information soon. Thank you so much for understanding, and have a lovely day."

She hung up, then sat down across from Frankie. "Damn. Sorry."

"You didn't have to do that," Frankie said. "Take the call, I mean. I had it under control."

Kayla watched her at length. "No one is expecting you to, you know."

That's where she was wrong, Frankie thought. Everyone would expect *exactly* that. But there was no use arguing—especially not with someone who so easily wore her emotions on her sleeve. "Besides, she's right," Frankie said. "I do need to find a new voice instructor."

In fact, there were probably a lot of things she needed to do that she wasn't yet aware of. But if she knew Estelle, there would be detailed instructions and lists somewhere for whatever software they used, the utility companies they contracted with, and the families that were enrolled. All she had to do was start looking.

"I can help," Kayla said. "Put together an ad?"

"That would be great." Frankie pulled out a drawer, riffled through it and closed it again. Then the next. "In the meantime, maybe Stefano can cover Estelle's students." He was their other vocal coach, hired part-time to work mainly with the male voice students. "With the library showcase Thursday, no one will want to skip lessons."

"Are you sure you wouldn't rather cancel the showcase this month? No one would hold it against you."

Frankie looked up. "Cancel? Why would I do that. Everyone loves it."

"I just thought..." Kayla's voice trailed off. "You're already dealing with a lot."

Frankie cocked her head. She wasn't used to this kind of involvement from anyone but Estelle, and she wasn't sure how she felt about it. On the one hand, if Kayla doubted her abilities, Frankie would rather she keep it to herself, but on the other, there was something vaguely comforting about sitting here talking just the two of them like they had years ago. So did she respond with dismissal or gratitude? What would Mom do?

"The community needs normalcy. That's my priority," Frankie said, adding, "I think we can pull it off together, don't you?"

*That's right. Everyone likes to feel needed.* Estelle nodded in Frankie's periphery.

"Of course," Kayla agreed. "I think I saw Stefano's car in the lot. I can go talk to him about puzzling the two schedules together if you want. I'm sure he'll be on board."

Frankie gave her a smile. "Thanks. That would be helpful."

Kayla left, and Frankie returned her attention to the desk. The third drawer was locked, but the key was on Mom's keychain, so she made quick work at getting it open. A stack of envelopes sprang free as soon as she did, spilling onto the threadbare Persian rug beneath the desk. She heard Kayla's footsteps recede and the front door of the school close, leaving a pregnant silence behind as she bent down to pick up the wayward mail.

She straightened, gathering the cascading stationery into a haphazard pile, her gaze trained on the envelopes as she flipped through them. They were all official-looking, all unopened, and several of them had red alerts stamped across the front.

"Final notice?" she mumbled, reading it like a question. What was this?

Frankie tore open the envelope and read the letter within, a chill seeping through her limbs. It was a bill for their property insurance, which had been due in January. She opened another one marked "PAST DUE," read it, then read it again. Internet service. Due two months ago.

All in all, there were five overdue bills and several unpaid others that Estelle for some reason had chosen to stow away instead of paying. Frankie's hands fell open on top of the desk.

Not once had Estelle mentioned financial troubles to her, and everyone on staff had received their paychecks like clockwork up until the day after Estelle's death. Was she to believe someone like her mom, who had always prided herself on facing challenges head on, had deliberately hidden something like this? As if bills go away when you put them under lock and key.

Frankie stood and paced away from the desk. Turned back to look at the stack of now-opened letters spread out on top of the leather table protector. Not only was this out of character for Estelle, but it also meant another entry on Frankie's long list of to-dos. No, scratch that. Not just another entry, a new top priority. If she didn't pay these bills, the school could be in trouble. So why hadn't Mom taken care of it? Or asked for help. Or... or... said *something*.

First that card and now this...

*What if the two are connected?*

The thought struck as the sound of voices reached Frankie from the hallway outside, but she quickly dismissed it as irrational imaginings. Back here in the real world, she had a morning meeting to get ready for, and besides, the only thing the petty note and the bills had in common was that their existence had surprised Frankie. That meant nothing. That was a *her* issue.

She hurried to tuck the bills back into their drawer, vowing to get to the bottom of this conundrum as soon as she had a minute to herself. The bank would be a good place to start. There would be a natural explanation. A logic Frankie couldn't yet see. Estelle had always been so good at thinking multiple steps ahead, so she would have had a reason for her actions. Once Frankie found it, all would be well. The opposite was unthinkable.

# THREE

## ESTELLE

Then

Estelle parked her blue Ford Escort in the driveway, turned off the engine, and tilted her head to the headrest. Her feet hurt, her back hurt, and her hair felt greasy from the kitchen fumes that always hung thick and cloying at Barnie's Bar and Grill. It was two in the morning, and in five hours, she had to be at her second job at a plant nursery two towns over.

She exited the car and approached the front door of the house with her gaze on the window, where flickering blue light illuminated the dark of the night. Greg had probably fallen asleep in front of the TV again. There weren't many nights when he didn't these days.

As quietly as she could, she unlocked the door and opened it, the familiar whiff of damp wood and Febreze washing over her. The floorboards closest to the entry creaked—they'd suspected for a while there was rot somewhere below—and she paused to see if he would stir from the sound. If he did, that would be a good sign.

Her stomach hollowed when he didn't, and maybe to provoke the desired response, she kicked off her shoes with more vigor than she needed.

Still no movement.

"God dammit, Greg," she mumbled as she rounded the couch and started gathering the empty beer cans that littered the pockmarked coffee table without a single look at her husband's limp form.

When the space was tidy again, she turned off the TV, hung up the jackets that had fallen off their hooks, arranged the pile of shoes she'd contributed to, then she moved into the kitchen where a pot of dried-in mac 'n' cheese still sat on the stove and dirty dishes lined the sink.

For a brief moment, she considered leaving them and going straight to bed, but they'd still be here when she got up, and seeing as all three of their mismatched mugs were somewhere beneath the stack of plates and bowls, the task would still fall to her if she wanted her morning coffee.

Had he at least picked up more milk like he said he would?

She opened the fridge, her lips tightening at the pungent smell and the sight of a six-pack of Coors inside. There were also several Tab colas, mayo, margarine, two apples, a takeout container (no doubt responsible for the odor), ketchup, and a bag with questionable lunch meat. No milk.

"God dammit, Greg," she whispered again, her gaze finally going to the man on the couch. His head was tipped back against the cushions, his mouth open and emitting a high-pitched wheezing sound with each exhale.

He'd been doing so well up until six months ago, holding on to a job, doing right by them, but then the layoffs at the lumber mill happened, and he had another brush with the law, unable to keep from running his mouth as he was. He'd applied for different positions since—at least so he'd told her—but nothing that had panned out. Not that Estelle was surprised; it was hard to portray professionalism while smelling like a brewery.

A fresh wave of indignation rolled up her spine that *she* had ended up *here*. Where living hand to mouth was an ideal to reach for. Where life itself was a millstone. Where the sheriff had more reasons than one to come knocking.

With one more glance Greg's way, she turned off the light above the stove and padded down the hallway past a closet and a door that seemed permanently closed these days into the only bathroom, where she brushed her teeth and removed the large gold hoops from her ears. She could get up fifteen minutes early for a shower in the morning she decided, well and truly done for the day.

Greg's jeans were on the floor at the foot of their bed, so Estelle picked them up, patting down the pockets for change he might have forgotten to spend before hanging them over the chair in the corner. She was in luck tonight—two dollars and fifty-three cents to add to the baggie she kept taped behind the headboard. Her dreams hidden from the greedy fingers in this place.

She got under the covers, her head finally sinking into the pillow as a deep sigh left her lips. She was thirty going on sixty, the weight of responsibility so firmly lodged on her shoulders that each day was a marathon. And in a few hours, it would start all over again.

She rolled onto her side, opened the drawer in her nightstand, and withdrew the well-thumbed photo from within. In it, she was sixteen with long, straight hair parted down the middle and standing on a stage with her eyes closed, a mic to her lips. Before life took a turn.

"It's not forever," she whispered to herself.

When she had enough money in her baggie, she'd get her guitar back from the pawn shop, get Greg to step up, and carve out time somehow to write, to sing, to get back up on that stage. It was all she'd ever wanted, and as she drifted off to sleep, she clung to that dream with every ounce of conviction she could muster, knowing in her heart she'd do anything to make it happen. Even escape.

# FOUR

## FRANKIE

Now

"Number thirty-one," the bank teller called, scanning the waiting area where Frankie was sitting.

Frankie looked down at her ticket. Two more to go. Five minutes to answers.

She had ended up cancelling her students and spending all day yesterday going through Estelle's office at the school and trying to get the bank on the phone to clarify what she was looking at, but when she finally got someone on the line, they'd informed Frankie she needed to appear in person to identify herself in order to access the accounts since Estelle had been the primary account holder.

So here she was.

Frankie plucked at the buttons of her yellow shirt, her gaze drifting to the impossibly blue April sky outside the tall windows. They needed to plant the peppers and tomatoes soon for a summer harvest. And maybe some sweet peas too. Those had done well last year, and the butterflies loved them.

A phone rang somewhere in the building, reminding her of

where she was and why. She closed her eyes briefly. No. *She* needed to plant them. She kept forgetting Estelle was no longer here. She opened the folder in her lap to distract herself and flipped through the assortment of documents she'd brought—bank statements, bills, a spreadsheet with inexplicable lists of numbers.

It was already clear that Starview was in trouble, but exactly how much trouble and how it had happened was hard to tell. She had high hopes that would change today.

"Thirty-three."

*Finally.* Frankie stood, almost dropping the folder before catching it in a shaky grip.

"Hi," she said, reaching the counter. "I called yesterday about going over my mother's accounts."

"Okay?" The teller looked at her as if expecting more information.

"Um, I spoke to Bob," Frankie said. "He told me to come in."

"Bob doesn't work Tuesdays."

The woman's curt responses would never have passed for politeness in Aspen Creek, but maybe Mooresville was different, and for whatever reason, Estelle had chosen to do her banking there.

"Then maybe you could help me," Frankie said. "My mother recently passed, and I'm trying to understand what's going on with the accounting for the school we run."

The teller picked up her phone and dialed a few digits. "I've got a client here saying she spoke to Bob yesterday. Could you take it?" She listened for a moment. "Yes. Mm-hmm. Yes, Frankie Lavigne. Okay." She hung up and pointed down a bright hallway. "Second door to your right," she told Frankie. "Robert says he's the one you spoke to, and he does work today, so you're in luck."

Frankie blinked at her, wondering if she should point out

the obvious, but decided it wasn't worth getting into the finer details of nicknaming when she had more pressing matters at hand.

Robert (or "Bob" as he, in fact, introduced himself) waited for her at the door to his office, offered her a bottle of water, then pulled out the chair opposite his at the desk. Already an upgrade from her initial experience at this branch.

"Happy to help you today, Ms. Lavigne," he said in a warm Southern drawl. "But first let me again offer my deepest condolences on the passing of your mother. I transferred into this branch not long ago, so I never had the pleasure of meeting her, but I know of her tangentially. Quite a lovely voice back in the day, and a colleague here has nieces and nephews who thrived at your school. Remind me of the name again..."

"Starview," Frankie offered.

"That's the one." He leaned forward, eyeing the folder Frankie was still clutching in her hands. "So, what can I assist you with?"

Frankie explained that she needed help understanding the transactions in the account but left out the overdue bills and her concerns for the school, and after she showed him her ID, Robert pulled up Starview's business account on his computer.

"I also have these spreadsheets that I don't understand, and I'm working to get access to the tax account," Frankie added. "I know that's probably not part of your job description, but if you have any advice..." Her voice trailed off as Robert's forehead creased in concentration.

"Okay," he said, turning his monitor so she'd be able to see. Then he pointed to various entries explaining what they were. "She had tuition transactions set up through our online platform, so when someone makes a payment, it looks like this. Here's a paid bill, business expenses, loans, all pretty straightforward. She had a credit card for the school too, which is normal, but it does concern me a little that the credit line is maxed out, especially since the account balance is so low."

Frankie leaned closer. "Maybe she was using the credit card to cover expenses?"

"Likely. Let's see." Robert opened the transaction history. "Looks like she's been using it to pay the second mortgage for at least a year."

"A second mortgage?"

He looked at her, sympathy in his eyes. "You didn't know?"

Frankie shook her head. Mom had never mentioned anything of the sort. "What are those payments?" She pointed to a few line items on the screen.

"Looks like paychecks." He clicked over to a different screen. "Here are the recipients. Does that look right?"

Frankie read the names. "I think so." She considered the list. "Are there other accounts connected to the school besides this one?"

"Let's see. If there is, you might not be... No, never mind. She has your name on this account too. It looks like her personal one though. Regular checking."

"Can I see it?"

Robert pulled it up, and they looked at it together. "Not much activity it seems. A small deposit once per month, then regular expenses—grocery store, pharmacy, hair salon, sundry shopping, credit-card interest payments. There's a maxed-out personal one too."

"Wait—can you go back to the paychecks in the other account?" Frankie squinted at the screen. "There," she said, pointing to an entry. "That matches the payment to her personal account, right? So that must be her paycheck."

He flipped back to the other account. "Yep, you're right."

"But that makes no sense. She worked more hours than anyone else at the school and that paycheck barely covers one week." Had Estelle stopped taking paychecks because the school was in trouble? "How far back has this been going on?"

Robert clicked on another button. "The small paychecks started about fourteen months ago."

Fourteen months. Frankie tried to think that far back. "That's right after we had that leak."

"It's possible she had other assets elsewhere," Robert said. "I can obviously only see what's available on our end."

"Yeah, I don't think so," Frankie said. No paychecks, maxing out credit cards, not paying bills—that didn't exactly point to stowed-away riches. "And you're sure there's nothing else? No savings account or something like that."

Robert angled the screen back toward him and clicked around while Frankie waited. "She used to have one, but she closed it two years ago it looks like." He paused, a low "huh" escaping him. "And there is one other account connected to her social security number, but your name isn't on that, so I'm not at liberty to share details with you at this time."

"Even though she's dead."

Robert made an apologetic grimace. "Not unless you have the death certificate and proof of relationship with you."

"They said it could take three to four weeks."

"Well, good news is the account isn't going anywhere, so when you have it, come back and we can take a look."

"You can't even tell me if there's money in it?"

"I'm afraid not," Robert said. "But you have my number."

That was all she'd get today. A handful of answers that raised further questions still.

On the drive back, Frankie was numb to everything around her except the road ahead and the swirling thoughts in her head. Starview had a full student roster, money *was* coming in. Granted, they also had bills and paychecks to cover, but had those so overwhelmed Estelle that she'd taken out a second mortgage, maxed out multiple credit cards, and stopped lifting a salary? Had she been in over her head with the upgrades they'd done in recent years? Banked on growth that never materialized? Was it the Covid dip?

A more disturbing explanation occurred next, which Frankie dismissed outright because there was no way Estelle would have hidden away money from the school into a personal account. No way she would do something so unforgivable.

Would she?

Frankie shrugged off the errant notion. That card was twisting her thoughts. There would be a perfectly logical explanation for this, but the sooner she could get access to that private account, the better. She should ask Matt if he would look at all of this too. He dealt with contracts and money all the time in his job, so maybe he'd see something she didn't. As soon as she'd pulled into the parking lot at the grocery store back in Aspen Creek, she texted him, and his response was instant.

*Happy to,* Franklin D. Roosevelt. *You know where to find me.*

She was still smiling at her phone when someone tapped on her window. Bonnie DeWitt, the mom of one of their newer piano students at the school smiled sugar-sweetly at Frankie. "Do you have a minute?" she mimed.

Well, she had to get out of the car sometime, and she couldn't avoid people forever, so Frankie exited but kept the door open between them as she stood. Call it instinct. "Hi, Bonnie."

"I'm out getting my run in," Bonnie said as if Frankie had asked. "And then I saw you and, well, I don't mean to be a bother, but Olivia was saying yesterday how *much* she misses lessons, and while I know you sent home new music for her to work on, it's not quite the same, is it? Ha-ha-ha." She gripped the top of the door, her French tips clicking against the window as her smile stretched even wider. "I suppose I'm wondering if yesterday's cancellation was a one-off and we can expect classes to resume soon or if it's a continuation of last week. That's all."

Frankie had had a reason to cancel yesterday; she was head of the school now and that had to take precedence. There was, however, also that small problem of her still not being able to play the piano that had made cancelling easier than it should have been. Not that she'd admit that to a parent. She inhaled deeply. "Most likely we'll—"

"Because she does have that recital in Charlotte in May," Bonnie cut in. "And I'm told someone with sway at Oberlin might be in attendance, which means we really can't afford for her to miss more lessons."

"I understand." Frankie paused to see if she'd get a word in edgewise. "And I'm sure you can appreciate that we've all been thrown for a loop." She shook her head, seeing the bank info scrolling past before her mind's eye. "Please tell Olivia to sit tight just a little longer."

Bonnie's smile faltered, and she let go of the door. "You're saying you can't promise not to cancel her next class too? Even with one of the school's core values being student focus? I remember when we first joined how *passionate* Estelle was about that. It's what made us sign up, and I'm not convinced this is how she'd want things run in her absence."

There was decidedly less warmth in her expression now, which made Frankie appreciate the metal barrier between them. The nerve. As if Bonnie knew a single thing about Estelle. But Frankie forced her face into an understanding smile. All was well.

"I would hate having to take Olivia elsewhere," Bonnie continued, oblivious to Frankie's struggle at keeping her breathing steady. "That's all I'm saying. I don't *want* to, but unless things go back to normal soon..."

Frankie balled her fists up at her side. The urge to argue for compassion, to wrench open her ribcage to show this woman the black emptiness keeping her from "normal," was overwhelming, but what would be the point? To some people, pain was invisible until they felt its jagged teeth for themselves. First Alicia and now Bonnie. They were so passionate, these parents. So involved, so committed. But that focus could leave empathy by the wayside.

*Because children are mirrors of their parents' dreams,* Estelle's voice reminded her. *They see their own worth reflected on that stage. Don't forget that.*

"Soon," Frankie said, closing the door and locking the car. She had to get her shopping done while she had some semblance of energy left, but she still forced herself to meet Bonnie's gaze. "And my mother and I shared the vision for Starview, so you can rest assured her wishes are being honored, absent or not."

Bonnie had the decency to look mildly chastised. "Of course. I didn't mean to insinuate... Like I told that woman asking around at the funeral reception, I have nothing but respect for the whole team at Starview."

Frankie had been ready to set off toward the store, but now her eagerness to escape fizzled. "What woman?" she asked.

"Oh, some curious biddy wanting to know what 'tone' Estelle set at Starview and if we were happy with the school. And don't worry—of course we all raved about it."

"This woman talked to several people?" Frankie asked, unease trickling down her spine. "Did you happen to catch her name?"

Bonnie thought about it. "No, I don't... Oh wait. She gave me this." She pulled her phone out of her belt bag and produced a card from the holder in the case. "Orla Monroe," she said, handing it to Frankie with a hint of pride in her voice at having come up with the answer. "Unusual name. Should have remembered."

Frankie stared at the simple business card for a long moment. This wasn't good. If parents like Alicia and Bonnie were already doubting Frankie's leadership, considering what she'd just learned at the bank, the last thing she needed was that particular reporter asking questions.

# FIVE

An excerpt from Orla Monroe's interview with Estelle Lavigne
Published in *Country Weekly*, January 1995

It will come as a surprise to no one that our first feature of the year is with none other than smash hit phenom Estelle Lavigne, whose emotional tearjerker of a hit, "My Only Child," dominated the airways in the last quarter of 1994. *Country Weekly*'s own Orla Monroe sat down with the newly minted star to talk inspiration, determination, and what's next so that you, our loyal readers, will have to wonder no more: Who is Estelle Lavigne?

## ORLA MONROE (OM):

Estelle, Estelle. The woman of the hour. I haven't been able to go anywhere in the past few months without hearing your song, and I must say I've loved every moment of it. It's relatively rare for a new artist to burst onto the scene like you have, so let me start by asking you how you got to this point. Where did you come from and what has this journey been like for you? I'm sure our readers are curious.

## ESTELLE LAVIGNE (EL):

So thrilled to be talking to you, Orla. Well, first of all, I'm not sure that I would call myself a new artist, but I understand why it may seem like I am to the wider audience. The truth is that I've been writing songs and performing since I was old enough to hold a guitar. My grandfather gave me my first one. Music is in my genes, you might say. His family ran a café in a small town outside Paris at the turn of the century, so he'd play for customers there. In fact, he'd later play for the soldiers during the Great War, and he used to say it saved the family—that extra coin he got for entertaining the weary men. He brought his love for music with him when they immigrated here.

With his encouragement, I spent all my free time after school growing up immersed in music. Singing is the only thing I've ever wanted to do, and while my parents might have preferred a more traditional path for me, they were still supportive, as was my late husband. My only regret with having reached this point right now is that none of them can be here to celebrate it with me. It's sounds cliché, but it truly is a dream come true.

## OM:

Would little Estelle have believed it if someone had told her we'd be sitting here today?

## EL:

I'd like to think so. I come from a long line of tenacious people and was raised to set goals and follow them. Failure wasn't an option. So little Estelle would have told you it was possible if she worked hard enough. Anything is possible if you set your mind to it. You just can't be too precious about your creature comforts. Success takes sacrifice and a willingness to make tough choices. And I've got that in spades.

# SIX

## FRANKIE

Now

Frankie's right hand was still wrapped around the mouse as she spun the chair out from under the desk at Starview and half stood while continuing to scan the subject lines in the school inbox for more emergencies. *That one could wait. That one too.* She'd been on her way out the door for a half hour, but at the last minute, she'd remembered she had to cancel a paper order they could do without for the month, and then she'd spotted a missed email from a parent asking about dress code guidance for the monthly showcase at the library that she was presently running late to.

Four days in, Frankie no longer had to wonder at Estelle's long evenings at the school. There was always something to do—from progress checks, performance arrangements, and staff meetings to creating lesson plans, parent communication, and now solving the financial issues and hiring too. At least she'd told Kayla and Matt about the bills just to have someone to talk to about it, and Kayla was showing up for her in a major way, always asking what she could do or if there was anything

Frankie needed. It made her feel guilty about the way their friendship had drifted—like it was her fault and Kayla had always been there—but maybe their life paths had simply diverged. Either way, it was nice to see more of her again.

Frankie's phone buzzed with a message just as she locked the door to the office and hurried toward the front door. She contemplated ignoring it because what if it was yet another busy task that would keep her from where she was heading, but then she sighed and pulled her phone out just like Estelle would have done.

*Where are you?* the text from Kayla read. *About to start.*

"Fudge." Frankie tossed the phone back in her bag and set off running.

The library was only a few blocks away, and she made it there as Grant, the guitar teacher, was introducing his newest students.

Every month, Starview put on a free performance at the public library as a stage experience opportunity for any student willing to show off their skills to the community. As with most other things Starview, this event was Estelle's brainchild and an effort she'd managed to get the town hall to sponsor since it fit neatly with their commitment to community-strengthening, literacy, and the arts. Over the years, it had proven to be a win on all fronts—each month, the showcase drew more visitors to the library, gave young musicians a chance to play in front of a friendly audience, boosted parent satisfaction, allowed the town leadership to mingle with the community and pat themselves on the back, and gave Starview a boost in exposure and a chance to entice new clients with little effort.

It was also plain fun.

Some of Frankie's earliest recital memories were from inside these book-clad walls, and she knew she shared that experience with both Tina, the violin teacher, and Stefano.

Frankie found a seat at the back of the full room, waving to

Kayla, who was overseeing a group of tiny ballerinas waiting their turn up front, to let her know she'd made it.

One of the librarians hurried back toward Frankie as three novice guitar players strummed up a shaky version of "You are My Sunshine."

"We have a reserved seat for you at the front," she whispered. "Come with me."

"Oh, I'm fine here," Frankie said with a polite smile.

"But Estelle always sat up front," the librarian insisted. "It's your seat now."

Frankie stared at her. She wanted to protest as if that empty seat was an invite that could reach the afterlife. As if Estelle might still show up. Besides, Frankie was not an "up front" kind of person. If that's who they expected, they'd be sorely disappointed.

*Don't be silly,* Estelle said in her head. *Expectations are opinions waiting to be formed.*

Frankie caved. For better or worse, she was the face of Starview now, and if they wanted to sign up more students, it would help if she was visible.

Before she could change her mind, she followed the librarian to the front and sat down with the eyes in the room burning at her neck. But Kayla gave her a thumbs up, and after another few performances, Frankie allowed herself to relax and enjoy the show.

Once the final musician had performed, all the students got up in front of their audience to raucous applause. It seemed to lift the ceiling today, and when Frankie turned around to face the room, she was surprised to see the audience spilling into the foyer. They'd never had so many in attendance before, but perhaps that was another sign of how much Estelle had meant to the community. A burst of grief threatened to shake loose the tears she'd locked up after the funeral, but it sputtered out as a glint of an idea ignited somewhere in Frankie's mind at the sight of the crowd.

Unfortunately, before she could follow its sparking fuse, a familiar bottle-blonde updo swept toward her where she stood near the piano at the front of the room.

"Impressive turnout," Orla Monroe said. She was dressed in a floral blouse and navy slacks today—more casual but equally as put-together as at the funeral. "I can see why the school is successful. You offer both music and academics now, right?"

Frankie studied the reporter for signs that she already knew something she shouldn't but found her expression friendly. Not that that necessarily meant anything. "We have an academic curriculum for grades one to six in addition to the part-time music conservatory," she confirmed. "But I'm sure you knew that already. What brings you here tonight?"

"Free musical entertainment," Orla said. "Who can resist?"

"But you don't live in Aspen Creek."

Orla cocked her chin in the affirmative. "True."

Frankie shifted her stance, keeping an eye on the people around them to gauge what she could and couldn't say. Her conversation with Bonnie earlier in the week had given her no rest, so when no one was in direct earshot, she took her chance. "Why are you walking around questioning parents about Starview and Mom?"

Orla's eyes widened briefly. "Oh, you're direct. I like it." She pushed a stray blonde strand off her temple. "Let's just say—"

"Frankie!" Grant strolled up to them picking a casual melody on one of the strings of the kid-sized guitar he'd slung around his neck. "We're heading out to catch the rest of the high school baseball game. Want to come?"

"Big one today," Stefano added as he and Tina joined.

"How so?" Frankie turned her back to Orla. She'd come back to her later.

Stefano looked offended by her ignorance. "They'll make it to state if they win."

"Which they will," Tina said. "Go Mustangs!"

Grant showed his agreement by plucking the first few notes to "Take Me Out to the Ball Game" on his guitar.

"I'm good, but you guys have fun," Frankie said. She could think of few things she found less interesting than watching people sweat over a ball.

She waited until they'd left before steeling herself for facing Orla again. "Where were we?" she asked, turning around, only to find the spot where the reporter had stood now vacated. She craned her neck but couldn't spot her anywhere. Typical.

She'd meandered halfway through the room looking for the woman while accepting occasional praise on behalf of the school and nodding at well-meaning condolences when a waving hand caught her attention beyond the family of one of the tiny ballerinas.

"Frankie!" a brisk voice called. Not Orla's.

She couldn't see who it belonged to, but it had to be someone short because the hand barely cleared shoulder height trying.

"Frankie, yoo-hoo. Over here." The hand waved some more.

Frankie's brow furrowed. She wasn't used to being yoo-hooed, but nevertheless, she pushed her way through the crowd until she stood before a lady clad in head-to-toe purple who grinned up at her with crinkled eyes from her wheelchair seat.

It was one of the Word Birds—a group of old ladies who'd made the library their daily hangout and who consequently showed up to every single one of Starview's monthly showcases.

"Mrs. Blunt," Frankie said, pulling the name from somewhere deep inside, even though she'd never exchanged more than a word in passing with the rather intimidating group of seniors.

"I'm not interrupting, am I?" Mrs. Blunt asked. "So many in attendance today."

Frankie offered her a smile. "Not at all. How are you?"

"No, no," Mrs. Blunt said sternly. "Not me. How are *you*?" She took Frankie's hand as if they were longtime friends. "I wanted to offer belated sympathy for your loss. I would have been at the funeral if only my gosh-darned knee hadn't needed replacing only two days prior. Hence the wheels."

The wheelchair was also purple, as was the brace spanning Mrs. Blunt's knee now that Frankie had a closer look.

"I can walk, mind you," the old woman added. "But I'm saving it for shorter distances for now. Plus, the chair gives Owen something to do." She peered up at Frankie, her pale eyes twinkling as she pointed behind her. "I trust you remember my grandson?"

Frankie's gaze shot up, landing on the man who had his hands on the wheelchair push handles. He'd been standing so still that Frankie hadn't noticed him before. Dark-blonde hair fell across his forehead, and several days of stubble covered his cheeks, giving what should have been well-known features a mildly boorish camouflage.

"Owen?" she asked, taking in the familiar slant of his eyes. Was it really him?

"Hi, Frankie." His voice was a low rumble in his chest. "I'm very sorry for your loss."

She managed to sputter out, "Thank you," while her mind threatened to short-circuit with memories. He was the only boy she'd dated in high school. He'd asked her out the summer before his senior and her junior year and for a brief while, she'd felt part of something bigger than herself. Then he'd gone off to college, and she'd stayed. He was the last person she'd expected to run into today. And yet here he was. She'd forgotten he and Mrs. Blunt were related.

"It's been a long time," he said, scratching two fingers against his forehead.

Frankie was about to agree when Mrs. Blunt continued. "Oh, everyone did so well today, but I had hoped to hear you play as well, my dear. You usually accompany an act or two." She turned in her chair and patted one of Owen's hands. "Such unbelievable talent."

A tightness wove itself into Frankie's smile. "It wasn't needed today," she said. "Maybe next month."

"But Owen might not be here for that," Mrs. Blunt said. "Perhaps something short right now? I'm sure everyone would love it." She gestured to the piano.

Frankie eyed the instrument as if it had teeth. "These events are really more to spotlight our students. I'm sorry."

Mrs. Blunt looked like she was about to push further, but thankfully, Owen placed a hand on her shoulder. "It's not necessary, Grams. I've heard Frankie play before, remember?"

He'd been on the football team back in high school—an unlikely match for her, she'd thought when he first asked her out—but he'd come to every one of her recitals that year, always bringing flowers that he'd hand her afterward.

Frankie gave him a grateful smile, ignoring the scrutinizing squint Mrs. Blunt was leveraging on her.

"You probably perform at bigger venues nowadays," Owen said, running a hand through his hair that made it stand even more on end. "Didn't that place on 1st Street have live entertainment at one point?"

Frankie had played there one summer in college, and she'd loved it—the pendant lights above forming a bubble around her and the piano, separate from the patrons who were too busy eating to pay her direct attention. She'd hoped to return the following summer, but by then Estelle had needed her for a summer intensive program at the school, so she'd turned it down.

"That place has been closed a long time," she said.

"And there's nowhere else?" Owen asked, bright blue eyes locked on her.

"No." Frankie shook her head. "I don't really perform. There's no time."

He bobbed his head in acknowledgement. "Bummer for me."

Something in his voice made her unsure what to do with her hands. Was he teasing her? She forced her attention back to Mrs. Blunt for safer waters. "In fact, I still have... um... things waiting for me back at the office, so if you don't mind...?"

"Of course, dear. You go. But I'll see you next month and for any Starview performance after that. Such a joy. Such a joy." She squeezed Frankie's hand again, and then Owen rolled her away with a nod Frankie's way.

Frankie watched them leave, vaguely aware that the librarians were starting to put the chairs away.

"Was that who I think it was?" Kayla appeared at Frankie's side as the crowd thinned. "What the heck is Owen Novak doing back here?"

"I don't know," Frankie responded without taking her eyes off the doorway.

"He looked a little rough, didn't he? I almost didn't recognize him."

Frankie glanced at her, then shrugged. "He's older. Like us." How many years had passed since she'd last seen him? Eighteen? Nineteen?

"What did he say?"

*You probably play at bigger venues nowadays.* Frankie cleared her throat. "Not much."

She spotted a leftover folder still sitting on the piano and that finally got her feet moving. Just as she suspected, it belonged to one of her second-year students who'd lose his head if it wasn't stuck on.

"Oh well. Good riddance, am I right?" Kayla said behind her. "Anyway—I'm meeting Matt at Portside Tavern for dinner, so I wanted to see if you'd care to join us?"

The excuse was on the tip of Frankie's tongue. *Sorry, I can't. Too much to do. You guys go ahead.* It was second nature at this point, though she couldn't remember when it had started. Maybe when Estelle had made her partner and stressed the importance of professional boundaries. Or was it when her friends got married? But standing there in the emptying room, with no one waiting for her elsewhere, the word that crossed her lips instead was, "Sure." If nothing else, she did still need to get Matt's take on the Starview documents she'd sent over for him to look at. It would basically be a working dinner. No need for Estelle to think she was getting distracted.

Kayla lit up. "Really?"

An unexpected burst of warmth spread inside Frankie at her friend's excitement. "I could eat."

"All right." Kayla gestured to the door. "Are you ready now or...?"

"Um..." Frankie's gaze skimmed the Starview poster board by the door and the stack of leftover programs that sat on its ledge. Then it skated across the makeshift stage, past the windows where cars were pulling out of the parking lot, and there, finally, was Orla. "There's actually one more person I need to talk to," Frankie said. "Can I meet you at Portside? I won't be long."

Kayla smiled. "Sounds good. See you there."

Frankie hurried out the door, determined not to let the reporter get away again, but she needn't have worried. Orla was wrapping up a conversation with a few of Kayla's ballet parents.

"Asking more questions?" Frankie asked when the parents left.

"Ah, there you are," Orla said as if she was the one who'd been looking for Frankie. "Only chit-chatting."

"About?"

"Oh, this and that."

Frankie sighed. "I believe you were about to tell me why you're here."

"Right." Orla lifted her chin. "It's that card. I haven't been able to let it go."

*You and me both*, Frankie thought. Out loud, she said, "But it's just a card. If you've been talking to people, you'll know how much Estelle meant to Aspen Creek."

Orla nodded. "True—the two are contradictory. But that's what makes it curious, don't you think?" She pulled out a small notebook from her purse and flipped a few pages. "Was there anything... unusual about her death?"

Frankie scoffed. "What?"

"I don't know," Orla said. "She was younger than me with no underlying health issues as far as I've discerned. Not the kind of person whose heart suddenly fails."

"But it did," Frankie said. "What are you insinuating?"

"Oh nothing, nothing." Orla lifted her hands in a show of yielding. "I was simply curious if there might be a parent out there who was discontent on behalf of their child. An overlooked solo perhaps, or lackluster progress. Anything at all that could have triggered a confrontation."

"A confrontation that led to her death?"

"Someone *was* unhappy with her," Orla said. "Per the card."

Was she right? Was it possible there was more to Estelle's death than they'd all thought? "No, the parents loved her," Frankie said.

"Doesn't have to be a parent. Could be anyone. Could be a teacher. Could be you." Her gaze remained steady on Frankie, but there was no telling if she was being serious.

"That's ridiculous," Frankie said, her voice thinner than she wanted. "You need to stop."

Orla shrugged. "Only doing my due diligence for an old friend."

Friend? Only if friendships were one-way streets. Frankie huffed but kept her thought to herself. "Well, can you do it away from the school please? It doesn't look good."

"And that's important to you? That things look good?"

"Yes. I mean, no. I mean..." Frankie sighed. This woman was infuriating. "I'm trying my best to do right by Mom and the school, and I don't have the bandwidth for whatever this is." She gestured between them. "It's hurtful. Mom died of a heart attack. I *lost* her."

For the first time since they'd met, Orla shrank back a step. Then she averted her eyes and nodded to herself. "You're right," she said. "Work habit, I'm afraid. To be a good journalist, you have to embrace your inner shark. I got carried away, and I'm sorry. Retirement makes for long days."

Frankie didn't respond, unsure if the tone change was genuine.

"I should get on the road," Orla said. "Head back to Charlotte. But here's my card in case you think of... anything."

"I have one already," Frankie said. "But there's nothing to think of, so I won't be calling."

Orla nodded. "Fair enough. Well, good luck to you."

Frankie squinted after the older woman, watching her retreat to the far end of the parking lot. She was pretty sure she'd won that exchange, but it didn't feel that way because somehow, she was certain she hadn't seen the last of Orla Monroe.

Frankie joined Matt and Kayla in a booth near one of the front windows, and after they'd ordered beverages, Frankie asked Matt to please give her some good news. After her run-in with Orla, she sorely needed it.

"I'm afraid you'll have to pick, Frankincense," he said. "Do you want good news, or do you want the truth?"

"That bad, huh?"

"It's like you said—the numbers don't make sense. I can't tell if it's because Aunt Estelle used her own system to track payables and receivables or there's some creative accounting going on, but Starview is behind on nearly every single payment including the two mortgages. Your best bet is getting into that private account, crosschecking every transaction over the last few years with the spreadsheet, and maybe talking to someone at the IRS."

"What do you mean by 'creative accounting'?" Kayla asked.

"Like money going where it shouldn't." Matt hesitated. "Like illegally."

What was it with people tonight? First Orla and now Matt. Frankie glared at him. "Yeah, right, because that was Mom."

Matt shrugged. "She could have outsourced the books."

"To a criminal?" Kayla gave him a scolding look. "I'm sure that's not what's going on."

*Someone was unhappy with her.* Orla's earlier sentiment caused a discomfiting twist in Frankie's gut. Involvement with the darker side of society, even if well intentioned, did get people hurt, at least on TV. Considering the loans and maxed-out credit cards, Estelle could theoretically have owed money to the wrong person. "Hey, do you guys think there's a possibility someone was with Estelle when she died?" she asked. "That the heart attack was—I don't know—provoked?"

Both of them stared at her, then Kayla slapped Matt's arm. "See what you did? Planting weird ideas..." She faced Frankie again. "No, there's no way. She would have told you if someone was giving her grief. You two were closer than most."

"So close," Frankie agreed as the waitress arrived with their drinks. "We didn't have any secrets."

"Oh, honey," the waitress said, setting Frankie's Moscow

Mule down before her. "Everyone has secrets. The things I hear..." She tapped her temple before distributing the remaining drinks on the table. "Now can I get any starters going for you?"

They requested more time to decide, and once the waitress had left, Frankie stirred the straw in her drink while considering that unsolicited truth bomb. Had Estelle had secrets? Frankie wanted to say no, but she couldn't completely dismiss the growing number of signs to the contrary. To Orla's point, the implication of the card was that at least one person out there had thought of Estelle with less than affection in their heart, which, in turn, meant there might be others. And that wouldn't happen without reason.

Nevertheless, Frankie forced confidence into her voice when she spoke again. "I'm sure we're just missing something. Once I get into that private account, I have a feeling I'll find some answers."

Matt nodded. "And in the meantime, I told Dad to give you a call."

Frankie stared at him. "You told him about Starview's money problem. Why?"

"Because I thought he could help."

"What's to say I want help?" This couldn't get out. The community would think she wasn't up for the task.

"I mean, you kind of need it." Matt had a sip of his beer. "You still have bills and paychecks to cover, right?"

"I'm figuring it out," Frankie lied. "As soon as we get back into the routine of things and I can see what the new day-to-day looks like, things will fall into place. No need to involve other people. I just emailed the staff about taking on more students, didn't I, Kayla?"

"You did." Kayla glanced at Matt, a silent beat passing between them.

"What?" Frankie asked.

"I don't know if that will be enough," Matt said. "It might drive up revenue a little, but for each extra lesson you offer, someone also has to get paid to teach it."

Kayla scrunched up her nose. "And you do need to hire a new vocal coach to take over Estelle's students, and that person is probably not going to be okay doing it pro bono."

Frankie's heart sank. Kayla was right; while Estelle hadn't taken a full paycheck for her hours, a new person would need to be compensated. How had she not thought of that?

"I'll figure it out," she said again, flicking her nail through a water droplet on the table and watching as it multiplied. Borrowing money was not an option. Estelle had clearly tried it with the second mortgage, and while it was out of character for her to make a wrong move like that, Frankie had to assume she'd had a good reason.

"But what happens if you don't?" Matt asked.

"I will," Frankie said. Failing wasn't an option. Not for a Lavigne.

*We dust ourselves off and we persevere,* Estelle whispered in her ear.

"Would you ever sell?" Matt asked in a softer voice. "If it came to that, I mean."

"Sell?" She stared at him in disbelief. She'd hit one little speed bump... "Starview is my life."

Matt pressed his lips together as if unsure he should continue, but since he'd never been one to hold back before, out it came even though Kayla shook her head at him in warning. "It doesn't have to be," he said, and Kayla hung her head.

"What do you mean *it doesn't have to be*?" Frankie asked. "It's all I know. My life is here."

"He doesn't mean anything," Kayla started, but Matt butted in again.

"You used to have other dreams," he said, taking a long pull on his bottle before resting it against the table. "Remember that night in Memphis? When my mom and I came out to watch Aunt Estelle play and she pulled you up on stage?"

The argument left Frankie in a rush. She'd been eight, and her accompaniment had brought the house down. Lights reflecting in the ivories beneath her stubby fingers, the base drum thumping in her stomach, the grown-up smell of sticky bar tables wafting by. "I do." A small smile tugged at her lips.

"You wouldn't shut up about it for the next two years. You wanted to be just like her."

"No, she was the star in the family," Frankie protested. "She had that it factor... or whatever you want to call it."

"My point is—that's what you wanted. To play. Not to run a school."

Her irritation rose again. "So what? Kids dream of all sorts of things. Didn't you want to ride around the world in an air balloon at one point?"

"You did?" Kayla asked, eyes widening as she looked at her husband. "That's so cute and also completely ridiculous considering your fear of heights."

Matt shrugged. "What can I say? Jules Verne made a big impression. But..." He held up a finger. "I *have* traveled to many corners of the world. What stages have you performed on, Frankfurter?"

Ugh, could he be any more obnoxious? Without a suitable comeback handy, Frankie bought some time by looking deep into her copper mug.

"I will save the school," she said after she finished drinking. "Because it's what I want, and because I owe it to Mom."

Matt was about to say something else, but this time, Kayla's elbow drove into his side, effectively giving him other things to think about.

Frankie sent her friend a grateful look. At least Kayla understood that this was something she had to do. Starview *was* Estelle, and you didn't turn your back on family.

# SEVEN

## ESTELLE

Then

Estelle shoved the knife into the jar of mayo as if she was plunging it into her fiercest enemy before sloughing the condiment onto the last slice of bread in the bag. The spongy piece flattened with the force, and even the frailty of this inanimate thing made her blood boil. Everything around her was spineless, drifting, undefined, averse. Including the food in her kitchen apparently.

She found a spotted banana and some chips in the pantry and shoved everything into a brown paper bag, not caring about the noise she was making. She was running late, but if she didn't pack this lunch, Greg would forget like he always did.

Setting it on the corner of the counter, she looked around. Over the last few months, Greg had moved on from beer to stronger stuff, and the smell of yesterday's binge seeped out of the garbage bin. It didn't matter that she'd straightened the pillows on the couch or wiped down the kitchen table. This place was gross.

Her home was gross.

A wave of shame heated her cheeks before she rolled her shoulders back and tightened her resolve. She'd tell Greg tonight after the gig that she was done. No more ultimatums or second chances. A long time ago, he'd been someone to count on who cared if she had a good or bad day, who supported her dreams, but every passing moment made that memory fade further into the fog of the youth they'd long since left behind. She'd be thirty-one in a few weeks; she had so much more life in her. But only if she left Greg. That was the conclusion she'd reached. It was time.

Somewhere down the hallway, a door opened, but instead of calling out a good morning, Estelle grabbed the car keys from their hook by the door and left. If she got roped into a conversation now, she'd hit traffic on her way to the plant nursery, and that was the last thing she needed.

After making sure she had her serving shoes in the car already so she could go straight from her day job to Barnie's later, she peeled out of the mobile home park, pretending she didn't see the face in the window watching her leave.

On Thursdays and Fridays, Barnie's Bar and Grill had live music from nine to midnight, and a month ago, Estelle had finally saved enough to get her guitar back and mustered up the courage to ask if she could get a spot. After playing a tune for Barnie, he'd agreed, as long as she "didn't expect to get paid for it." Which was fine. She knew nothing if not how to pay her dues.

She hadn't sung publicly since they'd lived in Waynesboro, but she'd been writing and dreaming, and when she'd played a cover of Dolly Parton's "It's All Wrong, But It's Alright" a couple of weeks ago, the patrons had enjoyed it. She hummed it as she drove through the countryside after finishing her shift at the nursery, her fingers mimicking strumming on the steering wheel. Tonight, she was getting the twenty minutes leading up to midnight, and she would be ready. She'd even included two original songs in her set list. It was a gamble seeing as she hadn't had that long to practice, but she was done playing things safe.

The restaurant was busier than usual for a Thursday, the kitchen vibrating with energy as she made her way through to the back room where there were lockers the staff could put their valuables in. They didn't fit a guitar though, so Estelle popped her head into Barnie's office.

"Okay if I put this in here?"

"Go ahead," he said, wiping his beading brow. "Damn, it's hot in here tonight."

"I can get you a drink," Estelle offered, tying her black apron around her waist. Barnie was a good boss. He paid fair wages and was low on the creep factor—two things that mattered more than they should.

He waved her off with a grunt while pulling the table fan on his desk closer.

"It's packed tonight," Estelle said.

"There's another trade show in town this weekend. The hotels are booked full from what I hear."

"Good for us," Estelle said.

"Good for us," Barnie agreed.

Estelle took off her rings and then pulled her shoulder-length brown hair into a ponytail before heading into the bar.

"Oh, thank God you're here," Sandy, one of the other bartenders said with a glance over her shoulder. "These guys are thirsty."

As if to prove her right, a blonde guy in a blue Polo shirt snapped his fingers to get Estelle's attention a second later. "'Scuse me."

"Seems like it," Estelle told Sandy with a smirk. Then she nodded to the guy. "What can I get you?"

"Could we get nine beers to that table over there?" He

pointed to a group of identical-looking men—sales guys no doubt—at a round table in the center of the room.

"Um..." Estelle scanned the floor for one of the waitresses that normally would take table orders, but they were all swamped. She had a choice to make. She could turn the sale down and risk losing a substantial tip, or she could step out from behind the counter this once. "Sure," she said. "Want to open a tab?"

"You know it." He tossed her his card, and she made a mental note to be protective of that table tonight as it had clear potential to be good for her pockets.

"Be right back," she told Sandy, picking up the tray with the beers and rounding the bar.

The guys were rowdy but not in a threatening way, seeming to know better than to mess with the staff, and several hands helped her unload the drinks while the conversation between the men jumped between quotas and tee times and other concepts Estelle had no interest in.

"Can I get you anything else?" she asked, putting the tray under her arm.

She regarded the group while they declined, one after another, her gaze landing on a man at the far side of the table who was observing rather than taking part in the interaction. He had feathered brown hair, tan skin, a strong nose, and piercing eyes that missed nothing. And right then, they were locked on her.

A shiver of awareness skated down Estelle's back, but she was forced to break their contact when a busser bumped into her.

"Enjoy," she told the table, then she pushed her way through the room back to the safety of the bar.

The next few hours saw nonstop bar traffic, which was good because it made time go by faster. The rhythm of the work—taking the orders, gathering supplies, opening the bottles, filling glasses, serving up—became a meditation with the loud backdrop of jovial voices cushioning the space where she worked. Estelle and Sandy exchanged a few words here and there, but it was mostly things like "right behind you" or "pass that opener," and on the few occasions when Barnie joined them to chat with some of the regulars, they included him in their dance too, moving swiftly around his sizeable shape.

The first act was about to start playing, and Estelle had just filled up a glass with water for herself, parched as she was after several hours on the go, when Sandy nudged her shoulder.

"Your guy is here," she said, tipping her head toward the end of the bar. "Want me to tell Barnie?"

Estelle's eyes snapped to the seat where Greg was currently shrugging out of his windbreaker and making himself comfortable. He spotted Estelle looking and waved her over.

"No," Estelle told Sandy. "I'll deal with it."

This wasn't the first time Greg had shown up to her work, but tonight wasn't going to be a repeat of last time when Estelle had had to beg out early to escort her drunken husband home. Tonight, leaving wasn't an option. She was playing at eleven forty, and nothing was going to keep her from it, especially not this man in front of her who she barely recognized anymore.

She set her glass of water down in front of Greg and tilted her head. "I thought we agreed you wouldn't come here when I'm working," she said. "I could get in trouble."

"But I never see you anymore," Greg said. "Can't a husband want to be with his wife on a Friday night?" He took a sip of the water, grimacing when it hit his tongue. Several droplets clung to his moustache when he set it back down.

"It's Thursday, and you don't see me because you're drunk when I come home and sleeping it off when I leave in the morning." She leaned closer to him over the bar to better gauge the glassiness of his eyes. "In fact, you're drunk right now. How did you get here?"

"Bus. And I only had one beer."

Estelle let out a tight scoff. "Right. And I'm the tooth fairy. Go home, Greg. You're not supposed to be out tonight."

"Come on, Stella. One drink." He smiled as if that would still work to get her sweet on him like it had when she was seventeen, and suddenly she didn't know why she hadn't put her foot down sooner. He wasn't her Greg anymore. He was someone else. A shell of the person who'd once made her laugh until her legs wouldn't carry her.

She hadn't laughed in years.

"We can talk when I get home," she said, reaching for the water glass, but his hand came down on her wrist, stopping her.

His lower lip wobbled as he blinked at her. "I'll do better," he said. "I promise. I'll find another job. We can be good again."

Estelle stared down at his hand on her skin. His grip wasn't so tight it hurt, just firm enough that she could feel the desperation oozing from him. "Let go please," she gritted out, not sure if she meant only his physical hold on her or if this was it—her plea for him to set her free.

Greg was about to respond when the attractive man from the nine-beers table earlier sidled up next to him, making him wobble as he looked up at the man's towering height.

"Everything okay here?" the man asked, his gaze going from Greg's grip on Estelle to her face. "Is he bothering you?"

Estelle's lips parted, a "no" on her tongue, but nothing came out.

"None of your business," Greg said, but he at least dropped her wrist. "Can't a guy have a drink in peace."

"I told you I'm not serving you tonight," Estelle said, forcing her gaze away from the stranger. "I'll call you a taxi, okay? Go home." She glanced the tall man's way again. "Everything is fine. Did you need anything from the bar?"

"A beer," Greg said.

"Not you." Estelle's voice was like a whip.

The stranger's eyes glittered in the muted light, a hint of amusement on his lips. "No, I'm all right," he said. "Just wanted to offer my services, but you clearly have things under control." He nodded to indicate Greg, then he winked at her and strode back toward his table.

How about that—the American gentleman wasn't quite extinct after all.

Once she'd lost him in the crowd, she returned her attention to her miserable excuse for a husband. For a split second, she considered dropping the bomb on him right then just to be done with it. The words swirled in her head, on her tongue, on her lips. *I'm leaving you.* But common sense won out, and instead she shook her head at him as he looked at her with bloodshot eyes. "Don't go anywhere," she said sharply. "I'll let you know when the car is here."

As soon as he was gone, it was as if the unpleasant interlude had never happened. Someone else took his seat, and Estelle carried on serving drinks. When had it become so easy to move right on along? Was it the first time he'd embarrassed her in public? That time she'd had to tell her favorite teacher she was dropping out of school? Or did it go even further back to her childhood when her own parents had thrown harsh words at each other at school functions and birthday parties, and she'd pretended not to notice. Maybe she'd always known that if she didn't acknowledge the shameful elephant, it didn't exist, and if it didn't exist, she didn't have to spend time figuring out how she felt about it. It was a good skill to have.

There was one benefit to Greg's interruption though—it had made Estelle too preoccupied to be nervous about her upcoming performance. Before long, it was her turn, and she hurried into the back to remove her apron, change her blouse, and retrieve her guitar.

The crowd had thinned substantially because of the late hour and it being a Thursday, but she didn't mind. She'd play for one person if she had to—each small step forward was still progress on this new journey she'd staked out for herself.

As the previous singer—a burly man with a banjo—left the small corner platform to make room for her, the audience returned to their plates and their company, so when Estelle introduced herself, not a single person in the room was looking at her. No, that wasn't true. The handsome guy was, his head tilted with curiosity as she strummed her first chord.

The stage had always worked like a time warp for Estelle, and that night was no different. Her twenty minutes felt like one, and when the echo of her final note floated toward the ceiling and the audience started clapping, she returned to her body as if her soul had been out adventuring in a place she hadn't visited in a long time. Every nerve ending tingled with familiarity and rightness, but since she still had an hour left of her shift, she hurried to thank everyone for coming out instead of lingering in that feeling.

"You were amazing," Sandy said when Estelle returned to the bar. "I can't believe you wrote those songs. Where did you learn that?"

Estelle shrugged. "My grandpa played, and he gave me my first guitar when I was six. I've loved it ever since."

"Well, you should definitely keep doing it."

Estelle smiled as she filled another glass with foaming beer from the tap and set it down in front of a patron. "That's the plan." She picked up a rag and wiped a spill from the bar before looking up, ready to take the next order, only to find herself locked in that intense gaze once again.

"How many different jobs can one girl do around here?" the handsome guy asked, one elbow casually resting on the edge of the bar. "Making drinks, serving, handling drunkards, musical entertainment..."

"What can I say? I have layers." Estelle smirked as she gestured to the tap. "Another one?"

He shook his head. "I don't drink after midnight."

"Why? Do you turn into a pumpkin?"

The full force of his wide grin hit her square in the chest as he nodded in approval. "Funny, but no." He leaned forward and lowered his voice. "See that guy in the green polo over there?" He nudged his head in the direction of the table he'd come from. "We're vying for the same contract, and I happen to know the guy making the decisions is golfing early tomorrow morning."

A man with a plan... Estelle found herself smiling back at him as something in her stomach made a double loop. "Clever. And what business are you in?"

"Construction currently. But I dabble here and there."

"I see." She didn't, but it was late, and her game was rustier than an old barn nail. A small flutter of the lashes seemed a safer bet than making conversation.

He straightened. "Which is why I wanted to talk to you actually."

She blinked up at him in surprise. "Oh?"

"That's quite a voice you've got there. It's not often that folksy Americana stuff captures my attention."

*Folksy stuff?* Estelle was about to call him out on the dismissive term, but the sincerity of his compliment stopped her. Or maybe it was his square chin and rapt attention. It had been a long time since anyone had looked at her that way. Like she was a woman to reckon with.

"Anyway..." he continued. "I think you have something special, and if you're interested, I might be able to help you out. I've got a lot of connections." He placed a business card on the counter and tapped it twice.

She took it, reading the words out loud. "'*Raymond Clark, Business Manager.*'"

"Hope to hear from you soon," he said.

# EIGHT

## FRANKIE

Now

The two violins chased each other through the sonata, the harmonies crisp and clear in the video that Tina, Starview's violin teacher, had sent Frankie of that morning's Easter Sunday service performance. Frankie had not been able to make herself return to the church where she'd said goodbye to Estelle, instead opting for a cup of coffee in Mom's red mug. She smiled at the students' perfected arpeggios, telling herself for the umpteenth time that if they could do it, so could she.

She was seated on the piano stool by the baby grand in Mom's living room. Her conversation with Matt the other night had driven home the urgency of the situation, which meant that she needed to get over her weird block not only for her own sake but to keep parents like Bonnie DeWitt happy. Her hope was that if she sat there long enough, music would happen. Now was not the time to risk losing students. If anything, they needed to enroll more kids, extend their hours, and possibly find some buried treasure to dig up too.

Outside the window, a sudden April shower created a wall

of mist, its sound hypnotizing against the wooden deck. The rhythm goaded Frankie to join in, but even though more than an hour had passed, she had yet to even touch the keys.

Estelle had given Frankie her first lesson when she was four years old. They'd been on the road somewhere, and after the gig, while Frankie waited for Estelle to finish chatting with the band, she'd sat down at the upright piano and started picking out tunes with one finger. After a while, Estelle had joined her, drawing the first five notes in a C scale on a piece of paper and matching them with the keys. While guitar was Estelle's first love, she did all right on the piano too, and she'd continued to teach Frankie until they settled in Aspen Creek, and she enrolled her in more formal lessons—first with a lady down in Cornelius and then at Starview once the school was up and running.

Frankie had understood the instrument from the start, quickly progressing through beginner books to more advanced ones. She wasn't necessarily a prodigy, but she loved everything about it. The smoothness of the keys, the muted tap at the press of them, the deep resonance of the lower register and the bright chime of the higher one. The thrill of a perfectly executed vivace passage. It was where she escaped after a stressful school day, where she refilled energy reserves, expressed her joy, and worked through conflicts. Estelle had used to say she could tell Frankie's mood from one single keystroke.

The piano had always been her ally, but now it sat before her silent and judgmental. Now, when she needed the escape the most, the door to it was locked and the key lost. The irony.

Maybe she could trick her hands to comply? She reached for the sheet music to a simple sonata from the shelf next to her and set it on the rack above the keys. This would be like decoding words in a book without caring about the story. Emotionless.

She placed her hands in the starting position, closed her

eyes, then opened them to the first measure. With an achingly familiar movement, the two eighth notes rose to the ceiling followed by a mournful minor chord, and as she shifted her hands, Frankie had time for one hopeful inhale—a glimpse of that other world where she could lose herself. Then a chill ran down the back of her arms, locking them in place, and her fingers slipped off the keys to a dissonant din.

She groaned out loud, slamming the fallboard down. Why couldn't she get past this?

She left the room, turning off lights as she went, and after locking up the kitchen entry, she jogged through the wet grass to her own little house. She'd have to keep being creative with her lessons, do more instruction than demonstration, and hopefully Kayla would understand if she had to use recorded music for her ballet class again rather than Frankie's accompaniment. It wasn't as dynamic, but it would have to do.

She sat down at her desk to have another pass at Starview's scheduling to see where they might be able to fit in new students since now, for the first time since she'd joined as partner, they'd have to actively recruit to keep the school afloat. She'd just started drafting an email to the three academic classroom teachers about possibly increasing the class sizes come fall when her phone rang. She sighed at seeing Uncle Ray's number lighting up the screen. Matt hadn't called him off then...

"Uncle Ray," she said in greeting. "Happy Easter. How is everything?"

"Frankie, dear. Yes, Happy Easter. Doing all right. Spending the holiday weekend at the St. James cottage with good friends. But how are you holding up?"

Matt's father had homes in three states and thriving property developments in even more. He still called Aspen Creek his base, but nowadays he split his time between North Carolina, Florida, and Tennessee depending on the time of year and where he currently had new projects in progress. Someone else might have thought it odd that he'd left town for Easter considering Matt was here, but Frankie didn't know him as a sentimental man. If she was to guess, his current company of "good friends" included at least one or two new business prospects who might be buttered up by a coastal retreat among the state's upper crust.

Frankie swiveled in her chair, her gaze trailing through the window toward Mom's house where her ebony nemesis resided. "I'm fine," she said. "Everything is under control."

"Such an immense loss, our Estelle. It must be very hard for you."

"It is," Frankie conceded. "But the work continues like I know she would have wanted. One day at a time." She frowned as the platitude crossed her lips.

"She'd be very proud, I'm sure," Uncle Ray said. Then he cleared his throat. "It's why I'm calling actually."

Here it came... "Oh?"

"I spoke to Matt the other day, and he told me Starview is having some financial problems?" He tipped the last word up, phrasing it like a question.

Frankie sent another mild curse Matt's way. She hadn't explicitly told him not to tell anyone, and perhaps she should have realized Uncle Ray would find out, but that didn't make this any less embarrassing.

"Nothing we can't handle," Frankie said, forcing her chin up. "I'm still, um... transitioning into the full managerial role, and once I have a clear grasp on everything, this will likely be a simple misunderstanding on my part." She sounded confident, right? It could be true.

"I see," Uncle Ray said. "Well, Estelle was a clever woman, so you're probably right. But..." He paused—a move of intentional suspense and an understated tactic for making people hang on his every word. He was a masterful puppeteer in conversations, but this wasn't Frankie's first rodeo, so she waited patiently for him to continue, which he did before long. "Should that not be the case," he said, "I'm only a phone call away. A small loan could ease your headache substantially. I did get Estelle started once upon a time, so you'd be in good company."

To Frankie's surprise, hearing the offer stated so bluntly, it was more appealing than she'd been prepared for. She even considered it for a split second. Their accounts back in black, a cushion. But loans needed to be repaid, and the thought of being beholden to anyone made her want to hang up the phone. Uncle Ray may have been the closest thing to family she had left, but he was a businessman, not a good Samaritan—that didn't make someone rich. No, she'd do this on her own or not at all.

"I appreciate the offer, but I have a plan," she lied.

"A plan." He guffawed. "You sound like me when I was your age. Very good. Then I look forward to seeing what you do."

She rolled her eyes. As if she had a mercenary bone in her body. No, the only thing they had in common was their fondness for Matt and Mom. "I'm sure Matt will keep you posted," Frankie said, unable to keep all the snark out of her voice.

If Uncle Ray heard it, he didn't say so. Instead, he began wrapping up the conversation, but just as he was about to hang up, Frankie's gaze snagged on the card from the funeral on the cork board above her desk. She'd pinned it there as a reminder that it was her duty to pursue the culprit, as if that task didn't already consume most of her waking thoughts.

"Oh, Uncle Ray—you knew Mom longer than most. Do you know if she had conflicts with anyone over the years?"

"Conflicts?" he asked. "What kinds of conflicts?"

"I don't know. Drama. Anyone who might have held a grudge."

"A grudge?"

"Yeah. Someone who, I don't know, maybe didn't... *like* her." She closed her eyes in the wake of what felt like a crude question to ask about her mom.

There was a beat of silence. "This is an unusual question," Ray said. "Estelle was a wonderful woman, and I can't say I ever saw her fight with anyone."

"Right." Frankie dug her teeth into her lower lip as she looked away from the card and its odd message. "So no one who would have had reason to think she needed forgiveness then?"

He was quiet even longer this time—enough for the fine hairs at Frankie's neck to rise—but then he chuckled. "Well, I am quite peeved that she dared go before me, but I don't suppose that counts."

Frankie huffed out the breath she'd been holding. "Right." What had she been thinking? That he knew something she didn't? Of course Estelle hadn't done anything to invite dislike.

There was a crackle on the line, then another pause before the commanding rasp of his voice returned, closer this time. "Is there a reason you're asking, Frankie dear?"

A cavalcade of snapshots ran through Frankie like a reel—Mom dropping whatever she was doing to ask about Frankie's day, her curious blue eyes crinkling and alive as she engaged with the stories Frankie told. Her back hunched over her desk late into the evening when Starview demanded it. Encouraging words before performances, not just to Frankie but to all the students. A straightened ponytail. A tuned guitar. How long it would take to walk through town with her because of how many people she'd stop to talk to.

Frankie should have thought this through better, should have known her question would spark curiosity, but she couldn't mention the card. Because no matter how pretty its glossy exterior, no matter that whoever had sent it was probably misinformed, the words inside cast a shadow at the edge of those memories.

"I don't know," she said vaguely, scrambling for an explanation. "I'm wondering if someone tried to sabotage the school or something. Just trying to think of why she made some of these financial decisions."

His breathy exhale made Frankie pull the phone slightly from her ear. "Ah. Yes. Success does draw in dark elements from time to time. Well, if you change your mind about the loan, let me know. There's no shame in it, you know. Without my Eton connections, I would have never gotten the company off the ground back in the day."

Frankie made a non-committal noise, thinking that day would never come, and then they ended the call, Frankie already planning to lock down Matt's line of communication about these things with his dad. Whatever was going on with Starview, she would handle it just like Estelle would have handled it—swiftly and professionally. There was no need to involve others.

The sun emerged from behind the dark clouds right as they hung up. Frankie stepped outside, inhaling the earthy air as water droplets winked and sparkled at her from every leaf and branch. There had to be another way to save Starview. *Think, think, think.* Lavignes didn't give up. Lavignes pushed through and they got the job done because at the end of the day, no one looked out for you but you.

She slipped on her rainboots and gardening gloves and wandered into the garden where some of Estelle's flowers were already in bloom. Frankie's vegetables and berries would not be ready for harvest for a while, but there was always something to do. Weeding, pruning, tying supports. She lost herself in the repetitive work while the sun sent the lingering damp evaporating into billowing swirls of mist around her.

She didn't notice her visitor until he was right upon her, that familiar, "Hey," making her drop her trowel. Owen was standing on the other side of the raspberry bushes with a towel-covered basket in his hands.

Frankie straightened, pulling off her gloves. "Hey." Maybe Kayla had been right—there was something unkempt about him. He was too pale for the sunlight, none of the glossy, all-American boy he'd been back in high school to be found in the man before her. Something must have happened along the way.

"I saw your car, so when no one answered the door, I decided to check back here. How are you?" he asked, a tightness she didn't recognize bracing his frame. Nerves or something else?

She blinked at him. This version of him was awfully curt for a guy who'd once sent her a note likening her complexion to the brightness of the stars in the Milky Way. Then again, much time had passed. "Fine. You?"

A grimace crossed his features as if he, too, found their exchange lacking, but he caught himself and held out the basket. "Grams made cinnamon hot cross buns for Easter. We have too many, so she asked me to drop off a few for you."

"For me? Why?" Frankie rounded the garden bed slowly.

Owen shrugged. "I don't know what that woman is thinking half the time, but I suppose she reckoned you could use a treat. What with your mom and everything."

He handed her the basket, and the most mouthwatering scent slipped out from under the cover.

"That's very nice of her." She carried it over to the weather-worn bench between the garden beds and sat down. "Want one?" she asked, gesturing to the spot next to her.

Owen hesitated, but then he joined her, taking a bun when she offered.

They ate in silence for a few minutes, nothing but the creaking of the seat and happy insects fluttering about them disturbing the peace.

"It smells exactly like I remember here," Owen said once he'd finished his roll, inhaling deeply. "Green. Warm. Happy."

He sounded lost to whatever memory had prompted the statement, so Frankie didn't respond. She wanted to ask where he'd been, where he'd lost whatever he was missing, but she wasn't that person to him anymore. She had no right.

He stood suddenly as if he'd said too much. "I should get going. I didn't mean to take up your time."

Frankie put her half-eaten bun down on the towel, squinting up at him as if she might spot something that would explain his jumpiness. "It's fine. They're delicious. Please tell Mrs. Blunt thank you from me. Do you need the basket?"

"I'll get it some other time."

"So I'll see you again?" Frankie didn't have time to stop the question before it was hanging in the air between them. She couldn't take it back either—that would give it more weight than she'd intended.

"Um..." Owen scratched the back of his head. "Probably. I'm helping Grams, so if she's about town, I am too."

"Like at the library," Frankie added.

"Right."

"I probably won't have the basket with me then though." Frankie tried for a smile.

Owen looked stumped at first, but then a shift swept past his eyes. A small crinkle at the corners. "No? I hear country chic is all the rage in Paris this season."

*There he is*, she thought, a grin spreading on her lips. He smiled back.

"It's good to see you, Owen," she said.

He nodded. "Same." He took a step back, then paused. "You are okay, right? I mean with your mom and the school. I can't imagine..."

"I'm fine," she said again. "Thank you."

"You'll do a great job leading it," he said. "I have no doubt. The turnout Thursday was impressive."

"Yeah, well, everyone loved Estelle."

He was right. A lot of people had shown up and with short notice too. Frankie had been unsure if their students would feel ready considering the interruption the week before, but everyone had stepped up, including the community. As always, they'd come to support the young musicians and for the entertainment, but Estelle's name had been on many lips as well. She was still a string that bound them together.

"They love you, too, and the school. That's Aspen Creek for you," Owen said.

Something simmered at the edge of Frankie's subconscious at his words. Aspen Creek loved Estelle, Estelle was Starview, so Aspen Creek loved Starview. And now Starview needed them.

"I wonder..." Frankie mumbled to herself.

"What's that?" Owen asked.

Frankie picket up the basket. "Nothing. Just realized I have some work to do."

"Oh. Okay." Owen started to back away. "I'll get out of your hair."

But Frankie was barely paying attention, the idea blurring her surroundings as it took shape in her head. The community was the solution. Once upon a time, they'd welcomed Estelle and Frankie into their midst, and Estelle had given her all right back. Maybe they'd still show up for her. What was it Estelle used to say? *Loyalty is more valuable than any currency.*

Yes. This could work.

Frankie watched Owen disappear through the gate, then she hurried inside to put her thoughts on paper. Tomorrow, she'd run the idea by the other teachers to see if it had legs.

If it did, she felt pretty sure she'd figured out a way to save the school.

# NINE

## FRANKIE

Now

It was decided. They would put together a grand In Memoriam event with live music, games, food, and a raffle and auction featuring unique prizes related to Estelle's life and work, to which they would invite all of Aspen Creek and the surrounding towns.

The more Frankie thought about it, the more she was convinced it would work. The only caveat was that they'd have to do it no later than May 17 which was three and a half weeks away. If they waited longer, they'd run into Memorial Day weekend, and then the end of the school year and summer break. This meant there was a lot to do and expedience was of the essence, but for the first time since Estelle's passing, Frankie had some genuine buoyancy to her step.

While Starview's finances were still a point of concern, now there was at least a chance they would catch up, and that had lightened the heavy load on her shoulders. She'd even decided to tuck the weird card from the funeral into a drawer to be able to give the auction her full attention. Who cared what had compelled some stranger to write those misguided words? Frankie knew Estelle and so did Aspen Creek, and that was all that mattered.

She let Kayla into her mom's house Tuesday evening because there was one thing the whole venture hinged on, and that was memorabilia for the live auction part of the event that would put Estelle front and center. She'd planned on going through Estelle's things herself, but then Kayla had volunteered, and in the spirit of efficiency, Frankie had accepted. It had been nice to spend more time with her friend lately.

"I'm caffeinated and ready to work," Kayla said as she kicked off her sandals. Then she called toward the ceiling, "You'd better have some treasures lying around, Estelle."

For a split second, Frankie listened as if an answer might carry on the air-conditioned wind, but then she scoffed at herself and followed Kayla into the living room.

"I found this," Frankie said, picking up a CD of "My Only Child" from the side table and showing her friend. "It's signed—that's good, right?"

"Yep. Do you have pen and paper? Let's start a list."

Frankie fetched what they needed from the roll-top desk in the corner. "I'm putting her guitar from school on the list too, and I've been debating if we should include the framed gold record? That could bring in a lot."

Kayla's face fell. "Frankie, no. You can't part with that."

It would hurt, that was for sure, but if it was between that and the school... Frankie pictured herself getting up on a ladder and hooking it off the wall above Estelle's desk at Starview, and her heart squeezed tight. "Okay. We'll keep it off the list for now," she said. "It can be a backup."

"We're going to find other things." Kayla gestured around the room. "So where do you want to start?"

Frankie's gaze was drawn to the stairs leading to the second floor. She hadn't been up there since it happened because she knew Estelle was everywhere in that space. Her scents, her colors, the textures of her clothes, and the silence she'd left behind. Ever since Frankie had moved into her tiny home, the second floor in this house had felt off limits—not because Estelle made it so, but because Frankie no longer had an obvious reason to be there. And if she'd had no reason to climb those sixteen steps while Estelle was still alive, she couldn't help but feel she had no business doing it now.

But Estelle would probably call nonsense on that. She wasn't the one who'd wanted Frankie to move out after all. A pang of guilt jabbed Frankie between the ribs. It was just that they'd already been working together, eating together, and sharing basically everything with each other. Frankie had needed something that was just hers if for no other reason than to mark her transition to college graduate.

"I guess upstairs," Frankie said.

"Then lead the way."

The setting sunlight streamed in through the large window on the landing, and Frankie paused there to settle the wobble at her core. A large portrait of her and Estelle from her high school graduation hung directly across from the window. In it, Frankie was perched behind her mom, leaning on her shoulder with their faces cheek to cheek. She could still feel Mom's soft skin like a brush of velvet against her own.

Frankie tore her gaze away from it and led Kayla down the hallway into what had once been her bedroom—the most neutral ground on this floor. Over the years, it had turned into a crafting room slash sheet music storage area, so it was a good way to ease into their task.

"Remember when we drew flowers all over that wall during a sleepover?" Kayla asked.

Frankie walked over to the wall and peeled aside the bottom corner of the wallpaper where her bed had once stood so Kayla could see.

"They're still there," her friend squealed. "Come on, Estelle, that's not a very good coverup."

Frankie smirked. "It definitely would have worked better if I'd been able to stop picking at it."

"As with most coverups." Kayla held up a knitted green scarf still attached to its needles. "How about this? Handmade by Estelle Lavigne?"

It was a lopsided effort, but they needed prizes and couldn't be picky, so Frankie agreed to add it to the list. If someone claimed it, it would likely be the first time one of Estelle's crafted creations had been worn since her normal MO had been to leave projects half-finished and discarded. *Life is too short not to go where your interest lies*, she'd often said, and that sentiment extended to any task that failed to hold her appeal.

"I don't think there's much of anything here," Kayla said after they'd done a cursory inventory of the room. "Unless you think we could include a stack of random sheet music?"

Frankie considered the boxes. "It couldn't hurt, right? If no one's interested, that's fine, but you never know."

Kayla nodded. "Good point." She dragged one of the boxes closer to where she was sitting on the carpeted floor. "Why don't I sort through these then, and you can move on?"

Frankie took a deep breath. Moving on meant going into Estelle's bedroom.

"You can do it," Kayla said gently. "Remember we're doing this for her. For Starview."

Frankie nodded. Kayla was right.

Standing outside her mom's room, Frankie resisted the urge to knock. Instead, she pushed the door open and braced for attack by the invisible force she knew would linger inside. The one with the power to throw her equilibrium. She'd loved the movie *Ghostbusters* as a child, cheering on the heroes as they vanquished ghouls left and right, but as she stepped over the threshold and allowed the comforting notes of orange blossom and white musk to wash over her, she would have welcomed an apparition no matter its intent.

"How are you gone?" she whispered into the shadows left by a half-drawn drape, wrapping her arms around herself.

She stood there, still and waiting for a response that would never come, until a ruckus from the other room snapped her out of her stupor.

"Sorry," Kayla called. "Dropped a box."

Frankie's gaze landed on the still-dented pillow on the bed where Mom had last lain her head, an ominous quaking rumbling beneath her skin at the sight. The temptation to allow herself to crumble yet again was overwhelming, but now that other people were counting on her, that people's jobs and children's dreams depended on her saving Starview, she would lock that chamber in her chest up tight and do what she'd set out to do.

Still, her heart pounded unevenly as she approached the bed, her fingers caressing the soft duvet. *You're my strong girl,* the ghost whispered on the wind. *My survivor.* Frankie flexed her hands once as if a concerto wanted to burst from her fingers, and then she pulled the drapes wide open, flooding the space with light. She also opened the window, and with the first gust of fresh air bursting in, her lungs regained their full capacity.

*Chin up, eyes forward.* She was here to do a job, and she would do it well.

The walk-in closet was first. She wasn't interested in the clothes and the shoes—most of those she'd donate at some point—and the small fireproof filing cabinet held only passports and other documents that were not for the public eye. But there was a photo at the school from opening day in which Estelle wore a knee-length floral dress with a matching red cowboy hat worthy of the Kentucky Derby, and that hat could make a fine auction item if she could find it.

Kayla appeared in the doorway with her arms full of music.

"I've had an idea," she said. "What if we make themed baskets instead for the silent auction—one each for piano, violin, guitar, voice, and ballet? I'm sorting through the stacks and there are some great scores here. We could add treats and other fun items that would be geared toward the students. The parents would eat it up."

Frankie lifted the lid off another shoebox on the floor and nodded. "I like it. Are you almost done in there? I'm looking for that hat."

"Halfway. I'll let you know when." She disappeared again.

Plenty of shoes and hats later, she still hadn't located the red one, and the closet hadn't yielded anything else for the auction. They needed that one high-value item that would draw interest for a bidding war, and so far, all they had were small potatoes.

"Guest room next," she called to Kayla.

"Okay, still got more boxes here," was her response.

The guest room held a queen-sized bed, a nightstand, a love seat, a small bookshelf, and an old armoire where they'd kept winter jackets and boots when Frankie was little. No one had stayed in the room since the early days of them living here when Estelle still had an occasional musician friend from her performing days visit. But at least twenty years must have passed since then, so it was a credit to Estelle that a freshly cleaned scent clung to the interior of the room.

The armoire was a natural first place to look for a hat, so she twisted the key that kept the ornate double doors locked and opened one of them carefully, half-expecting a slew of bumbling moths to fly at her. When the coast seemed clear, she set the doors fully ajar and examined the contents.

The first thing her eyes landed on was a clear garment bag with a frilly blue dress inside that made Frankie's breath catch. Her recital dress. They'd bought it at Loman's in Charlotte when she was thirteen, and she remembered trying on half the store before choosing this one. It had been her first big showcase, and she'd played "Clair de lune" to roaring applause at one of the wineries in the area. Estelle had just opened Starview that year and was pushing hard to get them visibility.

She unzipped the bag and pulled the dress free of the hanger, the familiar scratch of the tulle skirt calling up a memory of her smoothing it over her legs after sitting down on the piano bench. She held it up, marveling at its diminutive size. She'd eventually grown to her current five foot eight inches, but back then she'd always been the smallest in her class even though she technically was a year older than her classmates. Homeschooling and life on the road had left her with some gaps in her early elementary education, so the adults in charge had thought it best to hold her back a year.

How long had she fit into this dress? Two years? Three? Though as much as she'd appreciated her growth spurt once it hit, it had been a sad day when Estelle announced this dress had to be retired. To think she'd kept it all these years.

A cavalcade of other recitals brushed up against Frankie as she returned the dress to its bag. Chopin paired with a long, pale pink dress with an empire waist. Schumann and a flippy skirt with a bow at the back. A sophisticated black one for Rachmaninoff. None of those garments were here, but the memories were so vivid that she couldn't help but wonder what she might have chosen to wear on stage today if it had been her and not Maddie Forester who'd landed that job with the Chicago Symphony.

The thought made something dark and acidic snake through her, but she pushed the foreign feeling away as she continued searching the armoire. The past was in the past. "What ifs" and "could have beens" were better suited for country music tunes than her current task at hand.

"Aha," she said, pulling a milliner's box down from the narrow top shelf and setting it on the love seat.

The box had a metal latch closure that took some fiddling

before it snapped open to reveal its contents. Unfortunately, it was a black pillbox one she'd never seen before, not the bedazzled cowboy hat she needed. She let out a puff of disappointment and turned her back to the armoire to consider the rest of the room. "Where would I be if I was a hat?"

The bookcase held only books, a couple of porcelain figurines, and some puzzles, but when she looked under the bed, she spotted something that showed promise. She lay down on her stomach and pulled out a small gray guitar case. It was weather-worn and dull, but when Frankie opened it, she knew she'd found something that could make a difference. It was Estelle's first guitar—the one her grandpa had given her. Frankie recognized it from a framed photo downstairs. Two of the strings had snapped, but surely that would only add character and appeal to a collector.

"Kayla?" she called. "I've got something."

"Be right there. I think I found something too!" her friend called back.

Their luck was turning. Frankie could feel it.

While she waited, she looked deeper under the bed, spotting another guitar case and, behind that, a large suitcase, so she pulled those out too.

The clean floral smell that had first greeted her when she entered the room grew stronger, seemingly emanating from the two cases. Frankie's nose twitched as she unlatched the larger guitar case, her fingers crossed that it would be the black guitar from the "My Only Child" album. Now that would really be a find. She did recall Estelle saying that guitar had gone missing somewhere on the road, but you never knew. Sometimes lost things weren't truly lost.

She opened the lid just as Kayla entered the room, a notebook in her hand.

"Whew!" her friend exclaimed, wrinkling her nose. "That is potent. What did you find?"

Frankie stared into the guitar case, a frown weighing at her brow. Yes, what the heck was she looking at? It was definitely not a guitar—that much she was sure of.

"I don't..." She didn't finish the sentence. Instead, she reached in and plucked out one of the many boxes inside and turned it over in her hands. "I think it's tea," she said.

"Tea? As in for drinking?" Kayla joined her on the floor, her eyes widening as she took in the contents of the case. She reached for a different box and read the print before opening it. "This is a candle," she said, showing Frankie before dipping her nose to it and inhaling deeply. "Lavender," she said.

"The tea is lavender too," Frankie said before she dove on the large suitcase, her instinct telling her things were about to get even weirder.

She unbuckled the straps of the old trunk, and sure enough —stacks and stacks of the same boxes, plus several bigger ones that contained jars of honey. All in all, there were hundreds of boxes of lavender candles, tea, and honey tucked away under the guest-room bed.

"Estelle must have loved lavender," Kayla said, still smelling each box that she opened.

"I've never seen her use any of it," Frankie said. "She drank coffee and peach iced tea, and the only candle downstairs is a gardenia one, which I know because I bought it for her." She surveyed the spread before them, shaking her head. "Why would she buy all of this only to store it away?" An uncomfortable thought entered her mind. Was this where the school's money had gone? To some kind of compulsion?

Kayla sniffed between the two candles in her hands like she was emulating a sommelier. "Some smell stronger than the others," she said, setting them down and picking up two boxes of tea instead, one from the guitar case and one from the bottom of the suitcase. "Ah," she said as if she'd solved a great mystery. "This one expired in 2016, and this one is new.

That explains it. She must have bought them over several years."

Frankie set down the box she'd been holding. "It explains exactly nothing," she said, resisting the temptation to upend the suitcase all over the floor.

All she wanted was to ensure Starview's future. To keep her cool and make Estelle proud. These oddities that kept popping up—the card, the school's finances, the private account, Orla's insinuations, and now this horde of floral randomness—were burrowing under her skin at a moment when she didn't have time for such distractions. *Look at us*, they seemed to say. *Are you sure things are fine?*

"People collect all sorts of weird things," Kayla said. "My memaw collected playing cards, but only the queens. Had stacks and stacks of them. I honestly don't think it's that big a deal."

She could be right. Estelle's half of their raised garden beds outside was entirely dedicated to flowers, while Frankie preferred to grow edible things. Mom's proclivities might have simply spilled into this stockpiling of lavender products as a different kind of pastime. Except, why do it in secret?

"Did your memaw hide the cards under the guest-room bed too?" Frankie asked, looking to her friend.

"Well, no. She even had some of them framed on the wall."

Like Frankie had thought. Something wasn't right about this, and it was beyond frustrating that questions were piling up at the very instant Estelle wasn't here to provide answers.

She ran her hand over the contents of the guitar case and sighed. Everyone had quirks, and this could have been one of Mom's. An immaterial whim. But in the context of the relationship they'd always had, sharing everything, talking about everything, it felt like this did matter. Like it said something more about them that Frankie had yet to decipher.

"I don't get how I didn't know about it if it was just a

hobby," she said. "It doesn't feel like Mom. It's like... someone else put these things here."

"Maybe it was a phase," Kayla offered. "Like all those crafting materials she bought and didn't end up using. I sifted through a ton of that in the other room." She shrugged.

Frankie's gaze caught on the notebook Kayla had brought with her that was sitting forgotten on the floor. It reminded her that they were in the middle of something more important than understanding Estelle's unusual shopping habits.

She closed the lid of the suitcase and pushed it back under the bed. "You're right. Either way, we're not raffling off lavender tea at this event, so let's leave it for another day." She pointed to the small guitar case behind her. "But I did find Estelle's first guitar, and that we can use." She forced her lips into a smile. "How about you? What's that?" She pointed to the book.

Kayla's eyes glittered to life. "It was at the bottom of one of the sheet-music boxes. I think it's a songwriting notebook." She handed it to Frankie.

Frankie instantly recognized Estelle's handwriting as she started flipping through the pages. Kayla was right. It was page after page of cursive pencil scribbles. Some had full lyrics with chords noted above the words; others contained nothing but lists of rhyming words or scraps of verses.

"Here. This is where it gets interesting." Kayla reached over and flipped to a page toward the back of the book. The edge of it was wavy and stained with what looked like coffee so it was easy to find. "Look at the chorus."

Frankie followed Kayla's finger to the lines in question.

*Don't let me find sleep 'fore we are how we were*
*Just let it be over, oh please let me hold her*
*I'm not done counting heartbeats through days and nights*
*Give me a chance to set things right*

*Quiet places where laughter should be,*
*My only child is gone*
*Gone is she.*
*But I'll fight through the dark, and I'll chase down the light, you will see*
*Until my only child*
*Comes home to me.*

"Holy shit," Frankie said. This was where the hit had started—Estelle's process laid out for everyone to see. It didn't get much more personal than that.

Some of the lines had been struck through only to be reworded further down on the page, and Frankie spotted at least one whole verse that wasn't in the finished song. She traced the letters with her finger, imagining the emotional turmoil that had sparked these words.

Estelle hadn't often talked about Frankie's abduction other than to say it was the darkest two weeks of her life and that she preferred not to revisit them, and since Frankie had been too little to remember the ordeal herself, she'd had no problem respecting that. But here was an account at last, no matter how indirect. Lines of lyrics coated in anguish, fear, and hope that hadn't made it into the final song. Words of bargaining and surrender, but also of deepest love.

"I thought you'd like that," Kayla said. "Both this and the guitar would make great features. 'Never before seen'... etcetera." She painted the headline with a strike of her palm through the air.

Frankie was about to agree when her gaze snagged on a scribble at the top of the page that made her assent stick in her throat. She read it again, then one more time, certain she was misunderstanding.

"What does that say?" she finally asked Kayla.

Her friend leaned closer. "Um, June 20, 1987."

Frankie stared at her, unblinking. That's what she'd thought it said, but that couldn't be. "Are you sure?"

"Yeah, pretty sure." Kayla took the notebook and flipped through a few pages. "And see, the song before it is dated June 8, 1987, so it makes sense."

Frankie gasped. "No, K, it doesn't. It makes no sense at all."

Her friend's brow knitted in confusion. "What do you mean?"

"Don't you see?" Frankie tapped the page, icy tendrils shooting like glacial lightning through her limbs, freezing them rigid. "I was born in 1989. So how can a song about my abduction be written two years before I was born?"

# TEN

An excerpt from Orla Monroe's interview with Estelle Lavigne
Published in *Country Weekly*, January 1995

OM:

We've talked about how you got started with music, and it sounds to me like family has always played an important role in your life. You mentioned your late husband and how he supported your journey to reach this point. I understand he's been gone a few years now and, in fact, one of the songs on your album is an homage to him. Can you say more about that?

EL:

I'm sorry, but all I'm willing to share about Greg is that he was a wonderful man who backed my musical aspirations one hundred percent. But it's simply too painful to talk about his accident. I know he would have wanted me to move on, but that's not easy when you lose the love of your life.

### OM:

Of course, and obviously we'll respect your request to keep that close to your heart. But there is someone else who clearly has you wrapped around her finger. And this is probably something our readers don't know about you, but on top of being an amazing artist, you are a single mother of a darling little girl. Are you hoping to pass on your talents to her? Talk to me about what it's been like to juggle this success with motherhood.

### EL:

I think it's safe to say that Francesca—Frankie—has been immersed in music since the day she was born. She comes with me on the road, knows my whole setlist, and she's recently taken to the piano quite well for a soon-to-be six-year-old. We're very close, and one of our favorite things to do on the road is sing old showstoppers at the top of our lungs. So yes, she definitely has the Lavigne genes.

To answer the second part of your question, I believe it's a myth that motherhood is limiting. Because Frankie is with me all the time, there's not much juggling necessary. We go where the job takes me, whether to a nationally broadcast TV show or a local company picnic. Of course, there are times when I need to work, but then she has her schooling books to keep her busy.

### OM:

Yes, I understand you're homeschooling her. What a superwoman.

EL:

The truth is that I wouldn't have it any other way. I know it may seem unconventional, but this is what works for us. I love performing, and I love being Frankie's mother. Life is too short not to listen to your heart, so why should I have to choose?

OM:

Well said. Is it motherhood that also allowed you to mine the emotional depth that's made "My Only Child" strike gold do you think? A mother's ability to imagine the greatest loss of all?

EL:

Yes, I would say so, only this particular song was borne not from imagination but out of necessity. I haven't spoken about this before, but what I sing about happened to us. I almost lost Frankie when someone who was working close to me—someone I trusted—took her from me.

She was only a toddler at the time, and I'm bound by certain agreements not to divulge more details other than to say she was returned to me again after a two-week ordeal, but writing this song was my coping mechanism during those weeks. That glimpse of loss and pain was something I wouldn't wish on my worst enemy.

OM:

Oh my. You have me all choked up here, I'm afraid. You poor thing. I had no idea. It does speak volumes that you both have risen above and turned a horrendous experience into something that resonates with such a wide audience.

EL:

What can I say—Lavignes don't dwell. We move with purpose.

# ELEVEN

## FRANKIE

Now

Frankie swallowed the single-pour Scotch Kayla had handed her in one gulp, closing her eyes against the burn.

"Another," she said, holding out the glass.

"Frankie..."

"Another," Frankie insisted.

Her friend obliged, and after gulping down drink number two, her core finally started defrosting.

It was common knowledge that "My Only Child" was inspired by the harrowing events when a woman who worked with Estelle had abducted Frankie as a toddler. In Estelle's darkest moments, writing the lyrics had provided her comfort and hope—something to hold on to while she prayed for Frankie's safe return.

"I don't get it," Frankie said, her hands clutching the empty glass so tightly that her knuckles ached. "Why would she have lied about this?"

Kayla picked up the notebook that sat on the coffee table before them in Estelle's living room. "I don't know. Maybe she wrote it earlier, and then when you were taken, she came to associate the words with you? I admit it's a little strange, but it *is* possible there's a perfectly logical explanation."

Frankie let out a dark huff. "I seem to be looking for those a lot lately."

The world had always been a logical place to her before Estelle's death. The days had followed each other in predictable patterns. A school year led to summer break which led to another school year. Practice made perfect. Choices led to expected outcomes. Questions had answers.

She'd gotten up each morning and had breakfast with Estelle before they'd gone to work. At Starview, their days had unfolded like a perfectly choreographed dance—students arriving and departing, staff meetings, parent check-ins, a coffee run. Even the music that had flowed from the practice rooms followed organized principles and orderly rhythms.

She hadn't imagined these things. She'd lived them. They'd been real.

So why was it feeling more and more like that reality held things she'd missed?

"Even if you're right, I can't just let this go," Frankie said. "If we're auctioning off Mom's things, we have a duty to know they're legit. Mom always called this *my* song, but if it's not about me..." Frankie shook her head, willing the buzz from the alcohol to numb the hurt rising inside her. "I could even understand if she invented a story for the press, but why lie to me about it? That's what I don't get. I mean, did it even happen? Maybe she made the whole thing up." She flung her arms out and flopped back on the couch.

"Oh, come on, Frankie. That's the Scotch talking," Kayla said.

"Is it?" Frankie sat back up again. "You have to admit the questions are stacking up."

"And you'll figure them out. Everything will be fi—"

"Don't say it. Sorry, but that word is starting to feel like a jinx."

She gnawed at her lip, her gaze sweeping along white cotton curtains, full bookshelves, framed photos, and potted plants. It landed on the grand piano that Estelle had splurged on when they'd moved in—Frankie's first permanent home in her then eleven-year-old life, afforded to them by the success of "My Only Child." The lore of their early days had been threaded into Frankie's conscious mind as naturally as their lives unfolded, and never once had she questioned any of it. She'd had no reason to.

"So what are you going to do?" Kayla asked. "As much as I'm with you on verifying the legitimacy of our auction items, it's not like you can make your concerns public."

No, she had to be smart about it. Dig without seemingly digging. "Like you said, I'll figure something out," she said. "But in the meantime, the fewer people who know, the better."

Most of all, this could not reach Orla Monroe. Frankie hadn't heard from the reporter since the night at the library, but she'd be foolish to count her out. Something like this would surely be blood in the water for a woman who called herself a shark.

After several Internet searches about Estelle and kidnappings in the early 1990s that yielded little but references to the song and interviews where Mom had talked about the ordeal, Frankie conceded that it was unlikely she'd find what she was looking for there.

No one had ever been convicted of the crime, and Frankie was unsure if the woman responsible had even been arrested once the police found her. She'd been an acquaintance of Estelle's in the music scene, and since Estelle had known the woman's reason was desperation over not being able to have children of her own, she'd had compassion enough to solve the matter quietly on the condition that the woman sought help.

"Once I had you back, I decided I didn't want to ruin her life," Estelle had told Frankie when she'd asked years later, adding that everyone deserved a second chance.

Around age seven, Frankie had gone through a phase where she couldn't go to sleep, convinced that this faceless woman would return for her, but Estelle had assured her she was far away and that Frankie didn't have to worry, and before long, her fears had dispersed. Since then, she hadn't given it much thought because, in a way, it held no greater significance to her than an ancient account of her falling down while learning to walk or mispronouncing early words.

If not for the song of course.

The song complicated everything because at least one thing about it was a lie, and now that this strand had frayed from their neatly woven history, Frankie had no choice but to pull at it. Hopefully, this unraveling would lead to a place where she could verify both the authenticity of the song and its circumstances so that they could use the notebook in the auction without reservations, while also explaining the incongruences in Estelle's story. But if it didn't...

Well, Frankie didn't want to think about that. Not yet anyway.

The online searches offering no answers, Frankie turned to her second option—the library.

During her Thursday lunch, she strolled into the bright building where the sun flickered down in shafts from large skylights. She bypassed the information desk and set her course for the research corner and, more specifically, the small sitting area outside the microfiche room.

Hushed laughter reached her ears before she turned down the final stack, but it quieted when she reached the seated ladies responsible for the merriment.

The Word Birds were in the middle of a game of Scrabble, the board almost full on the round table between them. Discarded crossword puzzles sat on the couch between Irma and Vilma, two sisters who'd once run the town's flower shop, and a deck of cards stuck out of former third grade teacher Mrs. Villanueva's belt bag. The fourth seat where Mrs. Blunt normally sat was empty, but Frankie didn't let that stop her.

"Hello, ladies," she said. "How's the wordsmithing going today?"

Even though she didn't know these women personally, there had been no question in her mind where she'd turn for assistance when the Internet didn't deliver. It was common knowledge in Aspen Creek that the Word Birds knew their way around old records and a database or two—in fact, they'd once done the ancestry charts for the whole city council—and that was exactly the kind of expertise Frankie needed.

"If you hold your horses for another minute or two, we'll know," Vilma said, placing down a J, U, K, and E, to extend the already spelled out word "box" into "jukebox." She pumped her fist and turned to her sister. "Beat that if you can."

After another two tense rounds, Vilma was crowned the victor, and as Mrs. Villanueva started sweeping the tiles into their box, Irma asked Frankie to sit.

"I take it you didn't come to see sissy gloat," she said, pulling a pencil from behind her ear before spreading her crossword out before her. "How are you, Frankie dear?"

It should have felt odd to be so familiarly addressed by someone she'd barely spoken to before, but by now, Frankie had reconciled the fact that everyone knew of her and Estelle whether she liked that or not. And if she wasn't mistaken, Vilma and Irma had both been at the funeral.

"Keeping busy," Frankie said. "I'm sure you've heard I'm putting together an auction to benefit the school."

"So wonderful," Mrs. Villanueva said. "Will there be scratch tickets? I love me some scratch tickets."

"Not sure about scratch," Frankie said, "but there will be a raffle with prizes in addition to the silent and live auctions."

Mrs. Villanueva clasped her hands together in delight.

"Anyway," Frankie continued, treading carefully with how to phrase her solicitation without giving away too much. "I'm doing some research about, um, Estelle's early career and songwriting. Among other things. And since I could use some help with that, I figured I'd ask you all. No one knows microfiche like you do."

"That is true." Vilma nodded sagely. "Although technically, Thora is the one to talk to. Our eyes are not what they were." She gestured between herself and her sister. "And Ruthie finds the controls somewhat precarious with her tremors."

As if to corroborate that statement, Mrs. Villanueva held up a crooked hand, demonstrating its movement. "I can barely get through a game of cards these days I'm afraid."

"And where is Mrs. Blunt today?" Frankie asked.

"At home, I should think," Irma said. "She's got that poor grandson of hers mending fences and painting porch chairs and I don't know what else, and she couldn't possibly leave him to it without supervision, could she?" The three old ladies exchanged amused tuts and indulgent eye rolls. "Not very hands-off, our Thora."

"You should go distract her," Vilma said. "Give dear Owen a moment to breathe."

"And then tell her to get her bum knee down here," Mrs. Villanueva added. "Three people do not a bridge game make."

At the mention of Owen, something hummed to life in Frankie's midsection. A fluttering of wings that reminded her of the tiger swallowtails descending on the coneflowers on a warm afternoon. Her fingers fled there on instinct, pressing down as she shook off the unexpected reaction. It was because of their history, she told herself. A general curiosity, nothing else.

"I think I might do just that," she told the ladies.

If Mrs. Blunt was the best, then that's who she needed to enlist. It had no bearing on her decision that she could think of worse ways to spend a lunch than seeing Owen again.

Frankie pulled up at the address the Word Birds had given her ten minutes later. The house was a small, yellow two-story cottage with a wrap-around porch and green shutters that was set back from the street and surrounded by a thriving garden. No one was outside, but a tarp with paint supplies on the side of the building lent truth to what Irma had said about Mrs. Blunt keeping Owen busy.

The delicious scent of fried bacon drifted past Frankie as she marched up onto the porch and knocked on the screen door.

"Hello?" she called out.

"It's open," Mrs. Blunt called from somewhere inside the house.

Frankie hesitated for a beat, but then she let herself inside.

Wood floors and white wainscoting. Doilies and framed pastorals. Mrs. Blunt's wheelchair stood tucked into a nook beneath the stairs leading to the second floor on her left, and to her right was a bulbous chest of drawers topped with a vase full of fresh-cut flowers next to a portrait of an older gentleman.

Frankie jumped when Owen stuck his head out a doorway past the stairs.

"Hi," he said. "Grams says to come on back. We're in the kitchen."

"Hi," she said back, but he'd already disappeared, leaving her the only option to follow him.

"Frankie, dear—I thought it was you!" Mrs. Blunt lit up as

Frankie stepped into the modest kitchen. She was wearing a light-green dress today, but it was covered by a frilly patchwork apron. "Have you come for lunch?"

"Um..." Frankie's gaze went to the stove, where a pan with eggs and bacon sat next to a casserole dish of hash browns. Her stomach rumbled.

"Owen, get her a plate, will you? She's starved," Mrs. Blunt said from her seat at the table.

Frankie could have protested, but since she suspected both her stomach and Mrs. Blunt would take offense to that, she nodded her thanks instead and sat down in the only empty chair. Clearly, Mrs. Blunt was still intent on feeding her. "That's very kind," she said, finding her voice again. "How is the knee?"

"I've graduated out of the wheelchair completely," Mrs. Blunt said with a grin. "Now I've got this instead." She hoisted a purple crutch from her side, wielding it precariously through the air. "I should be spick and span in a jiffy."

"That's great," Frankie said.

"Here you go." Owen set a plate in front of her, then took his seat.

"Thanks." She let her gaze linger on him before picking up her fork. He'd shaved today, and his complexion had more color than when she'd seen him last, as if he'd spent the past several days in the sun. It made him look more like himself. Stronger. It also made his irises bluer.

"So..." Mrs. Blunt looked between them, a glint in her eyes. "To what do we owe the pleasure of Frankie Lavigne come to call? Did those hot cross buns have you wanting more of my prized cooking?"

Frankie smiled, swallowing a mouthful of hash browns. "As delicious as they were, Mrs. Blunt, I did have another reason for stopping by."

"As suspected. And call me Thora. We're all friends here."

"Very well. Thora." Frankie nodded. "I don't know if you've heard yet, but I've decided to throw a fundraiser for the school—an auction—and I've had a few, um... questions come up in relation to some of the items we're intending to include."

"What kinds of questions and what kinds of items?" Thora asked without hesitation, her keen attention leveled on Frankie.

"It's some of Mom's old things."

"Okay..." The old woman leaned forward. "And?"

"And I hear you're a maven at research, so I'm hoping you can help me."

"No, I mean—*and* what kinds of questions do you have about her things?"

"Oh." How was she going to explain this without explaining it? She reached for her water glass and drank. Set it down. Picked it up again.

Thora reached out and patted Owen's hand. "I believe the chairs should be ready for a second coat now, dear. Would you mind?"

He looked from Thora to Frankie, then stood without objection. Either he was okay being dismissed, or he was the politest grandson this side of the Mississippi.

Once he'd left, Thora angled her chair more fully Frankie's way. "I didn't send him away because I think he's loose-lipped, just so we understand each other," she said. "He's a good boy, and I trust him implicitly no matter what some folks about town might say about him." A brief but pained expression came over her before she caught herself. "But you seem to have something on your mind that's hard to name, so I figured I'd clear the room before you burst. Now tell me—what's got you bothered?"

Frankie wavered between stating her errand and asking who was talking about Owen and saying what, a protective urge rising within her, but since she had no claim to him anymore, she also had no reason to think Thora would share. Her own conundrum it was then.

Frankie explained about the notebook they'd found and why it didn't add up but left out the other questions not relating to the song that had arisen since the funeral. When she was done, her hands were twisted in her lap and her mouth dry. The words she'd spoken hovered between them: "I need to know if the story Estelle told about the song is true."

She might have said "the song and me," but she couldn't bring herself to do so. If she focused on the song alone, an item at arm-length's distance, the threat shrank from a tiger to a feral tomcat.

"Hmm," Thora said, her face tipping to the ceiling. "Estelle, Estelle..."

"Maybe it's nothing," Frankie said, the urge to backtrack overwhelming now that it was too late.

Thora smacked her palms down onto her thighs. "Well, let's find out, shall we?" She grasped the table and pulled herself to standing. "Be a dear and hand me my crutch. And my purse too—it's on the counter over there."

Frankie did as asked before following closely behind as Thora limped to the front door.

"I'll have Owen drive me since I have all afternoon, and you don't," the old woman said.

"I don't?"

Thora paused to look over her shoulder at Frankie. "You have a school to run, no?"

"Oh." Frankie shrugged to right herself in the whirlwind that was Thora Blunt on a mission. "Right."

"Ah, my apron." Thora untied it, pulled it over her head, and tossed it aside. "Close call. That would have had the whole town in a tizzy. Owen!" She pushed the screen door open and stepped out onto the porch. "Owen, where are you at? We're going for a drive."

"Um, and where are we going?" Frankie asked, taking Thora's arm to help her down the porch steps.

Thora squeezed Frankie's hand, her eyes crinkling in the sunlight. "To the library of course. It seems we have a mystery to solve."

# TWELVE

## ESTELLE

Then

Estelle leaned back from the microphone, her fingers strumming the final chords of a new song she'd been working on. "Return to Tennessee" she called it, and when she'd played the small towns around Knoxville and Chattanooga, it had brought down the house. Here in Mississippi, she found it didn't work quite as well, although that might also have been due to the beer garden audience having reached the stage of the evening when rowdy became riotous. County fairs were like that, but beggars couldn't be choosers, and she told herself she was grateful for any gig, no matter how small.

A bottle swished by her up on the small stage, and she ducked, her heart racing wildly as the bouncer located the brawling culprits and dragged them out. At least the bottle hadn't been meant for her. At a diner last week, she'd stopped playing when a piece of grilled cheese had lodged in her hair after an irate customer had taken issue with her playing anything but Garth Brooks.

After she finished her set, she packed up her guitar and

duffel and lugged them out of the tent into humid night air that was so thick with moisture it vibrated in place. Her dress clung to her back within minutes, and she wrinkled her nose as the smell of her own body reached her nostrils. She hadn't had a real shower in over a week, having slept in her car as she'd traveled south through Alabama, stopping wherever she found work.

Money had been tight since she'd left Greg four months ago. She'd brought whatever cash she'd been able to tuck away, but it wasn't like she'd been under any illusion it would last her for long. Which was fine; she was used to struggling. At least now, she was doing it for herself with a goal in mind and no one else holding her back. *This* hustle was worth it.

She made her way through the fairgrounds to the trailer where the organizer, a stout man named Morris, had told her to meet him after her gig. She'd gotten his number from a guitar player she'd met in Marietta as someone who often needed entertainers for his traveling fair, and Estelle had been in luck. Not only did he have an opening, but he and his wife also had a spare bed she could use for the night since she was playing again tomorrow. She'd get a hot meal, a shower, and money in her purse. The holy trifecta of a struggling artist.

She knocked on the door of the trailer, waiting for Morris to open it. Behind her, the music and screams from the fair rides rose and fell with the warm August breeze, and plenty of people still milled about. A low moan drew her attention to the side of the trailer, but she averted her eyes as soon as she realized what the two lovers were up to in the shadows, the sight of them forcing open the door she'd closed to the past.

She'd let Greg have her one last time before she'd finally had the nerve to tell him she was leaving. They'd fought so much over the past few years that it had felt like the only way to wrap up their fourteen-year marriage with something that wasn't miserable, but her effort to leave on some semblance of a high note had failed. He'd called her cruel. She'd called it closure.

She knocked again, and this time, a woman opened.

"Yes?" she asked with a bark.

Estelle asked for Morris, explaining who she was.

"Oh, the singer. Morris is asleep, but I'll show ya where it is. Hold on." She closed the door before Estelle could ask what she meant.

The woman opened the door again, this time with a sweater wrapped around her shoulders as if the Mississippi night might somehow threaten a chill. "Follow me."

Estelle had no choice but to do so, but her confusion grew when they set off toward a field adjacent to the fairgrounds. "I think maybe there's been a mix-up," she said. "Morris told me he had a spare room?"

The woman stopped abruptly and spun around. "A spare bed," she clarified. "What did ya think—that we have room in the trailer for ya?"

Estelle blinked back the way they'd come where the pale outline of the trailer sat like a beached whale occasionally lit up by the lights from the Ferris wheel. "Then what...?" she began asking, but the woman had already started walking again, so Estelle had to jog to catch up.

"It's the blue one over there." The woman pointed as a cluster of tents set up on a makeshift campground came into view. "There's a blow-up mattress and a blanket. The public washrooms are over there." She tipped her head left, and then she turned on her heel and walked off with a, "Have a blessed evening," thrown over her shoulder.

Estelle stared after her, various objections sticking in her throat. A tent? *Or you can sleep in your car again,* she reminded herself, her knees aching at the very thought of folding her five-foot-nine frame into the backseat of the Ford another night.

She sighed, hoisted her duffel over her shoulder, and pressed on.

The tent smelled of weed and mildew, but the mattress was mostly inflated, and the zipper closure worked. She considered heading back to the car to lock up her guitar, but it was late, and the parking lot was all the way on the other side of the grounds. Instead, she resorted to bringing all her stuff with her to the restroom as she went to clean up for the night.

Rubbing a wet towel over her skin was no shower, that was for sure, but she felt marginally better as the cool water dripped from her hair into the sink, and her make-up swirled down the drain. It was one night. She'd perform here tomorrow again, then she'd be on the road to whatever came next, each experience a brick in the foundation she was laying for her career. At some point, someone would hear her, and word of mouth would take off. She just knew it. It was only a matter of when.

Painting a future of accolades and ever-larger venues, Estelle crawled into the tent and closed the zipper behind her. There was no way she'd use the stained blanket that came with the mattress, so she dug up the small quilt her mother had made for her as a wedding gift years ago and willed it to cover at least her legs. She had to lie on her back to keep her weight spread evenly—on her side, her hip and shoulder sank through the mattress all the way to the ground—but it was nice to stretch out.

Before long, she was drifting off, the sound from the fair a faint backdrop that followed her into dreams where the noise was for her and her alone. She waved to a crowd of thousands, spotlights dazzling her. She joked with her musicians, all of them looking at her for pointers. She signed autographs, the crowd pressing up against her—a tug on her sleeve here, a whispered word of praise there.

Estelle huffed out a breath as the prodding of eager fans reached into the place between dream and consciousness, and when she couldn't make it stop, alertness rushed back in with a cold grip around her throat. Someone was in the tent with her. She knew it before she'd opened her eyes. The air was too cloying and in sparse supply, and the quilt no longer covered her legs.

Sensing danger, she played dead to the world while carefully opening one eye to gaze into the murky darkness, barely making out a large motionless shape near her feet. The zipper was pulled open, and beyond was safety, but how Estelle would make it there, she had no idea—not when this man was blocking her way.

As her mind struggled to solve this problem, the man lifted his hand and placed it lightly on her bare calf, one finger sliding along its side in a move that made Estelle's skin prickle all over. She had to do something. She had to move.

No sooner had the thought entered her mind than she sprang up, shuffling backward away from this stranger's touch. "What the fuck are you doing?" she hissed. "Get out now before I scream."

The man stilled. "Not sure you want to do that," he drawled in a low voice.

"I most certainly do," Estelle said, feeling the ground next to her for her bag.

"I don't know. You've got a free bed here and a paycheck coming in. I'm thinking my dad might change his mind about both if you make a ruckus."

Fuck. This was Morris's son, the great lug of a man she'd spotted hauling tarps earlier in the day. Her fingers found the duffel pocket they'd been looking for. "Look, I don't want any trouble, but you're not welcome here. I just want to sleep."

"And I say this tent was mine first." He reached for her knee this time, but she batted off his hand with the back of her hairbrush, the *thwack* ringing out between them.

"You bitch," he growled, cradling his fingers to his chest for an extended moment before lunging forward.

"Get off me!" Estelle shouted, clawing at him as his onion breath billowed into her face. "No!"

She bucked and shoved at the grunting oaf, protesting as loudly as she could with him crushing her beneath him, and finally, after what felt like an hour of struggle, another voice called out from nearby.

"What's going on?"

Then another, "Everything okay?"

It was enough to distract her attacker for the opportunity she needed to roll him sideways, and as she did, she drew her knee as hard as she could into his groin.

A strangled cry left him as she scrambled up and out of the tent into a small group of people who'd made their way closer.

"He attacked me while I was sleeping," she managed, still struggling to get a full breath into her lungs. "Someone call the police."

A guy sporting a wavy mullet crawled into the tent and pulled the guy outside. "Damn it, Fred. We've talked about this."

To Estelle's dismay, the other people immediately started heading back to their tents, muttered sneers between them. She stared at Mullet Guy where he was crouched in front of her assailant. "Why aren't you doing anything? He's a fucking rapist."

Mullet Guy looked up, giving her a once-over. "You look fully dressed to me."

Estelle scoffed. "Because I got away."

Mullet Guy turned back to Fred. "Had a few too many tonight, did you?"

Fred nodded, still clutching his balls. A small comfort.

"You'd better go home and sleep it off then." Mullet Guy

helped Fred off the ground and sent him off in the direction of the trailer.

"What?" Estelle balked. "That's it?"

"Nothing happened, right? You really want to make a fuss? Cuz I can guarantee you Morris won't take too kindly to that."

Estelle shifted her stance, her mouth opening and closing as she watched Fred's lumbering form disappear into the night. To her utter mortification, for the first time since she'd hit the road, tears burned behind her eyelids. It wasn't like she'd never before run into an asshole who thought he could walk all over her because she was a woman, but the complacency got to her. The complete acceptance of those around her that the cards were stacked against anyone who dared speak up.

She blinked hard against the moisture in her eyes, her fists balling up at her side. *No.* She had to say something. If Fred wasn't already a criminal, it was just a matter of time, and she had to think Morris would want to be alerted before it was too late.

"I don't believe you," she said, then she set course across the field.

She ignored the lingering tendrils of dread that refused to let go of her. It was possible following in her attacker's footsteps was inadvisable, but she wouldn't back down. She was not in the wrong.

She didn't pause when she reached the trailer, walking right up to it and knocking hard.

The door flew open as soon as her knuckles had left it.

"What now?" Morris asked, spittle flying and his face bright red as if he'd been in the middle of an argument.

"Hi," Estelle said. "Um, I..."

"Did you punch my son?" Morris asked.

Estelle gaped at him—at the notion that she was the one in the wrong. "He came into my tent. He *touched* me." She shuddered.

"Oh, he's harmless. Gets confused on account of being weak-minded. He probably thought you wanted him there."

Estelle steadied herself with her hands on her hips. "I've never even met him before."

Morris shrugged as if to say, "Oh well."

"You need to tell him to stay away from me or I'll call the police." Estelle put as much command as she could in her voice.

"Do it then. See whose side they take when they see the size of his swollen gonads."

"Oh please."

"You know what?" Morris reached behind the door and came back with a wallet in his hand. He took out three twenties and handed them to Estelle. "I just realized we don't need a singer tomorrow night after all. Take this and leave."

Estelle stared at the paltry sum. "This isn't even half of what we agreed on."

Morris looked down at her from his perch in the doorway. "Well, maybe you're not half the singer you claimed to be, which would make us even. Now goodnight."

"Hey!" Estelle called, but it was too late. He'd already shut the door, and she was left standing in the muddy grass staring at the dented aluminum. *Fuck.*

Shivering from fatigue and the adrenaline leaving her body, she made her way back to the tent to collect her things, muttering curses under her breath the whole way. So much for doing the right thing.

It took all of thirty seconds for her to shove the quilt into her bag and reemerge from the tent with all her belongings in tow.

"Things go well for you then?" Mullet Guy called out to her with a snicker.

She hoisted her duffel onto her shoulder and set course for the parking lot, flipping him off over her shoulder as she walked off. Another night in the car it was.

"It's temporary," she mumbled to herself. Things would get better. Everyone had to deal with the grind at first.

She put her things in the trunk but kept the quilt to use as a pillow, then crawled into the backseat and closed the door. The crumpled bills Morris had given her tumbled out of her pocket as she went to lie down, so she gathered them up and reached into her purse on the floor for her wallet.

"Ouch." She yanked her hand back, shaking her fingers as the sting from a paper cut swelled and sharpened.

What was that? She reached into her purse again, more careful this time, until her fingers touched something thin and angular. She pulled it out, squinting at it in the low light from a spotlight somewhere outside.

*Raymond Clark, Business Manager*, she read on the card, and a vague memory of an attractive man with intense eyes one night at Barnie's rose from the depths of her mind. Confidence and compliments. *Connections*.

Estelle sat up fully in the seat, flipping the card over in her hand. What if he'd meant what he said? That he could help her out? It had been months since that night, and he'd probably forgotten her by now, but she wouldn't know unless she called him.

She squeezed the card in her hand, allowing its edges to test her skin's resilience. When she chose it like this, the discomfort honed her senses. The night turned from black to blue, and sleep went from dreaded discomfort to a shortcut to potential. She tucked the card back into her purse and curled up on the seat, willing this possibility to be something real. She'd call the number tomorrow from the very first phone booth she came across on the road. With a little luck, the door closing on the gig tomorrow had opened a window to a different opportunity.

# THIRTEEN

## FRANKIE

Now

Walking into the library with Thora wasn't unlike going about town with Estelle—waved greetings and smiling faces aimed their way, getting stopped every ten feet by other patrons… It made Frankie stay as close to Thora as she could, as if to drink in the familiar second-hand connection she'd been so suddenly cut off from.

"Bridge!" Mrs. Villanueva called out as soon as she spotted them.

Thora pointed to the microfiche room and went on by. "Another time, Ruthie," she said. "I've got a job to do." But then she stopped without warning, causing Frankie to bump into her. "Although I believe Owen could do with a friendly game, couldn't you, dear?" She winked at him with such a lack of discretion that Frankie had to smile.

"Really, Grams?" Owen muttered.

"Just one. It'll let us get started in there." She patted his cheek. "That's a good boy."

Frankie's face flushed as he sighed and left them, knowing

she was the cause of his discomfort, but to his credit, he sat down and began shuffling the deck of cards he was handed without another word.

"You seem very close," Frankie said as she and Thora entered the small room with the microfiche machines. "I never knew my grandparents."

"We weren't always," Thora said. "His father, my son-in-law, kept him busy with sports when he was little—baseball, basketball, and then football, which was the one that stuck, as you know. If I wanted to see him, I had to show up at the games. Oh, and holidays of course." She opened an app on the desktop monitor closest to them. "After he went off to Boston for college, his parents moved north too, and I didn't see him for a while." Her fingers stilled as a memory took hold, but then she gave Frankie a tight smile. "The rest is a bit of a sordid tale I'm afraid, and it's not mine to tell. Now, let's see if we can find what you're looking for."

Frankie let herself linger on Thora's words. She'd been right then—life had thrown Owen a few curveballs, no football puns intended. She strained to hear the conversation outside the half-closed door, but if he was contributing, she couldn't tell beneath Vilma's and Irma's bickering.

"Now, what area are we focusing on? Did you all live around here back then too?" Thora asked.

Frankie blinked at the question. *Crud.* She should have figured this out first. "No, we didn't, and I'm actually not sure where we were at the time. Mom was performing wherever she could, so we stayed in a lot of different places."

"But here in North Carolina?"

Frankie scrunched her face up in an apologetic grimace. "Maybe. I'm sorry, I..." God, she must seem so clueless.

"Is there a way to find out? Someone you could ask?" Thora persisted.

Frankie looked up, the answer instantly appearing before

her. "Uncle Ray." She stood. "Don't go anywhere. I'll be right back." She rushed out the door, through the library, and into the parking lot, pulling her phone out as she came to a stop beneath a large sweet gum tree. Like Uncle Ray had reminded her last time they spoke, he'd helped launch Estelle's career, and even though the abduction had happened before that, maybe he'd already been around. She silently scolded herself as she dialed his number. She should have thought to ask him as soon as they'd found that notebook.

She paced as she waited for him to pick up, and right when she thought the call might go to voicemail, the line connected.

"Frankie?" His low voice was tinted with surprise. "Is everything all right?"

"Hi, Uncle Ray," Frankie said. "Back in town yet?"

"Tomorrow. Decided to take a few meetings in Raleigh on the way. Is Matt okay?"

A door closed, and she pictured him having excused himself from something important. She'd have to be quick, or he might revive the tired old joke about billing her for his time.

"Yes, yes. He's good," she assured him. "I'm just calling with a few questions."

"Oh?"

No point in beating around the bush. "Did Matt tell you I'm doing a fundraiser?"

"He did. It's a good idea. Make sure you count me in for tickets."

"Will do. Anyway, I was wondering if you knew Mom back when that woman took me?"

He was quiet for a beat. "You're talking about the abduction?"

"Right."

"Um, I wouldn't say I *knew* her, but we had met. I might have helped her find a few gigs at that point. Those were busy years for me. Darla and I had just gotten married, and she was pregnant with Matt. Why are you asking, Frankie dear? I can't imagine that agonizing incident being something you'd want to bring up at a fundraiser."

Frankie opened her mouth to tell him about the song in the notebook, but then she stopped herself. What if Kayla was right and there was a simple explanation for the date? She couldn't go around insinuating that Estelle had told tall tales until she'd verified the facts. On the other hand, Uncle Ray had been the money behind "My Only Child," so he might know something.

"Frankie?" he asked. "What's going on?"

She took a deep breath. How could she ask without jumping the gun?

"I'm trying to track the start of Mom's career for my speech at the auction," she lied, "and I've realized I don't know a whole lot. Like for example where she performed and where we lived during those years and when she started writing 'My Only Child.' Do you know, Uncle Ray?" She kicked at a crevice in the sidewalk while she waited for him to respond.

"So that would have been what? Early nineties. Ninety-one, ninety-two maybe?

"Right."

"Well, everyone knows she wrote that song once she had you back, and around that time she played mostly smaller venues in northern Mississippi and Tennessee from what I recall."

Frankie exhaled. That's what she'd needed to know. It made sense too since her birth certificate said Mississippi. Now they had a general area where they could start looking.

Uncle Ray continued, "Once I started booking her more frequently, we focused on gigs further north—Louisville, St. Louis, Nashville of course. I split my time between Nashville and Memphis at the time. Do you remember the Memphis house?"

"The white one with the pillars?" A memory of her and

Matt playing hide-and seek in the big garden flickered inside Frankie's mind.

"That's the one."

The bell tower in the church next to the library chimed two o'clock. Her first piano student of the day would be arriving in less than an hour. Frankie wrapped up the call with a promise to reach out again if any other questions arose, and then she hurried back into the library.

"I don't know, dear," Thora said when Frankie relayed the information. "We might have to get creative since we'd need film from out of state. But let's see—sometimes you get lucky."

She brought Frankie along to the archive where the film reels were kept, and together they searched for any news sources from the two states Uncle Ray had mentioned. Unfortunately, aside from one local Jackson, Mississippi paper, there was nothing that looked relevant.

Frankie checked her watch. Their search had taken up the better part of an hour, and now she was out of time.

"I need to get to work, but if you show me how to do this, I can come back later and—"

"Nonsense," Thora said. "You go do your thing, and I'll take care of this. Owen will be my second set of eyes."

Frankie released a breath, her insides still strumming with the urgency of needing answers. "Are you sure?"

"Of course," was Thora's chipper response.

"And remember we're looking for any mentions of abductions between 1990 and 1992."

"You got it. Leave me your number, and I'll have Owen text you what we find. I'm going to contact a few friends who are local to those areas too. They might have better luck."

Strangers would know about this search? Frankie wasn't sure how she felt about that.

As if sensing her apprehension, Thora patted Frankie's arm.

"They're good people. Bloodhounds for this sort of thing but discreet. Don't worry."

"Okay." Frankie scribbled her number on a scrap of paper next to the microfiche machine, and then she took her leave with ten minutes to spare before her lesson.

Frankie had always prided herself on being a good instructor. She had patience but knew when to push a student, and she was as detailed in her praise as she was with her expectations. Rarely did it pass her by if a student had neglected to practice. But today she couldn't focus. As soon as melodies started rolling off the keys, whether Chopin or Paganini, she was back at the library, her mind on the past.

Thora could be discovering evidence of her abduction that very moment. The mere possibility had Frankie on edge. Small-town papers ate stories like that up, so it must have been mentioned wherever they'd lived at the time. It could have been the Jackson area. There was a chance.

A dissonant jumble of notes brought her back to the practice room, her student hammering out a problematic measure again and again without getting it right. Frankie rubbed her forehead to erase an image of a press headline printed in all caps from her imagination.

"Okay, slow it down," she instructed. "Right hand only. One, two, three, four."

Tiny hands still tripped over the scale. "I can't do it," the second grader said. "My fingers don't move that way."

"The thumb goes under. Like this." Frankie placed her hand on the keys to demonstrate, and before the sound had died, a jolt at her core made her straighten. She'd played a melody, however short. Her hand had cooperated. She resisted repeating the move even though she itched to see if it had only been a fluke. Instead, she gestured to her student to have another go. "You can do it," she said, as much to herself as to him, forcing a tremble out of her voice. Tonight, when she got home, she'd try again. Lord knew she needed the outlet.

Owen texted a couple of hours later during a ten-minute break between lessons, the message as reticent as the man himself. At least this older version of him.

> *Found nothing today so Grams will call her contacts.*
> *TTYL*

Frankie pushed the bitterness of disappointment away. This was what she'd expected, she reminded herself. They'd only just started looking, and it had been a long shot.

She tucked her phone away again and was about to leave the office when two moms pushed inside, one calling, "Knock knock!" as if Frankie couldn't already see them.

"Glad we caught you," Mrs. Weaver said. Her daughter was a sophomore in high school and in their advanced ballet class. Right behind her was Mrs. Nolan, whose daughter Lauren had been one of Estelle's students.

Frankie checked her watch. Her next student would be expecting her in thirty seconds. "Little pressed for time, but how can I help you?"

The two moms shared a look, then Mrs. Weaver crossed her arms. "Natalie tells me they're still rehearsing to a track instead of your playing, and that this means more interruptions and less time on the floor. Is that true? Because if so, we have a little bit of a problem here." She dragged out the "l" in little with something that mimicked humor but was contradicted by her stance. "We are essentially paying the same amount for less practice time, and, well... it's *concerning*."

"As is the vocal coach situation," Mrs. Nolan added. "Stefano may be quite qualified for some of the younger voices, but

Lauren needs a teacher skilled at developing sopranos. How is the hiring process coming?"

Frankie was officially late to her lesson, and to make matters worse, she didn't have good answers for either of the women in front of her. She glanced over their shoulders, half-expecting her student to be coming around the corner looking for her.

"My husband tells me Lauren's lessons are paid until the end of the year," Mrs. Nolan continued. "Some deal he made with Estelle. But if things don't change around here soon, we'll be forced to ask for a refund and go elsewhere."

Frankie's gaze snapped back to her. She must have misheard. "What did you just say? You've paid in advance?"

That wasn't an official practice of the school, and not one Estelle had ever mentioned. Had it been an attempt at getting ahead of bills? Borrowing against the future? That was quite a gamble.

"Until the new year," Mrs. Nolan said. "Estelle approached my husband with the offer back in January. Little did we know..." She sniffed once, a blush spreading across her cheeks as if she'd just remembered the circumstances under which they were complaining.

"I never heard of any deal," Mrs. Weaver said. "Was it extended to everyone?"

"Only Estelle's voice students, I believe," Frankie lied. She had to buy herself some time to look into this. If more families had paid ahead, she'd need to adjust their expected income for the rest of the year, not to mention avoid at any cost those families leaving. Because if people started asking for their money back, it would soon become apparent to everyone that there was no money to be had.

Shoot. Now she was really late. She was going to have to think of a way to appease these parents or they wouldn't let her through. This was exactly the reason why she'd never minded

Estelle being the face of Starview. She always knew what to do. *Well, Mom, a little help?*

"Ms. Frankie," a small voice piped up behind the moms, forcing them to part.

Frankie saw her chance and squeezed past her visitors into the hallway. "I'll be just a minute, Kimmie. Start your scales for warm-up, okay." She turned back to the women, who were still standing in the doorway waiting for an answer. Above them hung a banner Estelle had kept from opening day. "WELCOME TO THE STARVIEW FAMILY," it said in all caps.

*Families who work together stick together.* Estelle's words echoed from the past.

*Yes, family,* Frankie thought. That was it.

"Thank you so much for bringing your concerns to my attention," she said. "I know you understand the transition period this has been for all of us—Estelle's shoes are not easy to fill—but I want to assure you I'm doing my best to get everything running smoothly. In the meantime, we're planning an exciting auction to celebrate Estelle's legacy, and I'm looking for a few parents to spearhead the committee. As both of you are engaged members of our Starview family, perhaps that's something you'd be interested in helping with?" She backed up a few steps before they could respond. "Now I really have to run, but I'd love to talk more about the auction another day. How is that?"

The moms looked at each other again, a tilt of the head, a nod.

"Yes, I suppose," Mrs. Weaver said.

"Great," Frankie called over her shoulder. "I'll be in touch."

She was home free for now.

# FOURTEEN

## FRANKIE

Now

Owen messaged Frankie a couple of days later to ask her to come over when she got a chance. Thora's contacts had come through, and she had information to share, "but not over the phone."

"So secretive," Kayla said as she helped Frankie close up the school after their newly added Saturday morning ballet class. "Do you think that means she found something?"

Frankie shrugged. "It's a long shot. Could be she just wants a visitor to break up her day. I get a feeling she's over the knee recovery at this point."

"But Owen is there, isn't he?"

Frankie paused what she was doing. "Yeah. But he's... different than he used to be. Quiet. I keep waiting for a good opportunity to talk to him, but it hasn't felt right so far."

"Maybe you need to create an opportunity then? We could use his help with the fundraiser. Is he good with his hands?"

A violent blush rushed up Frankie's face before she had a chance to turn away from her friend.

"Oh," Kayla said, tone insinuating. "Not what I meant, but good to know."

"Shut up," Frankie said before adding in a lower voice. "But third base with him *was* a formative experience."

Kayla wiggled her eyebrows. "Maybe you need to revisit it?"

"Don't even." Frankie crossed her arms. "That happened in another universe. No."

"Okay. Well—since you're no fun, now I'm leaving for real. See you Monday."

"See ya."

After stacking the chairs that lined the walls in the ballet studio so that Charlie would be able to sweep it Monday morning, Frankie, too, grabbed her things and headed out, and ten minutes later, she pulled up in front of Thora's pretty yard where Owen was in the middle of mowing the lawn.

The real smell of cut grass and remembered scents of Herbal Essence shampoo and sunscreen from that last summer they'd spent together mixed in such an overwhelming wave that Frankie could practically see a younger version of Owen pushing a different mower in a different yard overlapping with the man before her.

Maybe Kayla was right and Frankie had to create an opportunity to talk to him. If nothing else, she wanted to ask once and for all what she'd done wrong to make him ghost her like that. She didn't fault him for wanting to move on and be free of commitments when he went off to college, but even back then, it hadn't been like him to cut ties the way he had.

She shrugged off the memory and exited the car, waving to him as she strode up the porch steps.

She knocked twice, then entered, announcing herself as she did.

"In here," Thora called from the living room. "Will you be a doll and fetch the lemonade from the fridge too? I made it fresh this morning."

"Will do," Frankie called back.

"And three glasses. Owen will be thirsty."

"Got it."

Thora sat in an easy chair by the bay window with a ball of yarn and two knitting needles in her lap.

"Feeling crafty today?" Frankie asked, setting the beverage tray down on the coffee table.

"Not especially," Thora responded drily. "I thought I'd pass the time with what *Good Housekeeping* will have me believe is an appropriate activity for a woman my age, but Lord only knows how."

"You don't know how to knit?" Frankie asked, filling the glasses.

"See there—that's what I don't understand. Am I supposed to magically know how at seventy? Seventy-five? At exactly what age will I be bestowed this gift because it sure hasn't happened yet." She pushed the yarn and needles off her lap and made to get up.

"No, sit. I'll bring it to you," Frankie said.

Thora huffed. "And this gosh darn knee..."

"Is getting better," Owen said from the doorway.

Frankie looked up and met his gaze briefly before he ran a hand through his blonde strands and excused himself.

"Gotta wash up," he said. "Be right back."

"He's right," Thora said. "It is getting better. I'm just feeling ornery on account of not having been of more help to you, Frankie dear."

"Oh?" Frankie sat down on the couch and sipped her drink. The lemonade was on the sweet side, but that was better than too tart.

"Yes, I had my boys in the states we discussed search records these past few days, and not a one of them had any luck. As far as we can tell, there were no mentions of kidnappings between 1990 and 1992. Now that doesn't mean it didn't happen, only that no one wrote about it." She twisted her hands in her lap and drank from the glass Frankie had handed her.

"But?" Frankie leaned forward.

Owen joined them, wiping his hands on a kitchen towel he then slung over a side table on his way to the chair next to Thora. "What are we talking about?" he asked. His cheeks were rosy after exerting himself in the garden, and it was the most like his former self Frankie had seen him.

She handed him a glass of lemonade, which he took with a quick smile.

"I was about to tell her about Hattiesburg," Thora said.

"Ah." Owen gulped half the glass in one go.

Frankie looked between them. "What about it?" She set her glass down.

"Since you said your birth certificate lists Jackson, Mississippi, and given that the song in the notebook was dated 1987, I had someone check that area for kidnappings in the mid-eighties too, and..." She gestured for Owen to get her something from the dresser on the opposite wall. "We found something." She took the papers from Owen and passed them to Frankie.

The stack was made up of black-and-white print-outs of several newspaper articles dated December 1985, and the top one had a bold headline reading: "LOCAL FAMILY'S ORDEAL ENDS IN CHRISTMAS MIRACLE."

Frankie pored over the pages, absorbing the story as it played out—from the "MISSING CHILD" notice to the happy resolution.

Three-year-old Nellie Smalls had been kidnapped by the family's babysitter early December, and the two had vanished without a trace, leaving Nellie's parents in a nightmare that sounded all too familiar to Frankie. The babysitter had been pregnant earlier that year but lost the baby, and in one of the press photos, Nellie's mother was pleading with the other woman to bring her child back. If she did, all would be forgiven.

The plea must have worked because the day before Christmas Eve, the family had woken to Nellie banging on the front door, cold but unharmed.

The similarities were too many to be a coincidence, and with that knowledge, a stone lodged itself in Frankie's chest. She stood abruptly and started pacing, one hand going to her forehead as the implication hit home. This was the story that had inspired the song. She felt the truth of that at her very core.

"Like I said—this doesn't mean it didn't also happen to you years later," Thora said carefully.

Frankie stopped, swallowing hard against the knot in her throat. "Except there's no evidence that it did."

What had Estelle done? Had "My Only Child" been the topic of an interview one day (maybe even *the* interview with Orla Monroe), and she'd decided on a whim to attribute the emotional lyrics to a lived trauma? Or had she planned to do so all along? Had it been a calculated step to gain clout, sympathy, fame?

"Sorry, I need some air," she said, rushing to the front door and out onto the porch.

Once there, she sank down onto the top step and buried her face in her hands. The air was thick with wisteria and lilac, the sweetness engulfing her like a dear friend. As the minutes passed, she let her arms fall and allowed other impressions through her defenses. Rough wood against her fingertips. The mild breeze against her skin in the gap between her jeans and socks. The graceful bowing of the willow's branches at the edge of the yard.

The door opened behind her.

"Hey." Owen's steady footsteps came closer until his scent washed over her too. Bar soap and something warmer, like vanilla rolls.

"I'm not crying," she said, scooting a few inches when he sat down next to her.

"Didn't say you were."

They sat in silence while the sun passed its zenith, and the creek frogs took up their tune. She'd forgotten how easy it was to be quiet together with him.

"You know, Grams is right," Owen said after a while. "This doesn't mean Estelle lied about anything other than what inspired the song."

Frankie looked at him. Up close like this, the lines on his forehead were deeper and the story in his eyes longer. She resisted an urge to tug on his ear the way they'd teased each other back then. The fact that she knew what his soft lobe would feel like against her fingertips made her turn away instead.

"You don't actually believe that," she said, surprised at how little it bothered her that Thora had invited him into their circle of knowledge. "*I* don't believe that."

Owen stretched his legs out before him, crossing them at the ankles. "Fine, but that doesn't mean she didn't have a good reason."

Frankie glared at him. "A good reason to let me grow up believing I'd been abducted?"

He huffed. "When you put it like that." He paused for an extended beat. "So what are you going to do?"

Frankie rubbed a hand across her brow, a shiver rushing up her spine that had nothing to do with the air brushing her lower back. "What can I do?" she asked. "If she was here, I'd demand answers, but she's not."

There had to be answers, right? Even if they were ones she wouldn't like.

"And the auction? The school?" he asked.

"Starview still needs saving. This doesn't change that. I just can't include the notebook as a prize like I'd hoped."

"But you're not going to tell anyone?"

"No." Frankie bit down on the inside of her cheek. "At least not until I know more." And maybe not even then. For all she knew, Orla was still sniffing around somewhere out of sight.

Owen turned his head to face her. "You're going to keep looking into this?"

"Wouldn't you?"

He thought about that for a moment, his blue eyes inscrutable.

"Did you know that I haven't spoken to my dad in almost a decade?" he asked finally.

"No," she said, shifting so that she had the railing at her back. "I had no idea."

"Eight years, ten months, and four days to be exact." He smiled a wry smile. "I don't even remember what our last conversation was about. It's pretty fucked up."

Frankie tried to recall an image of Mr. Novak Sr, but high school was a long time ago, and the best she could do was a deep voice calling out, "Drive safely!" whenever she and Owen left his house. Maybe he'd had brown hair, she thought, more because she remembered Owen looking like his mother than because she was certain it was true.

"But you guys were close," she said. "Wasn't he assistant coach for the team?"

Owen nodded. "He was. And my hero when I was little. He never missed a layup shot, could juggle four tennis balls while standing on one leg. Important stuff." A genuine smile transformed his face for a second, but it twisted into a grimace too soon.

Frankie thought about her conversation with Kayla earlier. Owen was finally talking—the opportunity she'd been waiting for. "So what happened?"

He fiddled with the collar of his T-shirt as if it was too tight as he looked out across the yard. Then he flattened his hands together and lodged them between his knees. Rocked forward. Sighed. Looked at her. Blinked.

Frankie held her breath, sensing the possibility of revelations if she played her cards right. He needed a moment. She could give him one.

"I'm an alcoholic," he said finally, the words bursting from him on an exhale. "Recovering, but yeah. Eighty-four days sober."

"Oh." It wasn't an eloquent response, but his confession was so unexpected, Frankie wasn't sure what else to say.

"It's one of the reasons I'm here," Owen continued. "I got out of rehab, and I didn't want to go back to Nashville—that's where I was living—so Grams offered to take me in. It was good timing anyway because of her surgery. Keeps me busy."

"That's what she meant by you needing things to do?"

"Right."

"But so... How... um... I mean, when did you...?" Frankie scrunched up her forehead, trying to turn a cascade of new questions into words. When she failed, she switched gears. Maybe it was none of her business. "Ugh. Never mind. But I am really sorry you've been dealing with this. If there's anything I can do..."

"Nah." He rolled his shoulders back. "I'm okay. I didn't tell you for sympathy. I told you because I can see you're on this path right now, this quest—and I suddenly remembered that about you from back when we were dating. How you'd get hung up on something and be relentless about it."

Frankie smiled, ignoring the casual way he'd mentioned their past. "Remember Beethoven?"

"Oh my God, Beethoven. The project without end. You must have spent months reading everything you could on the guy for one stupid poster."

"What can I say—he was seriously impressive. Composing without his hearing?"

Owen rolled his eyes, but he was unable to hide his amusement. "I'm sure you're right, but that's not my point."

"Yeah, what is your point?"

"My point is this." He paused as if weighing his words. "My dad was this solid entity in my life, much like Estelle was for you. Never faltered, right? But what I never realized was that he was only steady because I didn't push up against him. Hell, I think he probably wasn't aware of that either." He ran a hand through his hair, making it stand on end. "And I know our situations aren't the same—believe me, I'm very aware I made my parents' life hell when I was drinking, and you didn't do anything of the sort to Estelle. But I would give anything to go back to a time when he was my rock, back before I discovered he had fault lines and that something I did could trigger a quake. Call it denial or what have you, but I would rather never have learned he had it in him to look me in the eye and tell me I wasn't welcome in his house anymore."

The quiver in his voice at that last word made Frankie reach for him, her palm covering his knuckles on the deck. "You don't think he'll come around?"

Owen's gaze went to their hands, lingering there before he pulled his away and into his lap. "Maybe, maybe not. I've sat with this a lot in therapy, and I've written him apologies, but I think he's still too scared of aftershocks to let me back in. This is something I have to accept—that I can't undo the past. I can't go back to 'before,' no matter how much I want to."

Frankie nodded. It was a lot to take in, and she still wanted to know more—what had happened to him, how his life had taken that turn.

Before she could ask, he stood and walked down a few steps before facing her again. The sky was a deep cerulean behind him. "All that to say—you asked me if I would keep looking into these things you're learning about Estelle, and my answer is, I don't know. You're still in the 'before' stage. Estelle is still mostly solid. Are you sure you wouldn't rather keep it like that than risk"—he gestured around them—"everything?"

Frankie watched the earnest set of his jaw, the somber depths of his eyes. "You're saying what if I find faults I'm not prepared for?"

He chuckled drily. "I know that sounds hypocritical as I stand here before you a self-confessed flawed man, but yes."

She wrapped her arms around herself to stave off the chill his warning had triggered inside her. "Never underestimate the power of denial?" she asked, referring to a quote that had adorned a wall in one of the high school social studies classrooms.

"I guess," he said.

"No. I don't believe willful ignorance leads anywhere good. And besides, it's too late."

He cocked his head in question.

"Do you know why I did that project on Beethoven instead of Mozart or Chopin?" she asked. "It was because of all the greats, he was the biggest enigma—a deaf composer was such an oxymoron. I needed to understand. It's the same with Mom; none of this makes sense. So you're wrong—I'm already past the before stage." *Well past it,* she thought. But Owen didn't know about the card, or the school's dire finances, or the suitcase full of lavender tea, so she'd forgive him for believing otherwise.

"I was afraid you'd say that."

"I can't just stop this overwhelming feeling that something is off. You get that, right? I can't shove it back down and pretend."

Owen nodded, a look of resolve coming over him. "No, you're right. And the reality is—my dad is human. He isn't perfect, and I shouldn't wish for him to be even if things were easier when I could pretend that was the case."

Frankie *had* always thought of Estelle as faultless. Was that a universal only-child thing—to put their parents on a pedestal? Clearly Owen had done it too. It had been such a natural spot for Estelle to inhabit that Frankie had never thought twice about it.

"Well, Mom is gone now," she said, pushing up to standing. "So what's the worst thing that could happen if it turns out she had a few flaws?"

Owen lifted his shoulders in a slow shrug as if to say, "You tell me," but he didn't contradict her logic.

"I should get going," Frankie said. "Will you tell Thora thanks from me?"

"Sure. And if there's anything else you need help with, let us know." Owen walked back up to the porch as Frankie descended to the path leading to the driveway.

"We could probably use a hand with the auction when we get closer," she said, remembering Kayla's suggestion. "If you need busywork."

He smiled. "Count me in."

She lifted a hand in farewell, but just as she was about to turn, he spoke again.

"Hey, Frankie?"

"Yeah."

"Whatever you find, I'm here if you want to talk about it, okay? Nothing too big or small."

She nodded, struck by how sincerity had replaced the glibness of youth on his features. "Thanks."

She almost asked him, then, why they'd lost touch. How he'd moved on so easily. Her lips parted, preparing for that first vowel, but nothing came out.

"Have a good rest of your day," he said, retreating to the door.

She bit down on her question. "You too."

Saving it for another time was probably for the best anyway. They'd had enough truths for one night.

# FIFTEEN

## ESTELLE

Then

Estelle paced back and forth behind the small, canopy-covered stage where she was about to perform, her long skirt swishing around the scuffed cowboy boots she'd picked up at a flea market outside Tuscaloosa back in July. Raymond—or Ray as he'd asked her to call him—had said he'd be there, but so far, she'd not had a single sighting. She peered around the corner again at the crowded lawn. Where was he?

They'd been trying to get their schedules to match up ever since she'd reached out back in August, but he was a busy man who traveled a lot, and she hadn't exactly been able to predict where she'd be from week to week. After the county fair fiasco, she'd headed back to Alabama for a while, landing a few gigs in the Huntsville area. One bar had even booked her two weeks in a row when their regular act got sick, so she'd been able to rent a room at a nearby motel for a change.

But then Ray had told her it wasn't likely he'd make it out that way any time soon so if she could find something closer to where he was in Memphis, that would be better. Consequently, she'd called every small town from Starkville, Mississippi to Dyersburg, Tennessee asking about work, and the Fall Fest organizer here in Tupelo was the only one that had come through.

The folk trio currently on stage finished their set to rowdy applause that made adrenaline course through Estelle's body like it always did before she went on. Her fingers fiddled with her favorite pick as she tipped her head and said a quick prayer. *Thank you for your blessings and please let Raymond Clark show up. Amen.*

After finding his business card that night in the car, his name had become synonymous with hope for Estelle. He'd been interested in her work. Encouraging. *Invested* possibly. She was vaguely aware that she might have embellished the memory of their conversation along the way, but with no other glimmers of light on the horizon, the dreamer in her had taken full reign of this one chance. She'd rather be disappointed later than never try at all, and in this case, that meant getting Ray to come watch her perform again. Something good would happen if he did. Something better than her current situation. Not that the bar was very high.

Her name was called, and the crowd's lukewarm welcome laid down the gauntlet for her set. She'd show them. Make them miss her when she was gone. They just didn't know it yet.

She sat down on the stool provided and slung her guitar into place. As she introduced herself, she tried to shade her eyes against the blaring spotlight to see if she could spot him, but it was no use. The audience melded together into a chattering gray mass, so all Estelle could do was play her best and trust that it would pay off. She needed a change like the farm fields around them needed water, and Ray Clark had to be the conduit because there was no one else.

She warmed up with a few crowd-pleasing covers, the guitar and her voice rising toward the darkening sky like a beacon in the night, drawing the attention of anyone with a soul within hearing range. She knew she had them when her first original song, "At My Father's Side," brought out lighters waving in time with her strumming, and when her forty-five minutes were drawing to an end, she noted absently that the talking had stopped completely. It was just her on stage, speaking to them, and there was no doubt they were listening.

The question was, was *he* listening too?

As Estelle got off stage to thunderous applause, she paused at the bottom of the stairs leading down onto the grass and closed her eyes to try to capture the feeling. Chances were, everyone here would have already forgotten about her tomorrow. The beer was flowing, and the next band was lining up to take her place, which meant the brief time she'd just shared with these people had been as fleeting as a dream the second you wake up. The only way to make it more substantial was to repeat it often enough that the memory of it didn't have time to fade between each encounter.

Her breaths came rapidly where she stood, skin damp and tingling as she tried her best to hold on to that rare lightness in her heart that only ever blessed her in the wake of a performance. It worked for a minute, but then the MC picked up his mic to introduce the next act, feedback cutting through both the cooling air and Estelle's oasis.

"Ugh," she groaned, her hands flying to her ears as she tipped her head up, and there he was, watching her from only a few yards away.

"Aren't you a sight tonight," Ray said, a grin stretching his lips wide. "Now that was a great show." He nodded toward the stage.

His skin was tan against a light-blue shirt, his hair sun streaked and longer than last time she'd seen him. She pictured him on board a sailboat, dominating the glittering expanse with a drink in his hand, certain that's how he'd spent his summer even though she'd never set foot on a boat.

Estelle dropped her hands to her side, smiling back. *He'd come. He'd seen her play. He...*

A pretty woman stepped out from behind him.

*He wasn't alone.*

Her greeting stuck in her throat.

"This is my friend, Darla," he said. "Her sister lives in North Haven, so she decided to come along."

*Friend?* Estelle covered her surprise behind a renewed smile as she took stock of the other woman. Darla was younger, mid-twenties maybe, and a true Southern belle, polished and prim. Estelle stepped forward and offered her a handshake. Darla's grip was delicate but her gaze snide.

"So you're the singer," she said. Not "hello" or "nice to meet you."

Estelle shook it off. "I am."

"And a damn fine one," Ray said, beaming between the two of them. "Now let's talk. Can I buy you ladies a drink?"

He steered them, one on each arm, to the beer garden where he paid someone off to clear a table for them. Estelle caught the cash changing hands but only barely—the move was so suave. Here, finally, was a man who knew how to carry himself in the world. Who made it work for him. Greg had always been clueless.

She watched Ray get them beers, aware of Darla's eyes being on him too.

"So how do you two know each other?" she asked to fill the silence.

"Our parents are friends," Darla said. She opened her clutch and checked her make-up in a pocket mirror. "So we go *way* back."

"Do you work?"

"No."

Estelle waited for Darla to elaborate, but she didn't, instead digging for a lipstick and reapplying. A perfect pout, fluttering lashes, a coquettish tilt of the chin...

Estelle looked down at one of the two nice blouses she owned and straightened its shoulder pads. She tucked her hair behind her ears and ran a finger under her eyes. Not that it would make much of a difference. She was a realist—next to Darla's gazelle-like grace, she was a wildebeest at best.

"So what *do* you do?" Estelle pressed on. There were other ways than looks to impress a man like Ray. Ambition for one. Purpose. She knew she wasn't imagining the mutual interest between her and Ray.

"I recently returned from Europe where I volunteered at a children's hospital among other things. My father thought I should 'see the world' before settling down after I got my degree in nursing. France was lovely. As was Portugal."

"You have a job lined up then?"

"No," Darla said again, wrinkling her nose at Estelle. "I have other plans."

Before Estelle could dig further, Ray returned with their beverages. "I see you're getting acquainted," he said. "What do you think, Dar? Isn't she fascinating?"

The two of them leveled assessing looks at Estelle, with one being decidedly friendlier.

Darla shrugged. "This kind of music isn't really my scene."

"And yet here you are," Estelle said, keeping her tone as cordial as she could muster.

"Perhaps there are more draws than one in a place like this." Darla flashed a white smile at Ray.

Estelle suppressed a laugh. She and Darla may never be best friends, but there was something unexpectedly impressive about her lack of subtlety, and she could respect a woman with goals. Not that she'd stand idly by and watch it happen. A man like Ray could weather storms both real and metaphorical, and if she was ever going to have someone by her side again, his type would be the sensible choice. His good looks were, of course, a plus.

Raymond lifted his glass and proposed a toast "to new endeavors," and when they'd finished drinking, he placed his hand, palm down, on the table between him and Estelle. "So," he said. "Let's get down to business. I have a proposition for you."

Darla stirred next to him but hid her face behind another sip.

"I like the sound of that," Estelle said.

"Come to Memphis over the holidays. I have an in with a good friend of mine who owns a restaurant that does live music. A professional sound booth. Ceilings and walls for a change." He gestured to the open-sided tent they were in. "We'll call it a... collaboration. See how things go. I've been wanting to dip my toes in new ventures, so why not talent management? Especially when the talent is so delightfully... *untapped*. What do you think?"

Estelle held his gaze while her fingers found a lock of hair at her neck to play with. The blush rising on her cheeks was equal parts gratification and strategy, the thrill of his pursuit made even sweeter when she glanced at Darla to see her lips flattened as if the beer was sour. If this was a competition, Estelle was currently the one with a leg up, and that was her favorite position.

She returned her attention to Ray. "Several gigs per week?"

"Certainly."

"Where would I stay?"

Ray paused, a small smile playing at the corner of his mouth. Then he turned to Darla. "You've seen the guest suite above my garage. Do you think that would be comfortable enough for a lady?"

Darla's lips popped open.

"Yes, I believe it would be," Ray said in answer to his own question before facing Estelle again. "Would that work for you? It's completely separate from the house, with a small kitchenette and a full bath."

Estelle wanted to say yes, but there was one small problem that followed her like a stubborn stain. She hated to bring it up but had no choice. "How much?" she asked. Her wallet was light, and her income stream slow.

Ray's eyebrows rose. "Oh no. You misunderstand. You'd be my guest. Free of charge."

She squinted at him. Tried to camouflage her confusion at his generosity with what she hoped was a playful sparkle to her eyes. "Out of the goodness of your heart?"

He lifted his glass and drank, watching her over the rim the whole time until he set it down. Turned it on its coaster. "Not at all," he said in a slow drawl. "I believe it to be a sound investment."

*Well then...* "It's tempting," she said, playing coy. More tempting than any flavor life had offered in a while.

"Then you'll come?"

It would be nice to stay in one place for a while. Get to know Ray better. And it would also allow her to hold on to the meager funds she'd saved. She probably needed to send something home to Greg too so he couldn't claim abandonment and make her look completely uncaring when she filed the divorce paperwork that was still sitting in her car.

Estelle smiled and raised her glass. "I will."

# SIXTEEN

## FRANKIE

Now

The moms were waiting for Frankie again after lunch on Monday. Both Mrs. Nolan and Mrs. Weaver were in athletic wear, though their hair and make-up suggested a morning spent at the salon rather than in downward dog, and they pounced on Frankie as soon as she got out of her car by the school.

"Ms. Kayla told us you were on your way," Mrs. Nolan said as if to explain the ambush. "We have a few things to run by you if you have time."

"What sort of things?" Frankie asked, making a mental note to give Kayla grief later for revealing her comings and goings so offhandedly.

Mrs. Nolan had a green folder tucked under her arm that she pulled out and opened. "We had a think about this auction you were mentioning and jotted down some ideas. Obviously, you'll have final say-so, but as your committee, we're here to help."

Committee? Auction ideas? Frankie's mind blanked out briefly before she remembered the off-handed request she'd made to wrap up their conversation the other day. "Right," she said, taking the folder from the other woman. "Very good."

The document in the folder was a three-page-long spreadsheet with color-coded columns and bolded lines.

"Wow," Frankie said, skimming the information. "You've been busy."

"So glad you like it," Mrs. Weaver said. "I just love a good spreadsheet, don't you?"

"What's all this?" Frankie pointed to a column full of numbers.

Mrs. Nolan leaned closer. "Those are the estimated costs. Obviously, we'll get donors to cover most of these, but this gives you a ballpark at least."

"Eight thousand for food." Frankie stifled a gasp. "Three thousand for tent rental. Um, volunteer T-shirts?" She looked up.

"Don't worry about that," Mrs. Nolan said. "Julie Boswell said her husband can print us some for free at work."

*That's all better then.* Frankie kept reading, her heartrate increasing with each line item.

"Exactly how much of this do you estimate being covered by donations?" she asked when she was done. Maybe she hadn't been clear that the event was meant to boost the school, not drain it.

"Well, that'll depend on how generous the community wants to be," Mrs. Weaver said. "But everyone loved Estelle, so I imagine you won't have much difficulty convincing them."

Frankie's eyes flew up. "Me?"

"We'll help of course," Mrs. Weaver said. "We'll be spreading the word at book club tomorrow, and my guess is the moms will cover most of the marketing and decor."

"And don't you think between us and our friends, we'll be able to put together several smaller baskets for the silent auction too?" Mrs. Nolan asked her fellow committee leader. "Maybe a dog-themed one that could include Lorilynn's handmade collars and treats. And Felicity makes those beautiful watercolor paintings."

"Oh—we should ask Lilliana if she'll donate a free service at the spa," Mrs. Weaver added. "And I'd be happy to offer a complimentary spin class."

Frankie's head moved back and forth like she was watching a ping-pong match as they brainstormed who of their friends would be best to ask and for what. Maybe it hadn't been such a bad idea to involve them after all.

"As you can see, we're more than happy to help," Mrs. Weaver said finally. "But when it comes to approaching businesses that may have had dealings with Estelle, we believe it's best if you make the plea as her daughter. Whether for raffle prizes like gift cards and other merchandise, or sponsorship donations in exchange for ad placement and the like, your name will lend legitimacy to the ask."

The two women looked at Frankie expectantly, and because their engagement already eclipsed Frankie's own to a shameful degree, she could only nod numbly. She'd had no idea what it would take to put together this kind of event, but now with the color-coded key in her hand, reality had come crashing down in organized grid format. She could either magically conjure funds to pay for all these things, though if she'd had that kind of cash, the auction wouldn't be necessary in the first place, or she could get out of her comfort zone and hit the phones.

"Oh, and some great news," Mrs. Nolan said, beaming. "I've arranged for some press coverage leading up to the event. I chatted with a lovely woman at the funeral reception who's well connected and used to be a reporter, and when I reached out to her after our talk Thursday, she agreed to interview you. Thinks *The Charlotte Times* will be interested. Her name is Orla Monroe. Isn't it wonderful?"

Frankie went rigid. On some level, she'd known Orla wasn't

going to disappear, but an interview? "No," Frankie said. She could practically hear Estelle lose it with rants of *What happened to privacy?* and *Some people just don't know how to mind their own business.*

Mrs. Nolan's smile faded. "No? But it's free publicity. A feature."

"Yes, you can't turn it down," Mrs. Weaver said. "We've already told everyone."

"Everyone?" Frankie's vision narrowed.

"*The Charlotte Times* is a big deal," Mrs. Nolan continued. "I would have thought you'd jump on the opportunity. Estelle certainly would have."

*Not with Orla she wouldn't.* A number of expletives Frankie had been raised not to say out loud bubbled to the surface of her mind like it was a putrid, boiling swamp. She was trapped. Estelle had turned Orla away once, so who knew what kind of agenda the reporter would have in this interview? She'd already shown a predisposition for sensationalist lines of questioning by suggesting irregularities with Mom's death. Not to mention that Frankie did have a few things she wanted to keep under wraps for now...

No, an interview was the last thing she needed, but without sharing her real qualms about having Orla in her and Starview's business, there was no convincing reason she could give without looking cowardly.

"Oh." She attempted a small laugh that she hoped only sounded feeble in her mind. "What I meant to say was, 'No way.' As in, 'It's such a surprise.'"

The moms relaxed.

"You'll do it then?" Mrs. Nolan asked.

"Of course." Frankie's voice was too high-pitched, but there was no reining it in. "Lovely idea. Pick a date and email me the details." She held up the spreadsheet. "Got to go now, but can I keep this?"

"It's yours. I have duplicates," Mrs. Nolan said. "My number is at the top if you think of anything to add."

"Let's hope not," Frankie said weakly. She started up the stairs to the school doors, but halfway there she turned. "Thank you for doing this," she said, trying her best to mean it. These women didn't know what they didn't know, and like it or not, she needed their help. "I couldn't do it on my own."

Both women lit up, that genuine glow overriding the perfect make-up and taking a decade of child-rearing and house-making off them both. Suddenly, Frankie saw purpose and connectedness where before their engagement had felt invasive. This ill-fated plan with Orla aside, she'd judged them unfairly.

*Estelle would never have done that.*

Frankie swallowed her remorse as she headed toward her office, the spreadsheet in hand. If she wanted to keep up Starview's good name, she'd have to find ways to emulate her mom's congeniality. An easy compliment here, a listening ear there. No issue too big or small. Now more than ever, she had to step up her game and be one with the community. Present a united and confident front. Because now, Orla was on her case.

After spending hours Monday evening thinking of all the local places that had a connection to Estelle (and not thinking about her upcoming interview with Orla, which had now been scheduled for next week), Tuesday morning she had a list of businesses in front of her that was the stuff of nightmares. Cold calling. Asking for favors. Talking on the phone. All things low on Frankie's list of enjoyable activities.

*You start with hello and see where it takes you,* Estelle seemed to remind her as she dialed the first number.

She could do "hello"—it was what came after she struggled with.

"Yes, hi. I'm calling for Mitchell Ross."

"This is him."

"Hi, Mitchell. My name is Frankie Lavigne, and I'm—"

"Estelle's girl," Mitchell said. "Of course!"

Huh. Maybe this was going to be easier that she'd thought.

Mitchell owned the plant nursery where Estelle had purchased whatever she needed for the garden every year, and the two had bonded over perennial choices from the get-go. It had been years since Frankie had gone there with Estelle though, so she was surprised he remembered her.

After accepting Mitchell's condolences, Frankie told him she was putting together an auction in Estelle's name to benefit the school and asked if he'd be interested in contributing anything garden related.

"It could be a plant of any size, or items for a garden-themed basket perhaps," she said. "Mom loved her garden, so it would mean a lot to have that represented in whatever way you think appropriate."

"Absolutely," Mitchell said as soon as she finished, and after another few minutes of talking, Frankie had a promise of a large "Estelle Marie" fuchsia plus a basket with seeds and tools.

Bolstered by her success, she jumped straight to the next business on the list and then the next. Almost everyone had something to contribute. The bookstore offered a gift card. Estelle's dental office agreed to raffle off a free whitening service. Even the kayak rental place by the lake whose services Estelle had never used as far as Frankie knew agreed to include a one-hour paddleboard lesson for an outdoor recreation basket.

Most of the people Frankie spoke to knew Estelle, but even those who didn't were at least familiar with the school and had some connection—niece, cousin, friend of a friend—who'd taken lessons at Starview. The apprehension Frankie had felt initially at the sight of the list evaporated as people she didn't know shared their sadness over Estelle's departure and willingness to celebrate her in this way.

"How did you do it, Mom?" she mumbled, noting down yet another contribution on a piece of notebook paper she'd stapled to the spreadsheet.

For as long as she could remember, people had wanted to be in Estelle's company, and her mom had invited them in, basking in forging connections and the attention that followed. But maybe that was par for the course for stage performers because Estelle had definitely had that special something. That star quality.

*That duplicity?*

The thought was there before she could stop it. Frankie was trying to keep saving the school separate from her new discoveries about Estelle. To think of them like two distinct problems to solve. But she couldn't deny the element of dissonance that came with simultaneously basking in the admiration people had had for her mom and hurting over the lie she'd told.

But maybe she was being too hard on Estelle. Maybe her mom had improvised the fictional tale in an interview and then fed it to Frankie to make sure her tongue didn't slip. Simple self-preservation. No ill intent. She *had* worked hard for them.

Frankie put her phone down and spun the chair around so she came face to face with the framed gold record. That one big hit had been it for Estelle. A feat never to be topped. Would she have gone further in her career if Frankie's dad hadn't died when she was a baby? Even though Estelle had managed to tour with Frankie tagging along, most likely it would have been easier for her to pursue her career if she'd had a husband to depend on. A home base.

She stood, reaching out to straighten the frame even though it was already perfect. Estelle had never made Frankie feel like she was the reason her success was brief, and when she'd made the choice to stop performing and settle in Aspen Creek, she'd never once expressed regret over what might have been. Instead, she'd taken every ounce of the effort she'd poured into her artistry and created Starview, so Frankie would be damned if she let it go to ruin now.

She sat back down and picked up her phone again. The next number on the list was the radiation clinic in Charlotte where Estelle had had her treatments during her cancer scare ten years ago. The breast cancer had been caught early, and she'd thankfully only needed radiation, but it had still been a time of upheaval that had brought the two of them even closer—all that time spent in the car together driving back and forth to appointments.

The call connected, and after Frankie asked the receptionist if there was an office manager or someone like that she could speak to, she was transferred.

"This is Sheila," a woman answered after two rings.

Frankie opened the same way she had in all the other calls. "Hi, my name is Frankie Lavigne, and I'm Estelle Lavigne's daughter."

"Okay?" the woman said, the inflection noting curiosity rather than the recognition Frankie had met in the other calls. That was to be expected though. Years had gone by, and Charlotte wasn't a small town where everyone knew each other like Aspen Creek.

"I'm calling because my mother was a patient of yours a while back, and I know how much the care you provided mattered to her."

"Oh, well that's lovely to hear," Sheila said. "Is she doing all right?"

"Um, no. She passed recently. Not from cancer," Frankie hurried to add, so Sheila would know she wasn't calling to complain about the treatment not working.

"I'm so sorry to hear that." There was a pause on the line, then, "So what can I do for you?"

"My mom ran a music school in Aspen Creek—Starview Conservatory—maybe you've heard of it?"

"Hm, no, can't say I have."

Frankie started to sweat. *It's okay*, she told herself. Not all calls could be smooth sailing. "Okay, well, I'm currently putting together a memorial fundraiser to support the school and celebrate Mom's life which will include a raffle, a silent auction for baskets, and a live auction for memorabilia, so I'm contacting everyone who was important to her to see if they would like to contribute something. Perhaps a wellness-related item or a small donation to sponsor a basket? I know it would have meant so much to her."

Sheila was quiet for a moment. "What did you say your mom's name was?"

"Estelle Lavigne. The school is called Starview Conservatory." Frankie switched hands, holding her phone so she could wipe her palm on her jeans. It was warm in here, wasn't it?

"One second. Just looking up her records," Sheila said, followed by the clacking of keyboard keys. "We don't typically participate in things like this unless it's for a specific health-related cause, but..." More typing followed.

Frankie waited.

"What's her date of birth?" Sheila asked.

"July 10, 1958."

"And Lavigne is spelled L-A-V-I-G-N-E?"

"That's correct."

"Yeah, I'm sorry, but we don't have a record of a patient by that name here. Are you sure you have the right clinic?"

Frankie's eyes flew to the computer screen, where she'd looked up the place. "Don't tell me I've..." she whispered to herself. Charlotte was big, and Estelle's clinic was undoubtedly one of many, but... She leaned closer to the screen and studied the map. No, it was the right place. She was one hundred percent sure because the coffee shop where she'd often waited for her mom's treatment to be done was across the street.

"Miss?" Sheila's voice returned.

"I'm sure," Frankie said. "Unless you've moved since then. Maybe changed owners?"

"No, we've been here since 2005."

It was as if someone flipped a switch, turning the office from sweltering to frigid. The hair on Frankie's arms stood straight up as the perspiration coating her skin cooled. Frankie swallowed. "Can you please check again? It would have been, let's see..." Was it late spring maybe?

She'd been dating Zach, a law student she'd met at a bar in Charlotte, for about a year at the time—she remembered because he'd wanted her to join him and some friends on a cross-country road trip that summer to celebrate graduating, which had sounded amazing. But then Estelle had fallen ill and needed Frankie's help getting to treatments and making the school run smoothly, and she'd had to back out. She'd received a few messages from Zach as he'd set out through Tennessee and west, but after that, contact had been sporadic, only to end with an "it's not you, it's me" text a month later. She'd never heard from him again.

"I think her treatments started late May ten years ago if that helps."

More typing, then Sheila returned. "I'm very sorry, but she wasn't a patient here. I don't know what else to tell you."

A small gasp escaped Frankie, as if someone had punched her in the sternum. "And you're absolutely sure?"

"I'm positive. But I wish you all the best with your fundraiser." She hung up.

Frankie remained in place, the phone pressed to her ear and her breaths still coming in irregular spurts. It couldn't be. She'd dropped her mom off outside that clinic several times per week for six weeks. She'd listened to stories about the staff and other patients who Estelle got to know, and she'd shared her excitement that the treatment was working.

Without thinking, Frankie dialed the number again, this

time choosing the nurse line instead of the administrative office, and when the call connected, Frankie told a different story. She said she was helping her mom access her medical records, but that her mom was unsure if this clinic was the right one, so could they please check?

But the answer was the same. They'd never had a patient by that name.

Frankie dropped the phone to the desk, the room spinning wildly around her. Before she knew what was happening, she had her head in the garbage bin next to the desk, her whole body heaving to expel everything she'd consumed earlier that day. Forgotten was the list of donations she'd procured, her next student, the engagement of the Starview parents, and every other good thing she had going.

Only one thought remained.

Here was yet another lie.

# SEVENTEEN

## FRANKIE

Now

She had to get out of there. Frankie shut off the computer, then grabbed her bag as she fled the school. Once down the stairs, she paused as the world flailed again, but this time she fought back the nausea with a long shaky inhale.

Had Estelle really lied to her about having cancer? It didn't seem possible because why would anyone do such a thing?

Frankie wanted to scream out the questions, but instead, she spun round, her eyes locking on the door to the school as if she might find the answer there. She stood there a long moment, the different corners of the town tugging at her with competing possibilities of where to go, what to do. But there was only one place that might offer clarity, and as soon as that thought had crystallized, she set off toward her car in the parking lot.

"Frankie—hey!"

She stopped with her key aimed at the car door and turned to see Matt come jogging toward her.

"Heading out for an early lunch? I was just stopping by to see if Kayla had a minute for a bite."

"No," Frankie said, the word cutting into her raw throat.

Matt didn't seem to notice. A message popped up on his phone, and he checked it, chuckling at whatever it said before shoving it back into his pocket. Frankie opened her car door, readying herself to get in. Her bag slid off her shoulder and bounced against the door frame.

"Here, let me." Matt dove forward and caught it before it hit the ground.

Frankie took it without looking at him. "Thanks."

Matt dipped his head to look at her. "Everything okay?"

Frankie swallowed down a threatening sob. How would she ever be able to explain *this* to another person? "Mm-hmm," she said. "Just in a hurry." Then she slid into her car seat and closed the door, ignoring the confusion on his face as she sped off.

Back at Estelle's house, she took the stairs two at a time with the single-minded goal to get to the fireproof safe in the walk-in closet. Any important medical documents would be there if they existed—health insurance, vaccination records, care summaries. Frankie knew as much because she'd had a folder in that cabinet too with annual health records going back to her first year in Aspen Creek until she'd created her own file box in her tiny home.

Frankie yanked out the bottom drawer the moment she sat down on the floor, and it rolled out so fast it slammed into her knee.

"Ow, mother trucker!" Frankie squeezed her hands into fists as she rocked forward. "Arrgh. Dammit." She rubbed at the sore spot, then inhaled deeply to try and force her pulse down. *Easy now.*

She flipped through the folders, scanning the labels as she went. Travel. House and Garden. Frankie College. Official Docs. Health.

Frankie pulled out the right folder and opened it on the floor. Over the next few minutes, she thumbed through Covid vaccine certificates, a referral for a blood draw and the subsequent results, an information page for a prescription that looked to be blood pressure related, ECG and mammogram results, a blood typing document, a rejected insurance claim due to an out-of-network provider that Estelle had contested, and more. She kept an eye out for anything cancer related, but even among the older papers, there was nothing from the Charlotte clinic.

Frankie's shoulders slumped where she sat in the middle of the closet, folders spread out all around her. There had to be something here. Something to prove either the clinic or Mom wrong. She went through the drawer again, but no other folder had to do with healthcare.

"Tell me you didn't lie to me about this too," Frankie pleaded into the still air, but there was no response but the steady hum of the HVAC system.

She started stacking the folders again, placing them back in the cabinet one by one, saving the healthcare one for last. She placed it in her lap and flicked through it once more, and this time, something stirred in her mind like a mosquito buzzing near your ear no matter how you wave it off.

She stared unseeingly as the pages flapped between her fingers, that vexing feeling growing until finally she emptied all the papers onto the floor and spread them out around her. Vaccines, blood typing, prescriptions, test results. Test results, prescriptions, blood typing, vaccines. Still, not a single mention of cancer or the clinic.

Frankie straightened, the mosquito's buzzing coming to a stop. *Not a single mention of cancer.* She examined the pile again, riffling through it for the various mammogram results she'd come across until she had a stack in her hands. With bated breath, she placed them down before her, organizing them by date, and when she was done, she studied the uninterrupted line of annual screens going back to the year after they'd moved here. None of them showed an abnormal result. There it was. No cancer.

A shuddering sob broke free in Frankie's chest.

It had been a ruse. Estelle had lied to her and not once but day after day after day. Frankie had brought her tea in this bedroom after her treatments. She'd run errands, worked extra hours at the school, been the chauffeur, and the support. She'd *worried.*

"Who does that?" Frankie gasped, letting the papers drop. Had it been some form of a joke? A cruel, morbid, pathetic joke? Because the mom she knew would never do something like that.

The air appeared to withdraw from the closet, but Frankie didn't move. She couldn't. Her thoughts kept her stuck in one inexplicable, never-ending loop.

Estelle telling the story that inspired "My Only Child," shuddering as she recounted Frankie being taken.

Estelle tired in the car after radiation, so grateful for Frankie's help.

Estelle giving new families a tour of Starview, touting excellence and reliability.

Lies, lies, lies.

But why?

Frankie's phone dinged, startling her out of her reverie.

It was Kayla. *Everything okay? Matt said you seemed weird.*

Frankie stared at the screen, thumbs perched to respond, but then she dropped her hands to her lap again. She couldn't tell Kayla and Matt about this. The song and the school's finances were one thing, but this? Who lies about cancer?

Frankie's face heated at the thought. She could barely admit to herself what must be the truth—that Estelle had feigned both the hardship of the diagnosis and the joy of recovery beyond suspicion—so how could she possibly admit it to others who had also loved her mom? Intentional or not, Frankie had been complicit. If anyone should have known, it was her, but instead she'd accepted gifted casseroles and get-well flowers from people around the community without blinking an eye.

Something built inside Frankie that made her tuck her phone back into her pocket and push herself off the floor. She'd had a happy childhood. Unconventional until they moved here perhaps, but good all the same. It had been filled with music, travel, and interesting people. She and Estelle had made a home of the Winnebago Uncle Ray had bought for them, and it had been as much a home as any other Frankie had been able to imagine. Estelle had homeschooled her on the road, and between field trips, libraries, and the varied folks they met on the road, it hadn't been a bad education, despite her being a year behind when they settled in Aspen Creek.

With the ever-changing scenery of their surroundings, the two of them had been each other's constants, so to now confront the notion that there had been more to Estelle than she'd let Frankie see almost cut deeper than death itself. Because how do you mourn what you don't understand?

No, nothing was okay and that would remain so unless she got to the bottom of all of this.

Frankie pulled out every single folder from the drawer, stacking them in her arms before leaving the health-related mess on the floor behind her and heading downstairs. The living room was bigger, and if she intended to go through every scrap of paper Estelle had filed away, she needed space. Whatever else was hidden within these documents, she would bring it out of the shadows once and for all. She wouldn't be able to rest until she did.

That evening, Frankie walked back into Estelle's living room with a single-minded focus after teaching her classes. She'd managed minimal interaction with anyone who wasn't her students, and since Grant taught his adult guitar class Tuesday evenings, he'd be locking up.

She flicked on the ceiling light, illuminating the papers strewn across the floor in stark clarity. She'd only had time to spread out the contents of the files earlier before she'd realized the time and hurried back to the school, but now the evening stretched out before her uninterrupted.

After setting her backpack down on the couch, she walked among the documents as if they might call out to her where to start. Estelle's passport lay at the top of one row, a drawing of a garden layout in another. She stepped over a payment schedule for her college loans, which they had finished paying off a few years ago, rounded a yellow envelope labeled "certification," then paused by an invoice for window washing.

The doorbell rang.

Frankie huffed at the sound. What now? She looked from the door to the papers surrounding her, contemplating pretending she wasn't here, but then the bell chimed again. It had better not be Kayla demanding entry because the mess would be difficult to explain without the truth.

Frankie peeked through the window next to the door before reaching for the handle. Her eyebrows rose. Not Kayla—it was Owen.

She glanced over her shoulder, an urge to hide the documents coming over her, but then she opened the door just enough to stick her head through. "Hi," she said, forcing her cheeks to comply with a smile.

A frown skated over Owen's brow as his gaze jumped above her to the space beyond, then back to her face. "Um, hi."

Her regret was immediate, the awkwardness of her position straining both her neck and likely his perception of her. She pushed through the opening instead, drawing the door closed behind her. "It's messy in there," she said, crossing her arms. "How's it going?"

He blinked at her, the deep blue of his eyes returning her briefly to poolside hangouts at Kayla's parents' house before he looked down at the foil-covered dish in his hands.

"We made cobblers," he said. "Grams wanted you to have one."

Frankie's stomach growled. She couldn't remember if she'd eaten today. "You baked?" she asked, her arms dropping to her side.

"I wore an apron and everything." He smiled, and a small trickle of warmth pierced the cool numbness that had locked Frankie in its grip since the call to the clinic. He handed her the dish.

The scent that wafted from beneath the foil made her mouth water. "Pictures or it didn't happen."

To her surprise, he whipped out his phone and tapped a few times before holding up the screen so she could see. The photo was blurry, and half his head was cut off, but there he was in a frilly yellow apron spooning flour into a bowl. "Grams is more enthusiastic than skilled at photography, but there you go."

Frankie hugged the cobbler closer, a genuine smile easing across her face. The next moment, she was crying, large tears tracking down her cheeks, unstoppable.

"Oh," Owen said. "Oh shit. What...?" His hands fluttered out before him as if he wanted to offer comfort but wasn't sure how.

"Sorry," Frankie cried. "It's just been a day, and this is so nice."

Owen came to a decision, taking the dish from her and setting it on the step. Then he pulled her into his arms and held her tight as she wept. His embrace was broader than she remembered, but the way his hands splayed on her back, firm and still, like he wouldn't let anything bad happen, was the same. She buried her nose against his collarbone and allowed the warmth from his body to ease the rest of her pent-up tension as her tears soaked into his T-shirt.

It was possible she stayed in that spot a little longer than she needed, but eventually, she lifted her head off him and sucked in a deep breath. A fleeting impulse to apologize for her behavior was there but gone just as quickly. She didn't have the energy.

"How about you go clean up and I'll heat up some cobbler?" Owen asked.

And because the thought of going back inside and facing everything again made her want to run far away from there, she said yes.

She opened the door, revealing the mess she'd made with a small grimace. "I'll explain after I..." She gestured to her face. "Kitchen is that way." She pointed.

"I remember," Owen said with a smile. "And your room was the first on the right up the stairs."

"It's storage now," Frankie said, ignoring the way her heart skipped a beat at the reminder of him in her life once before.

"Where do you sleep then?"

Frankie pointed out the window toward the tiny home. "That's mine."

Owen lit up. "Really? I watched those tiny home shows on HGTV when I was in rehab. Will you show me some time?"

Frankie's tears were fully dried now. "Sure, but it's hardly TV-worthy. I'll be right back."

After rinsing her eyes, she joined Owen in the kitchen. Two plates of cobbler were sitting piping hot on the table. He'd put on the kettle for tea too and was currently head-deep in the freezer.

"Looking for something?"

He jumped back at her voice, a sheepish look on his face. "In case you had some vanilla ice cream. Goes great with cobbler."

"I don't think we do." Frankie pulled two mugs off the shelf and grabbed a box of tea from the pantry. "Thanks for doing this, by the way."

"Not a problem."

They prepared their drinks in silence, moving around each other with ease until they were both seated at the trestle table. The first bite of cobbler melted on Frankie's tongue, and she stifled a moan as the sweet fruit sent bursts of delight across her tastebuds. When she opened her eyes, she found Owen watching her, mirth playing on his lips.

"Good?" he asked.

"Very good," she agreed. Almost good enough to erase the rest of the day, except outside this little bubble, she still had a trove of documents to examine and a life to make sense of.

"Will you tell me about it?" Owen asked as if he'd seen her thoughts shift.

She finished chewing another bite. "If I do, you have to promise to keep it to yourself. It's pretty messed up."

He didn't hesitate. "Of course. Is it about Estelle?"

She nodded. "You only know about the discrepancy in the abduction story, but there's more."

She proceeded to tell him everything that had happened since the funeral, including the weird lavender stash upstairs, and finally the cancer lie that had upended this particular day. "If it was just one oddity, I could maybe chalk it up to a quirk or something like that, but it's been one thing after the other, and added up..." She pressed her lips together before the panic could take hold and run with her again.

"It makes you wonder what else she lied about," Owen said.

Frankie slumped back in her seat. "How can I not?"

He nodded. "No, I get it. It would make me question everything."

"And to make matters worse, I now have to do an interview with this reporter, Orla Monroe, who's been asking questions since she read the card. It's a whole thing. What if she finds out about this? Estelle would be disgraced, and that would hurt Starview."

"Which is why you have all that stuff on the floor in there." Owen nodded toward the living room.

Frankie nodded. "I was about to go through it when you showed up. If there's something to find, *I* need to be the one to find it."

"Derailing plans one cobbler at a time." Owen shoved a big bite into his mouth and chewed around a smile. "Do you want help?"

An overwhelming "yes" resounded inside Frankie. She really did, and Owen was far enough removed from all things Aspen Creek to be a safer bet than Kayla and Matt. Owen didn't have preconceived notions of Estelle, and he wasn't invested in Starview or its success, which made him the perfect partner for this investigation.

"If you don't mind," Frankie said.

"Like Grams said—it's good for me to stay busy." He lifted another forkful but paused halfway to his lips and said as if on an afterthought, "I also don't like seeing you upset."

The unexpected honesty lightened the weight at Frankie's core. This version of him was so different than his eighteen-year-old self, all the edges rounded off, the depths explored and embraced, but when he said things like that, she got a glimpse of the unpredictability that had kept her on her toes back then. Like the raw undercurrent that had once simmered beneath his skin, exciting and intimidating her in equal measure, might still run deep.

Or, possibly, he just wanted to avoid further crying.

"I wonder if it started before the song," Owen said, setting his mug down on the table.

Frankie's analysis of him came to a halt. "What do you mean?"

"You said the lavender stuff went back what—ten-ish years? Same with the cancer. And whoever sent that note to the funeral certainly made it seem like they'd waited for her demise for some time. The financial issues are more recent, and we can't make assumptions about the private account until you get access. That means the lie she told about the song—and your abduction—is likely older than the other question marks you've found."

"Yeah?" She still wasn't sure what he was getting at.

"Look, lies are stories people tell for a reason. They can be honorable—like to spare someone's feelings—or completely self-serving, borne from a desire to deceive or a need to protect the self. I should know; I've lied to my parents, my employers, my friends, to my ex-girlfriend... I've lied about where I've been, what I've done, my habits, and my intentions. Part of the rehab program I was in required me to confront this in myself, but as hard as that's been, the real challenge was unearthing the origin of them all. *The one lie to rule them all*, if you will. Because once that first story takes root, it requires no effort to grow into something unwieldy that needs more lies to be maintained."

Frankie frowned, trying to match his words to what she knew of Estelle and failing. "But—and I mean no offense—Estelle wasn't an addict. There were no habits to cover up."

"That you knew of. Substance abuse is only one kind of habit."

"No." Frankie gathered her plate and mug and brought them to the sink. "Mom wasn't like that. I would have known." They'd both been so focused on the school, on their students, on the community. There would have been no time for secret extracurriculars.

Except Estelle did have a suitcase under the guest room bed that said otherwise, a small voice reminded Frankie.

Owen looked like he had more to say, but he backed down

when she didn't return to the table, opting instead to lean against the counter.

"I could be wrong," he said instead. "But her telling you that you were abducted? If that was a lie, I doubt it was the first one. It's too big to be the seed."

Frankie considered this, wanting to disagree with him but not quite managing. "You think the answers lie further back?"

"Maybe." Owen joined her and set his dishes in the sink. "What do you know about her life before she had you? Your dad died, right?"

"Yeah, I have no memories of him."

"So that must have been hard on her. Where did they live?"

"Mississippi. I was born in Jackson, but I'm not sure that's where they were from."

"Have you ever been back?"

Frankie pushed off the counter and headed for the living room. "That's a lot of questions at once. Are *you* secretly a reporter?"

He followed her, a low sound of amusement rumbling in his chest. "Sorry."

She stopped before the mess on the floor, and he did the same.

"I had no reason to go back," she said. "No grandparents, aunts, or uncles. She didn't talk much about her parents, but her grandparents were from France. She got her love for music from her grandpa. That much I do know."

Owen stepped out among the documents, as if he was setting off into a labyrinth. Frankie watched him, the placement of his feet, the way his gaze swept across these relics of a life, and it felt like he was looking at her instead. Like he'd be able to glean something in the spaces between the lines that she wasn't ready to own up to yet.

"What was your first lie?" she asked.

It had its desired effect. He stopped. Looked up at her.

"'Drinking helps me be myself,'" he said. "Rapidly followed by 'It makes people like me more' and 'I can stop whenever I want.'"

"Classic."

He shrugged. "I'd gone off to college and suddenly I didn't know who I was anymore. I was completely anonymous, and for a kid who'd had his name cheered throughout high school, that was like an icy shower of reality."

Frankie moved a roof-cleaning invoice with her toes. "I wish you would have told me," she said quietly.

"We'd broken up." His words were matter-of-fact. "I didn't want to mess up your senior year with my problems."

She was about to object when he bent down and picked up the yellow envelope she'd seen earlier.

"Certificates," he said. "Looks important."

"I think it says 'certification.' You know—for the school."

He flipped the envelope over again. "No. It says 'certificates.'" He held it out for her so she could see.

She squinted at the cursive. "Maybe you're right. Open it."

He did, pulling out a short stack of copies that he handed to her.

"'Marriage Certificate,'" she read, her thumb skimming the ornate font at the top of the page. Then her gaze trailed lower to where her parents' names were listed, and below them, their parents' names as witnesses.

"Is that your mom and dad?" Owen asked. "I didn't know that was her real name."

Frankie read the page to herself a third time, focusing on the swoop of her mom's signature to keep the knot that was forming in her throat in check.

According to the certificate, Greg Milne and Stella-Jane Sutton had been married in Franklin County, Alabama on November 1, 1975.

Frankie looked up, meeting Owen's gaze over the page. "Yeah," she said. "Neither did I."

"Well, shit."

Her sentiment exactly. Never once when Mom had talked about her past had that name come up, and here it was on her marriage certificate. Greg's penmanship was heavier than her mom's, the ink tip having debossed the squat letters into the paper, while hers flowed smoothly in a forward slant. *Stella-Jane.*

"Um, Frankie..."

"Yeah?" She looked up to see Owen with his hand shoved into the envelope, fishing for something at the bottom.

"There's something else in here." He pulled out two plastic straps, one bigger than the other, and held them out to her in his palm.

"What is it?" she asked, taking the smaller one and examining it. There was writing on one side, but it was smudged.

"Looks like medical wristbands," he said, turning the bigger one over in his hand. "Yeah," he said. "It is. Look." He showed her where Stella-Jane's name was written on the tag.

Frankie squinted at the smaller one again, trying to interpret the faded letters. "Probably from when I was born then," she said. "This must be the matching baby wristband."

"I don't think so," Owen said, the expression on his face saying enough that Frankie braced herself, her subconscious knowing something was coming around the corner that she couldn't have prepared for.

He gave her the bigger bracelet and pointed to the numbers below Stella-Jane's name. "This can't be yours because the baby who wore this was born in 1976."

# EIGHTEEN

## FRANKIE

Now

Frankie stared at the tiny plastic band in her hand, unable to draw breath. Estelle had had another baby? Frankie had a sibling?

"Frankie?"

Owen's voice sounded far away, even though he was right there. She looked at his face, saw the worry in his eyes, the movement of his lips as he said something else she couldn't decipher. Then her legs gave out.

A rumbling, "Oh, no you don't," sounded in her ear, and then strong arms caught her.

The next she knew, she was sitting on the floor, leaning against him. Her hands were splayed limply at her sides, and somewhere inside her skull, a deep pounding pulsed in time with her heart.

"You okay?" he asked.

The mantra she'd repeated daily since the funeral stung on her tongue—*I'm fine*—but her lips refused to shape the words.

Instead, what came out was, "Not really," which was closer to how she truly felt—that nothing would ever be fine again.

He supported her back as she worked to lean forward. "Reading between the lines here, I'm assuming you didn't know about this." He held up the wristband she'd dropped.

Frankie shook her head. They were still in Estelle's living room, still in a place that she'd have called home if someone had asked yesterday, but the supports around her were coming down. The wallpaper seemed to be curling toward the floor, the bookcases and all their contents seeping like paint into a murky puddle at their base.

"But I have so much to do," she mumbled, steadying herself against the wobbling floor. She looked up at Owen. "I don't have time for this. We're a cornerstone of the community. Aspen Creek is counting on us. Lavignes are reliable. Lavignes are true to their word."

She gasped, the collapse of all things familiar cutting through her and causing a rift through the very fabric of her being. She clutched at the front of her shirt and at her throat as pain of a kind she'd never felt before marred her mind. This was too much. One step too far.

How many times had she wished for a sibling when she was little? How many times had she pretended Matt was her brother? And all along, Estelle—who was really Stella-Jane—had only ever told her the two of them were enough. *We're two peas in a pod, and three would make it too crowded.* She'd had plenty of opportunities to tell Frankie about the other child she'd given birth to, but she'd chosen not to.

"Why?" Frankie asked of everyone and no one. The question she returned to again and again. "Why all these secrets? Why all the lies?" She faced Owen, who still had one hand splayed against her back, as if not trusting her to stay upright on her own just yet.

"I don't know," he said simply. "Could she have lost the baby?"

A tragic death? Frankie considered the possibility. "I don't think so. We talked about stuff like that." When he looked skeptical, she continued. "Matt and Kayla can't have kids. She had severe endometriosis when she was younger, and they've been through a lot. Several miscarriages among them. Estelle was always very pragmatic about it. Sympathetic, but not... affected if that makes sense. But who's to say? There's clearly a lot I don't know."

"You could look into it," Owen said.

Frankie shook her head. "The auction is two and a half weeks away. I still need sponsors. I need to hire a new teacher. I have a full roster of students, and the parents are unhappy that I can't play. And on top of all that, the interview I mentioned is only a week away. How am I supposed to talk about Mom as if nothing is amiss?" Her head jerked back, a new thought rearing its ugly head. "What if Orla already knows and asks me about this?"

"Okay, hey." Owen ran his hand up and down her spine a few times, forcing her attention. "Let's take a deep breath and think this through."

She nodded stiffly, her mind too mired in obligations to come up with a protest.

"If you didn't have the auction and the school to think about —if it was just up to you—what would you do about this?" Owen asked, reaching for the wristband.

"But that's not how things are," Frankie protested.

"*If* they were," Owen insisted. "Humor me."

"Fine." Frankie closed her eyes for an extended beat before opening them again. The walls hadn't melted; they were still standing tall around her, but there was something foreign about them now. "Then I'd get to the bottom of this. It feels like I don't know who I am anymore."

"You mean who Estelle was? You're still you." He gave her a crooked smile.

Was she? She reached inside, searching for that solid core that had always allowed her certainty in what she had, her sense of self, but found it gel-like and wobbly, like someone had taken a sledgehammer to it.

"Let's go over to Grams'," Owen said, pushing up to standing and offering her a hand. "I have an idea."

"Owen..." She looked up at him, staying firmly planted on the floor among the mess she'd made.

"Yes, I know. You don't have time. But do you really think you'll be able to tuck this away and pretend everything's business as usual? Beethoven, remember?" He winked and wiggled his fingers.

This time she took it, allowing him to pull her up to standing.

"My point is, you need answers," he continued, "and Grams is very good at finding them. You're not alone, you know. Come on. We can clean this up later."

She hesitated. He *was* right—that wasn't the problem. But if she allowed herself to go down this path, she'd be acknowledging that the course of constancy and stability she'd charted when Estelle died was a dead end.

On the other hand, maybe part of her already knew something had changed. She'd done fairly well not allowing the first few mysteries to derail her. She'd tucked away the card, approached the financial situation with action and patience, and shoved the suitcase full of lavender back under the bed. But the song, the cancer, and now this? These lies and omissions weren't slip-ups. They were personal.

"Okay," Frankie said. "Let's do it."

*Let's see who you really were, Mom,* she thought following Owen out the door.

And for once, there was no voice in her head offering a response.

Frankie let Owen explain to Thora what they'd found. The older woman made wide eyes when she learned about Frankie's sibling, but she didn't speak until Owen asked her if she thought she could help.

Thora turned her crinkled eyes on Frankie, sympathy warring with some other untold emotion therein. "Those are big secrets to keep," she said. "It will be safe to assume she had a reason. Are you sure you want to know?"

Frankie dug her teeth into her cheek, testing her certainty, but no matter the apprehension she felt, with Orla Monroe circling, Frankie needed to stay a step ahead if at all possible.

"I can't let this go," she said finally. "If nothing else, I need to know what happened to my brother or sister. Owen could be right that they died young. Or what if we're wrong about the inspiration of the song? Maybe it wasn't the Hattiesburg case. Maybe my sibling was kidnapped and never came back." If that had happened to Estelle, she might have rewritten that trauma into the more manageable one where Frankie was taken and returned. It would almost be enough to forgive the lie.

"I didn't even think about that," Owen said.

Thora nodded. "I hear you."

"Can you really help?" Frankie asked.

"Well, with her real name and a marriage certificate, I should think we'd be able to dig up something." Thora rocked forward, but before she could push off her chair, Owen was there, helping her up. "Let's head to the office. Owen, get my cardigan, will you?"

They followed her down the short hallway to a closed door that she pushed open with a flourish.

"I don't let just anyone in here," she said, flipping the light switch. "Ta-da."

It was like walking into a space shuttle cockpit. Shelves full of electronic equipment lined the walls, and the long desk that sat beneath the window was jampacked with cables, keyboards, monitors, and speakers.

"What is all this?" Frankie asked, moving deeper into the room and stepping over two extension cords that were taped to the floor.

"A bit of fun," Thora said, easing herself into one of the desk chairs. "My dearly departed husband dabbled with ham radios, and I suppose along the way I caught the bug too. But why stop at small potatoes?" She gestured to her setup.

"Grams can talk to people all over the world in here," Owen said, beaming at his grandmother.

"Like who?" Frankie asked.

"You never know," Thora said. "Depends on who's there. Divine shared frequency if you will. But mostly I use it to chat with my regulars."

Frankie looked from Thora to Owen, hoping he'd supply an explanation, and he must have caught her quizzical expression.

"Random folks she's met over the years. Most are in the southeast corner of the States—same time zone and all that."

"Mainly we check in once a week to make sure we're alive," Thora said. "People are lonely out there." She reached for a pair of headphones and put them around her neck. "But other times, we help each other with specific research. Mostly genealogical —lots of people curious about their ancestry at my age, looking for a tether to the past before entering the great web beyond perhaps. Other times it's book related, or, as in your case, past events, people, microfiche."

Frankie's eyes widened. "That's who helped you look for kidnapping articles?"

"Yep." Thora flipped on a few switches. "Did you ever watch James Bond?"

"Sure."

The old woman peered up at her with a glint in her eyes. "I like to think of myself as M, with the people on the other end as my agents." She rubbed her hands together. "Now let's see who's awake in the fine state of Mississippi. If we're lucky, Norman Clintock is at the dials—his brother was in state government, so he's connected."

Frankie watched as Thora did her thing, unsure what to think of this unusual method of communication.

"Couldn't you just call him?" she asked.

Owen chuckled next to her as if anticipating the answer.

"Where's the fun in that?" Thora said. "Every Tom, Dick, and Harry knows how to use a phone. This baby requires sophistication." She patted the box in front of her. "Oh, hold on." She yanked her headphones on and listened.

"Yes, this is Purple Partridge. Over."

"They use code names too?" Frankie asked Owen.

He grinned. "You don't know the half of it."

They were in luck, and Thora's contact was "on the air" or whatever they called it. Frankie stopped caring about the minutia of how the technology worked as soon as she heard Thora mention Stella-Jane and Greg and the year the baby had supposedly been born.

"I have their parents' information too," Frankie said, pulling the marriage certificate out of her bag and placing it in front of Thora, who gave her a thumbs up.

"Anything you can find on either of these folks would be much appreciated," she said finally. "Yes. Yes. Over and out."

"Well?" Frankie asked as soon as Thora pulled off her headphones, mussing her dark gray curls in the process.

"He's going to look," she said. "No guarantees, but if anyone can help us, it's him." She let out a great big huff of air and patted both hands on the desk as if she'd just finished a long day's work. "Now who's in for a game of cribbage?"

As unconventional as Thora's information network was, it did pay off. Less than twenty-four hours later, Owen messaged Frankie to stop by when she got a chance, and she was there within a half hour.

"Norman faxed me this a little bit ago," Thora said, waving a stack of papers in front of Frankie from her perch in her easy chair. "Greg Milne, born December 13, 1957, in Mobile County, Alabama," she read. "Stella-Jane Milne, nee Sutton, born July 10, 1958, Jones County, Mississippi." She handed the papers to Frankie. "This has a couple addresses, and their parents' and grandparents' information too. Norman's wife is big into genealogy, so if time wasn't of the essence, you might have gotten more than that. You need only ask."

Frankie poured over the information, skimming names she'd never before seen and places she'd had no idea she was connected to. Biloxi, Montgomery, Baton Rouge. She'd only expected facts relating to her parents, but suddenly her family tree had branches that stretched much farther skyward.

She sank onto the couch at once filled by the connection to her ancestors and stupefied by the fact that none of these names had ever crossed Estelle's lips. Well, except for her grandfather's, who she'd called Pepe. She ran her fingertip under his name, Joseph Martin Sutton, then onward to his wife's. "Imgr., Kildare," she read in parenthesis by their names before looking up. "What does that mean?"

"I assume they were immigrants," Thora said.

Owen typed something on his phone. "Kildare is a county in Ireland," he supplied. "That must be where they were born."

"No, they were French," Frankie said. "My great-grandpa was a bugle boy for the French army during the Great War and went on to play—" She was about to say "some of the finest venues in Paris" but cut herself off when something Estelle had said when they were struggling on the road rose to her mind's surface. *Music saved my pepe's life in the trenches. It will look out for us too.* Back then it had nipped any complaining from Frankie in the bud, but now, the words skewed dissonant when contradicted by the facts on the documents in her hands. It must have been another lie.

"I take it that's what she told you?" Thora asked gently.

Frankie nodded, feeling a headache creeping up her temples. "It rolled off her tongue like the truth. Like she believed it herself."

"Maybe she did. Or you misunderstood. Greg had ancestors in Baton Rouge—lots of French descendants there."

"I don't think so," Frankie said. "She'd have been more hesitant if it was speculation. This was fact. Something she was proud of even."

"Maybe she wanted it to be true," Owen said. "Some people lie because—"

Thora cut him off with a sharp glare.

Frankie's eyes trailed between them, sensing something solidifying in the building tension. "What?"

"It's not important," Thora said.

"If it's about my mom, I want to know."

Thora stalled, something Frankie hadn't seen her do before.

"Please?" Frankie said.

The older woman relented. "It's nothing," she said. "I didn't know Estelle, and I don't want to speculate."

"But?" Frankie urged her on.

Thora looked at Owen. "What my grandson was about to say is that some people lie because something within them compels them to. I learned about these things when Owen had his struggles. I was looking for an explanation, trying to understand."

"My family didn't know about my drinking at first," Owen said. "But they could tell something was off."

"So I wondered if there was a mental illness at play," Thora filled in. "That's how I learned about compulsive lying. It seems to me that Estelle might have had some trouble distinguishing between reality and imagination is all."

The knee-jerk urge to protest was too strong to resist. "No, she was a success," Frankie said. "In every part of her life. If she was ill, someone would have caught on. *I* would have caught on."

Thora peered at her for a long moment. "But aren't you?"

Frankie stared unseeingly at the papers in her hand. *Was she?* Had she been oblivious to the ruse all these years, or worse, had her vision been obscured? The answers were out there somewhere.

"I need to go there," Frankie said, more to herself than to the others. She looked at the first address listed, recognizing the county name from the marriage certificate. "Ferrisville is the only town in the right county, so it's probably where they lived when they got married. Someone might remember them." Heck, maybe she still had family there. She stood up, readying herself to leave. "Tell Norman thank you from me, okay?"

"You're leaving now?" Owen asked. "It'll be dark soon, and it's a long drive."

She checked the clock on the wall. He was right. "Tomorrow morning then."

"What about your job?"

"I'll figure something out." She had to. This wasn't something she could put off.

"Owen will go with you," Thora said.

"I will?" Owen asked at the same time Frankie said, "Why would he do that?"

"Those are backwater towns, not known for embracing strangers," Thora said. "And since you have no idea who you might encounter, you'll be safer traveling with a"—she gestured to Owen—"friend."

"But what about you?" Frankie asked. "Don't you need him here?"

"I can make do for a day or two," Thora said. "The Word Birds will look in on me."

Owen and Frankie looked at each other, the decision dangling between them.

Frankie reached for it first. "If you don't mind," she said.

He let out a breath. "No, no. I'm fine with it as long as you are."

It was settled. First thing in the morning, they'd head south.

# NINETEEN

An excerpt from Orla Monroe's interview with Estelle Lavigne
Published in *Country Weekly*, January 1995

## OM:

So far you've shared that several of your songs have been inspired by real life. Let's talk about process. How do you work? What does a typical day look like?

## EL:

I do find the world to be an inspiring place. People I meet, experiences I have, hopes, dreams, the trivial and the profound, good and bad, you name it. The very first song I wrote was called "Petite Potato," and it was for my grandmother. She was a great cook like all French women, better than any chef trained at Le Cordon Bleu, so I made it up while she had me scrub new potatoes from her garden. It was such a thrill to see the recognition on her face when I sang it to her. Even at such a young age, I understood that me putting words to an experience we shared was impactful.

So to answer your question, what I do is I pay attention. I follow the news, I talk to people, I read books, and then I write. I don't wait for inspiration, instead I sit down with my notebook and pen every day and jot down any thought or line of text that comes to mind. It doesn't have to be good—it's only a start.

When I have a few pages of scribbles like that, usually a line or two stand out. Those get kneaded into something better. Sometimes a melody appears at this point, sometimes not. But it is very much a deliberate process.

A typical day will be a few hours of that in the morning while Frankie does schoolwork. Then we explore whatever town we're in, which is important both for my creativity and her education. I do a sound check if it's a performance day, cook dinner, a load of laundry maybe. It's very normal-person stuff aside from being on stage. I'm a regular person. A regular mom.

## OM:

Oh, I think not. You're being exceedingly humble about everything you're juggling. I know your manager handles your bookings, but other than that, you do it all, *and* you write and arrange all of your own material, correct? No co-writers? A bona fide singer/songwriter.

## EL:

I do. Every chord, every word. But I don't think about it as merely lyrics and melody—it's a narrative the audience can get immersed in. That's why my music resonates with listeners—or at least I'd like to think so. I guess what I'm saying is that if we're going to parse words, I prefer to think of myself more as a storyteller than a songwriter. I hope that makes sense.

# TWENTY

## FRANKIE

Now

Owen picked Frankie up at first light, hair mussed, and a sleep crease still cutting diagonally across his cheek. Frankie hadn't slept much. Every time she'd closed her eyes, she'd seen endless versions of Estelle as if reflected in one of those trick mirrors at the fair. One version was real, but there was no telling which one, and the unknowingness followed her into restless dreams where she chased the ghost of her mother.

"Feel free to take a nap," Owen said after they'd left the town behind like he could tell she needed it. "It's early, and we have a long way to go."

But with the road ahead leading toward truth, how could she? Last night, she'd received an email from Orla expressing her excitement for their upcoming rendezvous, as if the woman was homed in on the sore spot.

The endless flat and green landscape rushed past her windows while a country station played at low volume over the speaker. Something mournful and guitar-heavy that was at once nostalgic and modern.

They didn't speak until they passed Greenville, and Owen suggested they pull off for a coffee. It was eight twenty in the morning, and while Frankie had not been able to doze off during their first two hours in the car, her mind had been blissfully blank.

"Thank you," she said as he handed her a to-go mug from a coffee chain drive-through. "And thank you for doing this. I'll pay you back for gas obviously."

He waved her off, stirring sweetener into his mug on the console between them. "It's nice to get away. I've been stationary for a long time now. First in rehab and now at Grams'." One of his shoulders lifted in a shrug.

Frankie eyed him over the plastic lid of her cup. "I still appreciate it."

He nodded once, his hair flopping over his brow. It had grown even longer since she'd first seen him at the library, making her fingers itch to push it back.

"What?" he asked, his blue eyes meeting hers.

She looked away. "Nothing."

"You want to cut it, don't you?"

He'd remembered too. His front porch, the sun caressing his bare back while she carefully trimmed his strands into something that would be more befitting his senior year homecoming dance than the mop he'd let it grow into. She'd done a terrible job, having never cut hair before, but he'd been a good sport about it, and the process itself had been... intriguing. Enough so that she'd volunteered to do it again multiple times in the year that followed.

A subtle shiver of longing raced up her arms.

"You can," he said, now facing the windshield again. "It's just not been a priority."

She took a moment, subtly tracing his profile. "Can I ask about it?" she asked finally.

He turned toward her. "About my hair?"

"About… what you've been through?"

"Oh." He sipped his coffee, then placed it in the cup holder and started the car back up. "Sure."

With that go-ahead, the curiosity she'd suppressed bloomed. She weighed her options for where to start as they left the city behind, but eventually she settled on a question that had been on her mind ever since learning of the challenging path his life had taken.

"You said you started drinking in college to feel more like yourself, but what made it hard to stop? Eventually I imagine you must have made friends and found your place, and you never drank when we were dating."

"It's an easy thing to put off when you don't see it as a problem," he said. "It took years before it was truly impacting my life, and by then, I was too deep in it." He sped up, overtaking a rusty hatchback. "You get to a point where you know it's a problem, you can see the disappointment on the faces around you, but to someone like me, that easily becomes another reason to drink. Kill the pain, blunt the guilt."

"That sounds so… sad," Frankie said, watching him.

The corner of his mouth stretched upward. "Maybe." He glanced at her, no trace of sadness on his face. "But I obviously wasn't thinking about it that way at the time. I was just a mess, leaving a bigger mess in my wake."

It seemed such a contradiction—Owen being messy. He'd been an athletic, white-toothed, polite-to-your-mom kind of guy back in high school. Did his homework, cut the grass, wore a seatbelt in his clean car. The image she had in her mind of someone too drunk to function didn't fit.

"What are you thinking?" he asked when she'd been silent for a long while.

They had hit the verdant plains of Georgia now, and the sun was climbing higher by the minute. Blue sky as far as the eye could see. Frankie folded a leg up under her. "I'm having a hard time picturing you like that," she said honestly. "You were so self-assured, so... optimistic. I keep wondering how things could have changed that much."

"I hadn't met much of life at that point," he said with a shrug. "You're different too."

"I am?"

He let out a soft laugh. "Frankie, come on. You were dreaming of Berklee, traveling the world, playing on the biggest stages. Aspen Creek in the rearview, remember?"

Unbidden, the recital dress she'd found in the armoire entered her mind. The excitement she'd once felt at what lay ahead. But even though she knew he was right, the memory of herself as that person was indistinct, as if her outlines had been smudged somehow along the way.

"We decided elementary education was a safer bet," Frankie said. "And besides—you and I had broken up, so it wasn't like I had a reason to follow you to Boston anymore."

Owen frowned, his lips parting as if he was about to object, but Frankie wasn't ready to shift the conversation away from him, so she hurried to ask her next question. "Was this your first time in rehab?"

His mouth closed, and he glanced at her, the deep blue beneath his brow swirling with a knowingness at what she was doing. But he played along.

"My second," he said. "First time was six years ago. Court ordered. I was working for a construction company and crashed the boss's car." He pressed his lips together as if the memory brought with it a bitter taste.

"But it didn't work?"

"It worked for a while. I met a girl, moved to Nashville, got a good job with a white glove service, bought a small condo."

"And then?"

He rested his arm against the window well. Glanced at her. "Arrogance," he said. "I stopped going to meetings, thought I had it under control. Next I knew, I'd started lying about it again, hiding bottles, that sort of thing. Showed up to work drunk one too many times, lost my job, and she dumped my ass."

"Sorry," Frankie said.

"Nah. It was my own doing, and it wouldn't have lasted long-term anyway."

Frankie wanted to ask why, but something about the topic of old girlfriends made her hold her tongue. It wasn't her business. "Then what happened?"

He let out a deep sigh. "More bad choices. I had four jobs in one year. I couldn't hold them down, so I had to get a roommate—who I owe quite a bit of money to, by the way. I just stopped caring about everything, and then... I broke my mom's heart."

The dejection in his voice was sudden and cut deep, so before Frankie could overthink it, she placed her hand on his shoulder. "But you're here now," she said. "That must mean something."

He straightened as if shaking off the darkness. "Yeah," he said. "She's a bigger person than me."

"How did you come out of it this time? Was it court ordered again?"

"No." He chewed on a corner of his lip. "I stole one of Mom's rings to pawn—for bills, you know. And right before I went to hand it over to the guy, I noticed an inscription in it. 'For Life' it said. It was an anniversary ring her dad had given her mom at one point. That stopped the world for me. It made me see *my* life and what I'd become, and I decided then and there this couldn't be it. I checked myself into rehab the next day."

Goosebumps prickled up Frankie's arms at his words. There he was—that decisive, grab-life-by-its-balls guy she'd known. After all he'd gone through, the core of him hadn't been lost. Did that mean the girl he'd known her to be still waited somewhere within too? Not that their pasts were comparable. There'd been no suffering for her, no drama—only hard work.

*So what's your excuse?* a small voice whispered, but it didn't sound like Estelle this time; it sounded like her younger self. And she didn't have an immediate answer.

"I'm happy you did," she said, even though that sentiment didn't come close to what she wanted to express. His decision had been admirable—impressive even—but she knew him. He'd brush off any such adjective.

"Not as happy as I am," he said. "And it's going to stick this time. Not because I have some idealized faith in my willpower, but because I'm going to work at it. Every day."

She nodded. "I believe you."

He flashed her a grin. "Thank you. That means a lot."

The miles stretched on, the road a never-ending gray belt through small towns, pastures, rolling hills, and leafy forests. They stopped on the outskirts of Atlanta to stretch their legs and have a bite to eat, but with Stella-Jane and Greg's old address burning in Frankie's pocket, they were soon on the road again.

The farther from Aspen Creek they went, the deeper in thought Frankie fell. She was about to visit a part of her mom's life that Estelle had never talked about, and with that came a pinch of disloyalty, as if she was going against expressed wishes, despite knowing that wasn't the case.

Even as a little girl, Frankie had always been very in tune with what Estelle wanted and needed, and it had made her feel important to oblige. It hadn't been a hardship—in fact, it had fostered a sense of importance and maturity that she was someone her mom could rely on, and some of her fondest memories were of bringing Estelle an icepack when a headache had come on or cups of her special, throat-soothing tea before a performance.

"I'd be lost without you, my darling," she'd always say, and little Frankie would grow several inches from the praise.

But this trip was different. The need stemmed from Frankie this time, and that was new.

Her phone buzzed in her purse, and she pulled it out. "It's Kayla," she said. Frankie had texted her before heading out that morning about covering those of Frankie's lessons she was able to and rescheduling the rest. Kayla was a decent piano player, so at least with the younger students it shouldn't be a problem.

Frankie accepted the call.

"That was a very vague message," Kayla said in greeting. "You're 'following a lead about Estelle'? What lead? Did you find out more about the song?"

"No, not yet. I'm..." *Trying to find my lost sibling.* No, she couldn't make herself say that. "I'm looking into her past. To see if there are clues."

"But there's so much to do here."

"I know, but this is important," Frankie said. "I'll explain more when we get back, but for now, please do me this favor."

"Fine. But it's just today, right?"

Frankie traced the outline of the window as she scrunched up her nose. "Actually, it's tomorrow too," she said. "It's a long drive, so... I was kind of hoping you could cover for me then as well?"

Kayla was silent a long while. Then she sighed. "Look, I know that you have a lot on your mind and that you need answers. I get that. But is now the time? All this stuff with Estelle—can't it wait a few more weeks until the auction is over? Even if she lied about what inspired the song, she still wrote it. Isn't that enough?"

Frankie bristled at her friend's tone. "You mean we pretend nothing is wrong?"

"It's a song," Kayla said.

"It's my life," Frankie countered.

"Which you'll blow up if you lose the school."

Frankie leaned her forehead to the cool glass. As if she didn't already know that.

"Frankie..." Kayla's tone softened. "We're worried you're letting yourself get distracted. We're worried about *you*."

"We?" Had she talked to the other teachers? Were they all discussing her behind her back?

"Matt and me. He agrees that your focus right now should be on saving the school and nothing else. Charlie just told us there's a mouse situation in the music building that needs to be addressed, there's an email from the moms asking your approval for the kids' performance order at the auction, and we're still short a teacher. Not to mention it's hard to explain to the parents that you're gone. It just feels like you're making this more difficult than it needs to be."

*What if it was your mom?* Frankie wanted to ask Kayla. *Your life?* But maybe that wasn't fair. Kayla didn't have all the information, didn't know about the cancer, the name change, or the other child, and her concerns stemmed from care. She also wasn't completely wrong; Frankie being here meant she was putting off things back home. Important things. It was just that she had no choice. Focusing on the school meant focusing on this because the two were connected.

"I'll be back as soon as I can," she said. "I promise."

"It's not like I have much choice," Kayla said, resigned. "But hurry, okay?"

"I will," Frankie promised. "And thank you."

They hung up.

"Trouble?" Owen asked.

Frankie tucked her phone away, ignoring a funny meme from Matt that she normally would have hearted, and responded with a non-committal noise.

What Kayla didn't understand was that Frankie had to do this *in order to* pull off the auction. Like it or not, she'd soon be sitting down with Orla to talk about Estelle to bring visibility to this event that was designed to honor her achievements, and that meant she had to hold all the cards firmly in her hands. She couldn't risk being blindsided by a past that someone else might have gained access to, and there were undoubtedly many things Estelle had kept to herself all these years. Orla might be older, but she was still sharp.

Now, whether the reporter had been on to something regarding the card being related to Estelle's death or if it was connected to any of the other questions Frankie had run into remained to be seen. The sender could be from Ferrisville. If Frankie was to believe Estelle had deserved that note, then it was as likely a place as any where the grudge may have been incited. Would she find someone there who knew Estelle before the lies? Someone who knew her family? Someone with answers?

Frankie was going to peel back each layer of this until she knew everything. Only then would she be able to go up on that stage and assure the Starview community that nothing had changed and that she'd carry Estelle's legacy into the future.

# TWENTY-ONE

## ESTELLE

Then

With Ray at her side, Estelle's middle name was *possibility*. At first, she'd balked at him taking a twenty-five percent cut, but since her take-home still equaled what she'd made on her own, she'd swallowed those qualms. Because that was just it—she wasn't completely alone anymore, and that was priceless. And besides, she'd been unable to pick up anything but temporary waitressing hours throughout November, so she was ready to jump through whatever hoops got her back on stage.

"You ready?" Ray asked, coming through the doorway next to her. He had a water bottle in one hand and a red cowboy hat in the other, which he offered to Estelle. "For the season, you know. Christmas in the country. Knock 'em dead."

Estelle shook out her hands to release her nerves and took the hat. It had a rhinestone band around the crown that glittered in the stray beams of the spotlights reaching past the stage.

"Thanks," she said. "Will you be watching?"

"I'll be at the bar. I'm going to use their phone to make a few calls, but I can multitask." He winked.

*As always.* If there was one thing she'd learned about Ray in the short time they'd spent together, it was that he always had another call to make. His pager went off several times an hour, but maybe that's what it took to build a business. He was making a name for himself in property development, and Estelle supposed that meant he needed to be accessible. She wasn't complaining though. His success meant connections for her. Or at least a *chance* of connections. She'd have to convince him she was worth it first, and tonight was the start of that.

She walked on stage looking out over the smoky interior, the air rich with bourbon and steak rather than the lukewarm beer and soil she'd grown used to, and in her mind, she was finally able to climb that first rung off the floor on the ladder of life.

"Happy holidays, folks," she said, sitting down. "Let's see if we can't put you in a festive state of mind as December rounds the corner, shall we? How about a little Hall & Oates?"

She started strumming as sporadic claps and whoops sounded from the tables. Her eyes landed on Ray and Darla at the bar as she began the first verse, Ray with a glass raised to her and Darla with a hand casually resting on his shoulder. She'd visited the house several times in the week since Estelle had moved into the garage suite, but since Ray was working so much and a lot of his current efforts were focused on this musical holiday test run, Estelle could afford to smile at them both. She already knew it was going to be a great set.

"How was that?" Ray asked her when she joined them an hour later. "Professional technicians, discerning crowd?" He gestured to the bartender to get her a drink, and before she'd had time to voice a request, she had a vodka soda in her hand. With a twist.

"How did you know this is exactly what I wanted?" she asked.

"Oh, he always knows what a woman wants," Darla cut in.

She was hanging on his arm, restricting his movements so he couldn't stray too far from her reach.

Estelle took the bait but directed her cheeky smirk at Ray. "Does he now?"

The corner of his mouth twitched. "I make it my business to know." He sipped his bourbon, watching her as his throat moved on a swallow, clearly not intending to elaborate beyond that.

"I see." Estelle let the chilled liquor coat her throat. "And to answer your question, it was great. Everything a gig should be."

"Glad to hear it. You have another one tomorrow."

Estelle lowered her glass to the bar, a second sip interrupted. "I do?"

Ray freed himself from Darla's clasp. "See the man over there in the white hat?"

Estelle turned, craning her neck. "Sure."

"He owns a bar down the street. I invited him tonight, and he liked what he heard."

She stared at him. "Just like that?"

He nodded. "It's not a lot of money, but it's a foot in the door. And I plan on having a few other guys show up for it too. Associates of mine," he clarified. "Word of mouth is the most powerful marketing tool."

"Doesn't hurt to be a Clark either," Darla said. "It's a big name around here, going back generations. Everybody knows the Clarks."

"Oh, you're sweet." Ray bumped his shoulder gently into hers, which brought color to her cheeks. "Not as many generations as you Everetts, though."

Wouldn't that be something? Estelle thought. To be known by everyone.

"I actually have a job for you, too, Dar," Ray continued.

Darla practically clapped her hands. "Of course. Anything."

"I need you to take my little prodigy here shopping." He gestured to Estelle's plain black skirt. "If you want to be a star, the first thing you have to do is act as if you already are one, and beauty alone won't cut it."

A compliment? Estelle willed her complexion to flush radiant to upstage Darla's. Juvenile perhaps, but you worked with what you had, and Darla's deftly disguised chagrin was dopamine straight to the brain. Would she even have tried as hard for Ray's attention had Darla not been there to make it a sport? The thought appeared out of nowhere, and Estelle had to admit it was possible. She'd never been one to give chase in the past.

"Oh." A multitude of expressions filtered across Darla's face to settle on something that looked like well-meaning concern. She was good. Estelle had to hand it to her. "I'm not convinced we share a style," Darla said. "Are you sure I'm the best fit?"

"I've seen your closet and it's the size of a small department store," Ray said. "You can do it. I believe in you."

"It's really not necessary," Estelle said. If it was up to her, she'd go to the nearest thrift store and that would be it. She didn't have extra funds to spend, but that was something people like Ray and Darla, who probably stuffed their mattresses with bills, wouldn't understand. "I prefer to save my earnings." That was good. Rich people did understand money in the bank.

Ray dug into his pocket and produced a credit card that he held out between them. "I insist," he said. "On me."

Estelle scrambled to think of a protest.

"I won't take no for an answer," Ray said, anticipating it. "Plus, it would thrill me to know you ladies are getting to know each other better."

Darla snatched the card from him while giving Estelle a pointed look. "Watch and learn," she said. "With this, you can turn yourself into someone else in no time."

# TWENTY-TWO

## FRANKIE

Now

They reached Ferrisville, a small, sleepy town in northwestern Alabama, a little before four in the afternoon under an overcast sky. Worn, two-story brick buildings lined the streets, many of them abandoned, and since the tiny downtown was largely empty of people at this hour, it gave the impression of a place forgotten by the rest of the world.

On their way to the address Norman had dug up, they passed a one-story town hall, three churches, a shuttered gas station, and several properties with rusted trailers decorating overgrown front lawns, but there were also glimpses of a persisting community here and there. A flowerbed bursting with blossoms. Freshly painted shutters. Children laughing on a playground.

Frankie took it all in while Owen navigated increasingly narrow streets in silence, as if he could tell that she was trying to sense her roots in this foreign place, but when he pulled to a stop where a country road lined with small ramblers turned into a parking lot, he cleared his throat.

"I think this is it," he said, peering out the window at the strip mall where half the storefronts were boarded up. Only a law office and a nail salon were still in business.

"No, it can't be." Frankie pulled up the address on her phone and double-checked it, finding him to be right.

"They must have torn it down to make room for this at some point," Owen said. "I'm sorry."

Frankie stared at the depressing building. Now she would never know what her parents' first home had looked like. "It's okay," she said, convincing herself as the words crossed her lips. This wasn't the most important stop on their journey. Tomorrow morning, they would visit city hall, and hopefully there would be some public records she could access about her parents and the sibling she'd never known. "Let's head back to town and see if we can find a place to eat."

"You sure?"

Frankie gestured toward the window. "There's nothing here. And I'm starving."

They backtracked to where they'd spotted a fried chicken joint, deciding on takeout since the atmosphere left a lot to be desired, and after they'd finished their food in the car, they headed for the motel Owen had found for them.

"Looks kind of cute," Frankie said when they pulled into the lot.

The motel was situated between a ball field and a Latter-day Saints church, and with its Spanish hacienda-style roofline and colorful siding, it couldn't have looked more out of place. They checked in, said goodnight, and went to their separate rooms with a plan to meet up for breakfast at eight in the morning.

Frankie sank onto the yellow coverlet blanketing the queen-sized bed, taking a moment to let the day's impressions wash over her, to catch up. They'd lived here once, her parents. Her family. And yet she'd never heard the name of the town until yesterday.

"Were you happy here?" she asked out loud, and perhaps the silence that followed was answer enough. Knowing Estelle, this would not have been an easy place to be. That was *if* Frankie had known her—something that seemed increasingly unclear these days.

She flopped back onto the bed and stared upward, tracing the uneven wallpaper edge where it met the ceiling. The air conditioning turned off with a clank, leaving only a faint buzzing noise behind. Occasionally, a car would pull into the lot, headlights flickering past the drawn curtain and drawing her gaze, but mostly she let the numbness of meandering thoughts sweep her away.

When it got dark enough that the shapes in the room blurred, she finally got off the bed and turned on a light. Then she brushed her teeth, changed out of her clothes, and pulled back the sheets.

The buzzing noise intensified tenfold.

Frankie paused, looking around the room. She dropped the sheet and stepped closer to the air vent, but that wasn't the source. In fact, the further from the bed she went, the fainter the noise.

She frowned as she retraced her steps, treading slowly so she could hear better. She took hold of the sheets again and shook them a little. The buzzing rose instantly, and at the same time, a handful of bees shot up from the foot of the bed.

"What the...?" Frankie dropped the sheet and stepped back. No way could that be what she thought it was.

After waiting a minute, she reached for her cell phone on the nightstand and turned on its flashlight. Then she squatted next to the bed and gently lifted the side of the coverlet to peer underneath the bedframe.

Thirty seconds later, she was knocking on Owen's door, her

backpack in one hand, her shoes in the other, and her travel clothes under one arm. "Owen!"

When he didn't immediately open, she banged her elbow into it a few more times.

"One sec!" she heard from inside, and a moment later he wrenched the door ajar, holding a tiny towel together at the hip with one hand. His hair was dripping wet. "Frankie. Is everything okay?" He looked over her shoulder as if searching for something or someone.

"Yeah," she sputtered, forcing her gaze away from a torso that bore no trace of the slender teen he'd once been. This was the build of someone who'd done years of manual labor, and she'd have to be a robot not to recognize that it suited him. But at the sight of his confused expression, she shook her head, her cheeks heating. "I mean no. There's a beehive under my bed."

"A what?" Owen took a step toward her, leaning forward to peer out the door as if the answer was there.

"A beehive. With honey and everything. I think. I didn't exactly stay to investigate. They did not appreciate my company." She shuddered at what might have befallen her in the middle of the night had she not discovered her companions beforehand.

"Come in," Owen said. "Let me put on some sweats, and then I'll call down to let the front desk know." He left her standing at the foot of his identical bed while he disappeared into the bathroom.

Frankie resisted the temptation to look beneath his bed too, trusting that the absence of buzzing was enough.

"Okay, let's see." Owen lifted the receiver on the nightstand and dialed zero for the motel reception.

Frankie listened as he described the issue and reassured them no one was hurt. "Would we be able to get a different room?" He paused, listening. "Mm-hmm. Yeah. No, that's no problem. Yeah, back to the same account is fine. Okay. Yes, you as well." He hung up.

"What did they say?" Frankie asked.

Owen used his forearm to wipe water dripping from his hair off his forehead. "Good news and, um, not so good news. They'll credit the cost of the room back to us, but all other rooms are booked. Which means you'll have to stay in here tonight."

"Oh."

They both looked at the one bed in the room.

"I'll take the floor of course," Owen said. "They said I can pick up extra pillows downstairs."

"No way." Frankie set her backpack down and unburdened herself from her other parcels as well. "That doesn't seem fair. I'll take the floor."

Owen looked at her for an extended beat, then he turned away, reaching for a T-shirt from the chair at the small wall-anchored desk. "You know as well as I do that I'd never let you do that."

"Then we share the bed," Frankie said before she could think better of it. "We've done it before, and it's only for one night."

Owen scratched the side of his head. "Are you sure? I might snore."

"So might I."

He let out a laugh. "I'm sure you haven't snored a night in your life. And those cute little sighs you used to let out don't count."

Her eyebrows rose at the unexpected throwback.

He looked away. "Um, I'm going to run down for those pillows." Was he blushing? "Why don't you... pick a side." He gestured to the bed, and before she knew it, he was out the door.

A sleepover with Owen. Now there was something she'd never thought she'd say. She'd never fully stayed the night with him in high school, but they had watched movies in his room, and she'd dozed off against his shoulder.

There would be no touching tonight though. This was a sleeping arrangement borne out of necessity, and all hands would be above the covers. Maybe she'd even tuck a pillow between them for good measure, so he didn't think she'd had ulterior motives for suggesting they share the bed.

Before she could decide, he was back, carrying two pillows in his arms.

She cleared her throat, then got in on the left side of the bed, avoiding looking at him as she settled underneath the covers. She'd brought a book that she'd stopped and started repeatedly over the past month to the point that she barely knew what it was about, so she pulled that out of her bag to distract herself with something while he got ready.

The bed bounced when he climbed in, forcing her attention. They exchanged a tight smile, but then she returned to her pages, where words swam together, making no sense at all. She hadn't spent the night with anyone since Zach, and the awareness of Owen right there next to her had her on high alert. The smallest movement of his hand shifting its grip on his phone sent a waft of his masculine scent her way, and the warmth from him transferred through the sheets even though she'd tucked the cover down in a V between them.

She flipped the page to give the appearance of reading.

It was normal to be this distracted by the situation. He'd been her first kiss. There were memories. At one point, they'd talked about a future together. He'd been a year ahead of her, but she'd planned to follow as soon as she graduated. They'd get an apartment together in Boston, see more of the world. And then a few months into her senior year, he'd sent her that letter and they were over. Just like that. He'd realized they were too different. That he wanted his freedom now that he was in college. She should make her own plans. He'd wanted a clean break, no contact, and she'd respected that. With him right next to her now, it seemed to have happened both in another lifetime and not that long ago all at once.

She turned another page.

"Okay, so this is a little weird, right?" Owen said out of the blue, cutting off her thoughts.

Frankie glanced at him. "So weird. I can still take the floor."

"No way." He pressed his lips together, pausing. "Weird doesn't have to mean bad. I'm not sorry you're here."

Her heart somersaulted. "No?"

His gaze met hers. "No."

She nodded, eyes returning to her book. Was it about an abandoned mansion? A florist? A florist finding an abandoned mansion?

"I'm setting my alarm for eight," Owen said, reaching over to turn his light out. "Is that okay with you?"

"A-okay." Frankie shot him a smile while internally scolding her chipper tone. Why were normal words suddenly failing her? "Goodnight," she said, turning off her own light.

"Sleep tight," he responded.

And she intended to. So tight on her own side of the bed, not moving a muscle.

Yellow light danced across Frankie's eyelids somewhere between sleep and wakefulness the next morning. There was a gap in the curtains, and a stream of sunbeams fell straight across her face, calling her out of the warm cocoon where dreamless hours had turned the leaf on a new day. She lay curled up on her side with her hands tucked under her chin and the covers wrapped tightly across her shoulder.

No, not the covers. Something heavier.

Consciousness fought its way to the surface, and she blinked her eyes open, squinting as sleep fully fell away. Her even breathing was echoed by that of another—Owen's heartbeats only millimeters away from where her forehead was resting against his chest. It was his arm cradling her, not the sheets. Sometime during the night, they must have both turned toward the other and ended up in this embrace, where his larger body nestled hers, the two of them fitting perfectly together.

This very comfortable, comforting embrace.

Frankie listened to his breathing, assuring herself that he was still asleep, while she contemplated what to do. She could move and risk waking him, or she could stay and close her eyes again, allowing the familiarity of his warm skin to lull her back to sleep until the alarm went off.

No sooner had the thought crossed her mind than it did just that, and Owen stirred awake. She was so close to him that she could feel alertness coursing through his muscles as he came to, and she had just enough time to regret the loss of this small carved-out piece of stillness before he moved.

She feigned sleep, wanting to avoid the awkwardness that was sure to follow as long as possible. A brushing noise against the pillow somewhere above her head suggested he'd turned his face to the ceiling, and she waited and waited for realization to land. He'd jump away from her, maybe let out a small curse to scold himself. It would be so Owen.

What she wasn't prepared for was the feeling of gentle lips pressing against the crown of her head before he carefully extracted himself from her, and how unwelcome the cooler air was that swept in to take his place.

"Frankie," he said gently. "Time to wake up."

"Hmm?" She rolled over onto her back in what she hoped was a convincing display of regaining consciousness. "Already?" She blinked up at him, stretching her arms above her head.

"Like a cat," he said, smiling down at her. He rubbed a hand over his face, then turned away from her to peer behind the curtain. "Looks sunnier today. Did you sleep okay?"

It was an innocent question, but because she knew what she knew, its answer held more importance. "Yeah, great," she said. "You?"

"Better than I have in a long time."

He disappeared into the bathroom, leaving her to sit with those words on her own. They probably didn't mean anything. They'd accidentally slept a little closer than they'd intended, but everything had been completely chaste. Even that little kiss at the end. Maybe it was like a thank you for the good night's sleep he'd had.

"All yours," he said, coming back out. "Are you showering?"

Frankie swung her legs over the side of the bed and yawned. What if she told him she'd liked waking up in his arms? The situation felt so oddly domestic that she could almost fool herself into thinking they were a couple again. After all these years.

"I probably should," she said. "Do we have time?"

"Oh yeah. I can head out for coffee and something to eat while you do your thing if you want."

They decided that was the best course of action. City hall would open at nine, and Owen's plan would put them there on time.

The shower was restorative, allowing purpose and common sense back into the nooks and crannies of Frankie's mind that had been muddled by skin-to-skin contact and nostalgia. By the time they'd had breakfast and were ready to check out, she had all but forgotten the whole incident, and that was for the best, she told herself. While she was enjoying Owen's company, she had too much else going on in her life to entertain whatever possibility was simmering beneath the surface where he was concerned, and she was certain he felt the same way.

# TWENTY-THREE

## FRANKIE

Now

The receptionist at city hall looked older than the building itself, but she was friendly and helpful when she directed them to their records department, which was one man in a small office down the hallway.

"Greg and Stella-Jane Milne," he said, typing something on his computer.

"And a child," Frankie added.

He glanced at her above his horn-rimmed glasses. "Property records wouldn't have children listed." He returned to the screen. "Like I thought. We've had some records from the eighties digitized, but since you think they might have lived here before that, I'm going to have to check the basement. It might take a little while."

"We have time," Owen said.

"You know what you could do in the meantime is ask the sheriff. He's down the street, three-minute-walk tops. He's been here since 1982, so if they lived here then, he'll know."

Frankie and Owen looked at each other and exchanged a nod.

"We'll do that," Frankie said. "Thank you."

"Let Lucy know when you're back, and I'll come get you when I'm done with my search." He stood, offering a smile showing teeth beset by age and bad habits, and indicated the door. "I don't often have reason to visit the stacks," he mused. "Here's hoping I find what you're looking for."

Indeed, Frankie thought, as she followed Owen back outside.

They strolled side by side down the street in the direction that had been pointed out to them.

"What do you think it's like living in a place like this?" Frankie asked.

Owen looked around. "It's probably different now than it was forty, fifty years ago. Most everyone has fled to the cities and bigger towns now, and that doesn't leave much community. It's almost a little dystopian. It would be difficult to be hopeful about the future here."

Frankie nodded. "Yeah, it must have been different then or why would they have settled here?" Neither family was from Ferrisville originally, and according to the sparse information they'd gleaned, both sets of parents had lived further south their whole lives.

"This is it," Owen pointed to the "SHERIFF" sign above the door.

The building was no bigger than the ramblers they'd passed yesterday, but it was better maintained, and the air inside was nice and cool.

"We're hoping to see the sheriff," Owen said to the man behind the front desk. He was in uniform and sported a goatee and moustache that were impeccably maintained.

"Who can I say is calling?" the officer asked, his eyes sliding to Frankie.

She took a step forward. "We were told he might have information about people who lived here in the eighties. I'm looking for my parents."

He cocked an eyebrow. "You adopted or something?"

"No, just interested in their roots."

He stared them down for a few more seconds, and then he spun his chair around. "Boss!" he called. "Visitors." He pointed to a couple of chairs along the wall. "You can wait over there if you like. He'll be right with you."

The sheriff was an imposing man in his upper sixties with a red-speckled nose and white eyebrows that had a life of their own. He invited them back to his office, then sat down, steepling his fingers together before asking them how he could help. Frankie explained that the man at city hall was looking through records for them, but that he'd said the sheriff knew everyone who'd set foot here in the past forty years or so, which made him the man to ask. She spread it on thickly, like she knew Estelle would have done in the spirit of catching more flies with honey.

"And what were your folks' names?" the sheriff asked, riffling through the piles of papers on his desk for a notebook and pencil.

"Milne," Frankie said. "Greg and Stella-Jane."

His head shot up. "You're Stella's girl?"

Frankie glanced at Owen, hope flaring inside her. "You knew her?"

The sheriff leaned back in his chair, his hands resting on his belly and the metal joint squeaking under his weight. "Ha! Everyone in the county knew Stella—she made damn sure of that. The mouth on that girl. Hoo-wee."

Owen straightened next to Frankie. "I'm sure I don't have to remind you that that's my friend's mother you're talking about."

Shrewd eyes peered at Owen above round cheeks. "Oh

now, I don't mean anything untoward. She was a spitfire, that's all. Great singer. Her husband on the other hand..."

"What about Greg?" Frankie asked. "I have no memories of him, so anything you can tell me..."

The sheriff considered her request, but then he cocked his head toward a door at the far end of the room. "Well, he was a frequent guest in our holding cells, I can tell you that much. House painter I believe but liked his booze a little too much." He hollered out the door, "Tom, can you check on a file for me? Name of Greg Milne."

"Sure, boss," came from the front room.

"It'll be just a minute," the sheriff told Frankie and Owen. "Those old records are still in paper form."

Frankie was about to ask him to expand on what he'd just said about her dad when Owen leaned forward.

"What about a child?" he asked.

"What about it?" the sheriff asked.

"Did they have one?"

"Well, she's sitting right there, ain't she?" He looked at Owen as if he was slow.

"He means while they lived here," Frankie said. "I was born later."

The sheriff's bushy eyebrows flew up. "Oh. Yes, I thought you looked on the young side to be her."

Goosebumps rose along Frankie's arms. "Her? They had a daughter?" She had a sister? A lump lodged itself in Frankie's throat.

"A quiet little thing from what I recall. But I suppose with those two as parents, there was commotion enough to go around."

"Do you—" Frankie cut herself off, her voice too brittle to finish, but then Owen's hand came to rest against her back. She looked at him, taking strength from his encouraging nod. "Do you remember her name?"

"You don't know?" The sheriff's brow furrowed.

"It's a long story," Owen supplied.

"Well, let's see..." The sheriff's eyes went to the ceiling as if the answer could be found written somewhere up there. His lips pursed one way then the other. "It might come to me," he said finally, "but seeing as we only overlapped a few years before they moved and it was long ago, I don't rightly know."

"What about schools in the area?" Frankie asked. There must be records of her sister somewhere.

"It's been closed since the late nineties, so I doubt it. The kids are bussed out nowadays. Sorry. Ah, here's Tom now."

The officer strode into the room and handed the sheriff a folder before making himself scarce again.

Frankie closed her eyes briefly and rubbed a finger across her brow, trying to force one life-altering fact aside to make room for another. She'd come back to her sister later, she vowed.

"Milne, Greg," the sheriff read on the label before flipping the beige cover open and sifting through the first few pages in the stack. "That's right, the blue Escort..." He continued reading, then pushed the file toward Frankie on the desk. "Public intoxication, disorderly conduct, DUIs, misdemeanor assault, criminal mischief, reckless driving, and the list goes on. If I remember correctly, he only did a couple of shorter stints in county jail though, so I'd say he got lucky considering his accomplishments."

Frankie rested her hands on the folder, her mind reeling at his words. Her father had been a criminal?

"It is sad," the sheriff continued. "Someone young like that already taken by the disease. I had a cousin went the same way."

"So it was due to drinking?" Owen asked at Frankie's side, at the same time flexing his hand against her back as if wanting to settle her. "Making poor decisions?"

Frankie pulled the folder into her lap and opened it, but much of the contents was sterile forms and checked boxes with only occasional notes. *Kept overnight. Charges? Medic called.* She read Owen's intent between the lines. She'd been too quick to label Greg. He hadn't been a bad person—he'd been an addict making bad choices—something that must be resonating with Owen in light of what he'd told her about his own past.

The sheriff nodded. "The devil's juice, my mother used to say. Certainly true for a fair share of people around here."

Frankie handed the folder back. The last records of arrest in Greg's file were from December 1984, and beyond that, she didn't need to read more. "What about Este—I mean Stella? Did she also have problems like these?"

"Oh no. She was just feisty. Opinionated." He let out an amused huff. "Did you know she scolded the mayor in front of God and everyone on Founding Day the year I moved here for 'a lackluster celebration'? She'd rallied a fair few people with her too and got some set against her. It caused quite the ruckus."

*Feisty* wasn't a word Frankie would have used about Estelle, but perhaps her mom hadn't yet learned about flies and honey at that point. Still, it wasn't hard to picture her gaining followers in whatever task she set herself. But that begged the question...

"Would you say she made enemies along the way?"

"Enemies?" The sheriff huffed. "I don't know about that. The mayor's wife wasn't happy about it of course, and there might have been a certain sense of relief when they moved, but that's it. Why do you ask?"

Because Estelle had needed forgiveness for something? Because she'd coated herself in lies? Because Orla thought it possible the past had caught up to her.

"No reason," she said. "It was just a thought." She turned to Owen. "Should we head back to city hall?"

They'd gotten everything they could there, so after thanking the sheriff, they took their leave.

. . .

"There you are," Lucy, the old receptionist, said when they entered the overly climate-controlled lobby at city hall. "He's ready, so head on back."

The records man lit up when he saw them, gesturing for them to sit down while he placed copies of a property deed in front of them. "Greg Milne," he said. "Looks like he bought the house from a John Milne—perhaps his father?" He aimed the question at the both of them.

"As far as I know, his dad's name was Fred," Frankie said. At least that's what the family tree Norman had put together showed. "But maybe an uncle." She turned to Owen. "That would explain why they moved here. Maybe he gave them a deal they couldn't refuse."

"A modest property," the man continued. "Just over nine hundred square feet, built in 1953."

Owen looked up from the document. "They bought it in 1978?"

"Um..." The man skimmed the information with one finger. "Yes, that's right," he confirmed. "May of 1978. And they sold it in March of 1985 at a marginal profit."

"But that means they weren't living here when my sister was born," Frankie said, disappointment making her stomach dip. "And there's no other address listed for this area. We're back to square one."

Owen gave her a sympathetic smile. "Not necessarily." He faced the man again. "There must be more information than that here, right?"

"Well..." The man pointed to the document. "On the back there you'll see a notice of late payment of property taxes the year before they moved, which would have resulted in a fine. Was the sheriff able to help you at all? He might have records of that."

"He was," Frankie said, choosing not to share Greg's sordid

relationship with law enforcement with this stranger since it wasn't necessary.

"But nothing else?" Owen pushed, and Frankie could have hugged him for understanding the need for more in her.

"Unless they were born, married, or died here, we wouldn't have such certificates in our records. I'm very sorry."

And Frankie already had the marriage certificate, so nothing new there. *Darn it.*

"We'll keep looking," Owen told her. "If this was their first home, they might have stayed with their parents until then. They would have been very young."

"Or they rented a place," Frankie argued morosely. "They could literally have been anywhere in all of Alabama and Mississippi, if not even farther than that."

The records man was following their conversation intently, and when Frankie noticed, she stood, offering her thanks since this part wasn't for his ears.

"Let me know if you need anything else," he called after them, but Frankie already knew they wouldn't be returning. There was nothing else here for them.

"We know where their families were from," Owen said once they were back outside where the sun was blazing down on the worn sidewalk. "We can start there. And we have an address in Jackson where we know you were born, so it's at least likely that's where they went after leaving here."

"Maybe." Frankie fought the temptation to sit down on the curb and mope. She didn't know what she'd expected—a comprehensive history of Estelle's and Greg's marriage, complete with listed reasons why Estelle had become a liar years later, and a written account of her older sister's whereabouts wrapped up in a bow? Could a person be more naïve?

"Hey." Owen nudged her shoulder. "Don't give up. We did learn some things. Let's go grab lunch, and we can decide what to do next. I need to call Grams too and check in."

Frankie let him escort her to the car, and she listened half-heartedly while he talked to Thora, who had nothing new to report. Was this it then? A dead end? Yes, her parents had lived here, and the little she'd learned about that was enough to paint a picture of strife and turbulence that added a nuance to Estelle that Frankie had never glimpsed before. To Frankie (and Aspen Creek), Estelle had always been the very image of composure, diplomacy, and goodwill, and yet the sheriff here had told a different story. That contradiction must be relevant in some way.

But there was still no sign of the truths Frankie was seeking. Why had Estelle never told Frankie about having another daughter? Why had she claimed a different heritage than her own? Why had she changed her name? Why had she lied about the song? About the abduction and Frankie herself? About the cancer? Who needed to forgive her? How had she ended up in debt? And where was her sister now? That question more than any other bored into her like a vicious thorn.

"You're not ready to go home yet, are you?" Owen asked after they'd ordered burgers at the counter of the Dogwood Saloon in the middle of town.

They were one of only three parties inside, even though it was noon on a Friday, and judging by the framed prints on the wall, the spider cracks on the green pleather booth seats, and the darkened wood paneling, there hadn't been funds for upkeep in this place for a while. According to Owen, it had a decent online rating though, so Frankie would reserve judgment as far as the food was concerned.

"No," she said, folding and unfolding the napkin in front of her.

"Jackson is less than four hours away. We could be there before city hall closes."

She looked up and saw nothing but sincerity in his eyes. "That's still a lot of driving—especially to get back home."

He shrugged. "I don't mind. We can take turns."

Frankie hedged as if she hadn't already decided. "And if there's nothing there? Then what?" she asked.

"Then you'll find another rock to turn over. Because that's what you do." He took a sip from his sweating water glass. "But at least you'd know."

"Kayla won't be happy," Frankie said.

"It's the weekend. And maybe if she knew what we're doing here, she'd understand." He raised an eyebrow.

"You noticed I didn't tell her yesterday?" Frankie asked.

"I guess it surprised me. But maybe it shouldn't have. I'm not close with anyone I knew back then."

"I've talked to her more the past two weeks than in a long time. But this...." Frankie swung her hand out. "It's... I don't know... embarrassing. That Estelle lied, that I didn't know."

"No one would hold it against you."

"Mom's reputation would never recover. I keep hoping to find an explanation before I tell anyone. Something to make it more... palatable."

Owen nodded. "Then you will. You can do anything you set your mind to."

His calm confidence in her ability to take action boosted her. She wasn't used to it. Estelle had always been so much more capable than her, or at least that's how it had felt.

"I'm going to run to the washroom before we head out." He jumped off his seat. "Be right back."

She finished her burger deep in thought until Owen called her name from the corner where the restrooms were situated. He was bubbling with some kind of pent-up excitement, so she hurried over. "What's going on?"

"Found something. Come look."

She followed him into a darker alcove where the walls were lined with pictures of smiling people having a good time.

"Looks like the Dogwood Saloon was pretty popular at one

point," he said. "And check this out." He led her to the far wall and pointed to a framed photograph. "That's your mom, right?"

Frankie stepped closer. In the picture, the bar looked more or less the same, but on a stool in one corner of the room sat Estelle, her guitar slung around her narrow torso, her mouth slightly open in song. Her hair was lighter, bleached perhaps, and her bangs poufy beyond reason as had been the style then. She looked so young—much younger than Frankie now. *Stella-Jane*. Married to Greg, a man with habits that no doubt made life a challenge for everyone involved, mother of a little girl whose fate Frankie had yet to learn, a star in the making.

Frankie's eyes stung. This was real. All the facts they'd learned today weren't just words on paper—Estelle had *been* here. Lived here. And that finally cemented the resolve within her. She was on the right path, and she wouldn't stop until she'd picked apart every clue in her quest to untangle the life of this woman before her, no matter where that would lead her.

# TWENTY-FOUR

## ESTELLE

Then

That holiday season was the most fun Estelle had had in longer than she could remember. It was hard work—she played several nights a week in different venues in and around Memphis and waited tables at a café during the day—but without having to worry about where to go and who to butter up for a gig, her mind blossomed with words and music.

On Christmas Eve, Ray's stately Greek Revival-style home was decked in red, green, and gold from top to bottom, with garlands weaving around the banisters, a ten-foot tree in the foyer, and a smaller one in the sprawling living room. The only thing missing from the idyllic Christmas card was a snow-covered lawn beyond the row of windows facing a deck strung with lights.

Guests were milling everywhere, with the large punch bowl being the most popular spot to congregate.

"Homemade sangria," Estelle heard someone say as she passed it. She'd have to try a glass of that later, but first she wanted to find Ray to show him the dress she'd bought for the occasion.

Darla had been right; shopping was a thrill when you didn't have to worry about the price tag. The lace-trimmed blouses and fringy dresses weren't necessarily her style, but with a little willpower, she could convince herself otherwise. Whoever she needed to be, she'd be, if that's what it took. She deserved more than what life had given her so far, and it was finally within reach. She'd saved this calf-length, wine-red wrap dress with flattering draping over the hips for tonight, and since Ray had shown approval for her stage selections, she couldn't wait to see his reaction to this.

She found him in the kitchen preoccupied with his pager, which must have gone off again. She couldn't imagine ever being tethered to a device like that where people could demand her attention all day long. She cleared her throat as she approached, and to his credit, he put the contraption away and turned.

"Wow." He touched a finger to his lips and nodded, eyes roaming over her. Then he held out a hand to her, which she took, and guided her in a slow twirl. "Gorgeous," was his verdict.

"Thank you." She held his gaze and forced her chin high.

She'd been staying with him for a month now, but so far, he'd made no move. Sure, they'd flirted some, and he was attentive as ever to her needs as a house guest, but he was a hard man to read. There were times when she caught him looking her way with a glint in his eye that spoke of something more carnal than how they were with each other outwardly, but other times he circled around Darla like she was the hub that anchored his existence. Estelle simply couldn't tell, but she hoped that might change tonight. If he had more to offer, she would willingly accept. She was a woman of flesh and blood after all.

"Are you having fun?" he asked.

"The most fun."

"Good." He picked up a glass of wine from the counter. "Talk to people. Make new friends. Tonight we party, but tomorrow we're going to talk business. I think there's still a lot we can do together."

An electric thrill zapped up her spine. "Sounds good to me."

"Off to mingle." He backed away, raising the glass, and then he was gone.

The timing was right for them too, Estelle thought. After the new year, she'd finally be free of Greg. She'd filed the divorce petition a few weeks back, listing Ray's number as a way to reach her. He'd been more than willing to help when Estelle had described the situation she'd escaped, and they were expecting confirmation any day now from the attorney Ray had found her that Greg had been served. She had no reason to think the court wouldn't grant the divorce. Everyone and their mother back home knew of his habitual drunkenness.

Unless he'd cleaned up with her gone of course. Out of necessity.

An unfamiliar pang struck her between the ribs at the thought of the place she'd once called home, followed by a tightness of the throat, but she reached for the open wine bottle on the island and had a gulp from it and then another, the bold warmth of the alcohol blurring the memories. Yes, she'd made some hard decisions down in Mississippi, but success didn't come without sacrifice. This wasn't the time for regrets.

She adjusted the belt on her dress and set her sights on the sangria.

Estelle woke with a start to unfiltered sunlight assaulting her retinas. She was still wearing her Christmas dress, and one shoe clung to the toes of the foot that was hanging off her bed. She covered her eyes with one arm and huffed out a breath that smelled so vile she would have dodged it had her head been bolted on right.

As it was, she no longer had a head. A heavy anvil had replaced it, and several sledgehammers were currently attempting to beat it to a pulp.

"I'm never having sangria again," she mumbled to herself.

"It's the fruit," a voice said somewhere in the room.

Estelle jerked upright with a yelp but lay back down just as quickly when the room spun and, with it, Darla, who was seated in a chair by the window.

"You scared me," Estelle said. "What are you doing here?"

Darla got up and approached with a bottle of water in her hand. "Making sure you're alive and inviting you to brunch. You were impressively out of it when we brought you up here last night. Someone should have warned you not to eat the fruit in the punch. It hoards the alcohol."

Oh no. Had she made a fool of herself in front of all those people? She wasn't sure if she wanted an answer to that question or not. "What time is it?" she asked.

"Eleven thirty. Christmas Day."

Estelle made a second slower attempt at sitting up, this time managing so long as she supported her forehead. "And you're still here?"

"I stay over sometimes," Darla said as if it was the most natural thing in the world. "And we're meeting Ray's parents at my parents' house later."

Estelle wanted to ask if she'd slept in the guest room, but it was too soon into wakefulness to calibrate her question to the right level of indifference. Instead, she asked for ibuprofen and for Darla to open the window to let in some cool air.

"You'll feel better once you get some food in your stomach," Darla said. "The casserole will be ready in thirty, so you have time for a shower."

She made to leave, but Estelle stopped her. "Did I... Who helped me up here?"

"Don't worry. You were fine, and I enlisted two of Ray's friends' wives when I noticed. Us girls have got to look out for each other, right? See you in a bit."

Estelle watched her leave. "See ya," she said, closing her eyes as a wave of affection for the other woman swept over her. Everything was fine. Too much to drink, that was all. She wouldn't do that again.

After cleaning herself up and changing, she joined Darla and Ray in the breakfast nook by the bay window facing the backyard. Jolly tinsel had been hung to frame the windows, and the room smelled of fir tree and bacon.

"There she is," Ray said, sitting down at the table with a loaded plate. "You disappeared last night. I was looking for you when the dancing started."

Estelle glanced at Darla, whose face remained neutral. "I was tired and, um... thought it best to protect my voice. It was a fantastic party though. Thanks for having me."

"Of course."

"For you." Darla set a mug of coffee and a plate in front of Estelle too.

Her stomach roiled once, but then settled, and after a few bites of a delicious egg casserole, she started to feel steadier.

"Speaking of your voice," Ray said after a while, producing an envelope from somewhere nearby like a magician. "This is for you. A proposal that I hope doubles as a gift. Merry Christmas."

Estelle took it. "For me?"

Ray exchanged a knowing look with Darla, who nodded encouragement his way. "I have some funds that I'd like to invest in your career going forward, if that's something you'd be interested in."

Estelle looked between them. "Funds?"

"Essentially, we'd keep doing what we've been doing but scaling up."

"Scaling up?"

"Oh, hon, just open it." Darla gestured to the envelope.

Estelle did, pulling out a ticket and a contract.

"What he means is, he'd be managing your career," Darla explained. "He can provide training, book you studio time and venues, and get your name out there to make sure the right people pay attention. You wouldn't just be playing around here; you can go further—even to Nashville if you're lucky."

"Luck has nothing to do with it," Ray added. "It's all talent, and you've got it in spades."

"What's this?" Estelle held up the ticket.

"It's for a cruise, but the ticket is mostly for show. If we're going to do this, you need a different kind of stamina and focus than you've been used to, so I talked to a buddy of mine about getting you a gig for a month or two onboard his ship. Daily shows, lots of time to write. Covers will only get you so far. You'll need a full set of your own material for what I have in mind."

"You want me to go on a ship for two months?" To leave Memphis. Leave him and Darla to their own devices. She knew the offer was sound. She wanted what he was describing. But also...

Ray tipped his head to Estelle. "What do you say? Are you interested?"

No, her head was still foggy. She shouldn't be hesitating. Whatever it took—that was the deal. Whatever he asked of her in the name of her career, no venue too small or odd or far away, no hours too long. This meant no more sleeping in the car. No more waitressing. She'd be a real artist. A name. Someone people admired.

With a whoosh of energy, all hesitation left her. "You know

I am," she said, knowing she'd let nothing and no one come between her and this dream he'd just presented her.

"Fantastic." The phone rang just as Ray reached for a beignet from a plate Darla had put out. "Give me a minute. It might be the office."

"On Christmas?" Darla asked, but Ray had already disappeared into the kitchen.

"No rest for the wicked," Estelle said, sipping her coffee without tasting it in her current elated state of mind.

Before Darla could respond, however, Ray reappeared in the doorway to the kitchen. "It's for you," he told Estelle. "Mr. Stringer."

Estelle frowned. That was the attorney. But surely he hadn't served Greg on Christmas Day.

"Okay," she said, joining him.

"You can take it there." Ray gestured to a wall-mounted phone by the fridge. "Want me to stay?"

She nodded before picking up the receiver. "Hello, this is Mrs. Milne." The formality tasted oddly on her tongue, but perhaps that was the hangover.

"Thank goodness," the attorney said. "I've been trying to reach you, but I must have had the number jotted down wrong."

"Why? What's going on. Is there a problem with the papers?" Estelle turned where she stood, the spiral cord tangling around her.

"Well, sort of," the attorney said. "And I do realize it's Christmas and everything, but this couldn't wait."

"Okay..." Estelle frowned. "So are the papers served or not?"

"No." The man sniffled. "I would have called sooner, but as I said..."

"You had the wrong number," Estelle filled in. "I understand."

Ray tapped the counter to get her attention and mimed a question about what was going on.

Estelle covered the receiver with one hand. "Not sure."

He took a step closer. "Want me to talk to him?"

Estelle shook her head. "Mr. Stringer?"

"Yes." The word was followed by a sigh.

She rolled her eyes, inviting Ray to share her frustration. "I'd like to get back to my holiday lunch here, so how can I help you?"

"Well, ma'am." He huffed again. "I did try to serve Mr. Milne the papers this past week, but I couldn't find him."

"The address is on the documents."

"Yes, that's not it." Another pause.

Raymond gestured for Estelle to give him the phone, and this time, she did.

"Stringer," he said. "Ray here. What's going on? We're in the middle of—" He fell silent, the other man clearly having found his voice again. "Uh-huh," Ray said. "When? Mm-hmm. I understand."

"What?" Estelle asked, but Ray held up a finger to make her wait.

"Yes. Yes. Yeah, I'll let her know. Okay. I'll talk to you soon."

They hung up.

"What?" Estelle demanded. "What's going on?"

Ray tipped his head back briefly, then leveled his gaze on her. "He found out a few days ago," he said. "Apparently, Greg is dead. I'm so sorry."

Estelle staggered back a step. "What?"

"Stringer's going to find out more details and get back to me."

"Dead?" All the heat drained out of her arms, pooling like a liquid weight on the floor around her and threatening to pull her down. "No, that can't be. He's supposed to..."

Ray pulled her into his arms, pressing her close to his chest.

"What's going on?" Darla asked from the doorway.

Somewhere above Estelle's head, Ray answered her, explaining what had happened.

Two seconds later, another set of arms crushed Estelle from behind. "Oh, hon."

They led her back to the table, probably expecting tears, but Estelle's eyes stayed dry and unseeing. She'd mourned the man Greg had once been for a long time, and she'd already left him in the past, so while part of her wanted to keep protesting, to tell them they'd got it wrong, deep in her heart, she knew that wasn't the case. This was exactly the sort of inconvenience Greg had laid at her feet untold times before.

And all Estelle could think was that she wouldn't let this change a thing. No matter what.

# TWENTY-FIVE

## FRANKIE

Now

It was midday on Sunday when they finally returned to Aspen Creek. Other than a death certificate for Greg that stated he'd died from cirrhotic cardiomyopathy—a direct result of his drinking—Jackson had been a bust, but like Owen had pointed out, Frankie couldn't have *not* gone.

They'd had no luck at either city hall or the sheriff's office, both of which required electronic requests for records being submitted with a wait of up to two weeks. The school district Frankie's sister might have attended flat out refused to share information, stating it was protected by privacy laws, but considering Estelle had homeschooled Frankie her first few grades, it was perhaps fair to assume she'd done that with her oldest daughter too. That's to say, if Frankie's sister had even been with them through the Jackson move. Anything was possible at this point, and Jackson was too big a city to try finding someone who might have known the Milne family back in the eighties. It would have been the definition of looking for the proverbial needle.

Yesterday, they'd gone to see the trailer park that Estelle and Greg had called home, but like their house in Ferrisville, it was long gone, replaced by a commerce center at some point in the past twenty years. After that, they'd driven half the way home and spent the night at a hotel outside Atlanta. Frankie hadn't slept well.

"Are you awake?" Owen asked from the driver's seat as they approached Estelle's house.

Frankie had only dozed the first hour in the car, but the weight of information still uncovered had marred her desire for conversation. Without knowing what had happened to her sister, she couldn't help but feel like she'd left something behind in Mississippi, but what choice did she have? Until she found another piece of the puzzle, like it or not, she was needed here.

"Yeah," she said, adding with honesty only he brought out in her, "I think I'm just sad. I don't know how I'm going to go back to work tomorrow as if everything is fine."

He pulled into the driveway and turned her way. "We won't give up. We'll submit those requests for records and hope that gives us new leads. We'll find out what happened to your sister. I'll ask Grams to activate her full agent network." He tried for a smile, but when she didn't respond, it faltered. "Come on—I'll grab your bag. What you need is some solid sleep in your own bed tonight." He got out of the car, and before she'd unbuckled, he'd opened her door, stepping back so she could get out.

He was right. She was tired and mentally drained, and perhaps tomorrow things would look better.

She grabbed the mail, then followed him as they rounded the house to the backyard. "Thank you," she said. "For everything. For caring about this. I know I seem a little unhinged, but..."

"Not at all." He stopped outside her tiny home, something both familiar and new flashing through the shadows beneath his brow. "I'm glad I came along," he said. "It's been... good."

Frogs and crickets sang about summer in the thicket behind the house even though it was still only early May. Tomorrow she'd be back at the school, back to students, colleagues, parents, bills, cold calls, performances, marketing, the looming piano. To expectations and demands. She didn't want to. If she could turn back time to Friday morning, and that feeling of safety and hope that had simmered through her at waking up accidentally wrapped in him with the day ahead filled with possibility, she would.

As if he had the ability to banish the disappointment she'd returned with, she let herself into his space and wrapped her arms around him. He followed her lead, pulling her closer and resting his cheek against her head.

"I'm glad you came too," she said, inhaling deeply to soothe that still-flailing part inside her. Then she let him go and unlocked the door. "Talk tomorrow?"

He nodded. "You know where to find me."

After unpacking and showering, Frankie texted Kayla to let her know she was back, and then she opened her work email to see what she'd missed. Matt had also texted to check in, but she put off responding. She'd known him for so long that it felt better to say nothing than to lie.

While the page loaded, she sifted through the stack of mail she'd brought in. There were a few bills, some ads, and a couple of straggling condolence cards, but one envelope in particular caught Frankie's eye. It was from the Register of Deeds office, and she tore it open immediately, hoping it would be what she'd been waiting for these past few weeks—the death certificate that would allow her access to Estelle's private account.

"Finally," she mumbled as she scanned the page.

What time would the bank open tomorrow? Eight? Nine? No, she'd have to go to the school first or she'd never hear the end of it. She'd go at lunch, she decided, and she'd bring her birth certificate too to prove her identity beyond a mere driver's license. She wasn't about to give the bank another reason to turn her away. If Starview's struggles had been the result of any kind of financial duplicity on Estelle's part, Frankie would soon know.

The thought made her feel better, but the relief was short-lived as the email at the top of her inbox was from Mrs. Nolan reminding her that the interview with Orla would take place at Estelle's house Tuesday at noon, and did she need help getting things in order?

*I'd be happy to send my cleaning lady over, and how about some fresh flowers?* she wrote.

Frankie started typing a declining response, Estelle's voice ringing in her head. They'd always cleaned the house together every Saturday morning like clockwork because "caring for your things is good for the soul."

*What about caring for your daughters, Mom?* Frankie thought, a pang of some serrated emotion cutting deep without warning. It surprised her, and she blinked it away before it could take hold, but she also erased the message and started over, this time responding in the affirmative and with gratitude. It would free up time she already didn't have. Maybe Lavignes didn't ask for help, but they sure as hell could accept it when offered.

If Frankie had worried that the hours leading up to Monday noon would drag on, she was woefully mistaken. Two days she'd been gone from work, and yet the stack of messages left on her desk added up to double digits. The moms must have directed vendors to reach out with proposals for table, chair, and tent rentals because several of the messages listed dollar amounts in Kayla's florid handwriting that were well above what Frankie wanted to spend.

Hope surged at two messages from potential sponsors she'd

contacted last week though, so she returned those first. One was a florist in Cornelius whose daughter had been a Starview student several years ago, and she wanted to donate a few arrangements for the occasion as well as two gift certificates for classes she offered in her shop to be included in the auction. The other was from the owner of a successful sporting goods chain who'd asked Estelle out on several occasions in the past. Frankie wasn't sure what he might want to contribute, so she'd left her request open ended.

She called the number Kayla had written down, and he answered in the middle of a booming laugh.

"Whoo, sorry about that," he said. "This is Cal. What can I do you for?"

"Frankie Lavigne returning your call," Frankie said.

Cal hushed someone on his end, and when he returned, some of the joyfulness in his voice was gone. "Oh Frankie, Frankie. What a blow to us all. Sorry I missed your call last week."

"No worries," Frankie said, wishing she could fast forward through the commiserating part of the call. "Glad I got hold of you now."

"As am I. It's a wonderful thing you're doing, and I absolutely want to be a part of it."

Frankie's spirits lifted. "Oh yeah? That's great. Did you have something particular in mind? Sponsoring a basket perhaps? A gift card to your stores?"

"Oh, I think I can do you one better," Cal said, and Frankie could practically hear him rubbing his palms together. "I'll give you a check for ten thousand dollars, and in exchange, you put our logo in your print materials..."

Frankie's stomach went into freefall. That was by far the most generous donation they'd received so far, and she was about to tell him as much when he continued. "And play the exit tune at my son's wedding this weekend. I'm thinking a gorgeous piano version of 'Evermore and Always.' The cellist we'd booked broke her wrist biking of all things. What do you say?"

Frankie gripped the phone tighter. She must have misunderstood. He wanted *someone* to provide the music, not her specifically. "I'm sure we have a couple of students who'd be available," she said.

"No, no. It has to be you, Frankie. Everyone we know will be there, and as Estelle's daughter, you're a name now. It will lend the event a certain something extra—you playing one of her songs."

Cold sweat broke out at Frankie's temples. Of all the things...

So far, the few notes she'd managed to play to help one of her students had provided nothing but false hope. No matter how she tried at home, her hands still wouldn't cooperate, which meant if she said yes to Cal, she might very well make a fool of herself.

On the other hand, if she told him no, they'd lose all that money, and it was a big check to turn down. Maybe too big for there to be a real choice. Her ability to play could return in the next few days, and if it didn't, wasn't that future Frankie's problem? Today's Frankie had an event to plan, students to teach, an interview to prep for, and, more immediately, a bank appointment to get to that may or may not reveal the woman Cal so adored embezzling school funds and who knew what else.

"You have yourself a deal," Frankie said, forcing conviction into her voice.

*That's right. Fake it until you make it,* Estelle said in her head, and Frankie suppressed the urge to swat the sentiment away like an annoying fly.

What if she'd told him the truth instead, she thought as soon as she'd hung up. That her fingers hadn't cooperated since Estelle's death. Maybe he would have understood and chosen to support her and the school anyway because he was a decent man. Had Estelle thought about that?

*No, not Estelle.* Frankie's eyes swept across the motivational posters on the walls, the shelves stuffed full of music, artwork from former students. Had *Frankie* thought about that? Wasn't faking it assuming the worst of people? Was that who she wanted to be?

"There you are." Kayla strode into the room unaware of Frankie's inner conflict and sat down in the chair across from her. "How was the trip?"

Frankie forced all thoughts of Cal out of her mind. What was done was done, and they did need that money. "Not as enlightening as I'd hoped."

"Aw, that's too bad," her friend said. "But you're back now, right, and we've got work to do." She launched into a detailed account of what she'd heard the mom committee discuss and where Frankie was needed most according to them, before relaying lesson notes about Frankie's students. "Oh, and I put the invoice from the mouse guy over there." She pointed to a pile of papers at the corner of the desk. "He thinks he got them all."

"He thinks?" Frankie reached for the invoice and balked as she spotted the amount. "Fifteen hundred dollars?"

"I called around, and he had the lowest price."

Frankie sighed. "It's fine. I'll... pawn some of Estelle's jewelry that she never wore or something."

"Right." Kayla chuckled, but it caught in her throat when Frankie didn't join her. "Wait. You're serious?"

"You know there's no money," Frankie said. "So yeah. I guess I am. Whatever it takes." She stood. "Which is why I'm heading back to the bank now. Cross all your fingers and toes that that private account isn't as empty as her other ones."

. . .

This time, she called ahead to the bank to make sure she could get in to see the same banker as last time, and he was ready for her within minutes of her arrival. He tried to make small talk as they sat down, but Frankie's objective was single-minded—get into the account and get some answers.

"I brought the death certificate as you requested," Frankie said, adding because she couldn't help herself, "Though by now her passing should be easily verifiable by a simple online search."

"That may well be the case," Bob said, "but rules are rules." He navigated to Estelle's accounts on his computer. "I'll take your ID too, and do you have a birth certificate by chance? I'd need that to establish your relationship."

With a sense of triumph, Frankie produced exactly what he'd asked for, practically seeing Estelle nodding approvingly before her mind's eye. *Lavignes come prepared.* She handed Bob the documents and sat back in her chair. Finally, she'd be able to put at least one of the many conundrums that were bothering her out of her mind.

"Hmm," he said, reading over her birth certificate before looking up. "Do you have the original of this?"

Her confidence quivered. "What do you mean? That is the original."

He turned the page over, read it again, held it up to the window, scratched his temple. "No..." he said. "There's no watermark and no embossed seal." He placed it down on the desk between them and looked something up on his computer. "And in fact, this stamp here"—he pointed to the page—"is not actually the seal of Mississippi."

"I was born in a different state?" Had she misread things? Misunderstood? Frankie pulled the paper closer so she could see, but no, the place of birth clearly said Jackson, Mississippi.

"I don't know about that," Bob said. "But I do know this isn't a real birth certificate."

# TWENTY-SIX

## ESTELLE

Then

"You're back." Darla closed the patio door behind her and joined Estelle on Ray's deck.

It was the morning after Estelle had returned from her cruise, and she was still finding her land legs after two months on board a moving vessel. Coffee was helping, as was the steady tree line on the horizon.

Darla sat down. "How was it?"

"Great."

Estelle had another sip of coffee. With Greg gone, the timing of the whole thing hadn't been ideal, but Estelle had made the most of it. She'd performed, developed her stage act, written new material, and tried to forget about anything and everything that might be going on back on the mainland. For the most part, it had worked. "What's new here?"

"Oh, not much." Darla's lips pursed around a small smile. She looked different. Softer somehow.

Ray stalked through the door dressed in a light-gray linen suit and a white shirt. "There you are." His words were directed at Estelle. "I'm setting up a meeting with Glaston Park about their summer series, and I want you there. It'll probably be next week some time, and then I'm going to have you do a jam session that following Thursday with one of the best guitar players in Tennessee. He's not performing anymore but a great person to know. Also, the Riverwide Entertainment gig is this Friday—you should plan on staying after to mingle."

"Let the woman settle in," Darla said with a smile. "Give her a chance to breathe before you bombard her with your plans." She leaned over the table and touched Estelle's arm. "I'm sure you must be exhausted."

She was, but she was also ready. This was what the weeks between New Year's and departure had been like. Gigs, meetings, sessions with other musicians she didn't know, guitar lessons (because good can be better), and everything else between the sun and moon that Ray deemed necessary for her to hone her craft. Estelle had had no idea what such an effort would require of her—she'd thought singing on stage would do it—but Ray had quickly burst that bubble. Not that she was complaining. She'd jump through any hoop, go any extra mile, ignore any inner whisper suggesting the sacrifice was too much.

Except there was that letter that had been waiting for her upon arrival last night...

Darla moved her hand, and something caught the sunlight, reflecting it into Estelle's face. Was that...? She reached for Darla's wrist, staring in disbelief at the large rock on her finger.

"You're engaged?" she asked. "That's..." She cleared her throat. "That's amazing. Congratulations."

"Yes, we're very excited." Darla gazed lovingly up at her betrothed.

That explained Darla's more serene demeanor. The hunt was over. Estelle had left, and here they were. Though perhaps the odds had always been stacked against her.

Estelle's gaze flicked from Darla to Ray, finding those

intense eyes of his locked on her face as if searching for something. Credibility? Jealousy? Disappointment? She schooled her features and reminded herself that this had always been about the music first.

"I hope you'll be very happy together," she said. Then she withdrew her hand from Darla and rinsed down that jagged pill with a mouthful of cooled coffee.

*Chin up, eyes forward.* This was nothing to be morose about. She was made of stronger stuff. And it wasn't like Ray had left her emptyhanded. In fact, considering how busy she was about to be, the way things were working out was probably the better of the two scenarios anyway. She didn't need more complicating factors, and men were always good at supplying those.

"Oh, you should play at the wedding," Darla said, lighting up further.

"We'll see," Ray said, his hesitance making Estelle's confidence plunge as if the floor had given way. But then he tipped his head with a wink. "She might be playing bigger venues by then. You never know."

Estelle let out a breath and forced lightness back into her smile, annoyed with herself for being so easily affected by his opinion. But when you'd never had someone to truly believe in you before—someone to expect success and not be surprised when it came knocking—the threat of losing it was bleak indeed.

"I'll play wherever they'll have me," she said. "You've set a date then?"

"July 28."

"Oh wow. That's soon."

Darla reached over her shoulder for Ray's hand. "We're not telling anyone, but that's the only way I'll fit into my dress. If you know what I mean."

Estelle blinked at her. They were pregnant too? A glance at Ray told her she'd come to the right conclusion, though next to

Darla's radiance, his expression held a touch of ambivalence she wasn't used to seeing in him.

"Congratulations again," she said.

His lips tightened briefly. "Thank you."

"You'll be one of my bridesmaids of course," Darla said. "And come with me shopping for the nursery."

This openness toward Estelle was another shift in Darla's personality. They were no longer rivals, Estelle realized. If they ever had been. Darla had won her prize, so now she could afford to let Estelle closer.

"Sure," Estelle said. "If I'm still here."

"Wonderful." Darla stood and placed her hand on Ray's chest. "Looks like you're off the hook, darling. Thank goodness for Stella-Jane." She made for the patio door and swept out of sight with a, "See you tonight," thrown over her shoulder.

As much as Estelle hated to admit it, engagement and pregnancy suited the other woman. Her friend? She was happy for her. For them. She told Ray as much.

He sat down and rested his elbows on his knees. "Obviously, we'll need to talk about your living arrangements in light of this."

He was close enough that she could smell his expensive cologne. Close enough for her stomach to do its instinctive dip. But it was a knee-jerk reaction, nothing more. The rules had changed.

Estelle thought of that letter in her room again. "Yes, I was already going to tell you I can't stay here. My sister has taken ill, so my niece needs to live with me for a while."

Ray retreated a few inches. "Now? And how is this the first I hear of a sister?"

Estelle ignored his question. "I'll need a bigger place. A home base where she has access to schools and whatnot."

"But you'll be touring."

"She'll be fine. She's an... independent sort. Didn't you say you have a small place in Nashville that you barely use? Maybe as a temporary solution?" If there was a way for Estelle to avoid having to watch Ray and Darla's domestic bliss unfold, she'd find it.

He stared at her a long while, then his lips curved in a smile. "Still a woman with a plan," he said, nodding. "That could work. Anything else?"

"Yes." She'd thought about this while on the boat. A new life was unfurling before her, and she wanted to meet it free of the restrictive contours of the past. "*Stella-Jane Milne* sings at hoe-downs and seedy bars, but she doesn't record hits or get her name lit up in neon. It's clunky and small-town, so it's time to change it."

Ray frowned. "Change your name?"

"It's necessary," Estelle said. "Think about all the other female stars out there."

Ray nodded, warming to the idea. "Something classy. Something with rhythm." He grabbed a napkin from the table and pulled a pen from his pocket. "What about... Cindy LaRue?" Another few scribbles. "Georgia Lovitt?"

"Estelle," Estelle said. "Estelle Lavigne. It still feels like me, like *Stella*, only more polished."

"Estelle," Ray said, and she loved how it rolled off his tongue. "That's good. It adds mystique, and I can sell that. A young, charming, eligible songstress who lives for her music. I always thought *Stella-Jane* was a solid name, but you're right—it's not alluring, and that's what we're going for. *Estelle* on the other hand... I'll be booking her at every company function, upscale restaurant, radio station, and music hall I can find."

"Then do it," Estelle said, holding his gaze. She could be alluring if stardom called for it, and that's what was now on the horizon.

She could feel it in her bones.

# TWENTY-SEVEN

## FRANKIE

Now

Frankie sputtered out something that resembled a laugh. Not a real birth certificate. What else would it be? "Sure it is."

Bob shook his head. "I'm sorry. You'll have to come back when you have the real one."

"No!" She stared at him, the word having burst from her lips propelled by the crush of yet another thwarted path. She remembered Estelle giving her this document when she'd sorted out Frankie's important papers from her own. There had been no sign of deception. She *remembered* dammit.

Bob shrugged. "I don't know what to tell you."

He was close to kicking her out, Frankie realized, pushing the implications of what she'd just learned out of her mind to focus. That tremor at her core. For all he knew, she was the one who'd forged it, and that was probably a crime, not to mention it meant the answers the account might provide would remain out of her reach. This would require another tactic.

"But you know who I am," Frankie said. "You know who Estelle was. Can't you make an exception?"

"That's not how we do work here."

"What if I have someone vouch for me?"

"I'm sorry, but—"

"Please. You don't understand." She needed to know what was in that account. Needed it more than it probably warranted, but with so few answers available to her, every possibility was high stakes.

Bob looked at her with a mix of sympathy and discomfort. "I think it would be best if you left now."

Frankie sucked in a long breath, and then she nodded. "I'll be back," she said, the words sounding more like a threat than she'd intended. But she wouldn't give up on this. Couldn't. The very idea of driving back to Aspen Creek felt like admitting defeat.

She stopped before her car in the parking lot, the sun reflecting off the windshield. There must be something else she could do. Someone who could help. Her eyes swept over the surrounding buildings. When she'd come here the first time, it had seemed so random that Estelle had decided to do her banking here and not in Aspen Creek, but Estelle had always been an intentional person. If she chose this place, she must have had a reason.

Someone could have recommended it to her, Frankie thought. Someone who'd advised her mom in business for a long time. *Ugh.* Frankie didn't want to call Uncle Ray again—he'd think she was incapable of handling her own business—but if there was a small chance he could help, she had to take it.

He answered after the second ring with his big rumbling, "Frankie, dear."

"Hi, Uncle Ray," Frankie said. "How are you?"

"Oh fine, fine." He was silent for a beat. "I hear you've been out traveling."

Matt again. Did he have to tell his dad everything? "I found my parents' marriage certificate, so I got curious where they started out. Just a little road trip."

"And did you find it?" he asked.

"Yeah, but the house was no longer there." Why did she feel like he already knew the answers to the questions he was asking. Was it just his salesmanship, a trait that came with built-in self-assurance? Or maybe he did know more than he said. She decided to test the theory. "Hey, Uncle Ray, do you know where Mom's family came from originally?"

"Sure. They were Irish, I believe."

So she hadn't lied to *him*. "I always thought they were French," she said. "But then again, I didn't know her real name was Stella-Jane Sutton either." She held her breath, waiting to see what his reaction would be.

"I always thought Estelle Lavigne suited her better," Ray said. "And it was certainly better for the stage. She was a smart woman, suggesting that change."

An artistic choice then. If Frankie was going to be generous, she could admit it had a snappier ring to it than Stella-Jane. What she still didn't understand was how she'd lived for thirty-six years and never known.

"She never told me," Frankie said. "No one did. Did she want it kept a secret?"

"I wouldn't know. It wasn't something we discussed."

Frankie pursed her lips. *How convenient.* Then another thought occurred. "When did she change it, do you know?"

"Oh, that must have been early nineties sometime. Before her career took off."

That confirmed Bob's assessment of the birth certificate as fake because on it, her mom's name was listed as Estelle Lavigne, and with the knowledge Frankie now had, that should have been Stella-Jane, and Frankie's last name should have been Milne. Which brought her back to why she'd called him in the first place.

"Speaking of names," she said. "I'm trying to access Mom's bank accounts—you know, for the auction—and I'm running into an issue because I..." She weighed her words so they'd be close to the truth without opening the can of worms falsified documents were wont to do. "Because I don't know where my birth certificate is," she said. "Do you happen to know anyone affiliated with Lake Norman Bank in Mooresville? I'm there now."

"Of course," he said immediately. "The manager is a close friend. In fact, I'm only ten minutes out. I could swing by."

Frankie closed her eyes, chin slumping to her chest. It would be so much harder to guard what came out of her mouth in person. "Oh, I wouldn't want to inconvenience you. I'm sure a phone call would suffice."

"Nonsense." A car door closed on the other end. "I've not seen Jeremiah for some time. Hang tight, Frankie dear." The call disconnected.

She let her hand drop to her side. *Great.* Now she'd have to contend with his shrewd perception while actually lying. It was bad enough when she had nothing to hide. When they were little, she and Matt had been convinced for the longest time that Ray had spies following them. How else would he have known about the contents of the cookie jar being "magically" transferred to a pillowcase that ended up in the tree house? He wasn't even home at the time. No, he wasn't a man who let anything slip him by.

Uncle Ray's Mercedes pulled up next to her eight minutes later. "Need a few strings pulled today, do we?" He grinned at her as he exited the car.

As much as she hated to admit it, she did, which made her no better than the nepotistic cronies he normally surrounded himself with. At least he knew *she* had nothing to offer in return.

"I called ahead," he said at the same time as a rotund man with jet-black hair that belied his age exited the bank.

"Raymond Clark. Will you look at that," the man said.

"Jeremiah!" Uncle Ray straightened to his very tallest as he shook the man's hand. "Good to see you, old friend."

"Who are you calling old?" Jeremiah slapped Uncle Ray on the shoulder.

They jabbed each other like that for a minute, then Uncle Ray introduced Frankie and explained she needed access to Estelle's account.

"Lovely Estelle," Jeremiah said. "Such a tragedy. My deepest condolences to you, young lady."

"Thank you," Frankie said, though her gratitude was more for them not questioning her story about her misplaced documents than for the sympathy.

"So what say you, Jerry?" Uncle Ray leveraged the full weight of his gaze on the other man. "My word still good with you? We don't need to worry about this certificate, do we?"

Jeremiah rolled back on his feet. Cocked his head. "Are the greens at Pinehurst still true and fast?"

Uncle Ray let out a deep guffaw. "Why don't I take you out there one of these days and you can see for yourself?"

Frankie wanted to sink through the concrete. This was what she'd stooped to—being an accessory to tit for tat. She reminded herself as she had many times before never to get on Uncle Ray's bad side. Someone who could pull strings like that for you could also pull them against you.

The two men wrapped up their conversation with more handshakes and shoulder slaps, then Uncle Ray turned to Frankie, wide smile still in place. "Anything else I can do for you before I head off, Frankie dear? Got places to be, but you know I'm always happy to help."

Frankie glanced at Jeremiah, who was waiting to escort her back inside. Something about being the focus of the two older men's attention like this made her feel like she'd failed herself. Like she'd somehow shown incompetence when tested. It was all in her head of course. *Lavignes are self-reliant.*

"I don't think so," she said, making sure to keep her chin up. "I really appreciate it though."

"Tell you what. You join us for dinner next time I have Matt and Kayla over and we'll call it even." He nodded once to mark it a done deal, and Frankie didn't protest. That dinner would likely never happen anyway. In Ray's world, invites and commitments like these were throwaways synonymous with goodbye.

"I'll be in touch, Jerry," he called while unlocking his car as if to make Frankie's point. "Better warm up that swing."

Jeremiah demonstrated the move. "You know I will."

Frankie couldn't help but feel a little bad for the branch manager.

Still, minutes later, she found herself in front of Bob once more. To the principled banker's credit, he didn't seem put off that she'd gone above his head as he finally accessed Estelle's private account for her.

"Okay, let's see what we've got here." He turned the monitor her way and pointed to the balance. "Fifty-three dollars and seven cents," he said.

Not any hoarded-away riches then. From the way her stomach hollowed at the low number, Frankie realized she'd held out hope this whole time that this account would fix Starview's problems. A secret stash. A nest egg for a rainy day. But no.

"Looks like that's not changed in a long time," Bob said. "The last deposit into this account was ten years ago, and it's been idle since. A shame she kept paying for it if she didn't need it." The last comment he said more to himself than Frankie.

"Can you see the activity in it before then?" Frankie asked. "Did she use it as a regular checking account?"

"I'm not sure why she would have," Bob said, clicking around on the page. "She had that other checking account you already saw."

"Maybe she forgot she had this one too?"

"Hmm..." Bob opened a page with a list of transactions and scrolled down farther and farther on the page. "No," he said. "It's odd because there are exactly twelve deposits per year into this account from her other checking account—one per month—and one payment totaling all of those funds to the same recipient once a year on October 28 going back... well as far as I can see."

Frankie jerked as if someone had slapped her. "October 28? You're sure?"

Bob pointed. "There."

"That's my birthday," Frankie breathed. This was getting stranger and stranger. Why would Estelle have made annual payments of six thousand dollars to someone every year on her birthday?

A terrible foreboding snaked up her limbs, sending her pulse galloping at the base of her throat. No birth certificate. Payments to someone on her birthday as if settling a shameful debt. What had Estelle done?

"The recipient seems to be an overseas account." Bob navigated through a few menus and let out a satisfied hum. "Ah, yes, the receiving bank is in the UK," he said as if that explained everything when the opposite was true.

"Can we see whose account?" Frankie asked, her voice coming from someplace far away.

"I'm afraid not. You'd have to contact them directly if you have more questions, but they'll be closed for the day right now. I can give you the number if you'd like?"

Frankie nodded, barely holding it together while her mind screamed at her to flee.

As soon as Bob had handed her a slip of paper with the

information, she was on her feet and moving, her feet flying across the floor tiles through the bank and out onto the sidewalk. She stopped there, her breath coming in choppy gasps, before she stumbled to her car and got in.

She pulled herself together enough to start the engine and leave the lot, but she was out of directions. Behind her was all she'd known, the bright colors of a familiar life now seeping together into abstract shapes as she raced toward the unknown. She had no idea where she was heading until she saw the spire of the church on the outskirts of town, and even then, she had no conscious plan to pull into the parking lot of the cemetery next door before she did so.

She parked across two spots, paying that no heed as she locked the car and took off at a hurried pace toward Estelle's gravesite. If there were people around, she didn't notice, and quite frankly, she didn't care. She needed to unload the torrent of dread swirling inside her onto the one person who might once have been able to offer reassurance.

She fell to her knees in the grass before the stone that was still ringed with flowers, her fists tight in her lap. The same question she'd asked herself at the bank came spilling out as soon as her eyes landed on the inscription.

*Beloved Mother, Shining Light*
*Estelle Lavigne*
*1958–2025*

"Did you steal me?" Frankie's voice broke when she put words to what had started as a tremor at her core upon finding out her birth certificate wasn't real. "Please tell me you didn't. Please tell me I'm yours and I've got this wrong."

Tears spilled down her cheeks as she sat before the silent stone. The missing sister, the abduction story, the song that hadn't been about her, the lies upon lies. It all pointed nowhere good. Had Estelle's first daughter been lost somehow? Was she the one who'd been kidnapped? Maybe not returned? The grief could have made Estelle act irrationally, taking Frankie to fill the void.

*No, she would have never.*

"I don't understand," Frankie sobbed. "Tell me how it fits together. Who were you paying? Were you bribing someone? Settling a debt with money from the school? What did you do, Mom?" Her hands fell to the grass, and her face turned skyward as she struggled to hold herself together. "Who were you?"

*And who am I?* she thought. At best, the daughter of a liar, an unwitting co-conspirator, complacent and enabling. At worst, a casualty of a twisted mind, meant to be somewhere else.

*My darling daughter*, Estelle whispered on the breeze. *My only child.*

"But I'm not," Frankie said, an edge to her words. "So why would you say that?"

Was it denial? A need to forget the daughter who'd been lost?

"What happened to her?" Frankie asked, frustration building like steam in a kettle at the void where answers should be. "Why didn't you tell me?"

She wiped the tears off her face and stood, her eyes hard on the gravestone. "I won't be back until I know," she said. "I don't care how long it takes." Then she turned and strode back to her car, those never-ending questions carving raw fissures into her soul.

That evening, Frankie was halfway home after sitting through a staff meeting, an auction run-down with the moms, and several lessons while mentally so checked out that there was no hiding it. She couldn't even feel bad about phoning it in.

Kayla was the only one who'd commented, but Frankie

hadn't been able to make herself explain, so she'd gone with "bad headache," and for once Kayla had let it slide. Possibly she was satisfied that Frankie was physically back where she was supposed to be.

*If, in fact,* here *was where she was supposed to be.*

As the fears from earlier reared back up, Frankie made a U-turn in an intersection and sped back the way she'd come, setting her sights on a house at the other side of town.

*Lavignes walk tall no matter the burden,* Estelle seemed to protest.

"Oh, shut up," Frankie huffed, turning into Thora's neighborhood. The phone number for the UK bank burned in her pocket, and if she was going to stay up until they opened over there, she didn't want to do it alone. There was no weakness in that.

Owen opened the door laughing as if he and Thora were mid-conversational sparring, and as the sound rolled over Frankie into the evening, her insides softened enough to allow a smile of her own to greet him.

"Frankie, hey." He ran a hand through his hair, his eyes still twinkling with mirth. "Didn't know you were coming."

"Me neither." She shrugged, both of them rooted in place for an extended beat before Owen backed up, gesturing for her to come inside.

"Did something happen?" he asked.

Frankie toed off her shoes. "Is it that obvious?"

"Is that Frankie?" Thora called from the living room.

"Hi, Thora," Frankie called at the same time Owen called, "We'll be right there."

He caught her arm to keep her in the foyer, sincerity settling across his features. "Are you okay?"

The warmth of his hand seeped through the thin fabric of her shirt, sending a burst of calm blooming from the point of contact. She could breathe again.

"I don't know," she said truthfully. "Everything's a mess."

He nodded, his hold on her pulsing tighter in a barely there movement of his fingers. "Then I'm glad you came here."

Heat crept up Frankie's cheeks. "Me too."

"What's taking so long?" Thora called from the other room.

Owen let Frankie go, and together they joined the older woman, who was watching them with narrowed eyes as they entered the room. "I sure hope you didn't tell him all your secrets already," she said.

"What?" Frankie sputtered. She didn't have secrets. Not from Owen. If she hadn't told him how much she was enjoying having him back in her life, that was a simple omission. No need to make a big deal out of nothing.

Thora smirked. "Why you're here, I mean."

"Oh." Frankie sat down.

"Tell us," Owen said. "What's going on?"

And Frankie did. She shared what she'd learned about her birth certificate and the strange activity in the private account. Her worries about what that might mean. How she didn't understand how everything fit together but that she was convinced it did. That she needed to call the UK bank as soon as they opened.

"What's the time difference?" Owen asked.

"I haven't had time to look," Frankie said.

"Five hours," Thora supplied as if everyone knew that. "So nine in the morning there is four a.m. our time. You'll sleep in my guest room then."

Frankie hadn't realized she had that many hours left. "I don't want to be any trouble. Maybe I should just go—"

"No. Stay," Owen interrupted her. "It's not a problem. Are you hungry?"

Frankie looked from him to Thora, who was pressing her lips together as if suppressing a smile while she returned her attention to the crossword puzzle in her lap. In the past, she always would have answered such a question with a firm "no." It had been ingrained in her not to accept charity, but she'd told Estelle off in the car, so why not now?

"I am actually," she said. "I came straight from work."

Owen lit up. "I'll make us something. Grilled sandwich? French toast? Hmm..." He squeezed his eyes together as if trying to recall the contents of Thora's fridge. "An omelet?"

"Whatever is easiest," Frankie said.

"A croque monsieur it is," he said, which to Frankie sounded anything but easy. "Be right back."

Thora grinned. "I've created a monster." When she noted Frankie's puzzled expression, she clarified. "It's a grilled ham and cheese sandwich, but teach him the difference between frying and sautéing and suddenly we're using French terms."

"Tea for you, Grams?" Owen called.

"Thank you," she hollered. "Not that I mind," she added in a low voice to Frankie. "Whatever makes him happy."

"He seems to be doing better," Frankie said. Was it really less than three weeks ago that she'd first run into him at the library? He'd been a shadow at the time, quiet and hidden beneath a layer of uncertainty. No one she recognized. Now, he was Owen again, if a version that life had knocked about a bit. And she didn't mind that part at all.

"Like I always knew he would." A serene expression settled on Thora's face, taking years off her appearance. "He just needed to believe it himself."

Frankie nodded. "I'm glad he has you."

"And you, my dear." She returned to her crossword.

Frankie sat with that while an old Sean Connery movie played mutely on the TV. What if they hadn't broken things off back then? If she'd followed him to Boston like they'd planned? Would they have stayed together? Would the alcohol still have gotten its claws into him? Would she still be here running Starview?

Something nagged at Frankie amid those "what ifs." Something to do with Estelle and the school and the lies, but before she could put her finger on it, Owen entered the room carrying a tray, the accompanying scent sending her thoughts in a more alimentary direction.

Oh well. How did that saying go again? *The past is in your head; the future is in your hands.* Maybe the point wasn't that they'd broken up but that they were both here right now.

She picked up her knife and fork and cut into the golden bread, sending melting cheese onto the plate.

"Blow on it. It's hot," Owen said, handing Thora her tea.

"I don't know that I care," Frankie said, testing a corner on her tongue, a small moan escaping her as the savory bite lit up her taste buds.

Owen elbowed Thora gently. "Why don't you react like that to my cooking?"

"Yes, I wonder why?" Thora deadpanned, which might have made Frankie blush again if she hadn't been so busy chewing.

Once they'd finished eating and the movie credits were rolling, Owen helped Thora up the stairs to her room. She was walking well with a cane now, but he thought it safer if she had someone below her on the stairs. When he returned, he showed Frankie where she'd be sleeping.

"I put an extra toothbrush on the sink in the hallway, and I'll set my alarm for three fifty so we can call right when they open."

No, she doubted she'd still be in Aspen Creek if things had worked out differently between them in high school.

"Thank you," she said as he lingered on her threshold. "Really."

He glanced toward the bed. Nodded. "Let me know if there's anything else you need. Pillows, blankets, noise maker..."

"Would you stay for a bit?" she asked, the words hanging in

the air between them before she could stop them. "Just for, um, company I mean."

He hesitated, but she held still while his gaze roamed across her features. "I can do that," he said finally. "Left still your side of preference?"

She smiled at his nod to their motel night. "Yep."

It should have been awkward, getting into bed with him again, but it wasn't. They stayed on top of the covers still fully dressed, just heads on pillows facing each other.

"What are you most worried about?" he asked, knowing without her saying so that her primary reason for avoiding solitude was what was brewing on the horizon.

Frankie folded her hands underneath her cheek, wondering if she'd be able to shape the words. But when he looked at her that way, with nothing but acceptance, it wasn't that difficult. "That I'm not hers," she said. "That she was the abductor."

He shook his head gently. "There's no way, Frankie. You look just like her, except your hair is darker." He reached out, pushing one of her strands back from her forehead. "I can see why you'd go there, but I don't think that's it."

He withdrew his hand and let it rest on the mattress by his chest. It was probably not good that she wished he'd keep playing with her hair.

She sighed. "I hope you're right. And I hope the bank can tell us who she was paying."

"It might not have been about you at all. It could be career related—something to do with her music or the school."

"But why were the payments on my birthday?"

"To help her remember to make them? I don't know."

That was a reasonable explanation, Frankie supposed, and for a while they sank into companionable silence. She thought about all that Estelle had been to her—mother, caretaker, best friend, counselor for both support and guidance, role model, landlady, boss, business partner. For the first time in her life, it occurred to her that their relationship had been unique in that way. Everyone else she knew had different people filling those roles. There was no doubt that Estelle had centered Frankie in her life and made sure she wanted for nothing, but it was also easy not to question a person like that—so easy to let the days slip by in predictable comfort.

"Why stir a pot that's simmering nicely?" she mumbled, opening eyes that must have fluttered closed at some point.

"Are you asking me cooking questions in your sleep because of my excellent croque monsieur?" A corner of Owen's mouth tugged up.

"Wasn't sleeping," Frankie said.

"Was too." He dragged a finger gently from her forehead down between her brows and along the bridge of her nose, making her eyelids fall closed again. "And you stir because otherwise it'll burn at the bottom, and you get nasty brown bits ruining everything."

Wasn't that the truth, she thought as she drifted off. Everything about her life had looked perfectly fine on the surface, but along the way, she'd forgotten to stir, and now that she was, here were those unpalatable burnt scraps floating up.

It seemed only minutes had passed when Owen shook her shoulder, rousing her from a deep, dreamless sleep.

"Frankie, it's almost four," he said. "You ready to make that call?"

And she was. She would stir and stir and sift away every bitter morsel until what remained was good again.

# TWENTY-EIGHT

An excerpt from Orla Monroe's interview with Estelle Lavigne
Published in *Country Weekly*, January 1995

## OM:

I, for one, am thrilled to have had this chance to learn more about the Americana scene's newest darling. So what's next for this storyteller? What's on the horizon, Estelle?

## EL:

Life as a musician doesn't change with one success. My goal remains as it's always been—to write and perform music that people want to listen to. To grow my fan base. To make a comfortable living on my own terms. The success of "My Only Child" has opened doors that I'm excited about, and we're currently working on touring dates for the coming year. If you're anywhere in the southeastern United States, chances are I'll be visiting a town near you. Beyond that, my number one focus will continue to be my daughter.

OM:

Is there a long-term plan? Hopes and dreams? Perhaps a special someone? Handsome men must be swarming around you.

EL:

Oh no. My life is full as it is, so I'm not looking. Frankie and I are quite all right on our own.

As for dreams, I hear the Mayor of Nashville sometimes bestows keys to the city to esteemed individuals. Wouldn't that be something? Perhaps as a lifetime achievement award. No, but in all seriousness, my goal is to continue doing what I do best—weaving together tales and music—until the day I die. There is always another melody, another turn of phrase, and another listener to capture. Perhaps new countries to visit. So, barring anything unexpected happening, you'll keep finding me and my guitar on a stage somewhere living the dream.

OM:

Sounds wonderful. I certainly am eager to see where your journey takes you. It's bound to be far with the strength and determination you've shown. Hopefully, I'll run into you at one of the upcoming awards shows this year too.

EL:

Your lips to God's ears, Orla. It's been wonderful talking with you.

# TWENTY-NINE

## FRANKIE

Now

"I apologize. Could you repeat that, Miss? I'm not quite clear on what you're asking," the British banker said in a perfect imitation of the actor Hugh Grant.

Frankie restated her request to find out who owned the account Estelle had made payments to from her perch at the edge of the bed where she sat with a notepad at the ready, and then she gave him the account number again too for good measure.

"Hm," Hugh Grant said. "I'm afraid I'm legally prohibited from sharing any such information with you unless you are the account holder."

"I'm obviously not," Frankie said, her lack of sleep making it harder to feign politeness.

"Right." Hugh's last consonant was sharper than necessary. "Well, you could always try a court order if it's of great importance to you, but such processes are lengthy and rarely fruitful in my experience."

Frankie's eyes roamed the paper that had the account

number and transfer information. "Could you at least tell me if it's a private or business account? And what about these letters next to the account number—SSTGTAFY—can you tell me what they mean?"

Owen followed the conversation from next to the bed. "No luck?" he mimed, absent-mindedly rubbing a kink out of his neck.

She shook her head, then turned the phone on speaker so he could hear.

"Miss, I do so wish I could help you, but unfortunately my hands are tied," Hugh said.

"Even decoding those letters for me?"

"Again, I'm very sorry, but I can't confirm any details about that reference over the phone."

Frankie hung her head, but Owen waved a hand to get her attention. "He said over the phone," he whispered. "What about in person?"

Frankie covered the microphone with one hand. "And how would that work?"

"Just ask," Owen prompted.

Frankie inhaled deeply. "What if I visited in person? Could you tell me more then?"

"Well..." Hugh appeared to take a moment to think. "I suppose if you did visit a branch with the relevant documentation in hand—IDs for you and your mother, death certificate, and US bank records showing the payment and account details—we might be able to offer further assistance."

Owen nodded eagerly, excitement lifting his brow as if this was good news and not merely a small step up from being stonewalled.

"Okay," Frankie said, dejection weighing heavily on her already exhausted shoulders. "Thank you."

"Not a problem," Hugh said, more chipper now. "Happy to be of service. Is there anything else I can do to assist you today?"

*Not be in the UK*, Frankie thought. Out loud, she declined his further so-called help, and they hung up.

She tipped backward and closed her eyes. "Fudge," she whispered.

The bed dipped as Owen sat down next to her. "It's still a lead," he said. "Not a dead end."

She opened her eyes to look up at him. "I currently have a Ziplock bag full of Mom's old jewelry in my purse that I need to pawn to pay off an exterminator because while mice are cute in nature, they are unhelpful to ballerinas trying to dance. The school is months away from bankruptcy, I have to hire a new teacher *and* pay them, don't you know, and the moms spear-heading the auction think we have a money tree growing out back. In what world do I have spare change for airplane tickets lying around waiting for me?" She pushed herself up to sitting. "I appreciate your support, but this *is* a dead end. Wishing it wasn't doesn't make it so."

She reached for her bag and stuffed the papers back inside, then got off the bed. "I'm going to go home and try to get a few more hours of sleep."

"Frankie..." Owen watched her make her way across the room.

"Owen," she said, offering him a tight smile. "I know you mean well, and I am so, so grateful for all your help." She gestured to the room. "For being here right now."

"We'll think of something," he said.

"Maybe, maybe not." She reached for the door handle. "But right now I have to be at work in four hours and at Estelle's in another three to be interviewed about my mother's legacy by a woman who may or may not be looking for a scoop." She huffed out a glum laugh. "So I'm going to try to put all this out of my mind for a bit and see where that leaves me, okay?"

Owen nodded. "I get it. Sorry, Frankie. I know you're dreading this interview. I'll be here if you need me."

"I know. Thank you."

The urge to run to him, to seek shelter in his strong arms like that night in the motel, forced her feet out the door and down the hallway. He'd said no thanks to her once before back when they were teens and he broke things off, and there was no need to add insult to injury with everything she already had on her plate.

"Head in the game," she said to herself as she unlocked her car and got in. Sleep, work, interview. *Professional* was the word.

The rest would have to wait.

When Frankie arrived at Estelle's house after a morning at the school, she found the living room transformed. The couch had been moved closer to the window, the blinds were open, there were freshly cut flowers on every surface that allowed it, and the piano had been polished.

Mrs. Nolan was hovering by the front door, ready to usher Frankie inside as if she was new to the building.

"Orla is ten minutes out, but I thought we could get a couple of pictures for the auction brochures first," she said. "I'm sure she's bringing her own photographer for the feature, so look at it like a practice round. Do you need help with make-up?"

Frankie looked into the hallway mirror. "What's wrong with my make-up?"

"Oh, I didn't realize you were wearing any. You'll want to go heavier for the camera."

"I do?" Frankie spun in place as Mrs. Nolan rushed past her to where the cleaning lady had left a roll of paper towels sitting out on a sideboard.

"Definitely," Mrs. Nolan said, turning back to her. "You're the face of the school now, Frankie. Let's look the part. Make Estelle proud." She put a palm over her heart.

Frankie didn't have it in her to object, mostly because she suspected this whole affair would only drag out if she did, and after some added blush and eyeliner (plus setting powder because "no one liked an oily forehead"), she was deemed presentable. It was right on time, too, because no sooner had Frankie been released from Mrs. Nolan's clutches than the other woman let out a squeal of excitement announcing Orla had arrived.

"We meet again," Orla said upon entering, extending a hand to Frankie. "I must say I didn't expect the invitation based on our last conversation."

Frankie shook her hand, taking a few seconds to recalibrate. Orla thought Frankie was behind this, which could only be a good thing. It meant the reporter might be less likely to think Frankie had something to hide.

Sensing the power dynamic shifting slightly in her favor, Frankie allowed her shoulders to relax. "Of course. The more people learn about this auction, the better." She nodded a greeting to the too-young-looking photographer Orla had brought along.

"My grandson," Orla said, gesturing to the young man. "But don't tell anyone or I'll be accused of nepotism."

Frankie shared a conspiratorial smile with her, then she guided them into the living room, following the prompts Mrs. Nolan had given her. "I thought we could sit over here. Can I get you something to drink?"

"Iced tea if you have it," Orla said.

"I'll get it." Mrs. Nolan hurried into the kitchen.

While they waited, Frankie tried to make herself comfortable, but the light and angles in the room were all wrong with the seating moved. "Thank you for doing this," she said just to say something. "It means a lot that you would take the time."

"I've always liked a good cause. Besides, at this point in my life, I only take jobs that interest me, and this did."

"Oh?" *Act friendly, play dumb.* She could do this.

"I followed Estelle's career obviously, short though it may have been. She was an interesting person—fun to talk to, thoughtful, enterprising—and I admit it surprised me when she settled here and opened the school. I never got a chance to talk to her about it since she stopped giving interviews, so I'm excited to learn more." The reporter's gaze held Frankie's for an extended moment—a life of honed perception shining within them.

Frankie swallowed, her tongue drying up in her mouth. Still no mention of the botched second interview. Was Orla holding back too, or did she consider Estelle's snub a professional failure that she preferred not to think about? Frankie had no idea if such situations were par for the course for reporters. What she did know was that she should have asked for something caffeinated to help her step up her game over the next two hours, or this had the potential to turn into a big mistake.

Once they had their beverages in front of them, Orla placed a recording device on the table between them and sat back against the cushions, one smooth leg crossed over the other. "Should we get started?"

Frankie nodded, putting conviction behind the move. "Let's."

"Excellent." Orla lit up. "So, Frankie—or do you perhaps prefer Francesca now that you're older? Named for your great-great-grandmother, was it?"

"Frankie is fine." She couldn't remember the last time someone had used her full given name, and in light of what she now knew, she wouldn't be surprised if that little factoid also was based on a lie. She'd been too cocky before; this wasn't good. Her back was already sticky.

"Do you remember the first time you realized your mother wasn't like other mothers?"

Frankie blinked at her. She'd just thought about how

different other people's relationships with their moms were. Was this woman a mind reader?

"That she was famous, I mean," Orla clarified.

*Oh. Right.* Frankie told her about the night when she'd discovered the piano after Estelle's show, and how she'd looked out across the room from the stage, seeing for the first time what her mom saw every time she performed. "I recognized the magic in it that evening," she said. "And after that, it was like my eyes had opened to how people would circle around her, would come to see *her*. I don't know that I would have known to call it fame at the time, but it definitely made her stand out."

"That she did, and I'm sure her loss must be a hardship both for you and for Aspen Creek. Can you share a bit about your life here, and perhaps a few sentiments from the community that you've heard since her passing? What has it been like to share your grief with others who didn't know her as well as you did?"

*If only she knew*, Frankie thought, not loving the direction the questions were taking. She talked for a while about their years in Aspen Creek, the way the community had taken them both under their wings, the boards Estelle had been on, her championing of the arts. "Everyone has been so supportive and encouraging," Frankie said, choosing a few select condolences to include in the interview. "Estelle meant a lot to so many people, and all I can do is try to fill the space she left behind the best I can, which is why I'm doing this auction—"

Orla interrupted before Frankie could move them down a safer path. "Yes, I talked to a few citizens earlier today and the word *legend* was mentioned. Do you feel that word described her well?"

"No," Frankie said before she could stop herself.

"Oh?" Orla leaned forward. "How so?"

Frankie's gaze flicked to Mrs. Nolan, who'd taken a seat on the other side of the piano. She was on her phone but no doubt listening, and Frankie could be sure the other moms would hear all about this before the day was over. "Legends aren't real," Frankie said. "They're blown-up stories designed to make the subject look bigger, braver, better..." Her voice trailed off. *The Legend of Estelle Lavigne* had quite a ring to it. Might a story like that not include fame, a perfect mother, a town matron, everybody's friend?

"Frankie?"

Frankie blinked away the wisps of fog that blended reality with fiction. "What I mean is—Estelle was a real person to me. And let's face it, no one thinks of their parents as legendary." She tried for a smile and forced it to reach her eyes.

It worked. Orla let out a pealing laugh before sitting back again. "Speaking of your father," she said, making Frankie prepare for the next obstacle course. "You never knew him, is that correct?"

"Right."

"His accident was a topic Estelle didn't want to cover during our interview. She said it was still too raw for her. Knowing she never remarried, is it safe to say she never got over him?"

Was that how she'd described things back then? Frankie held back a scoff. No word about him drinking himself to death then. What a minefield the past had turned into. She had to find a way to steer this interview to the auction instead.

"She didn't have time for romance," Frankie said. "Starview was her partner, and she put every ounce of herself into that place to make it the school it is today. The upcoming auction is in many ways a love letter to her from everyone whose lives have been touched by her music—whether on stage or off."

"But there was one man who played a big role in her success, correct? In fact, some would say she, um... followed him here?" She checked her notes in a weak imitation of someone who couldn't recall. "Raymond Clark."

"Uncle Ray?" Frankie's chin drew back. "Sure, they were friends and worked together."

"But there was nothing to the rumors?"

Frankie blinked at her. "What rumors?"

"Oh dear, how awkward," Orla tittered. "I'm sure it was wild speculation, but in *some* circles, there was talk of the two of them being more than that. An affair."

A disbelieving laugh bubbled out of Frankie. "Estelle and Ray? Hardly." Orla needed to check her sources.

But the reporter persisted. "He was always nearby—that's all I'm saying. And for a man with a young family back home..."

Frankie's hackles rose at the insinuation. "This sounds an awful lot like you were part of those speculating circles."

Orla shrugged. "She was a beautiful woman. He was an attractive man. And... she didn't care much for me asking questions about him."

Frankie's objection stuck in her throat. Was that the real reason why the second interview had been cut short? But surely that couldn't mean...

"You were young at the time," Orla continued. "If they kept it a secret, you might not have known."

*Great. More secrets...*

Frankie shook her head, willing logic back in. Not once had she seen anything remotely inappropriate between Mom and Uncle Ray. Orla was bluffing. This was a red herring designed to knock her off-kilter. "No. Absolutely not," she said, finding her voice again. "He was her manager, so of course they had to spend time with each other. End of story." There was no way.

"His wife did leave him," Orla pointed out.

"Years later. Besides, Estelle and Aunt Darla were good friends too. But I thought we were here to talk about Starview, not Uncle Ray."

It was sweltering in the room now. Frankie wished she

could open a window but didn't dare move for fear of being analyzed.

Orla paused, scooted back in her seat, and rested her notepad in her lap. "How was their relationship as of late?"

Frankie's head dipped toward her chest, and she rubbed one hand across her forehead in defeat. "It was good. He travels a lot, so we don't see him as much anymore."

"But he was in town when she passed."

Frankie cocked her head to the side as the realization set in. "You're still suspicious of her death."

"Just doing my due—"

"Diligence," Frankie filled in. "Yes, you said."

"Old manager, potential lover... Could be disagreements over money or royalties."

Frankie stared at her a long time. Mom's death had been natural. Talking to Matt and Kayla, hearing Charlie describe finding her, and reading over the coroner's report again had struck out any notion that it wasn't. Undetected coronary artery disease had caused a clot. It could have happened anywhere at any time.

But she'd never considered Uncle Ray being somehow connected to Starview's financial situation. She didn't think it likely, but perhaps it warranted a look.

"Their relationship was always amicable," Frankie said, putting as much pathos into her voice as she could. "And I'm going to draw the line here. We can talk about Estelle, me, and Starview, but not about people who aren't present and can't defend themselves, or this interview is over. Surely there's some journalistic integrity to that effect that you have to follow."

Orla pressed her lips together, but then her features smoothed again. "You remind me a lot of her," she said finally. "It's good to know her memory lives on."

It was a weak olive branch, but Frankie had to take it.

"Okay," Orla said, wrenching back control of the interview

before Frankie could catch her breath. "So no relationships, only work. Did she not get lonely?"

"Lonely?" Frankie's eyes flew to the quiet spines lining the bookcases. The stairs leading up to empty rooms. Then she spotted her tiny house through the window. "No, I'd like to think she was satisfied with how her life turned out. She had a whole town behind her. She had me."

"Yes, I understand you were very close," Orla said, sympathy coating her words as if their spat from a minute ago had never happened. "I would have thought it hard to grow up in the shadow of someone so adored by the public, but you stayed." She paused, watching Frankie with her head tilted.

"Um... was there a question in there?"

Orla laughed. "I suppose I wonder why. I've done my homework, and from what I've heard, you were quite the piano prodigy once upon a time. So why not take center stage yourself? Did you worry your talent wouldn't live up to her legacy?"

Frankie sputtered out a protest. "No. That's not what it was like at all."

"No?"

"No," she said again. "I stayed because I wanted to—because we had an opportunity to build something lasting." She could hear the cadence of Estelle's voice as she spoke the words, but she persisted anyway. "I was never as comfortable in the spotlight as her, so staying here was the right thing to do." Not that she'd been *un*comfortable on stage. And she'd liked the applause. But that was neither here nor there. She couldn't play right now anyway, and the way her emotions simmered mercurially inside her showed it. She was a shaken soda bottle of trapped feelings with the cap still on. The pressure had nowhere to go without her normal outlet.

"Okay." Orla's voice was placating, a small smile tugging at her lips as if she'd asked for a treat and Frankie had delivered. "It's obviously known to all that 'My Only Child' was directly inspired by you, but do you think being a mother influenced Estelle's music in other ways and also her decision to retire from performing relatively soon after that big hit?"

Frankie wanted to go to sleep. Just curl up in a ball right there, pull the blanket over herself and drift off. Every single question had pitfalls that required her to either do verbal gymnastics or flat out lie, and she wasn't sure how much longer she could go on.

She wished Owen was here. He would lean against the doorjamb to the kitchen, rolling his eyes or doing some other grimace to distract her. How would he have answered the question?

"I think every aspect of an artist's life is fodder for inspiration," Frankie said finally. "Good experiences, distressing ones, and everything in between. Being a mother was obviously a big part of Estelle's life, so I have to assume her songs might have been different if she'd not had me." *Us*, the voice inside her whispered. *Two daughters*. She cleared her throat and continued, the second part of the question easier. "And yes, her choice to move here and stop recording did have a lot to do with me. I was getting older and needed better schooling than she could provide on the road. She wanted stability for me. And herself too I assume."

Orla brushed something invisible off her sleeve and said as if in passing, "I notice you call her Estelle."

Frankie's heart constricted in her chest. Did she know about Stella-Jane?

"Did she prefer that over *Mom*?" Orla continued.

*Oh*. Frankie reached for her water glass to hide the breath of relief rushing out of her. "I called her both," she said. "Sometimes it was easier to use her name since so many people knew her in a professional capacity."

"Got it," Orla said. "Okay, so let's talk future plans for the school. This auction—what do you hope it will achieve?"

*Finally.* Frankie set her water glass down and squared her shoulders. "Well, Orla, it's expensive to run a school, and my hope is to continue my mother's legacy of offering first-class, music-centered education to the children of Mecklenburg and Iredell Counties and beyond for years to come."

For the next half hour, Frankie listed sponsors, auction prizes, and activities that would draw attendees to the auction. She gushed about the Starview staff and the engaged parents (giving a special shout-out to Mrs. Nolan), teased performances, and thanked a long line of people for making it happen.

"You should come," she told Orla. "See what Estelle created." No matter how complicated Frankie's feelings about her mom were, she couldn't deny that the school, at least, was something to be proud of.

"Maybe I will," Orla said. "Will you put your own stamp on Starview now that it's yours, do you think, or will it remain Estelle's?"

"I'm not sure there's a difference, and why mess with perfection?" Frankie said with a smile. She'd made it through the interview in one piece. Now she could only hope Orla wrote it up in a favorable light.

"Huh." Orla squinted at her. "Interesting."

Frankie should have let it go, but something about the other woman's tone got to her. "What do you mean?"

"Oh, nothing." Orla's voice was breezy. "Something she told me back then that I haven't thought about in years. What was it again? 'An artist's relevance is determined by her most persistent fan.'"

"And?" Frankie prodded.

"Who needs fans with such a loyal daughter?" Orla reached for her recorder and turned it off. "You could teach mine a thing or two. God forbid I even had an opinion on the food my grandson ate when he was little."

"Yeah, well, Estelle didn't have grandchildren," Frankie

said, even though part of her knew that wasn't the point Orla had been making.

"How about some photos?" Orla asked, waving the grandson in question to her. "Do you have a preference for inside or outside?"

And like that, the interview was over.

Frankie got in her car a little later feeling as if she'd stumbled out of the washer after a particularly intense spin cycle. She had only a vague recollection of the photo shoot—of angling her head this way and that, smiling when asked, looking "like a leader." Whatever a leader looked like.

Orla had thought of Estelle as one, that much was clear. She'd even suggested Frankie imitate one of Estelle's poses from the original interview. Frankie had complied, even though on some deep level, the comparisons and accompanying expectations were morphing from complimentary to oppressive. Not that long ago, Frankie had been proud of the closeness she and Estelle had shared, but with Orla's insinuation fresh in her mind and Estelle's dishonesty ruling Frankie's every waking thought, that bond was beginning to seem more like blurred boundaries.

The problem was that she had no idea how to redefine them because where did Estelle end and Frankie begin?

# THIRTY

## ESTELLE

Then

"You're made for this," Ray told Estelle when she came off stage at Mississippi Nights in St. Louis to an audience that had been electrified by her cover of Tom Petty's "Runnin' Down a Dream."

She was sweaty and happy and in denial that they were coming up on Thanksgiving when obligation would have her return to Nashville for a week before her December events kicked off. She already knew what that would bring. Sullen glares. Slammed doors. Phone calls to return from the school. No gratitude or cooperation. Here she was making concessions and arranging comforts while at the brink of professional significance... She didn't know why she bothered.

"I know," she said, letting him buy her a drink.

She'd seen more of him lately, and while he wasn't saying so outright, she suspected he was keeping out of Darla's way while she nested. If she was to believe her friend, Ray had neither taste nor judgment when it came to preparing for their baby boy. She supposed that made them both persona non grata in their homes.

"Excuse me." A woman tapped Estelle on the shoulder. "Would I be able to get an autograph?"

Estelle blinked at her. "From me?"

"Yeah, I love your voice so much. I saw you in Paducah this past summer too."

Estelle's heart grew several sizes. This was a first. "Of course," she said. She wiped her hands on her skirt and accepted the pen and notebook the woman handed her. She'd practiced her signature endlessly since the name change, but her fingers still trembled when she put the tip to the paper.

After the woman had left, a low squeal of delight rose up her throat. A fan. She had a bona fide fan.

"Happy?" Ray asked over the brim of his beer glass.

His eyes were dark in the muted light, but a shimmer of something triumphant still made it to the surface. Like he was proud of her.

No one had ever been proud of her before.

"I am," she said.

Across the room, she spotted the woman showing the autograph to her friends. A piece of paper with her handwriting on it that now was special to a stranger. The sight had her float up another few rungs on the ladder she was climbing.

"It suits you," Ray said.

She turned back to him, recalling that night at Barnie's when they'd first met. How he'd looked out for her when Greg had shown up. How he'd seen more than a waitress from the start.

"Thank you," she said. "I don't think I say it enough, but I really am grateful for everything you do. None of this would be possible without you."

He set his glass down and reached out, letting one finger

briefly skim her jaw. She recognized it for what it was—a display of chaste affection, nothing else. But since that was the best she could do in terms of male attention at present, she accepted it.

"You just stick with me," he said, "and we'll do great things together. That's a promise."

# THIRTY-ONE

## FRANKIE

Now

Loud voices reached Frankie after she'd finished her three o'clock lesson the following day. The argument was coming from her office, so she hurried through the hallway and entered the space.

"Oh good. There you are," Kayla said as soon as she saw her, a visible wave of relief sweeping over her.

On the other side of the desk were Mrs. Weaver and Mrs. Nolan, and neither of them looked happy. In fact, they were glaring at each other with such animosity that Frankie suspected she'd interrupted just in time to prevent a physical fight.

"Everything okay here?" she asked, her gaze sweeping over the two irate women to Kayla.

"Small disagreement," Kayla said.

"It's not small," Mrs. Weaver hissed. "I had already secured a tent supplier, and now Alicia wants to go with her husband's contact instead. Not only was that not her job, but we're down to the wire, and pulling out of my agreement will make me look terrible."

Mrs. Nolan threw up her arms. "Forgive me for thinking a better deal would be more important than your standing with a vendor."

"It's about being true to one's word," Mrs. Weaver said. "But I guess to some people that doesn't matter."

"You mean like when you said you were fine with Lauren getting the final solo at the show and then you told Lorilynn and Felicity behind my back that Mira Kopp would have been a better pick?"

"Okay." Frankie approached the desk, sharing a commiserating look with Kayla. "You're both working so hard to get this done, and no one appreciates that more than me, but how about we take a small step back and breathe. We're on the same team."

"You've not exactly been around," Mrs. Weaver sniped.

"My responsibilities here pull me in many different directions," Frankie said. "My point is, we all want this fundraiser to be a success." She waited until the women had agreed with her. "As far as the vendor goes, I'm inclined to agree with Mrs. Nolan—if her person is offering a better deal." She put up a hand to stop Mrs. Weaver from launching a protest. "But to ensure there's no blowback on you, I'm happy to contact your person myself and take the blame. How is that?"

Mrs. Weaver huffed out a breath. "I suppose that would be acceptable."

"Okay, good." Frankie offered them a smile, the same one reflected back at her from the many framed photos of Estelle in the room. *We're all friends here,* it said. *Work with me.*

"And what about the performance order," Mrs. Nolan asked. "Like I said, we have a preliminary list put together already."

"A great start no doubt," Frankie agreed. "But the other

teachers and I will finalize that. Everyone will get their chance to shine."

Both moms nodded, looking down at their hands, and Frankie had never felt more like the principal of a school.

"Now if you don't mind, I have to get ready for a lesson. Was there anything else urgent?"

"I'll have quotes for sound systems for you tomorrow," Mrs. Weaver said.

"And I'm sending you a list of all our donations," Mrs. Nolan added.

"Thank you both so much," Frankie said. She nodded to Kayla, who stood and gestured for the moms to follow her to the door.

As soon as they were gone, Frankie sank into the desk chair and covered her face with her hands, and that's how Kayla found her a few moments later.

"You okay?"

"Mm-hmm," Frankie said from behind her hands.

"Um, I have some résumés for you to look at. Voice teachers. When you get a chance. And the exterminator called about payment again. He's kind of being a *pest* about it. Get it?" She snickered at her own joke.

"How did Estelle do this?" Frankie asked, her hands dropping to the desk. "There aren't enough hours in the day. I was planning on driving up to Mooresville to pawn this stuff after my five o'clock." She pulled out the plastic bag from her purse. "But now I also need to reach out to the tent guy and call potential job candidates. Not to mention figure out how the heck I'm supposed to play at that wedding this weekend." She held up her useless hands.

Kayla leaned against the desk. "Well, first of all, I think part of why you're in this situation is that Estelle, in fact, did not 'do this.' You're trying to clean up a mess that she created, so don't compare yourself. Second of all—you still can't play?"

Frankie shook her head. "Not even a simple sonata."

Kayla's brow furrowed. "What's going on with you?"

Frankie gestured around the room in response.

"No," Kayla said. "There's more. Things you're not sharing. Don't think I haven't noticed. Matt says you're not texting him back either."

A pang of guilt hollowed Frankie's gut. It was just that once she'd decided to keep what she was learning about Estelle from them, the secrets had piled up, and it wasn't like she didn't have reasons. Kayla was friends with Tina and Stefano outside of work, Matt talked to his dad, they both had their own loyalties to Estelle, and word traveled fast in a small town like this.

"We used to tell each other everything," Kayla said. "I know it was a long time ago, and that people grow apart. Matt and I found each other and built a life together. You've had Starview and Estelle. But we're both still here. I'm still trying. Maybe I can help."

Something tightened inside Frankie as Kayla's words cracked a lens in the rose-colored glasses that she'd always viewed her life through. *Work and her mom—that's what her life had amounted to.* What had happened to her dreams? To the girl Owen had kissed senseless on the bleachers?

She considered her former best friend; the woman Kayla had become. She would listen, Frankie knew that, but would she understand? Would anyone? "I'll think about it," she said. "It's just... a lot."

"Okay," Kayla said. "But don't take too long. You can't go on like this."

Frankie nodded, unexpected tears stinging behind her eyes.

"Will you at least let me help with this?" Kayla said, reaching for the bag of jewelry. "I don't have class until seven, and I'm an excellent negotiator. I can go to Mooresville."

Frankie looked up. "You'd do that?"

"Of course. And I'll text you if I have questions. I'll leave now."

As soon as Kayla had left, Frankie pulled out her phone and opened Matt's last message from yesterday. It was the third one from him that she'd ignored.

> *What's up, Frankenweenie? Haven't heard from you in a while. BBQ this weekend?*

She typed out a quick response. *Sorry. Things are busy. BBQ sounds good.*

Kayla had been right—they were still trying, still including her after all these years. Frankie was the one who'd pulled back. It wasn't that she'd regretted letting Estelle introduce them, but she also hadn't considered at the time that from that point onward, the two of them would have each other, independent of her. Estelle was the one who'd pointed that out to her—that couples, especially new ones, didn't need a third wheel always tagging along, so maybe it was best she skip that movie outing or hike or dinner.

She frowned at the memory, sucking in her lips as if something bitter had touched her tongue. It had been difficult in the beginning, had felt like her life had shrunk a little even if Estelle had done her best to make sure Frankie had things to do. Distractions.

*Distractions.*

A hot flush surged beneath Frankie's skin. There was something there trying to get out. Something nauseating with deep roots that her instincts fought against.

The timer on her phone went off, reminding her that her next student would be there in five minutes. She still hadn't made copies of the music he needed, so she pushed all other thoughts out of her head in favor of being practical.

It worked through her students' warm-up scales and beginning measures, but then her phone started ringing.

"Sorry," she told the kid, declining the call in her pocket.

"Phones off in the practice rooms," the kid said.

"You're right about that," she said brightly. "Now from the top."

Her phone rang again, this time only buzzing against her hip. She twisted away from the kid so she could peek at the screen without him seeing, while he stumbled through the piece she'd assigned for homework last week.

Thora's name lit up the screen, and the rejected one from a minute ago was also from her. Frankie frowned. Something must be going on.

"Do that one more time and focus on dynamics," she told her student. "Remember crescendo means...?"

"Stronger."

"Good. I'll be right back."

She left the room in time for a third call to come through, and this time she answered it.

"Thora, is everything okay?" She hunched in a corner of the hallway with her fingers covering her free ear to block out the faint notes of violin and guitar trembling through the air from the other practice rooms.

"Put the phone down," she heard Owen say somewhere in the background on the other end. "Frankie is working right now."

"I don't care." Thora's voice was loud and up close. "Marv will need a decision ASAP."

"Grams..." Owen again, even fainter. "Unlock the door please."

"Yes, everything is fine," Thora told Frankie. "Owen's just got his shorts in a knot."

"And you've locked yourself in the bathroom," Frankie guessed.

"Well, he didn't want me to call you, but it was important, so I went rogue."

"Do you need me to text him to back off?"

"Oh, would you? He'd listen to you, I'm sure."

"Okay, hold on." Frankie typed up a short message with the promised sentiment and sent it off.

Owen's response was quick. *Clearly she hasn't told you why she's calling yet...*

What was that supposed to mean?

"Okay, he's been benched," Frankie told Thora. "Now tell me what's going on please. I have a student waiting."

"Well, Owen told me about the bank situation," Thora said. "So I made some calls."

Frankie straightened. "Don't tell me you have contacts at the bank."

"No..."

"Agents in England who have contacts at the bank?" Frankie guessed.

Thora let out a raspy giggle. "No, dear, but thank you for playing along with me and calling them agents."

Frankie looked toward the closed door of her practice room. If she didn't get back soon, that little guy might mutiny. "What calls then?" she asked.

"Right, so I have a friend in Atlanta whose sister's husband's brother was a pilot for American, and he can get you on a flight early Friday."

The air stilled around Frankie. "What?"

"A flight. To London," Thora said as if that simple explanation said it all.

"Friday," Frankie filled in. Then she squeezed her eyes together and shook her head. "For me?"

Thora chuckled. "Of course, for you. Who else has important business at an English bank right now?"

"I can't," Frankie said on instinct. Now it made sense why

Owen had been trying to stop his grandmother. "Sorry you went through the trouble, but I already told Owen I can't afford it. It's disappointing and frustrating, but there's nothing I can do about it."

"Oh, it's free," Thora said. "I guess I left that part out."

Frankie's objections stuck in her throat. "What do you mean it's free?"

"You'd use his buddy pass. Technically, it's a standby ticket, but he knows there are open seats on the five-a.m. flight. He needs to know by eight tonight."

Frankie's hand went to her forehead as she paced the few feet of space available to her in the hallway. She could go to London. Possibly find out where Estelle's payments had gone. She'd only have to be away for the weekend so she wouldn't miss many lessons, except... *Darn.* Cal's son's wedding was this weekend. That was ten thousand dollars for the school that she shouldn't walk away from. But going later also wasn't an option. She'd already missed lessons while in Alabama, so she couldn't be gone several weekdays, and the following weekend was the auction.

"I don't know," she said.

"Of course you know," Thora said.

"I really don't." Frankie's voice took on a note of desperation. "I'm going to need to think this through. There's a... a lot at stake. People who are counting on me."

"But what about you? What do *you* want to do?" Thora's voice was full of compassion. "Isn't that what matters most?"

Frankie crouched down in her corner, leaning her forehead against the wall. This was an amazing chance but one that came with consequences. She clutched at her collar as if that would make breathing easier, then she stood abruptly. "I have to get back to my student," she said. "I promise I'll think about it and call you when I'm done here. That's the best I can do."

Thora was quiet for a beat, then her voice returned, still

gentle as if Frankie was a skittish foal. "You're not doing it for me, dear. I'll be fine either way. This is all about you."

If that wasn't a novelty, Frankie didn't know what was. Maybe she could do this.

But then she found her student sitting under the piano playing games on his phone when she returned because she was a terrible teacher and possibly an even worse representative for Starview, so no—she definitely couldn't.

"All right, back to the keys we go," she said, urging the kid back onto the chair. "From the top. Show me your dynamics."

He played, and she didn't hear a single note, her thoughts far away across the Atlantic. The key to everything could be there, and if it was, didn't she deserve to know?

The scales tipped again.

She took stock of everything she'd learned, spreading all the different pieces out before her and turning them this way and that—an unexpected death, someone wronged, secret payments, a hit song based on lies, a missing child, compulsive collecting, an invented heritage, a fake diagnosis, a failing school—but no matter how she tried, the pattern remained elusive.

She was at her desk, still trying and failing to spot the bigger picture when Kayla returned a little later.

"Success," her friend announced. "Or, well, some of the items were costume jewelry and not worth much, but you got twenty-four hundred dollars out of it. Enough for the mouse guy and then some."

"That's great," Frankie said, forcing enthusiasm into her voice. "Thank you so much."

"I did keep one piece," Kayla said, pulling a necklace out of the now almost empty baggie and dangling it in front of Frankie. "I didn't think you meant to pawn it—it seems more like a keepsake."

The locket at the end of the chain caught the light from the window, prompting Frankie to take hold of it. She didn't recognize the etched gold oval, but then again, she'd been in a hurry when she'd gone through Estelle's jewelry drawer. She flipped it over, her fingertip catching on an ornate A decorating the front. Not E for Estelle, F for Frankie, or even G for Greg. *A*. The hairs on Frankie's arms rose with awareness before she'd even opened the dainty thing.

"Aw, such a cute picture of you," Kayla said as the image within was revealed.

Frankie fought to maintain control of her breathing as the smiling toddler looking up at her in the photo made the past undeniably real. Same eyes and cheeks but lighter hair and a different time.

"Yeah, that's not me," she said, finally choosing to entrust Kayla with the truth. "That's my sister."

# THIRTY-TWO

## ESTELLE

Then

Estelle had protested when Ray had handed her the tickets to England and onward. She had things to do back home, and she didn't want to leave so soon after her friend had given birth, especially since baby Matt was colicky, and Darla was fraught with lack of sleep. To travel now felt ill-timed, but nevertheless, he'd insisted. She'd go to England and meet up with his contacts, do what needed to be done, and then spend the summer in Scandinavia. She'd be playing a few gigs here and there, but mostly he wanted her to write and record songs for her first album.

"You've been under so much pressure lately," he'd said. "Sweden is wonderful this time of year, and the change of scenery will do you good. We'll still be here when you get back in August, and then you'll have your head on straight again."

Maybe he had a point, she thought, looking out at the creampuff clouds on the other side of the airplane window. Her head was somewhat askew at the moment. So much had happened since she'd moved to Nashville a year ago. Professionally, it was all good, but she wasn't used to having someone else in her business all the time.

A drowsy groan came from the seat next to her as if to underscore that crowded feeling. Estelle put her elbows up on the tray table and rested her forehead in her hands. What it boiled down to was—she trusted Ray. So far, he'd never steered her wrong, which meant this was the right thing to do.

"Is everything okay here?" a stewardess asked above her.

"It's the turbulence," Estelle said. "Motion sickness. Do you have another bag?"

"Of course. I'll bring some water too."

It would be over soon, she told herself. This detour didn't mean her path forward had changed. Like Ray had said, it would pick back up exactly where she'd left it upon her return. She might even be better off. More experiences meant more material to draw from in her writing. Better stories.

She leaned back in her seat again as the bright blue sky outside softened into lilac and yellow with the setting sun.

Yes. Everything would be all right.

She was Estelle Lavigne now, and unlike Milnes, Lavignes prevailed.

# THIRTY-THREE

## FRANKIE

Now

It rained at Heathrow when Frankie stepped out of arrivals onto British soil. If she didn't count two hours of fitful dozing on the plane, she was going on over thirty hours of no sleep, but adrenaline and hope carried her forward to the taxi ramp.

The discovery of the locket had made up Frankie's mind. Even if she put all other question marks aside and decided lies and financial irregularities were unimportant, she had to keep digging for her sister's sake. That picture of baby A, which was how she'd come to think of her, had been a sign. If the payments to the bank had anything to do with her, Frankie needed to know.

In the car on the way to her hotel, she texted Owen first to let him and Thora know she'd made it safely, and then Kayla.

Frankie had expected Kayla to put up a fight about her leaving again, but after she'd explained everything that had happened, her friend had hugged her and told her she'd keep everything back home on schedule. Losing out on the ten thousand dollars was a hit, but Kayla had promised she'd offer Cal musicians free of charge for the procession and let him know he was off the hook for the donation. Frankie would go see him in person when she returned, and in the meantime, she had to trust that they'd pull in enough money at the event anyway.

The only caveat she'd added after telling Kayla everything was to keep Matt out of it until Frankie got back. While Frankie didn't believe for one second that Estelle and Ray had been romantically entangled, Orla's comments had shone a spotlight on just how close the two of them had once been. The more Frankie thought about it, the more convinced she was that Uncle Ray knew more than he'd let on about something—exactly what, she didn't know—and she didn't want to risk Matt's ear getting bent by subterfuge until she had the facts to counter them.

*Cal was disappointed but gracious about it,* Kayla texted. *Mira is going to play. Where are you now?*

*Almost at the hotel*, Frankie responded.

London traffic was chaotic, but at least they didn't have to dive into the fray of downtown to get to the small boutique hotel Owen had found for her last minute near Waterloo station.

"First time visiting?" the driver asked when Frankie plastered her face to the window to see the River Thames joining them on their right.

"Yes," Frankie said.

"Business or pleasure?"

"Um..." Frankie sat back in her seat again to avoid getting car sick as they dodged another traffic jam. "Business I guess." Of the unfinished kind.

Her phone dinged again. Another message from Kayla. *Hope you can get some sleep.*

That made two of them. Tomorrow could be a big day, and she needed to be ready.

. . .

The branch of the bank Frankie needed to visit was in Guildford, about an hour's train ride from Waterloo station. She'd left herself plenty of time by taking a train out of the city that would get there thirty minutes before the bank opened. It was a sunny morning, though still cool enough to warrant a jacket, but Frankie turned her face to the sky as she headed toward the high street and let the morning rays fortify her.

She hadn't expected the town to be so charming. Cobblestoned streets, narrow alleys here and there, skewed storefronts that spoke of history, a river. Saturday foot traffic had yet to pick up, but she had no doubt that the cute shops and cafés would be teeming with people in a few hours—especially on a nice day like today. It was almost enough to help her forget the real reason she was there.

The branch was in a block of unassuming yellow-brick buildings that lacked the character of the quaint structures she'd passed on her way. *At the bank*, she texted Owen once she'd located the side street where her destination lay. He'd insisted on getting up early for moral support, even though she'd told him he didn't have to.

*Break a leg*, he responded, true to his word. *And don't take no for an answer.*

"I'll do my best," Frankie mumbled to herself. Then she pushed open the heavy door and entered.

There was only one teller working, and she was helping another customer, so Frankie took her place in line and pulled the envelope that held all the documentation she might need out of her bag. She didn't have to wait long until a second teller took his place behind the counter and called her forward.

"Morning, Miss, how can I help?"

"Hi," Frankie said, placing the envelope on the polished wood while choosing her words. "I have a somewhat unusual request I'm hoping you can help me with. I spoke to someone on the phone a few days ago and they suggested I come in person, so I flew here from the US just for this."

The teller's eyes widened. "Oh my," he said. "Must be important."

Frankie explained what she was trying to do. That her dead mother had made payments to a UK account and that she was trying to figure out what for.

"I have this," she said, pulling the sheet with the payment information out of the envelope. "See. Here's the account number and payment reference. I also have my mother's death certificate and a notarized letter from her bank stating that I am the beneficiary." She presented him with everything she'd brought, sending up a silent prayer that it would be enough.

"Hmm. Let's see." The teller studied the documents, a crease forming between his brows. "I'll be right back. One moment." He disappeared through a door to the right, leaving Frankie hanging on to the counter to support her increasingly jelly-like legs.

*Please*, she thought. *Give me something.*

The man returned with an older woman with a gray perm and readers on a cord around her neck. She was the embodiment of a stern school ma'am, but her pale blue eyes were friendly as she slid the documents back to Frankie.

"I hear you've traveled far," she said. "But unfortunately, we cannot disclose account information to anyone but the account holder. That's the law."

Frankie dug her nails into her palms. *Not again.* "But I'm not asking for account activity on your end—only where my mother's money was going."

"Be that as it may, our hands are further tied by the fact that there is no active account matching the details you've provided."

"But I know it's here." Frankie pointed to the address on the page. "This is the right branch."

"Like I said," the woman continued, glancing at her colleague. "There are no *active* accounts matching your information."

Frankie was about to protest again when the inflection of the woman's voice stopped her. The emphasis wasn't accidental. She was trying to say something.

"The account is inactive," Frankie said. "Closed?"

"We're simply unable to find an active account with that number," the male teller said, a pointed glint in his eye. "That's all we can tell you."

*Okay*. Frankie pondered this. As disappointing as it was to learn the account was inactive, these two tellers were being helpful. Maybe she could push her luck a little. "Let's forget about the account then," she said, offering a smile. "I'll start over. I'm here to understand the reference for an international payment to your bank. It's not important to me who the account holder is or was—I just want to know what these letters mean." She indicated the eight letters next to the account number, deliberately covering the numerical digits in a demonstration of just how much the account itself didn't matter.

"Let's see," the older woman said, placing her readers at the tip of her nose. "SSTGTAFY." She turned to the computer monitor next to her and typed something on the keyboard."

"AFY—is that Aftbury?" the man asked.

"What's Aftbury?" Frankie asked.

"A village south of here. Used to be a Benedictine monastery hundreds of years ago."

The woman scribbled something on a note and handed it to Frankie. "Looks like this abbreviation is for St. George's Trust in Aftbury."

Frankie looked between the two of them. "A religious trust? Like a church?" Why would Estelle have been sending money there?

"Could be for land management, education, charity,

building upkeep..." The older woman gave a little shrug. "We couldn't say."

Couldn't or wouldn't? Frankie nibbled at her lip as she looked at the note. "How far away is it?"

"Oh, about a twenty-minute drive, I'd say," the man said. "Not more."

"And the trust is still there?"

"It's possible," the woman said. "It's a historical landmark, so someone must still be overseeing it, one would think."

So the account was inactive, but there might be someone there with more information about the trust. Frankie gathered everything and shoved it back into the envelope she'd brought, a decision forming. "Thank you for your help," she said. "Do you happen to know where I could rent a car around here?"

"There are cars for hire at the train station," the man said. "Do you know where that is?"

"That's where I came from." Frankie tucked the envelope back in her bag, backing away from the counter. "Thank you again."

"Best of luck," the older woman called.

Frankie retraced her steps through the town to the station, not stopping to admire the old-timey charm again. She was getting closer. She could feel it. All she had to do was get to Aftbury.

She practically ran up to the rental desk, out of breath and sweaty. "One car please," she panted. "To rent, I mean. I'd like to rent a car." She'd never rented a car before, which was obvious to anyone judging by the clerk's amused expression.

"American?" he asked.

"Is that a problem?" Frankie asked.

"No, no." The man smiled. "Just curious. We don't get a lot of walk-ins from overseas."

"Oh. Yes. Poor planning." Frankie let out a self-depreciating laugh.

"Not to worry. And how long will you be needing it for?"

"Um..." Frankie did some mental math—travel time, boots on the ground, that sort of thing. "Maybe four hours. At most."

The man looked up from his computer. "Oh, we have a twenty-four-hour minimum."

"But I don't need it for that long."

He shrugged. "Company policy. You can return it sooner, but the charge is the same."

"Fine." She handed him her emergencies-only credit card and hoped it wouldn't be too expensive.

After signing the necessary paperwork, the guy walked her to the car. "Have you driven in England before?" he asked, unlocking it.

"No, but roads are roads, right?" Restless energy bounded inside Frankie. She wanted to be on her way five minutes ago. "Don't worry, I'm a safe driver."

"And you have insurance, which is what I care about," he said. "But what I meant was—have you driven on the left before?"

Frankie pulled up short, eyes drawn to the small sedan where, yep, the steering wheel was on the wrong side. She'd forgotten about that detail.

"I'm a quick learner," she said, holding out her hand for the key.

He hesitated for a beat, then dropped it into her palm. "If you say so. There are some great videos online of how we do roundabouts and intersections. You might want to check them out. Friendly suggestion."

"Thanks." She opened the door and got in, looking around at the backward interior. Fluttery critters started circling in her belly, but she forced a smile as she waved the guy off. She could do this. Lavignes didn't back down from a challenge.

As soon as he was out of sight, she took him up on his advice and viewed several short videos of common pitfalls of left-side driving for tourists, and then she started up the car, thanking her luck that he'd at least given her an automatic transmission. She took it slow at first, singing a made-up song about "staying to the left" any time she had to make a turn, but once she was out of the city, it was easier.

She reached Aftbury in twenty-two minutes and even managed to parallel park along the narrow street that ran through the small village.

If Guildford had been cute, Aftbury was downright picturesque, with hollyhocks lining the cobblestoned streets in front of quaint cottages adorned with thatched roofs. It was like entering a fairy tale.

"Excuse me, do you know where I can find the St. George's Trust?" she asked the first person she came across.

The woman pointed ahead. "Second right," she said. "Past the church."

"Thanks." Frankie set off in that direction at a quick pace, forcing herself to ignore the scenery. Everything but the task at hand could wait.

After searching for a few minutes, she found a sign on a brown-brick building with the name of the trust and knocked on the door. She waited, her pulse thrumming erratically both from her quick walk and the potential for answers. The squat stone church with its ornate square tower rose on her right, its medieval features poised as if to launch knights and dragons from its belly any moment, and beyond its cemetery was an even larger matching building that Frankie guessed had been the monastery.

She knocked again when no one came to the door, fighting the urge to peek through the lace-curtained windows.

"Come on," she whispered, knocking a third time.

"No one's there," a voice said from somewhere behind her.

She spotted a man in the shade of a tree at the edge of the

cemetery. He was resting his hand on top of a rake handle, a bushel of yard debris at his feet.

Frankie took a step toward him, shading her eyes against the midday sun. "Do you know where I can find them?"

He looked off toward the village. "I suspect they're at home with their families. You know it's a Saturday, right, love?"

Right. And maybe a trust wasn't the sort of place where urgent work happened around the clock. "I need to speak to someone about... something," she said, not wanting to get into it with this groundskeeper.

"That's to do with St. George's?" he asked, gesturing toward the church.

"Maybe," she said.

"Well, the priest is here. You could try him."

Frankie looked wistfully at the trust sign again, then accepted the change of plans. "Inside the church?" she asked.

"Last I saw him."

She thanked him and directed her steps to her new destination.

The inside of the church was steeped in muted light, the air stale with old mortar and dust, but the brightly colored cloth on the altar spoke of an active space, as did the small children's play area near the doors.

"Hello?" Frankie called, entering the central nave.

The rustling of paper reached her ears from somewhere not far off, then footsteps headed her way.

"Hello there," a heavyset man in his fifties said upon approach, his collar telling Frankie she'd found the right person. "Can I help you, Miss?"

"I hope so," Frankie said.

She shared what she'd learned at the bank and that it was important to her to understand why her mother had made payments to the trust but that their offices had been closed. "The last payment was ten years ago, and I have reason to believe the account is no longer active," she said, being intentionally vague to protect the tellers who'd helped her more than they should have. "Any idea where her money ended up?"

"Hmm," the priest said. "About ten years ago, you say. Could I possibly see the document?"

Frankie retrieved it from her bag and handed it to him, pointing out where the account number and code were located.

"Do you mind waiting while I make a call to someone who might know more?"

"Of course." Frankie nodded, hope returning.

She paced the aisles while she waited, the priest's muted voice skimming the walls around her as the sound traveled from what she assumed was his office. *Please, find some answers*, she pleaded silently, eyes drawn to the stained-glass windows up high. She snapped a picture and sent it to Owen with the caption *Following breadcrumbs in Aftbury.*

*Look at you sleuthing*, was his response. *Grams is so proud.*

Just then, the priest returned, so she tucked her phone away. "Anything?"

"I don't know why I didn't think of it before," he said. "But at least I confirmed it for you. We believe the payment was a donation to the boarding school."

"A boarding school?" Frankie frowned.

"See the first S in the code would have earmarked the funds for the school, but it was closed permanently a little over eight years ago," the priest continued. "Dwindling enrollment and the cost of building maintenance made it unsustainable. A shame. It brought energy to the community for so many years."

"But why would my mother in North Carolina make payments to this school?" Frankie asked. "And why stop paying two years before it closed if it had financial issues?"

"Was she an alum perhaps? We did get a handful of overseas students each year. Or her church might have directed her charity our way if they knew of a struggling partner parish."

Frankie shook her head. None of it fit well. Mom had attended church regularly for the past twenty years, so maybe the priest's second suggestion had some merit, but it still didn't explain the connection to Frankie's birthday or why Estelle hadn't used her regular checking account to make the payments. The only comfort was that it at least didn't suggest Estelle having paid someone off for a criminal endeavor.

"Would she have had reason to sponsor a student?" the priest asked.

Frankie was about to say no, but then a thought struck that made her gasp. "What age were the students?" Could her sister have come here? She quickly calculated how old baby A would have been when Estelle started sending payments, but her excitement faltered as soon as she realized the years didn't add up. Her sister would have been an adult by then if she was still alive. Her heart squeezed at the thought.

"Twelve to eighteen. Such a fun age," the priest said. "I joined the parish five years before the school's demise and didn't have much to do with the academic side of the trust, but we all felt the quiet after they were gone."

"Do the names Lavigne or Milne mean anything to you?" she asked just in case. "Or maybe Sutton? First initial A? A girl."

He thought about it. "Nothing comes to mind. I think there was an Anthony Milner toward the end possibly."

"What about Estelle Lavigne? Ever heard that name?"

He shook his head. "I'm sorry, no."

Frankie sighed. Was this really going to be another dead end? She might have found out where Estelle's money had gone, but the big "why" remained infuriatingly veiled.

She thanked the priest and returned outside where the sunlight blazed her retinas as she adjusted to the light. She stood for a while on the church step, the village quiet before her. The heaviness in her heart didn't fit this beautiful May

Saturday. She was in England—her first trip ever crossing an ocean—but as much as she wished she could enjoy it, that wasn't why she'd come. She was on a mission, and if she wanted to prevail, she had to think.

She opened a browser on her phone and searched for St. George's Academy in Aftbury to see if anything would pop up and spark an idea, but her roaming internet was too slow to load anything.

"Crap," she muttered, dropping her phone to her side, her mind working.

If she was Estelle, why would she donate money to a school so far away? Had she come here at some point? Did she have ties to someone local? Was it merely a religious donation?

An old couple passed the church walking their small dog in the direction of the village center. The school had infused energy into this place the priest had said, and Frankie believed it. Was this what would happen to Aspen Creek if she wasn't able to save Starview? A decline into lassitude? No doubt the median age had gone up by about forty years here in the near decade since the school had been gone. Frankie had a feeling this was now the kind of place where people remained into old age.

In the midst of the absolute knowledge that she didn't want such a shift on her shoulders, the thought sparked something else. If Estelle had spent time here, someone in the village could remember her. It was a weak lead, but the best she had.

*Can you check and see if Mom's church had any ties to St. George's Academy in Aftbury?* she texted Owen while she walked. Best to cross all the Ts.

The village center was made up of a cluster of shops surrounding a triangular, grass-covered town square. There was a small chain-store grocer, a florist, a realtor, a pub, two cafés, a souvenir shop slash craft gallery, and two clothing stores. Hanging planters adorned every entry, and the shop signs displayed the kind of charm reserved for places with a history going back more than a couple hundred years. People were moving about, but as it wasn't yet tourist season, their pace was unhurried and focused on meeting neighbors rather than seeing the sights. That meant locals and exactly the people she wanted to talk to.

Within an hour, she'd all but exhausted her sources. Yes, most people she met had lived there when the school was operating. No, no one recognized Estelle's name or picture. She didn't even meet a single person who'd been a student at the school, and most of the shopkeepers were too young to have worked there for more than ten years. The pub owner was an exception, and he'd known most of the teachers at the academy, but beyond that he was no help.

"You've been talking to a lot of people," the woman running the souvenir shop said when Frankie entered her store. "I've seen you through the window. Are you a journalist?" She was dressed in linen overalls with her graying hair up in a messy bun.

"No, just curious about the school that used to be here," Frankie said, looking around at the keychains, soaps, and quirky pottery that lined the shelves inside.

"A shame I can't help you with that," the woman said. "We opened two years ago. Moved down from the city to get some peace."

Which meant this woman would be of no help to her either. "It is peaceful," Frankie agreed, offering a brief smile before picking up a pair of novelty socks with red phone booths on them—not because she needed socks but to give her hands something to do while she dealt with the ramifications of the constant squashing of her hopes. No one knew Estelle. No one had first-hand experience of the school. No one.

"Are you looking for anything in particular?" the woman

asked. "You're American, right? Perhaps some treats for your loved ones back home. The fudge is always popular."

"Just browsing for now," Frankie said, moving away from the register to give herself space. Her fingers trailed a tabletop with folded scarves, her eyes sweeping over the silk creations and accompanying novelty earrings on stands. A counter full of crystals was next, then a shelf with handmade ceramic incense stands and packs of fragrant sticks.

"Are you on a solo vacation then?" the woman asked, coming up behind Frankie. "We typically don't get a lot of tourists until late June here.

Frankie knew she should leave. She wasn't in the mood for chit-chat, but as soon as she stepped back outside, she'd have to admit defeat. "Something like that," she said, picking up a tester of hand cream and smelling it, then another.

"Sounds mysterious," the woman said. "Oh, those creams are bestsellers. Locally made. We had a cinnamon and vanilla one that was all the rage over Christmas, but I fancy the floral ones myself." She handed Frankie a tube adorned with roses and waited expectantly while Frankie tried it on the back of her hand.

"It's a little strong for me," Frankie said. "But thank you."

She continued her cursory perusal of the wares, building up to the moment she'd have to confront reality again. She was almost there, almost ready, when she spotted a pair of dangling earrings in the shape of ballet slippers on the table by the window. Those would be perfect for Kayla. "I'll take these," Frankie said, glad to have bought herself another few minutes' respite.

"A fine choice," the woman said. "I'll wrap them up for you, shall I?"

"Thank you." Frankie watched as her gift was rung up and bagged.

"And just because," the woman said, tucking a small tube of

hand cream into the bag. "On the house. It has calming properties."

Was it so obvious she needed it? Frankie smiled as she handed over her card. "Thank you so much." And then she was outside again on the wrong side of the possibility Aftbury had presented.

Frankie dragged her feet back to her car, her movements slow and heavy as she unlocked the doors and got in. She tipped her head back against the headrest, wishing Owen would appear in the passenger seat, his unending optimism bolstering her.

No, she hadn't found answers here either, but she was a pair of earrings and—she reached into the bag—a tube of lavender hand cream richer. She opened it and rubbed it into her skin, wishing whatever magical calm it possessed would imbue her. It smelled much better than the rose one, that was for sure, its sweet herbal fragrance filling the small space.

"So you paid the school for fifteen years," Frankie recapped under her breath. "Then ten years ago the payments stopped, but not because the school closed since that happened later." It struck her that the made-up cancer had also taken place ten years ago. A coincidence?

She took a deep breath of the fragrant air, something else tugging at her subconscious that she couldn't place. It wasn't to do with the cancer. The boarding school payments then? Were they connected to the situation Starview was in? It seemed unlikely since so many years had passed, but perhaps it would be unwise to dismiss the possibility. Frankie still didn't know if something Estelle had done had caused Starview's predicament. As far as Frankie could tell, the school's accounting books hadn't looked doctored, and the only regular expenses Estelle had had were daily life upkeep ones. Plus, the weird collection of tea and candles of course.

No sooner had Frankie recalled the guest-room discovery

than the scent of lavender around her intensified, bringing with it the echo of Kayla's voice telling her that the oldest products in the suitcase were about ten years old.

"Something happened ten years ago," she mumbled to herself. Estelle had sent money to the school, then stopped only to start buying lavender products. Almost as if one replaced the other.

Frankie pulled the hand cream tube out of the bag and squinted at the fine print beneath the product name. Like the shopkeeper had said, it was locally made, the name of the company in swirly italics next to the listed ingredients. Frankie tried to recall the packaging of the teas and candles in her mom's stash, but at the time, she'd been more focused on the strangeness of the collection than such details. The packaging had been different for the different products, but she couldn't remember if they'd been from multiple sellers or only one.

Frankie fumbled with the zipper of her bag to get to her phone, her fingers clumsy and slow as she dialed Kayla's number.

"Hey, it's me," she said when her friend picked up. "I have a favor to ask."

The minutes elongated into an excruciating wait while Frankie pictured Kayla driving to Estelle's, unlocking the door, walking upstairs, pulling out the trunk and guitar case, and opening them.

She stared at her phone as if that would make it go faster. Any minute now.

When Kayla finally called, Frankie picked up before the first ring had finished playing.

"Different or the same?" she asked.

"They're all the same," Kayla said. "The logo seems to have been redesigned maybe three years ago, but it's all from the same place—Midsomer Lavender Farm."

Frankie's pulse kicked into high gear. This was important.

She didn't yet know exactly how it fit together with everything else, only that it mattered. "Can you look it up for me? My internet sucks here."

"Sure, one second."

Frankie drummed an uneven rhythm against her thighs while she waited.

"Looks like it's not too far from where you are now. A couple of hours west, south of Bath."

"Phone number?"

Kayla gave it to her. "What are you going to do?"

"I'll call them—ask if they knew Estelle. She didn't buy all that stuff to use it, so she must have had another reason. If we figure that out, maybe we'll figure out why she paid the school too."

They hung up after Frankie promised to keep Kayla posted, and Frankie immediately dialed the phone number Kayla had given her. Several seconds of silence went by, but then it finally connected. One beep, two, three.

"Midsomer Lavender," a woman answered. "This is Amber speaking. How may I help you?"

# THIRTY-FOUR

## FRANKIE

Now

A soft gasp escaped Frankie at hearing a cadence so uncannily familiar in a stranger. Everything stilled around her, the already quiet interior of the car pressing against her eardrums like a vacuum. It couldn't be... Her lips prepared to speak, but no sound came.

"Hello?" The woman again. *Amber.*

No, Frankie must be imagining things. The British accent was playing tricks on her. The name was a coincidence, and this was simply a clerk manning phones at a local business. Nothing else.

"Anyone there?"

But that husky alto that always sounded a second away from slipping into song...

"Um, hi," Frankie said. "I'm calling because I think my mother was a customer of yours. My name is Frankie Lavigne, and—"

There was a rustle on the line, and then it went dead.

"Hello?" Frankie said. She looked to see if her phone was still connected, which it was, then listened again. Nothing.

She hung up and sat staring at the screen until it blurred. Had she just spoken to her sister, or was she losing her mind? She huffed out a little laugh. Was such a thing even possible?

She dialed again, holding her breath as it connected, but this time it went straight to voicemail. That same voice again that sounded so much like Estelle.

"You have reached Midsomer Lavender, where we aim to set your life in bloom. We're unavailable to take your call right now, but please select one of the following options. For hours, press one. For our address, press two. To leave a message, press three. Have a wonderful day."

Frankie waited too long to make her choice, the call disconnecting while her phone was still at her ear. Her hand shook as she lowered it to her lap. Was her sister there? The possibility swirling in her mind shouldn't have made sense, but Frankie had to admit that it gave Estelle a reason for her floral purchases. Had it been her way of supporting her oldest daughter's business? But surely there were many easier and more direct ways to do that, not to mention how it still didn't explain why Estelle had kept it to herself.

Frankie called the number again, willing Amber to pick up this time, but she got voicemail again. She cursed under her breath, debating what to do as the voice listed the options again. Finally, she tapped the number two on her screen for an address and scrambled for a piece of paper and a pen in her bag to jot it down before the call disconnected.

She looked out the windshield down the cobblestoned street where she'd parked what felt like eons ago. The car was hers for twenty-four hours, so she wasn't in a hurry, and she'd come this far. She could do a couple more hours on the road.

Her phone dinged with a message, and she yanked it up so

fast it almost hit her face. But of course it wasn't the lavender farm. No reason for them to be texting. It was Owen.

*Asked the priest and he's never heard of St. George's Academy. What's happening over there?*

That settled it. Frankie was willing to bet that whether or not this Amber was her sister, there was a connection between the lavender farm and the boarding school, and she needed to know what it was more than anything.

*Found a woman named Amber working at the lavender farm Mom bought all those products from,* she typed. *I'm heading there now.*

Then she started the car.

It was mid-afternoon by the time Frankie approached her destination. Two hours of endless green expanses lay behind her, the sky as big as she'd ever seen above the rolling English countryside. She'd not paid it much attention though, her eyes firmly on the horizon straight ahead and the promise of a resolution, no matter what shape it would take.

Her heart pounded furiously in her chest as she made the turn off the main road, following the signs to the lavender farm, the sound of it dizzying as she spotted a two-story brick farmhouse rising beyond fields of not-yet-blooming shrubs. She was so close, but the uncertainty of what she'd find still loomed before her.

She pulled into a small gravel parking lot outside a wood structure with a "SHOP" sign above the door and took a few steeling breaths before exiting. There were three other cars in the lot, so Frankie assumed they were open, but the prospect of entering the store, of confronting the woman she'd heard on the phone, made her stomach roil. She'd have a look at the fields first, she decided. Give herself a moment.

A cool wind blew across the sprawling landscape, making Frankie wrap her arms around herself despite the sunlight as she wandered along the rows of lavender mounds that would soon stretch on in endless purple.

A figure became visible at the far end of the row she was in, carrying a large basket under one arm and occasionally stooping down to pull something—weeds presumably—from the ground.

Frankie looked back toward the shop, but there was still no sign of life, so she set off toward the field worker instead. Sooner or later, she'd have to find someone to ask, and this person was no better or worse than the next.

She had the sun behind her, so when she was twenty yards out, she cleared her throat to make sure she didn't sneak up on the poor woman—because it was a woman. Clad in jeans and a flannel with sunglasses and a wide-brimmed hat covering her head, Frankie couldn't tell much else, but she stopped all the same when the woman stood up tall. There was something about how she jerked her gloves off her hands and lifted an arm to shade her eyes from the light that drove the air from Frankie's lungs like a punch to the stomach.

"Can I help you?" the woman called.

It was her. The woman from the phone. Amber. And seeing her like this, there was no doubt in Frankie's mind that she'd finally found her sister.

She swallowed against the thickness in her throat, then cleared it. "I called earlier," she said. "My name is Frankie."

Amber's arms fell to her sides, her gloves dropping to the ground. "You're here?"

"I'm..." Frankie fought to find the right words as she realized that Amber knew who she was. "The phone call disconnected. I... I think I've been looking for you."

A harsh noise escaped Amber like she'd fought to hold back a sob but lost the battle, and then she dropped to her knees where she stood. "Oh," she cried. "No, it can't be real."

Frankie looked about her in a panic, briefly struck rigid by the unexpected reaction. Then she continued toward the other woman, who had pulled off her hat and turned her face to the sky as tears flowed down her cheeks. Hair a shade lighter than Frankie's and with a few gray streaks at the temples spilled down her back in a loose braid.

"I'm sorry," Frankie said. "I didn't mean... You know who I am?"

Amber looked up at her. Nodded. She wiped her cheeks with the backs of her sleeves, then pushed off the ground.

"You knew Estelle?" Frankie asked, wanting to be sure. "Estelle Lavigne?"

Amber nodded again, a straggling sob making her hand go to her chest as if to soothe it. "She was my mother," she said, a sharp exhale following the statement.

Goosebumps broke out all over Frankie's body. She'd really found her. "I have so many questions."

A sad sigh crossed Amber's lips. "I know." She took a step closer to Frankie, her eyes roaming over her features. "I can't believe you're here. How did you find me?"

"It's a long story." Frankie lips twisted with wry humor at the understatement.

"I can put on some tea," Amber said. "If you want."

Frankie wasn't alone after all. She had a sister. A family. "More than anything," she said.

Another airy sob escaped Amber, but this one was accompanied by a smile. "Oh my God. My husband is going to lose it," she said as if underlining Frankie's thought.

"You're married?" she asked.

"Fourteen years." Amber's expression grew radiant, so reminiscent of Estelle that Frankie ached. "And my twins are twelve."

Frankie laughed. She was an aunt too? "Amazing."

Amber stilled. "It is," she said. "And now you're here." She opened her arms. "Can I?"

Frankie didn't hesitate, letting her big sister pull her into an embrace that smelled of lavender and the outdoors. She inhaled deeply and noted absently that Amber did the same.

"Come on," Amber said, leading Frankie toward the farmhouse with one arm around her shoulders.

They entered through a patio door that led straight into a large kitchen with light-green cabinets and white counters. An oak trestle table sat on a colorful woven rug at one end of the space, covered with what looked like a school art project. On the walls were a mix of framed art prints, photos of the farm and its inhabitants, and taped-up kid drawings. The space was lived in and immediately felt homey to Frankie.

"Have a seat," Amber said, gesturing to a round stool tucked under the small kitchen island. She headed for the sink, where she took her time washing her hands and filling a kettle.

Frankie was thankful for the minutes of inertia. She needed them to catch up to the reality of suddenly sitting in her sister's kitchen, out of place and right where she belonged all at once. There was so much she needed to know, but every possible question she came up with felt insignificant in the face of this momentous development.

"Now please tell me how you ended up here," Amber said as she set first a mug down in front of Frankie, then a plate of what looked like lavender biscuits.

"You kind of stole my question there," Frankie said, stirring honey into the steaming tea. "But fine, since you asked first."

Amber leaned back against the counter, crossing her feet at the ankles like Estelle often had. It distracted Frankie enough that Amber had to ask again.

"Sorry. You just... You look a lot like Mom."

Amber frowned, squinting at Frankie as if she wanted to argue, which made Frankie curse her tongue. Whatever had happened between Estelle and Amber, it had caused a deep rift. She should have assumed Amber wouldn't welcome the comparison.

Instead of kicking that hornet's nest, she forged on to answer the question, hoping that would steer the conversation right.

"The short version is that the school we run is having financial trouble," she said. "After Mom died—" She stopped herself again, her gaze flying to Amber's in alarm as if she'd said too much. What if she didn't know?

"It's okay. I knew," Amber said, reading her mind like only a sister could, then bringing her mug to her lips. "Continue."

Frankie explained about the account she'd found and the payments, leaving out the other, unrelated lies for now. "I was trying to find an explanation for all the weird things that have surfaced since she passed. And I'd learned about you—that she'd had another child, I mean." Frankie glanced at Amber, who was listening with a guarded expression. "Anyway. I came here to find out where the payments went. Found the boarding school—and I'm still not clear on how it's connected, by the way—then I remembered the stash of lavender products under her guest-room bed."

Amber's eyes widened. "She kept everything?"

Frankie nodded. "So I followed the trail. I didn't expect you to be here, but when you answered the phone..."

"Yes, about that," Amber said, setting her mug down next to her. "I didn't mean to hang up on you—I was just so shocked at hearing your voice that I dropped my phone. The screen cracked, and I... I guess I didn't know what to do."

"I tried calling again."

She bit into the corner of her lower lip. "I know. I'm sorry."

For a while, neither of them said anything, the magnitude of them being in the same room reverberating again through Frankie. She couldn't be upset with Amber for not picking up the phone. By all objective standards, this was the kind of surprise that needed digesting.

"Did you work at the school?" Frankie asked, picking up that loose string instead. "Is that why she sent money?"

"Work?" Amber frowned. "No, but I was a student there a long time ago. Oh." She craned her neck as she spotted something outside the window. "That's John and the kids back now—they've been at his parents' today. Let me give them a heads-up."

"Of course." Frankie's head swam with the information that Amber had been at St. George's Academy. So maybe the abduction story had been inspired by the Hattiesburg family after all. Maybe Estelle and Greg had simply decided to give Amber a solid education. She would have been twelve in 1988, which fit the timeline. If the more recent payments were the tail end of a lengthy payment plan, that would also explain how they'd afforded to send Amber there, though it did strike Frankie as a little odd that anyone would send their young child abroad for school, especially since Estelle had homeschooled Frankie. Then again, Uncle Ray always talked about his time at Eton as some of the best years of his life, so what did she know?

Footsteps outside the door put Frankie on alert, and she stood as Amber's family entered the kitchen.

"Frankie, this is John, Evie, and Daniel. Family, this is Frankie."

Frankie waved at her niece and nephew and shook John's large hand when he offered it. He was a broad man, not much taller than his wife, but with shoulders and arms that spoke of hard manual work. Kind eyes that reminded her of Owen.

"Frankie," he said, curiosity and something else more emotional lining his features. "It's so nice to finally meet you."

"You as well," she said, even though she hadn't known he existed until a few minutes ago.

He and Amber shared a look, then he turned to the twins, who were watching them from a few yards away, disengaged enough to almost camouflage their interest in that off-handed way only tweens could pull off. "Come on, kids—let's run out and pick up something for dinner, shall we? Leave the ladies to it."

Evie looked over her shoulder at Frankie as she stepped outside, their eyes meeting long enough that Frankie saw herself reflected therein. Evie may have had John's reddish-brown hair, but the Lavigne family resemblance was still strong. How odd to have such a connection thrust in your lap when you'd thought there was no one.

Amber was watching her when Frankie returned her attention to her sister. "So that's my family," she said, a fond smile lingering on her lips.

"They seem wonderful," Frankie said, and she meant it. Her sister had made a nice life here. "I'm happy I got to meet them."

Amber nodded before sipping her tea. She frowned as the beverage hit her lips. "Urgh, cold," she said. "Can I get you a refill?"

Frankie declined, eager to continue their conversation instead. "Um, you were saying you were a student at St. George's Academy?"

Amber set the kettle down after pouring hot water into her mug. "Right." She pulled out another round stool and sat down at the short end of the island.

"Whose idea was it for you to go to school in Aftbury of all places?" Frankie asked. "Did Mom have a connection there? Or Dad maybe?" It could have been Greg, she thought. It didn't quite fit with the few things she knew about him, but there were large gaps in her knowledge.

"It was after Dad died," Amber said. "Frankie..."

After Greg? But then she would have already been born. Frankie's brow creased as she tried to puzzle a new timeline together where she and her sister had met before as children. That meant Estelle would have been a single mother of two. A boarding school could have relieved some of the parenting burden.

"Did you want to go?" she asked. "I mean I assume you did since you ended up staying here permanently." She gestured around the room as the sun passed behind a cloud outside the window, muting the light. The horizon was dark beyond the shop, like a front was gathering. Was rain good for a lavender farmer?

"Frankie..." Amber said again, clasping her hands together.

"But why did she never tell me I had a sister? That's what I don't understand." Frankie turned back to meet Amber's gaze and found it shifting from wavering to resolute.

"Because..." Amber sighed. "Because you don't. Frankie, I'm not your sister. I'm your mother."

# THIRTY-FIVE

## FRANKIE

Now

Frankie knew the truth of Amber's words the moment they were suspended in the air between them. Felt it, saw it, heard it. There was pain in her voice, regret, sorrow, resignation, and yet Amber kept her shoulders back, not wavering in the face of what she'd laid out before Frankie.

"I realize this must come as a shock to you," she said. "I figured she never told you. But I can prove it." She walked over to a robust armoire in the small room off the kitchen and unlocked the bottom door. After rummaging inside it, she returned to Frankie and handed her a short stack of stapled papers. "They're the maternity notes they gave me after you were born."

Frankie took them without a word, afraid of what might come out if she spoke. At the top of the page was Amber's full name, and her date of birth. Then followed a brief medical history, test results, various appointment notes, and a recommendation for a caesarean section.

*Because she'd been a child,* Frankie thought, nausea rising in her chest.

On the final page were notes about the birth. Full term, healthy baby girl, October 28, 1991.

"What?" Frankie looked up from the paper. "I wasn't born in eighty-nine?"

Amber stared at her. "That's what she told you?"

Frankie nodded numbly. "Why the hell would she lie about that of all things?" She dropped the papers to the island and pressed her hands to her head. "I don't..." She sucked in a deep gulp of air. "I don't understand. You were what—fifteen? And she sent you to St. George's?"

"Here, have some more tea." Amber put the mug into Frankie's hand and encouraged her to drink. "I'm so sorry."

"You're sorry?" Frankie coughed as a gulp threatened to go down the wrong pipe. "She's the one who should be sorry!"

It was laughable, the version of herself she'd been a few hours ago—so naïve wondering about bank accounts and ancestors, questioning the dishonesty that was coming to light. But this? This meant nothing about Frankie's life had been real.

A balloon of static energy expanded inside her, compressing every organ in her body. She needed to get up, to move, to scream and thrash, but she was frozen in place, the only giveaway to her internal chaos a tremor in her hands that threatened to upend the mug she was holding. "Please tell me," she whispered. "Tell me everything."

Amber was watching her with caution in her eyes, as if preparing for the hurricane swirling beneath Frankie's skin to make landfall. Finally, she agreed. "Let's go sit on the couch. I'll grab you a blanket."

Frankie let Amber lead her into the living room. She hadn't even noticed she'd started shivering, but a throw around her shoulders eased some of the tension inside.

"How much do you know of the years before?" Amber asked, taking Frankie's hand in hers.

"Close to nothing." Frankie told her about going to Ferrisville and Jackson and how little that trip had yielded. "Just start at the beginning. Please."

Amber nodded. "Okay." She scooted back into the other corner of the couch and pulled her legs up underneath her. "First of all, you know Stella was only eighteen when she had me, right?"

Frankie acknowledged that she did.

"I think it's safe to say I wasn't planned, and that she didn't really want to marry Dad. Probably, the parents arranged it, and it was a doomed situation from the start. There were some good years. I remember kicking a ball with Dad in our yard, saying grace before dinner, Christmas presents. But even when things were decent, they were never not fighting. I think Stella blamed him for her ruined life. Blamed us both maybe.

"She was beautiful, talented, charming, but all the plans she'd had went out the window with me and Dad, and she never let us forget it. Don't get me wrong, she still tucked me in, made my school lunches, and took me to the doctor when I was sick, but now that I'm a mother myself, I see the difference. I would do *anything* for my kids. She would only do the bare minimum."

It was difficult to reconcile Amber's description of Estelle as a mother with the image Frankie had of her as such. She'd been Frankie's constant companion, always in her ear, her care and concern vocal and insistent.

When Frankie told Amber as much, there was no immediate response; instead, a shadow of something heavy swept across Amber's face.

"I don't know why she was different with you," she said finally. "Maybe at that point she was ready? She'd chosen you? Or maybe she needed to prove to herself that she wasn't completely horrible."

The last word came out barbed, but Frankie kept quiet. She wanted Amber to tell the story at her pace.

Amber's gaze drifted away from Frankie to a series of family portraits on the wall next to them, but after a minute, she found her resolve again.

"Anyway," she said. "Dad started drinking. I was maybe four, five. First it was just on the weekend, but then he started missing work, getting into trouble..."

"Yeah, the sheriff told me about that."

"Stella had to pick up the slack, and to her credit, she did. I never went hungry, and our bills were paid. She took jobs waiting tables and bartending, and sometimes she'd sing at those places too. I think those were the only times she was truly happy back then—in front of a microphone with everyone's eyes on her."

"The center of attention," Frankie said. "Yeah, that never changed."

"After we moved to Jackson," Amber continued, "she worked at this place called Barnie's. Long hours. We lived in a trailer, and Dad never got his feet under him. They had hoped he'd have more options for work there—clean slate and all that—but instead it was like he gave up. And the more they fought, the more he drank. I was left to my own devices a lot."

"That must have been hard," Frankie said.

"It was," she agreed. "I was this quiet country girl, and Jackson seemed enormous. The school..." She shook her head. "I was used to several grades in the same classroom, but there you'd get swallowed up in the hallways. I think I was eleven when I got drunk the first time. Mom would go off to work, and I'd slip out the door with whatever bottle I could find and hang with some of the older kids in the trailer park. No one knew, and no one cared. I still showed up to class and got decent grades, so... God, it feels so long ago."

"Because it is," Frankie said. Then she added, "But your

accent gets different when you talk about it. Did you notice?" The pronounced British inflection had slowed and incorporated a Southern drawl the longer Amber spoke. Evidence of a distant past.

"I didn't," Amber said. "Huh. And here I was thinking I'd scrubbed my soul of everything from that time." She gave Frankie half a smile that faltered as the bigger implication of her statement sank in. "I didn't mean..."

"Me?" Frankie asked. She hadn't missed that while Amber described Estelle's lack of maternal instinct, Amber herself had been completely absent from Frankie's life. But there had to be a reason, and she would reserve judgment until the story reached its conclusion. "I know. Please go on."

Amber pulled a throw pillow into her lap and tugged at a strand of its fringe. She was quiet for a beat as if bracing for the next part, but then she dove in. "Stella left in April of eighty-nine," she said. "I watched her drive away—I don't think she ever knew I used to do that. I'd like to think she believed we'd be fine without her, but at that point Dad was already in such bad shape that I don't see how she could have. She was just done, I guess. I'm not sure where she went or what she did, and to be honest, I don't remember much of that year. I was out a lot. Had my first boyfriend—a real piece of work, but he showed me interest, and I was a sucker for that."

"You were thirteen?" Frankie asked.

"Yes. He was seventeen."

"And is that how I..." Frankie tried to find a delicate way to ask if this juvenile delinquent might have been her father.

"Oh no," Amber said, catching on. "Not Auggie."

"Okay." Frankie didn't know if she should be relieved or not. If not "Auggie," then the story continued.

"Dad died in December that year, and a neighbor took me in. Stella was trying to make a go of her music at the time, and she was hard to get a hold of, so for a while there was talk of foster care. I didn't want that, so the following spring, I stayed on my best behavior. No partying, nothing. And then one day, she was there. She'd come to pick me up." Amber's voice cracked, her eyes filling with tears. "I hadn't seen her in a year, and I barely recognized her. She was so much... more... than she'd been before. She had nice clothes, her hair was done, she smiled at me. I thought... I thought maybe she'd decided she wanted me after all." Amber pinched the bridge of her nose. "But she was only doing the bare minimum again, drawing the line at making me a ward of the state."

Frankie pulled the blanket tighter around her shoulders. It was like watching a horror story unfold, the innocuous details and orderly contours of her life with Estelle morphing before her into something that was inevitably heading in a sinister direction. "I'm really sorry," she said, though those words hardly seemed sufficient.

"She basically put me up in an apartment in Nashville that she'd borrowed from someone, enrolled me in school, and took off. Her career was picking up, and she had gigs all over the place. She'd call occasionally, but more often than not, I didn't know when I'd see her next. Sometimes people she knew would stop by to check on me to make sure I had food and stuff, but other than that, I was on my own. I went to school, took up with the wrong kind of friends again, and this time I had even less of a reason to keep up pretenses. I don't know how I wasn't expelled."

"It's difficult to picture that now," Frankie said, looking around at the cozy room.

"Oh, I was feral." Amber stretched out one leg and ran a hand down the fabric of her jeans as if smoothing a crease. "And then one weekend, I was getting ready to go out when one of Stella's associates came to do his check in. I'd already had a couple of beers, so I offered him one too, thinking that would make him less likely to tell on me. He checked the fridge and ran down to the corner store to pick up some stuff I was out of. We talked about school, how well Stella was doing..." She swallowed. "And then he raped me."

"Oh." The word burst from Frankie's lips as she stared at Amber, one hand flying up to cover her mouth. "No..." she whispered.

Amber's gaze was elsewhere, but she pressed on as if needing to get the words out and have it over with. "I got pregnant with you and sent to St. George's. At first, I lived with one of the nurses who worked at the clinic that was part of the school, and then after you were born, I was enrolled as a student. It was very hush-hush. Stella came back once six months after, but not for me." She focused on Frankie again.

"Only for me," Frankie filled in, horror clogging her every cell. Estelle had cast out her only child in the most vulnerable of times and left her behind. She *had* stolen Frankie after all, but not the way Frankie had feared. No, this was worse. She'd orchestrated a lifelong ruse, and she'd almost gotten away with it.

"I was told it would be better for everyone if I forgot about the whole thing and focused on my education." A streak of bitterness coated Amber's voice. "But I was fifteen. I felt ruined, and I suddenly had nothing and no one. I left the school on my eighteenth birthday and didn't look back. The path of self-destruction I'd turned to at eleven lured me further along, and for a long while, I lost myself completely. I'm not proud of that. Homelessness, drugs, petty crime..."

"Did Estelle know?"

"I don't think so. I was doing my best to pretend my past didn't exist, so even if she tried, I doubt she was able to find me. I was a ghost."

"I wonder if that's why she started sending money to the school," Frankie said. "Maybe once we were settled in Aspen

Creek, guilt caught up with her, and when she failed to track you down, the school was second best."

Amber let out a bitter huff. "I don't know that she was capable of the feeling. I think she was a sociopath or whatever you call someone who doesn't care about the way her actions impact others. Stella was always number one in Stella's world. Not Dad, not me, not you. Just Stella and her ambitions."

Frankie pondered that. A few months ago, she would have protested the statement with vehemence, but now she wasn't so sure. Estelle *had* always managed to get her way, but her gift was never to be overt about it. Everyone loved her because it felt like she was on their team. The question was if she'd played them all. More and more, the signs pointed that way.

"So how did you get away from that life?" Frankie asked.

"Luck," Amber said. "I broke my leg—walked into traffic when I was drunk and high and got hit by a car."

"Doesn't sound lucky to me."

Amber smiled. "I went through withdrawal in the hospital, and one of the nurses there took pity on me. She'd lost a son years earlier to drugs, and now she was about to retire, so she offered me a chance. She was moving back to Wales where she was from. I went with her. Celebrated my thirtieth birthday pruning lavender and rose bushes in her garden, six months clean. A couple of years after that, I met John. She passed in 2020, but Evie is named after her. She was my guardian angel."

"That should have been Estelle," Frankie said, her anger seeping through. "That's a mom's job. I'll never forgive her for this."

Amber clutched the pillow in her lap tighter. "What about me? Will you forgive me?"

Frankie startled at the question. "For what?"

"You said it yourself—it's a mom's job to protect her children. And here we are—strangers to each other."

Frankie struggled to untangle the mess of emotions that

churned inside her. No doubt her life would have been different if she'd known the truth. She'd already be part of this other family for one. Yet no anger emerged.

"You were a child yourself," she said.

"Not fifteen years ago, or ten, or five." Amber's gaze was watchful, as if preparing for the lashes she thought she'd earned. "I did write Stella about a decade ago. In a moment of weakness, I thought she might want to know that I was alive. I was in the throes of early motherhood and imagined naïvely that that might connect us. I asked about you—if you knew about me. She said that it would wreak havoc on your life. That it would be selfish of me after all this time." She lifted her shoulder in a small shrug that didn't manage to hide the writhing emotion underneath it. "I could have insisted," she said, casting her eyes down. "But I was scared that she might be right, scared I'd hurt you and lose myself again. I couldn't risk it for the twins."

Frankie nodded. "I understand."

"I hoped one day..." Tears swelled in Amber's eyes again. "Oh my God, Frankie, I'm so sorry." She covered her face as her shoulders started shaking. "I'm so sorry."

Frankie scooted across the couch and wrapped her mother in her arms. "It's okay," she said in soothing tones. "I'm okay."

Amber pulled back, her hand cupping Frankie's cheek. "Are you?"

Frankie leaned into the tender touch. "I promise."

"Okay." Amber sniffed, her thumb caressing a stray tear from beneath Frankie's eye. Then she reached for a tissue from a box on the side table behind her and blew her nose. "Phew," she said. "I'm too old for this." She rubbed at her eyes and inhaled deeply. "So now you know."

Frankie leaned back against the cushions and let everything sink in. A few of the cracks that had formed as Estelle's house of cards had come tumbling down were filling in, but others remained open gashes. Amber wouldn't have all the answers, but there was one that she still hadn't touched upon.

"What about the man who raped you?" Frankie said at the ceiling. "Did you tell Estelle? Did she know?" She pleaded with the fates that the answer would be *no,* fearful she'd only learned half of Estelle's betrayal so far.

Amber was quiet for a few seconds. "I tried to tell her, but it was his word against mine. All he had to do was point to a few of the guys I was running with and there was enough plausible doubt for her to latch on to. For the record, I wasn't sleeping around. There was only ever one possible father. But he had her ear, and I didn't."

"Who was he? Do you have a name?"

"I think he was her manager at the time. Which was probably another reason why she didn't question him. It would have ruined her career before it even got started."

Cold sweat broke out down Frankie's back. "Her manager?"

"Raymond Clark." Amber spit out the name. "May his soul rot in hell."

# THIRTY-SIX

## FRANKIE

Now

The room tipped around Frankie. Uncle Ray was her father? The man who'd launched Estelle's career, who'd organized their tours for years, who'd recommended Aspen Creek as a place to settle, who they'd celebrated holidays with.

Frankie pushed off the couch and paced the length of the room, her heart beating furiously. She spun back to face Amber, who was watching her reaction with wide eyes. "When you said that thing about his soul—you know he's not dead, right?"

"Sure he is," Amber said. "There was an obituary years ago."

"No, there wasn't." Frankie ran a hand through her hair. "Maybe it was his dad or someone else by that name, but the Raymond Clark who was Estelle's manager is very much alive. I call him..." The words stuck in her throat. "I call him Uncle Ray. I've known him all my life. His son Matt is one of my best friends." She sucked in a breath. Oh dear God—Matt was her brother.

She sank down onto the floor, a lifetime of interactions with the man who'd broken Amber running a reel in her mind.

Amber's face had paled as Frankie spoke. "She kept him in her life?" she asked. "She didn't even believe me enough to be wary of him? She let him around you?" Her voice rose on the last syllable.

"He's never hurt me," Frankie hurried to assure her.

"But he could have." The words were like flint and must have felt as such too because Amber brought a hand up to her throat as if needing help to swallow them down. "Whatever it took, huh, Mom?" she sneered. "That's what she'd tell me every time she'd been home and had to leave again. Now I know. Success was truly all that mattered."

"She was a fraud," Frankie breathed, the pieces coming together. "She sent you off..."

"Actually, I think he arranged and paid for it. He was always going on about his network of contacts here. Better for them both to be rid of me. No one would ask questions, and she could keep taking his money without me there reminding her that she was aligned with the devil."

That made sense. And Frankie had to assume Ray had known. He'd always been generous with her for birthdays and holidays. It was enough to make bile rise in her throat. "So she sent you off, you had me, for some reason she decides to come get me and raise me as her own, but she lies about how old I am."

"Wouldn't that have been pretty obvious?" Amber asked.

"I don't know—we were traveling. A six-month-old can be nine months. A one-year-old, eighteen months. A two-year-old almost three. If you're never in the same place for long, no one is going to question stated fact. She always described me as small for my age and blamed the trauma."

"Trauma?" Amber's brow creased.

"Do you know the song that made her famous? 'My Only Child'?"

"I've heard it, but I obviously wasn't a fan."

"She told everyone it was about me. That I'd been abducted and returned. I've been speculating that she said it because it brought her more attention, but maybe it was also a vague explanation for whatever age-appropriate skills I may have lacked. Greg could have only been my dad if I was born before he passed."

"She made you believe you'd been kidnapped?"

Frankie nodded.

"Holy hell..." Amber tossed the pillow she'd been holding away from her. "The gall of that woman. I swear I thought I was over her, but this brings everything back."

Frankie got off the floor. "I'm sorry."

"No. Do not apologize for her. None of this is your fault."

"None of it is *our* fault," Frankie amended.

Amber nodded. Then she got up and came over to hug Frankie again. "But you're here now," she said softly, running a hand over Frankie's hair. "My firstborn."

Frankie let out a small laugh. "I've gone from being an only child to having three half-siblings in a day." But then her thoughts darkened. "I don't know that Matt is going to believe me though. He's close with his dad."

In fact, if this came out, it could make for a bigger problem than just Matt. Raymond had just as much sway in Aspen Creek as Estelle had had, if not more. His development company was pouring money into the area, and he had friends in high places. But it had to come out, didn't it? There was a criminal in their midst.

"When do you have to go back?" Amber asked.

"I have the car until ten tomorrow morning."

"Will you stay the night? We have a guest room, and I'd love for you to better meet everyone."

Amber looked so hopeful that Frankie said yes on the spot. She could put the messy turns of this story on hold for one night and let herself just be. Spend time with family she'd never expected to find. Tomorrow was inevitable, but it wasn't here yet, and Frankie had a feeling she'd need to gather her strength before then.

Saying goodbye was harder than she'd thought.

After an evening of listening to her brother and sister talk about their schools and interests, of eating good food, and learning everything she could ever want to know about lavender processing, there was still so much unsaid between her and Amber.

"We'll stay in touch," her mother said, walking Frankie to her car early Sunday morning. "And if you ever need anything, I'm here."

She'd made clear she didn't expect Frankie to go after Raymond.

"I have a good life now," she'd said. "I don't want you to upend yours over me and a past that's long gone. He's old—he'll die soon enough."

But Frankie wasn't sure. She needed to process and to talk to Owen. He'd give her his honest opinion—she was sure of it. So much was at stake.

"Oh, I forgot to show you the shop," Amber said as they approached the building. "I've got to send you with a few gifts. Come on."

They entered the small building, and Frankie was immediately engulfed in fragrant air that brought her back to Estelle's guest room and snapped another piece of the puzzle in place.

"Did you say you wrote her ten years ago?" Frankie asked.

Amber handed her some pillow mist and a tub of bath soak. "Yes, about then. Why?"

"That would explain why the payments to the school stopped. She only sent money there because she didn't know where you were. After you wrote her, she started buying products from you instead."

"A more direct way to offer her thirty pieces of silver?" Amber asked. "Maybe."

"Did you know she was ordering from you?" Frankie asked.

"I did." Amber piled several lip balms and small lavender bags into Frankie's arms. "But we're a seasonal farm so it wasn't like I was going to turn down her business. Every sale matters." She looked around the store as if to make sure she hadn't forgotten anything. "I suppose you don't need any candles or tea since Stella had that covered?"

It was a good sign that after all the revelations they'd shared, they could still find levity in the situation.

"I'm happy to pay for it," Frankie said, setting her stash down on the rough-hewn counter. "Now I know all the hard work that goes into this."

"No, Frankie. You're my daughter. This is as much yours as it is mine."

Frankie's cheeks flushed with elation at Amber's words, another rift healing inside her. Being Amber's daughter was already different than being Estelle's because it came without strings. She'd never noticed how complex Estelle's mothering of her had been until she'd experienced the ease of being in Amber's presence. It was true that she was an adult now and didn't need the oversight she might once have required, but there was something else intangible at play too.

"Let me wrap everything up for you." Amber reached behind the counter for tissue paper, and while she worked with nimble fingers, Frankie perused the cute displays and handmade signs that lined the shop.

Finally, her eyes came to rest upon a card stand next to her on the counter. She stared at it for a long moment before reaching for one of the prints. Familiar purple fields beneath a sunset sky. "It was you," she said. "You sent the card to her funeral."

"You saw that?" Amber asked, using a sticker with the farm's logo to keep the tissue paper in place.

"It's what set everything in motion," Frankie said. "Without it, I probably wouldn't be here."

Amber paused what she was doing, placing her hand over Frankie's. "Then the sentiment served a purpose."

"Did you mean it?" Frankie asked. "Have you forgiven her?"

Amber withdrew her hand and proceeded to place all the small parcels into a paper bag. "Yes, I forgave her for what she did to me." She handed Frankie the bag. "But now it's going to take just as long to forgive her for what she's done to you."

"A few lies hardly compare," Frankie said.

Amber came out from behind the counter. "But it's not just lies, is it? It sounds like you did everything together—like you were always presented with curated choices that suited Stella's plans. I'm not saying that's necessarily bad, or that they might not also have been your plans, but I wonder—would you have stayed if you'd known?"

The question lingered as Frankie drove away, her real mother growing smaller and smaller in the rearview until a turn in the road hid her behind a towering hedge. Her life hadn't been bad, and she certainly hadn't suffered any traumas that came close to what Amber had been through. Yes, she'd had some heartbreak and regrets, and she was still single at thirty-six...

*No, thirty-four*, she corrected. That was going to take some getting used to.

But aside from the lies, Frankie still struggled to see herself as a victim of any real injustice, and yet Amber's voice had burned with vehemence when she announced the withdrawal of her forgiveness.

Wrongs needed to be righted, there was no doubt about it, but throughout the drive back to Guildford, the train ride to London, the last night at the hotel, and the hours on a plane far above the Atlantic, no clear answer materialized. Estelle had been a liar and a con artist, and she'd aided the worst kind of monster. Raymond had got off scot-free for something that should have landed him in prison. Both of them were part of the very fabric of Aspen Creek.

If she told, would the town believe her when she wasn't even sure Matt and Kayla would? She could come off as unhinged, could face charges for libel. She could lose her whole community. And what would that do to Starview? Aspen Creek needed the school and the reputation it carried, but whether people believed her about Estelle, or they thought she was telling tall tales, Starview would be disgraced either way.

*Everything is fine*, Estelle whispered at her shoulder as the plane touched down in Charlotte late Monday afternoon. And as Frankie looked out at the familiar blue sky above the tarmac, the leafy green tree line in the distance, and heard the pilot welcome her home, she wanted to believe it. Maybe the show could go on for a little while longer. The auction was five days away, and everyone from students and teachers to vendors and parent volunteers had worked so hard to make this event happen. Afterward, she'd make this right. She'd confront Raymond, she'd do another interview, she'd force justice for Amber somehow, she'd... she'd...

But as soon as she spotted Owen in the pick-up lane, she burst into tears, the idea of keeping things to herself going up in smoke. She hadn't told him anything over text beyond saying she'd found her sister, and the delay in sharing the truth weighed more heavily on her than she'd anticipated.

Owen jumped out of the car and pulled her into his arms

despite the lane attendant yelling at him. "Hey, hey, hey," he said softly, one hand stroking her back. "I've got you. Here, let me take your bag." He guided her into the passenger seat and put her things in the trunk, then pulled away from the curb. "I can stop somewhere, let you catch your breath," he said, glancing her way as she wiped her cheeks. "Did something happen, or are you just glad to see me?"

Despite everything, that coaxed a smile from her. "I am glad to see you," she said, meaning it. "But yeah, everything is messed up." She leaned her head back and closed her eyes. No, things were not fine, and she wasn't Estelle—no amount of pretense was going to make it so. The show ended here. "You don't have to stop. I'll just tell you."

By the time they reached Aspen Creek, he knew everything.

"Estelle was your grandmother," Owen said, his gaze resting solemn on Estelle's front door as he let her story sink in. "You have another family. Matt Clark is your brother." He made a hand gesture next to his head to indicate that his mind was blown.

"And Raymond is my..."

Owen turned to her with murder in his eyes. "Don't say it. He'll never be that. That pompous fucker."

She nodded, looking down at her hands. "I don't know what to do," she said. "I'm supposed to celebrate Estelle in a few days, and she doesn't deserve it, but if I don't, Starview is done."

"You can't lie," he said. "I know you."

Their eyes met over the console, the short distance bridged by something indefinable that had grown deeper in her absence.

"But what if they don't believe the truth," she said. "I barely believe it myself."

"Grams will, and she can be very convincing."

"I have to tell Matt and Kayla before I tell anyone else." Frankie's palms grew damp at the thought.

"You think they'll doubt you?"

"Would you believe something like this about your father?"

"It's not difficult to prove."

He made it sound so simple, and perhaps it was, but as Frankie crawled into her own bed that night, resting her head on a pillow scented with a spray of her newfound mother's crafting, apprehension still ruled supreme. Because in the morning, she wasn't just telling her friends the truth about her parentage; she was doing to Matt what Estelle's death had done to her—dismantling everything he'd held as true about his life until this point and rearranging it into a pattern he'd never asked for.

# THIRTY-SEVEN

## FRANKIE

Now

Matt and Kayla stared at Frankie across their breakfast table. She'd asked to see them first thing to get it out of the way, but now she wondered if that had been wise. Jetlag and this level of skepticism didn't mix well.

"There's no way," Matt said for a second time, pushing off his chair and stalking to the sink. He opened the faucet, then closed it again as if he wasn't sure what he was doing there. "Dad would never."

"I realize how it sounds," Frankie said. "It was a shock to me too."

"Then maybe it isn't true," Kayla tried. "Maybe she... misremembered."

Frankie cocked her head forward. "You think that's the kind of thing blurred by memory? She said Estelle's manager did it. She named him."

"Yeah..." Kayla glanced at her husband across the room, wringing her hands on the table as if she at least wanted to believe Frankie.

"You've only just met this woman," Matt tried, sitting back down and leaning forward. "You don't know anything about her. How are you so sure she can be trusted?"

Frankie met his gaze head on. "I know Estelle lied about a lot of things. And I know Amber is her daughter—that would be obvious to anyone who saw her. Her story also matches the other things we've discovered, which means your dad met her and he's never mentioned her to either of us."

"Hardly evidence of guilt." Matt's voice was clipped.

"Maybe not," Frankie conceded. "But at the very least, he would have known Amber was sent away and why, *and* that I wasn't Estelle's."

"So he was loyal to her and kept her secret." Matt crossed his arms over his chest. "You've got to do better than that. This is a serious accusation, Frankie."

If he used her actual name, he meant business, but so did she.

"There is no doubt in my mind that Amber's story is true," Frankie said. "You weren't there." She cut her gaze between them. "But I do understand needing proof, so if that's what it's going to take, I'll get it for you."

"How?" Matt scoffed, his expression eerily similar to his dad's in that moment.

"From you," Frankie said. "Thora knows someone whose granddaughter works for a lab in Charlotte. We'll go in today, get a quick cheek swab, and she'll expedite it for us. We should have the results tomorrow."

Matt didn't respond, the silence growing to fill the entirety of the large open kitchen until Kayla turned to him and took hold of his arm. "You have to do it," she said. "If it shows that you're siblings, you'll know."

Frankie watched Matt battling for another argument in his head. She'd backed him into a corner, but if that's what it took to get him on her side, she had no choice.

"Fine," he said finally, dragging a hand down his face. "Fuck." He pointed to Frankie. "But we go now. I have a meeting at eleven, and I want to get this shit over with."

Frankie raised her hands palms up in defense. "Whatever works for you."

"I'll grab my purse," Kayla said.

Faced with the results of the test, Matt's reaction was diametrically different. He cried, which in turn made both Frankie and Kayla cry, and then he raged, one expletive after the next reverberating through Frankie's tiny house where they'd gathered.

"How could he do this?" he howled. "How could he...? To a fifteen-year-old girl." He sat down on her love seat and buried his face in his arms, sobs wracking his tall frame.

Frankie and Kayla held on to each other near the kitchen counter where the laptop still sat open displaying the test results. Frankie had never seen him like this, but her instinct told her to give him space for now, so she kept Kayla back.

"And then to send her away... To lie about..." Matt gasped for air. "Everything." He moaned into his hands once again, shaking his head as the horrible image conjured from Amber's tale no doubt played before him. "I will never speak to him again," he announced abruptly. "I will change my name. I will fucking ruin him."

"Okay..." Kayla broke free from Frankie and went to her husband. "Here." She handed him a tissue and waited while he blew his nose. "I know this is awful, and you have every right to be angry, but let's not be rash."

Matt let out another gasp. "Do you think my mom knew?"

"I don't know," Frankie said. "It sounds like Amber was in the Nashville apartment the whole time, so maybe not. She also overheard Estelle referring to her as 'her niece' on several occasions, so who knows what she told people."

Another sob shook Matt's shoulders, perhaps this time in relief at being able to maintain esteem for one of his parents.

Frankie joined them, crouching down in front of Matt. "I'm really sorry," she said, placing a hand on his knee. "If it's any consolation, I couldn't wish for a better brother."

A half laugh half sob slipped out of him. "That would be the only good thing to come out of this. I always wanted a sibling, and you're the very best, Frankwurst."

Frankie hugged him, relief flooding her when he relaxed against her shoulder. Kayla wrapped her arms around them both.

Once they'd all settled enough to wipe eyes and noses and, in Matt's case, down enough water for a marathon runner, they went outside and sat down on Frankie's small porch. The early evening air was the kind of lukewarm that you barely felt on your skin, and for a while, they just sat there, listening to the birds in the thicket behind Frankie's house and the bees zooming in and out of Estelle's flower patch.

"He'll never admit it," Matt said eventually. "Not even with the proof we have. And I think it's too late for the law to intervene."

Frankie nodded. That's not what Amber had wanted anyway.

"So he gets away with it?" Kayla asked. "That doesn't seem right at all."

That had been Frankie's fear too. Owen and Thora had let her lament the impossibility of the situation many times over since she'd been back. She'd slept in their guest room again last night, hoping company would distract from the obsessive thoughts about the pending DNA test that had haunted her when she was alone. She and Owen had stayed up past midnight turning this conundrum over and over, along with how Frankie should handle the looming auction, without ever settling on a solution.

It was a shame that she'd planned it as a celebration of Estelle's life when she'd first hatched the idea. A simple fundraiser for Starview would have been one thing, but now that Estelle was the figurehead, Frankie couldn't help but feel like she was following in her deceptive footsteps. Her grandmother's first guitar, the signed CDs, and the framed gold record Frankie had decided to part with after all were still the big-ticket prices, and it wasn't like she could withdraw them. The school needed the fundraiser to be successful, and the community would hardly open their wallets if they knew what Estelle had done.

Unless...

Something about what Matt had said about it being too late for the law stuck with Frankie.

"Your dad is planning to attend the auction, right?" she asked him.

Matt frowned. "Yeah. Why?"

Frankie's gaze was drawn to a large butterfly fluttering above the black-eyed Susans at the edge of the patch. *It's a Giant swallowtail,* she could hear Estelle explain to her. *They have the ugliest larvae, but look at it now. No one would know.*

Except people did know. That's what Estelle had gotten wrong. No one admired the giant swallowtail less because of its plain beginnings; that wasn't the measure that mattered. If anything, it made the creature more impressive. But Estelle had never cared to acknowledge flaws other than to cover them up, so that's what Frankie had learned. Well, no more.

"You've thought of something," Kayla said, recalling Frankie's attention.

"Maybe."

"You can't accuse him in public," Matt said. "As much as the bastard deserves it."

"I might not need to."

Frankie turned the different parts of her plan around in her head, testing their merit. The court of law may have run out of time, but the court of public opinion had not. It would be a bit of a gamble, and there was more than one chance of it backfiring, but she had to do something. For too long, Estelle and Raymond had been allowed to wash their hands of their murky past. It was time to acquaint Aspen Creek with the real people behind the glossy surface. Frankie just hoped she wouldn't take down Starview in the process.

# THIRTY-EIGHT

## FRANKIE

Now

The evening before the auction, Frankie was invited to dinner with Thora and Owen. Thora's knee was finally healed enough that she didn't need the cane to move around. She'd celebrated this newfound freedom by cleaning the house, so when Frankie arrived, she was resting on a chaise out back at Owen's insistence.

"I've put some chicken on the grill," he said. "Grams made potato salad earlier, and I've poured you some lemonade already. Only the garlic bread left." He nodded toward the garden, urging her out there before she'd had a chance to offer him help in the kitchen. His bangs flopped over one eye, and because his hands were covered in marinade, he blew a breath upward to move the strands.

"That's it," Frankie said. "After dinner, I'm giving you a haircut."

"Threatening me with a good time, are you?" He winked.

Frankie played off his innuendo. "Depends. You've got to

look respectable if you want to be my date for the auction tomorrow."

His smile vanished, and his eyebrows jumped. "You're asking me out?"

She shrugged, heading for the patio door. "Are you going to let me cut your hair?"

"Damn straight I am."

She grinned as she left him behind. This was exactly what she needed on the eve of what was sure to be a day of sweeping change in her life. A meal with two people who had always accepted her, flaws and all. More time with Owen.

"Hand me that pillow over there, will you?" Thora said. "Not that I couldn't get it myself, but you're closer."

"Of course." Frankie's smile lingered. Everyone needed help from time to time. Someone to lean on. That's what connected them. Maybe she needed some new mantras, especially now that she meant to take Amber and Greg's last name. *Milnes ask for support. Milnes admit struggle.*

They settled in, watching the swallows swoop and play above the magnolia trees while the savory smoke from the grill permeated the air.

"Are you ready for tomorrow?" Thora asked after a while.

Frankie had shared her plans with a select few that included her current dinner company, Matt, Kayla, and the other teachers at the school. They were most likely to be impacted after all, so she'd wanted their blessing.

"I think so. I'm nervous, but if I can drive on the left side of the road, I can do this." She sipped her lemonade, her thoughts going to Amber. They'd been in touch daily since Frankie returned, and she, too, had approved of what Frankie was about to do. "I don't know if I said so before, but thank you again for arranging that flight. None of this would have happened if you hadn't. I wouldn't have found my mom."

"Oh, nonsense. I was happy to."

Frankie studied the older woman for a beat. "You've done nothing but help me since I came to you that first time. Why? I was no one to you, but you've rallied your whole network for me."

Thora reached her hand across the small table that separated them, and Frankie took it. "You know I live for this," she said, a tender glint in her eyes. "The search. The mystery. The impossible quest." She squeezed Frankie's hand, then let go to pick up her glass instead. She sipped it thoughtfully before setting it back down again. "But you're wrong. You weren't no one. You were Frankie. And if I needed another reason, it's that you put some life back into my grandson's eyes again—just like I knew you would. You were the one who got away. Didn't you know?"

Frankie's lips parted in surprise, but just then, Owen joined them, carrying plates and silverware that he set down on the patio table. "Could you grab the potato salad, Frankie?" he asked. "I'll be right behind you for the bread. Grams, need help up?"

"Oh no you don't," Thora said, swinging her legs over the side of the chaise. Then her voice softened. "But I will take a refill of that lemonade if you're already going inside."

Thora's words rang in Frankie's ears while they ate. She hid it well enough—or at least she thought she did—but she couldn't help her gaze sliding to Owen when he laughed that unbridled laugh she remembered from their youth at something Thora said. Had he regretted breaking it off with her then? Thought of her enough afterward that Thora had picked up on it? But if he'd regretted ending it, he could have said so. He'd known where to find her.

After they cleaned up, and Thora had settled inside with a crossword puzzle and *Dr. Zhivago* playing on TCM in the background, Owen brought a chair out onto the deck and handed Frankie a pair of scissors and a comb.

"Do your worst," he said, pulling his shirt over his head and sitting down. "I know you've been dying to get your hands on it."

Frankie stood behind him, eyes lingering on the width of his tan shoulders, but then she took hold of herself. "Right," she said, placing the tools on the table next to them. She hesitated, then let her fingers slide into his hair to see what she was working with.

"Oh my God," Owen grunted on a deep chuckle. "That feels so good."

Frankie's cheeks warmed, but his words boosted her nerve, and she dug in with firmer fingers, reveling in the feel of his soft strands against her knuckles.

"You could stand to lose a couple of inches," she said. "It's a bird's nest up here."

"It hasn't been high on my list in a while."

"Yeah, I get that." She reached for the comb and scissors. "Ready?"

"Mm-hmm." He sounded like he was drifting off, and when Frankie peered over his shoulder, his eyes were closed.

"Tilt your head a little that way." She adjusted him, then got to work.

For a long while, the only sounds around them were those of the garden and the metallic snip of the scissors. The golden hour was tinting the few clouds on the horizon pink and bronze, and it highlighted the blonde in Owen's hair as it fell to the floor.

Frankie's fingers grew more confident as she worked, her movements falling into a known rhythm that made the present blend with the memory of all the other times she'd done this. It may have been a long time ago, but when she let herself relax into his space, it was like riding a bike.

Driving with him had felt the same. Eating together. Sleeping curled up next to him.

Like no time had passed.

"Why did you break up with me?" she asked, the question posed before she could second-guess herself. "I know it's been a long time, so it doesn't really matter, but would you tell me anyway?"

"What?" Owen looked up at her, forcing her to pull the scissors back.

"I mean, I know what your letter said, and I get not wanting to be attached to anyone starting college, but was that it? Or was it me?"

"Frankie..." Owen had turned in his chair while she spoke, so he was facing her more directly. "What are you talking about?"

She dropped her hands to her sides. "What do you mean, what am I talking about? It's a pretty simple question—why did you break up with me? I'm curious." She shrugged one shoulder to show just how *casual* the question was.

He squinted up at her as if gauging if she was joking. "But I didn't," he said. "You broke up with me."

"What?" She huffed out a laugh. "Why would I have done that?"

"Because you started dating that baseball player guy. What was his name again? How do you not remember this?"

Frankie pinched the comb tighter in her fingers. "Because it didn't happen. You wrote me a couple of months after leaving for Boston and said you needed space."

"What?" Owen shook his head, blinking into the distance like he was trying to retrieve the details of that fall. "No..." He faced her again. "You wrote to me. *You* broke up with me."

They stared at each other for a long while, confusion mixing with old hurts in both their eyes until a single word spilled across Frankie's lips. The syllables formed on her tongue more on instinct than with conscious effort, as if she'd been guided there by countless signs over the past month.

"Estelle." She sank onto the next closest chair, something inside her clicking into place. Something like the final piece of the puzzle.

"Estelle what?" Owen asked.

"She wrote the letters."

Frankie pulled on the memory of that fall, urging it to the surface. She and Owen had spent as much of the summer together as they could. They'd both had jobs, so there were days when they couldn't see each other, but when they didn't, they'd text on their Nokias—three fours for I, three fives for L, three nines for Y—and sometimes Owen would leave notes on her porch on his way to and from his construction gig.

They'd both been tearful saying goodbye when it was time for him to leave for Boston, but they'd had a plan, which made it bearable. She'd finish high school, and then they'd be together again. The world would be at their feet, and they'd have each other. Until then, they'd write all the time, they promised, and she'd read his first letter almost to pieces, attempting to absorb everything he was describing of his new world up north.

She'd started her senior year, and there had been no honeymoon period before she was swamped with assignments. She'd also had her own little group of piano students to keep her busy, so she'd spent a lot of time at Starview. They'd had some issues with theft at the school that fall. Her backpack had been snatched from the staff room one day and was found outside near the garbage bins missing her cell phone and make-up bag, and Estelle's car had been broken into and a scarf she loved taken. But none of those events overshadowed the way she'd counted the days until his next letter would arrive, so when it had taken longer than she'd expected, she'd been thrown off by it. The tone inside had been the same as always, and yet she'd not quite been able to shake the delay.

"Do you remember how many letters you got from me that fall?" she asked.

"Two," he said, as if it wasn't ancient fact. "The second one was where you told me you'd met someone else. To respect your decision."

This betrayal had a sharper tang than the other ones—a poison drip designed especially for her. "I can't believe she did that," Frankie whispered, rubbing a hand at her chest where the serrated truth had stabbed her.

Owen stood, fine hair clippings drifting off his shoulders in a cloud as he moved to her. He squatted and placed his hands on her forearms, pausing as if unsure how to phrase what he needed to know. "Are you actually telling me Estelle ended us?" he said finally. "That my heart broke for nothing?"

Frankie's insides twisted at the sorrow in his voice. That's what Thora had meant when she said Frankie was the one who'd got away from him. "She could have taken your letters before they reached me, and I always put outgoing mail on her desk so she could add stamps. It would have been easy for her to take the envelopes and copy out new letters if she set her mind to it."

"But why?" Owen asked.

Another string of images from her life with Estelle popped into Frankie's mind at once. Touring with her, being home-schooled, eating together, reading together, gardening together, the story about the song, college decisions, job decisions, the tiny house in the yard, partnering at Starview. *Mother of the year.*

"She wanted me to stay," Frankie said. "She needed me to stay." She could see it so clearly now, like a curtain had parted to reveal the plain facts behind a magic trick. Owen had been a complicating factor in Estelle's plans for Frankie's future after high school—a factor that she likely sensed would hold more sway than a mother.

One by one, Estelle's machinations snapped into view. The decision to choose a "safe" major instead of pursuing music had likely been to prevent Frankie landing a career that would have her touring or moving to hard-to-come-by jobs. The need for help at Starview increasing at the same time Frankie had a lead on a teaching job in Charlotte now seemed less of a coincidence. The tiny house appearing—such a thoughtful gift if not for the lack of buy-in from Frankie, who'd felt she couldn't turn it down.

Then there was that other time she'd come close to leaving—with Zach and the road trip.

"That's why she lied about the cancer," Frankie said now, not caring that she was omitting context for Owen. "To keep me close."

Whether Estelle's deceptions had stemmed from a fear of loneliness, a misguided attempt at alleviating guilt over what she'd done to Amber, or something pathological, Frankie would never know, but regardless, it was now clear they'd been more fit for a puppet master than a loving parent.

Frankie had been tethered to Estelle and Aspen Creek, not voluntarily like she'd thought but like a prisoner in body and soul, unable to leave because the choices she'd been offered had presented no such option. And there it was, Estelle's finest con laid bare, because Frankie had never even realized.

She didn't notice she was crying until Owen wiped a tear from her cheek with his thumb. She covered his hand with hers and held it against her skin. "I didn't meet anyone else," she said, needing him to hear it. "I promise."

"I know," he said. "And I didn't want my freedom. I just wanted you."

She bridged the space between them in a heartbeat, their lips coming together in a gentle conjuring of times gone by. The salt from her tears lent a biting edge to the solemnity of the moment—one she'd no doubt carry with her into tomorrow's activities—but Owen's touch was nothing but sweetness.

He leaned back, his pupils dark with warring delight and agony. "I should have texted you or sent you an email too—not just relied on the letters. If I had known... I just didn't suspect..."

"I think she counted on that," Frankie said. "Both of us wanting to do right by the other. And I didn't have my phone anyway. Someone took it from—" Her mouth snapped closed. *Of course.* Estelle would have wanted to minimize the risk of Frankie and Owen finding other ways to communicate, so she'd taken the phone from Frankie's backpack at Starview. The surrounding details were made up like so many things had been in Estelle's life.

"I'm still sorry," Owen said, resting his forehead against her knees like he was bowing to her.

She threaded her fingers through his now shorter strands, lingering there for a while before lifting his face to hers again. "Me too," she breathed against his lips.

She finished cutting his hair, each touch and movement drawn-out and more tender than when she'd started. Their discovery was a glinting soap bubble between them—beautiful and complex, its swirling colors reflecting the many versions of the two of them they might be.

Frankie wished nothing more than to press pause on everything else and look closer, but the bubble was also fragile to the world it existed in. This moment on Thora's deck with her garden surrounding them was a carved-out sliver of time. Here, it was easy to forget all the years that had passed since the two of them had made their plans. That Owen had his sobriety to focus on. That regardless of what happened tomorrow, Frankie now had real choices to make about her life that could not be based on anything or anyone other than herself.

As Owen walked her to her car, they both knew there

would be no promises made this night. No plans or commitments. And that was okay.

"How does it look?" Owen asked, running a hand over his neat new cut. "Decent enough to be your date tomorrow?"

Frankie smiled. Well, she thought, no *long-term* plans or commitments at least. "I'll pick you both up at one."

# THIRTY-NINE

## FRANKIE

Now

Frankie sat at the electric piano that had been set up on the stage inside the big auction tent. It was five minutes until the event would officially kick off, and she'd decided to do it with music. Her hands would cooperate today, she'd decided. No one determined what she could or couldn't do but herself anymore. She was in control. If she said she'd play, she'd make it happen.

One of the guys who'd come with the rented sound equipment stepped up next to her and adjusted the microphone stand on the other side of the piano because today she was singing too. Nothing like having your sense of self stripped down to nothing and built back up to venture into unknown territory. Plus, she needed the lyrics fresh in the audience's mind.

Matt and Kayla and the other Starview teachers had already taken their places on the other side of the stage, and she reciprocated when Matt gave her a smile and a nod. *Her brother*. Kayla hinted subtly toward the audience that was milling in to take their seats, and Frankie's gaze followed her indication, spotting Raymond seated in the third row. *Good.*

Owen and Thora were two rows behind him, and from the looks of things, Owen was currently working hard at burning holes in the back of Raymond's head with his eyes. Despite what she'd told herself last night, the sight of Owen buoyed her heart. There was something there, she couldn't deny it, and maybe when all of this was over, they'd get a chance to see what might have been.

How lucky she was to have these people in her life. Frankie could see now that the way she and Kayla had drifted apart was not from Kayla's lack of trying. It was the natural progression of one of them marrying and the other not. For all Frankie knew, this fact might also have been of Estelle's design. Like with Owen and Zach, Estelle could have seen threats to her total control of Frankie in Matt and Kayla, so what better way to eliminate that than introducing the two of them. Two birds with one stone. Frankie was willing to bet Estelle had hoped they'd move away too, but thank goodness they hadn't. Instead, Estelle had made Frankie partner and kept her busy at Starview—busy enough not to get too close to anyone else.

It was possible the school had never been able to afford that shift and expansion. The school's finances ending up in shambles still baffled them all, but all signs pointed to simple poor management. Renovation costs that were never recuperated. Interest on loans. An unwillingness to increase prices. Pride.

Well, that ended today.

Frankie placed her hands on the keys. It was time.

The audience quieted as soon as the first chord rang out. Frankie's hands trembled initially, but when the notes came sure and true, she relaxed and let herself breathe into the music. The dam inside her finally broke as her fingers moved; each new key depressed melting another measure of tension until, finally, stillness settled at her core. A collective inhale swept through the space when she leaned forward and started singing. This would be the last time she ever played "My Only Child." After today, this chapter would be in her past, and there it would stay.

Her performance brought down a swell of applause that seemed to lift the tent as she brought the microphone with her to go stand in front of Matt, Kayla, and the teachers. The tent was filled to the brim just like the church had been at Estelle's funeral, and the wall panels had all been strung open to allow the air to circulate and for more people to partake in the festivities from picnic blankets and lawn chairs in the park beyond.

Long tables lined the right-hand side of the tent, overflowing with baskets of varying sizes ready for the bidding. Frankie had contributed one of her own last minute—a woven one with a purple bow stuffed with lavender products from Amber's shop. She'd sent her mom a photo this morning, to which Amber had responded that she was so proud of everything Frankie had accomplished. Frankie couldn't remember one time when Estelle had expressed something similar without making it out to be a joint achievement.

She took a deep breath, then brought the mic to her lips. "Hello and welcome," she said, spotting Orla Monroe at the edge of her seat in the first row. Frankie had personally called to leave a message encouraging her attendance, as well as expressing a wish to amend their interview whenever there was time.

Squealing feedback cut through the tent, making everyone squirm, but Frankie got it to stop and let a smile settle her nerves. She found Owen in the crowd and kept her eyes on him as she continued speaking.

"Thank you all so much for being here today. We have a wonderful afternoon ahead of us with live music by our talented students, games and activities outside, a raffle and silent auction with donations from our generous community, and of course the main event that will take place at four o'clock when we auction off our big prizes that you can see over there." She gestured to a table below the stage.

"But first I'd like to say a few words about the woman without whom we wouldn't be here today." She paused, her gaze sweeping through the crowd of smiling and eager citizens. This was it.

"Estelle's too-early passing was a blow for the Aspen Creek community. We all have our personal memories of her, but I think there's also a communal sense of who she was to us. Entertainer, idol, teacher, friend, colleague, advocate, champion. To me, she was Mom."

Several tuts of sympathy reached the stage, but Frankie forged on. "To come to terms with her loss, I embarked on somewhat of a journey to... understand her better after she died. And I think I did, but what I found was something I never could have expected. You see, Estelle was not always Estelle. She was born Stella-Jane Sutton in rural Mississippi to Irish immigrants, and as I've learned more about her, an image has crystallized of someone who always wanted to be more than she was. Who possibly even felt that she was owed a better life and did whatever she could to claim it."

Maybe that had even been Estelle's original lie, Frankie thought. That she deserved more for no other reason than wanting it. Was that what had set everything in motion?

The first inklings of unease stirred pockets of the audience, but Frankie faced them head-on. "We all know this about her. She was ambitious. She was charismatic. She had talent. But the woman you all think you knew was also self-serving and manipulative."

The whispers rose around the room, and outside the tent, Frankie spotted some people moving closer.

"How many of you in here know the story behind the song I just sang? Of what happened to me?" Frankie asked.

Almost everyone in the tent raised their hands.

Frankie nodded. "Well, the truth is that the song was inspired by an abduction in Hattiesburg in 1985. It turns out it's not about me at all. In looking for things for this auction, I discovered the original draft of the song which is dated several years before I was born. She lied. To you and to me."

The whispers rose in volume, with a few audience members growing visibly agitated.

Owen stood. "Let her finish please. Listen to what she has to say."

"Thank you," Frankie mouthed, allowing herself another private moment with just him before facing the audience again. "I know this is difficult to hear, but that wasn't the only lie she told. And I'm sure you're wondering why I'm choosing to share this here. Now. We are gathered to celebrate her, after all. To honor her legacy. But while she did have an admirable career both as a singer and as champion for our town through the school, I stand here before you today with the truth because anything else would mean allowing the deception to continue, and the truth is that Estelle wasn't who we thought she was."

At the core of everything lay a simple fact. Estelle had always done whatever she needed to do to get what Estelle wanted. First with her career and Amber, and then with Frankie and Aspen Creek, and she'd pulled it off. She'd arranged her world so that she'd always felt adored and important—an inspired songwriter, a caring mother, a matron of the arts, a cornerstone of society. The tenacity would have been admirable if Frankie hadn't been on the receiving end of her grandmother's fixations.

Frankie's lips parted on an inhale, then she let the words go. "Estelle was not my mother; she was my grandmother." She ignored the ripple of shock through the room and continued. "My real mother had me when she was fifteen, and I was just able to reunite with her this past weekend. Needless to say, this has come as a shock to me, as have the intricacies of the lies Estelle told, but I'm choosing to see it as separate from the task at hand, and my hope is that you will too." She gestured to the room as if underscoring that hope. It was, of course, an understatement. She'd seen first-hand in Aftbury what could happen to a community when its heart disappeared, so she *needed* the people here to rally despite what she was telling them.

"The truth is also that our school needs money to survive. Starview has been in financial jeopardy, and none of us up here knew about it until after Estelle's death. There is no downplaying what this school has meant for Aspen Creek—I know it, and you know it—but I can't in good conscience ask for your support without you knowing what you're contributing to, and that's why I'm choosing to lay all of this out for you.

"After today, the school will no longer be called Starview Conservatory. We are renaming it Aspen Creek Academy to represent the town, to acknowledge our academic one-to-six curriculum, and to sever its close association with Estelle. I am also stepping back from its leadership. It's time for me to move on. The very competent teachers you see behind me will take over operations of the school and, I'm certain, ensure its continued success."

The room broke out in chatter, and this time there was no stopping it, but Frankie remained at the mic, her gaze going to Raymond, who was looking visibly pale beneath his tan. At the same time, Kayla and Matt stepped up closer behind her.

"Do the feedback thing again," Kayla suggested when no natural lull in the conversations appeared.

"Good idea." Frankie brought the mic closer to her lips and said, "One more thing."

The siren-like note had the desired effect, and in two seconds, the room had stilled once more.

"In light of what I've shared with you, we up here all understand if you choose to forgo the festivities today or even to withdraw from the school altogether, but I want to plead with you not to make any rash decisions for Aspen Creek's sake. When Estelle and I moved here twenty-five years ago, this was a waning town. Rich in history and tradition, but not a place with a real future. But it turns out that people move where their children can thrive, and while I'm not so conceited as to think it was all Starview's doing, we did turn the tide. For that, if nothing else, we have Estelle to thank, and while her legacy is now tainted, I believe the school's legacy is one to preserve. *You* are all part of that.

"That said, should you choose to leave today, and the auction fail to reach our funding goal, I want to assure you that we are not in dire straits anymore. We have a generous benefactor among us who has pledged to fund the school to ensure its continued success for at least another fifteen years—please give it up for my biological father, Mr. Raymond Clark." She gestured to the man in question while locking him in her iciest glare.

Sporadic clapping commenced as some of those in attendance needed longer than others to put two and two together. It was easy to tell who still remembered her remark about Amber having her at fifteen by the craning necks and loathing gazes that followed.

To ensure there would be no public protestations from Ray, Frankie knew that Matt was currently gesturing the letters D-N-A to his dad. There would be no way for him to get out of this. He was now publicly committed to this ongoing patronage, while small-town talk would likely drive him out of Aspen Creek for good. Matt had also promised that if his dad did put up a fight behind the scenes, he'd be happy to let Ray's business associates in other cities and states know exactly who he was and what he'd done.

When Frankie had wrapped up the most unorthodox

welcome speech of any fundraiser, Kayla pulled her into a tight hug. "You did the right thing," she said.

Out of the corner of her eye, Frankie spotted her brother stalking out of the tent after their father. "Is Matt okay?" she asked. She knew what it felt like to be left without family, and she hated that she'd done that to him.

"He's upset naturally," Kayla said. "But he'll be fine. I think he's more worried about you. Starview has been your life. Aspen Creek is your home. Giving everything up seems so... drastic."

Maybe so, but it wasn't like she was planning on catching the first flight out tomorrow. She'd take her time, complete the transfer of the school to the other teachers, sell Estelle's house, make a plan. She needed to talk to Owen. They'd both been through enough to bypass playing coy. Maybe this exact moment wasn't theirs, but someday soon she hoped that would change, and she thought he did too.

"There could be a multitude of places out there that fit me better," she told Kayla. "That's the thing—I won't know unless I go. And I'm too closely tied to Estelle to stay with the school. If we want to contain the blowback, it's better to make a clean cut. I want to see what else I can do."

"So no regrets?" Kayla gestured to the audience that was still milling about the tent.

"No. They deserved to know. Estelle will always have her gold record and her standing as a vocalist, but it wouldn't have been right to let these people continue to idolize her. The only thing I still wish is that I could have done more to get justice for Amber, but she's moved on and says she wants me to do the same."

"And will you be able to?"

Amber had assured Frankie that Ray suffering financially and socially, plus losing his only son's esteem, was more than she'd expected or hoped for, and if *she* could look ahead, who was Frankie to cling to the past?

No one was leaving, she realized, looking out at her fellow Aspen Creekers. A mass of people had congregated in front of the table with the baskets, two students who'd switched their violins for fiddles had their own audience clapping along outside, and beyond them, howls of laughter rose from the three-legged sack race. The town, too, had chosen to put Estelle's past aside and focus on the future of the school.

Kayla was right. Frankie's life had played out here in this town, good parts and bad, and starting over someplace else would be a major change. But in that lay adventure, possibilities, and freedom. After everything she'd learned, after having been so wrong about that which she'd taken for granted, it felt okay to invite in a little ambiguity.

"I believe I will," she said, looking out over the crowd below the stage.

There were the parents who alternated between rejoicing in and worrying about their children every day in the hopes of them thriving. The teachers who relied on equal parts patience and passion to teach the next generation of musicians. Her friends who'd saved a space for her in their hearts even when she was too preoccupied to inhabit it. Thora, whose age brought both fragility and impressively strong connections. Owen, who'd fought his way back to the surface against currents that worked to keep him down but lit up at the sight of her.

There would be ups and downs ahead, that much was certain. But as Frankie joined the festivities, she welcomed what Estelle had kept from her for so long—the autonomy to choose and to meet the consequences of those choices head-on, no matter what they were.

It was possible, likely even, that everything wouldn't always be fine. But why that had once scared her, she could no longer remember.

# A LETTER FROM ANNA

Dear reader,

Thank you so much for choosing to spend a few hours of your time in Frankie's (and my) company. I hope you enjoyed reading *My Mother's Lie* just as much as I did writing it, and if you did, I also hope you want to stay connected and up to date on all my releases. To do that, just sign up at the following link. Your email will never be shared, and you can unsubscribe at any time.

*www.bookouture.com/anna-e-collins*

A few years back, I was really into genealogy and researched family trees for several friends and relatives. That's when I learned that a grandparent of someone I know grew up under the same misconception as Frankie. The woman he thought was his mother was, in fact, his grandmother, and the woman he called sister was his mother. The identity of his father remains unknown until this day. Unlike Frankie, this man didn't discover the truth until his mid-forties, which obviously threw him for a loop, and these family secrets were what ultimately sparked the idea for this book. Because of its connection to a real-life kernel of truth, I think it will always have a special place in my heart.

Hearing from readers is always exciting, so if you loved following Frankie as she set off forging her own path in life separate from Estelle, I'd be thrilled to have you leave a short review or get in touch through my social media or website.

Always so grateful for your support.

Anna

www.aecollinsbooks.com

instagram.com/AECcreates

facebook.com/aecollinsbooks

# ACKNOWLEDGEMENTS

I wrote this book during a supremely busy time in my life. Birthdays, graduations, travel, college planning, international visitors, you name it. It shouldn't have been possible really, yet here we are, so naturally some gratitude is in place.

First, thank you to my family for allowing me as much time as possible in the "writing shed," which was really the only place where I could focus during those three intense months. You are my reason for most everything I do, and I love you more than life itself.

Second, to my friends for cheering me on in the race to finish, but especially to Megan for early feedback and for whisking me out of town for a writing weekend right at the midpoint and getting me out of my head when I needed it the most. You know I'd do it again anytime!

Also thank you to my fantastic Bookouture team, without whom there would be no book—especially to my editor, Brittany Golob, and to Jennifer Hunt for believing in the story. I continue to be impressed with how this team works together, and I can't wait to see what the future holds.

Lastly, thank you to my readers, whether loyal or new, for reading, reviewing, and recommending my books, and to anyone else who's gone out of their way to support my writing in general, and this, my eighth book, in particular. Nothing makes me happier than knowing something I wrote might have provided an escape for a few hours or provoked some thoughts or feelings that lingered beyond the pages. I appreciate each and every one of you more than you know!

# PUBLISHING TEAM

**Turning a manuscript into a book requires the efforts of many people. The publishing team at Bookouture would like to acknowledge everyone who contributed to this publication.**

**Commercial**
Lauren Morrissette
Hannah Richmond
Imogen Allport

**Cover design**
Emma Graves

**Data and analysis**
Mark Alder
Mohamed Bussuri

**Editorial**
Brittany Golob
Ria Clare

**Copyeditor**
Laura Kincaid

**Proofreader**
Liz Hurst

**Marketing**

Alex Crow
Melanie Price
Occy Carr
Cíara Rosney
Martyna Młynarska

**Operations and distribution**

Marina Valles
Joe Morris

**Production**

Hannah Snetsinger
Mandy Kullar
Nadia Michael
Charlotte Hegley

**Publicity**

Kim Nash
Noelle Holten
Jess Readett
Sarah Hardy

**Rights and contracts**

Peta Nightingale
Richard King
Saidah Graham

RAISING READERS

Books Build Bright Futures

Dear Reader,

We'd love your attention for one more page to tell you about the crisis in children's reading, and what we can all do.

Studies have shown that reading for fun is the **single biggest predictor of a child's future life chances** – more than family circumstance, parents' educational background or income. It improves academic results, mental health, wealth, communication skills, ambition and happiness.

The number of children reading for fun is in rapid decline. Young people have a lot of competition for their time, and a worryingly high number do not have a single book at home.

Hachette works extensively with schools, libraries and literacy charities, but here are some ways we can all raise more readers:

- Reading to children for just 10 minutes a day makes a difference
- Don't give up if children aren't regular readers – there will be books for them!

- Visit bookshops and libraries to get recommendations
- Encourage them to listen to audiobooks
- Support school libraries
- Give books as gifts

There's a lot more information about how to encourage children to read on our websites: **www.RaisingReaders.co.uk** and **www.JoinRaisingReaders.com**.

Thank you for reading.

Printed in Dunstable, United Kingdom

79278964R00211